THOROUGHLY MODERN MONSTERS

THOROUGHLY MODERN MONSTERS

J.L. Aldis, Editor

E.E. Weber, Assistant Editor

Story Spring Publishing
Cincinnati, Ohio

Gallowglass and the Fiddler copyright © 2013 by Abby Phelan
Verisimilitude copyright © 2013 by Lin Thornhill
Nothing But the Best copyright © 2013 by Jae Eynon
Seeking Single Human Male, No Stakers copyright © 2013 by Libby Weber
Little Monsters copyright © 2013 by Caireann Shannon
Grace Abounding copyright © 2013 by M.R. Glass
Cold Cuts copyright © 2013 by Michaela Vallageas
Learning Curve copyright © 2013 by Jae Eynon
The Freakshow File copyright © 2013 by Murphy McCall
Morrigan Mine copyright © 2013 by Wendy Worthington
The Proper Task of Life copyright © 2013 by Antioch Grey
The Skin of My Teeth copyright © 2013 by Libby Weber
The Devil Makes Work for Idle Hands copyright © 2013 by Antioch Grey
Provender copyright © 2013 by Wendy Worthington
Pretorius copyright © 2013 by Jonathan Waite

All rights reserved. No part of this publication may be reproduced, distributed, or transmitted in any form or by any means, including photocopying, recording, or other electronic or mechanical methods, without the prior written permission of the publisher, except in the case of brief quotations embodied in critical reviews and certain other noncommercial uses permitted by copyright law. For permission requests, write to the publisher, addressed "Attention: Permissions Coordinator," at the address below.

Story Spring Publishing
P.O. Box 9727
Cincinnati, OH 45209
www.storyspringpublishing.com

Publisher's Note: This is a work of fiction. Names, characters, places, and incidents are a product of the author's imagination. Locales and public names are sometimes used for atmospheric purposes. Any resemblance to actual people, living or dead, or to businesses, companies, events, institutions, or locales is completely coincidental.

Book Layout ©2013 BookDesignTemplates.com
Cover Design ©2013 by Jennifer Ramming

Thoroughly Modern Monsters/ J.L. Aldis, Editor— 1st ed.
ISBN 978-1-940699-10-3

For Theresa—Thanks for all the nagging.

Contents

Foreword	iii
Gallowglass and the Fiddler *by Abby Phelan*	1
Verisimilitude *by Lin Thornhill*	17
Nothing But The Best *by Jae Eynon*	37
Seeking Single Human Male, No Stakers *by Libby Weber*	57
Little Monsters *by Caireann Shannon*	69
Grace Abounding *by M.R. Glass*	95
Cold Cuts *by Michaela Vallageas*	117
Learning Curve *by Jae Eynon*	137
The Freakshow File *by Murphy McCall*	149
Morrigan Mine *by Wendy Worthington*	181
The Proper Task of Life *by Antioch Grey*	207
The Skin of My Teeth *by Libby Weber*	233
The Devil Makes Work for Idle Hands *by Antioch Grey*	255
Provender *by Wendy Worthington*	271
Pretorius *by Jonathan Waite*	285
About the Editors	297
About the Authors	299
About Story Spring Publishing	305

Foreword

Welcome to the shiny modern world, where we adapt everything to our whim, and any shadows we may encounter are of our own making.

A journey of a mere few hundred years brought us to this brightly lit space, once we turned our backs on the Dark Ages. The Age of Enlightenment raised our minds above superstition and taught us to treat the horrors of imagination as metaphor. The Industrial Age saw us scramble to take control of our world and bend it to our service whether it would or no. And finally, we brushed the soot and oil from our clothes and sauntered blithely into these hi-tech times, where we meet our old fantasies face to face in the anodyne guise of shiny animations and computer games.

But, as we battle our CGI orcs and smooch the sparkly princes of the night, we really ought to pause and consider where the real monsters have gone. Surely we left them behind in the Dark Ages? What role could they possibly play in this cynical age where adventure and thrills present themselves to us on demand, at the touch of a button? What place do the real monsters, those denizens of myth, legend, and nightmare, still have in a world where their avatars are served with popcorn on the side?

This is the question that eleven fearless authors have set themselves to answer in the fifteen stories of this collection, *Thoroughly Modern Monsters*.

In the pages of this anthology, we will encounter creatures who are simply seeking to live undisturbed, perhaps even finding redemption in these open-minded times, and we will discover others who are adept at turning an all-too-willing world to their monstrous purpose. In humour or in horror, on the margins or in the mainstream, in the house next door or way beyond the boundaries, our authors have sought and found their monsters living, working, *feeding*, just as well as they did before we tried to domesticate them—and in some cases, rather better.

J.L. Aldis
2013

ABBY PHELAN

Gallowglass and the Fiddler

There was a rhythm to night driving, like a heartbeat, a soft pulse underlying the world. The rush of wind outside the helmet, the throaty rumble of the engine. The flash of the sodium lights as they drifted past, one by one, painting the night in yellow and black. In the small hours, on the rumbling hiss of the tarmac, the world was a ribbon of lights in darkness, threading forwards and dwindling behind, the muted roar of movement and the solitary unity of drifters moving through the darkness.

There was a kind of tranquility to it, Aoibhe thought. There was a joy in the cocoon of white noise and rumble of the bike, the ache in the limbs and the strange, distant awareness of the world. In all the world, it was the closest thing she knew to peace.

It wasn't enough, though, at least not tonight. Not enough to disguise the aches beneath her motorcycle leathers, the deep muscle bruising under her ribs and along her right hip. Not enough to erase her memory of the draugr, its monstrous arm slamming into her chest and flinging her across the road. Not enough against the memory of the debt she still owed tonight, under the owl moon, the night of boundaries and the time of crossing through.

There was nothing in all the world that could take that away right now.

She switched off the East Link up East Wall Road, leaving

the quays and the city centre behind her. The port drifted past to her right, the bike moving like a living thing beneath her, smooth and savage. The toll plaza for the Dublin Port Tunnel loomed up ahead, floodlights and witchlights bathing the expanse of road in yellow, and suddenly there was no time left, and no peace either.

She pulled over onto the shoulder just below the toll gates, kicking into neutral and switching the engine off, removing her helmet with short, angry motions. The remaining threads of traffic heading through the Tunnel before its scheduled closure, ten minutes away, mostly ignored her. The Others lining the shoulders below the plaza, the supernatural traffic waiting for the changeover... not so much. She, however, could ignore them. And did, along with the soft clenching of her stomach and the twinge of bruises beneath the freshly scarred leather on her hip.

"You're late, Gallowglass," a voice said softly. Not really accusing, mildly curious at best. Aoibhe, reaching into the saddlebags, felt herself stiffen anyway.

"Waylaid," she explained shortly, as she lifted a slightly dented hauberk out of the luggage, the chainmail silver and ringing softly in her hands. It had already done duty earlier. Hopefully, the Devil notwithstanding, it wouldn't have to do duty again tonight. She shrugged into it carefully, pulling it down over the armoured leather, barely wincing at the ache in her ribs, and reached back down for the long tube holding her weapon.

There was silence behind her for a very long, almost trembling second while her new companion digested that, while he considered the implications and decided whether or not he liked them.

"On my account?" he asked, tone light and thoughtful, with nary a glimmer of danger. So very soft-spoken, this creature. "In your opinion, anyway. Were you delayed to damage me?"

Aoibhe paused for a second, leaning heavily on her bike, her shoulders tight and hunched beneath her armour. She could feel the St Christopher's medal beneath her leathers, the warmth of the silver on her skin as she drew strength up from her machine and the distant, shining regard of her Patron. For a moment, she simply breathed against the corpse stench of the draugr still staining her nostrils and the silent, impassive danger at her back.

Then she stood up, the telescoping metal of her spear's haft ringing out beside her as she drew it to its full length, her helm in her other hand as she turned to him. Gallowglass of the Clan McCabe, and Guardian of the Ways to top it.

The Devil looked back at her calmly, his grey-green eyes twinkling softly from the worn lines of his face, the middle-aged visage of his human guise. He was a handsome enough man, she thought absently. Fortyish, prematurely grey, with a face that said it had been beaten a few times in its day. His clothes were soft and warm under the heavy jacket, and the violin case on his back was as scarred as the leather at her hip. Possibly for the same reason. He wore it the way another being might wear the scabbard of a sword.

And for the weapon it held, well he might.

"No," Aoibhe decided, after a long moment. She thought over the incident critically, ignoring the spike of remembered adrenalin, and let the lurking conclusions she had come to on the drive up gently present themselves. "I don't think it was directed at you, Old Man." She smiled crookedly, shrugged. "Draugr on the coast road. I think it was simply fresh from the sea, and the whim of Manannán or Ægir put it in the path of a Way Guardian."

He raised one bushy eyebrow at that, a supremely skeptical expression, but appeared to accept it. It was possible that the draugr *had* been sent to interfere with this job. They both knew that. It was even possible, considering where they were going and under whose auspices, that a 'whim of Manannán' might be both coincidence *and* directed at them. The god of the Otherworld was inscrutable that way. But it made little difference now, when neither of them had the choice but to go, and both of them were still fit enough to try.

"Well, then," the Devil murmured, a slow, sly grin that might be humour or anticipation or both creeping across his features. He held out an arm towards her, his expression flashing to true mischief and back as she glared, and bowed her up towards the toll gates and the portals to the Otherworld they veiled. "Shall we, Gallóglach?"

Aoibhe curled her lip at him, in something that might, possibly, have been a smile and bowed him on in turn. "After you, my lord Scratch," she demurred and met the flash of his teeth with her own. She might be Gallowglass, hereditary mercenary, but she was a Way Guardian first, and he would do well to remember it. She owed him an escort on the back of services rendered, but she did not belong to him, nor serve him in the long run.

He looked at her for a long second, his distant, secret smile marked in that weathered face, ancient and malevolent. And then he straightened and laughed softly to himself, turning his face onward with an odd, wry expression.

"Yes," the Devil mused. "Yes, I suppose I ought to lead, at that." He shrugged a shoulder lightly. "I was ever first, you know. The light of morning. Perhaps you're right, and I shouldn't change that now."

He laughed again, shrugged his violin case higher on his shoulder, and turned now to the arc of the toll awning higher up the plaza. His shoulders stiffened, rolled lightly under his heavy jacket, and she followed his gaze, her own spine straightening as she saw it too. The electronic boards announcing the scheduled Tunnel closure had fallen dark, the streams of cars moving through the gates had petered out, and what sat beneath the toll awnings now... was another set of

Gates entirely.

The Boundary Time had come. In the silence and the yellow light beneath the owl moon, All Hallows Eve, Aoibhe stood behind the Devil at the Dublin Port Tunnel and watched Manannán's Gates open beneath the city to beckon travellers north and through, into the Barrowlands and the Old World beyond.

Dammit, she thought silently, her hand clenching on her spear, her muscles taut and ready beneath her leathers. This was what you got for owing the Devil a favour.

She should never have let him take the blow for her, never have let him step between her and the arc of blood that the Gan Ceann threw to mark her for death. But there hadn't been *time*. If she'd been able to do anything, if she'd had *time* to do anything, she would have simply avoided the attack herself. But she hadn't. She had met the eyes of the Gan Ceann, the Dullahan, by accident as it passed her by the roadside, and the creature's dark rage had boiled to the surface in seconds. The next she knew, the hitchhiker beside her had stepped between the ghost horse and her and flung his coat in the path of the steaming contents of the Dullahan's basin, catching the mark of death for his own.

Then the hitchhiker had sneered, soft and mischievous and darkly amused, as both she and the Dullahan realised exactly what, and exactly *who*, he'd turned out to be.

And now, four months later, here she was, escorting him into the Barrow Courts themselves in payment for that omen averted and that death turned aside, about to march with him before all the Old Gods of the Isle, the Sídhe and the Tuatha de Danann, and older things besides. All because she'd been stupid enough to meet a Dullahan's gaze, stupid enough not to realise the Devil himself stood beside her, stupid enough to let herself owe Old Scratch a favour.

If she weren't poised so very tenuously between so many forces right now, Aoibhe would have been tempted to try taking a god's name in vain. Some god. *Any* god.

On the heels of the thought, the medal at her throat cooled, flashing cold as they passed through the gates. The distant gaze of her Patron dimmed, her power stuttering as the force of another presence pressed down.

Mannanán, the God of the Boundary, had laid his hand upon her.

Aoibhe grimaced and paused just past the awning, her hand shifting on the haft of her spear. Scratch turned, looking back at her curiously, but she ignored him, her attention turned inwards, threading down past the medal to her feet, to the feel of her armoured boots on the tarmac. Otherworld or no, Manannán or no, she stood on the roads, and that meant she could have power. That meant she *would* have power. She pressed inwards, pressed through the barriers, and ground the butt of her spear into the tarmac.

And after a moment, sharp and bright, a stab through a reluctantly parting veil, she felt warmth and strength rush back through her. St Christopher's casual strength, that had once borne up the weight of the world through the rush of a river, flooded through her limbs, and the medal at her throat warmed once again. Aoibhe grinned, slow and fierce beneath her Patron's gaze, and offered her spear in salute.

He might not approve of the cause, her Patron. He might not approve of a Guardian of the Ways, the travelling brotherhood, marching guard on the Devil himself. But he didn't approve of Manannán's interference, either. It was in breach of the Crossroads Treaty, after all, the agreement of the gods and goddesses of travellers and mariners, of roads, crossroads, gates and doorways, of all the ways through and between and onward. By that treaty, any Way Guardian could bear the blessing of their Patron past any gate and along any path. Whether they escorted enemies into the heart of a people's power or wandered aimlessly on nothing more than a whim, the Brotherhood could not be waylaid by any one signatory's power.

So Manannán, Devil or no Devil, could *shove* it. She was the Devil's contracted Guardian. Scratch had been invited, the gilt-edged invitation to the Barrow Courts of Meath signed by the Leannan Sídhe herself. And even if that lay in Manannán's realm, even if none of them, not her, not her Patron, not the Old Gods of the Otherworld, knew what plan the Devil had in mind... between the treaty and that invitation, she had a right to her power, even though none could tell how she'd use it.

The Devil was watching her when she opened her eyes. Patient and amused, his gaze was fixed unerringly on the medal hidden beneath leather and mail, the soft burning of a familiar power undoubtedly clear as daylight to him. She wondered absently if he remembered Christopher, the barbarian who'd chosen God over him because the Devil had been too weak to hold his interest. She wondered if Scratch remembered that.

She wondered if she might be here because of it.

"Trouble?" the Devil asked mildly, waiting just at the northbound Tunnel's mouth. The sodium lights, flickering here with more intent than usual, the electrical leer of their elemental spirits visible now that they were past the Boundary, made him look oddly normal. Grey and scarred and tired, at the mouth of a Tunnel that wasn't his. Aoibhe blinked at him, slowly.

"Manannán doesn't like me tonight," she said, walking forward to catch up with him, the ring of her armoured boots heavy as they moved into the Tunnel itself. The Devil fell into step beside her with casual ease, a faint smile caught at the corner of his mouth. She shook her head at him. "Do I want to know what you did last time, that the entire Otherworld seems petrified at the thought of your rematch?"

An escort to a duel, he'd told her, when he'd called his favour in. He'd patted the fiddle case on the seat beside him as he hunched over a table at a petrol station seating area, bad coffee in hand, her motorcycle helmet resting beside his violin. Every century, he'd said, he had a standing appointment with the Leannan Sídhe, the dark fae of music and inspiration, for a duel of music, to see who could make the heavens weep the hardest. Actually, he'd confided, he had such standing appointments with most of the muse spirits, the gods of sound and fury, the musicians of the spheres. His little personal amusement, he'd said, his quest.

But the humour in his voice had been only surface deep. And underneath it, there had been something darkly luminous. The monster, maybe. The bright-dark thing beneath that human veneer.

"It was a fine duel," he told her now, matching her pace easily as they marched beneath the Tunnel's lights, passing under Dublin and deeper still, passing under time, into the Other places beyond. "She had such a beautiful champion, back then. Her best, I think." He smiled thinly. "Utterly mad, of course. So deep in her grasp that he barely knew the difference between one world and the other. I don't think he even realised who his opponent was. But he was beautiful. Oh yes. And he was talented. Mad passion and utter brilliance. He played fit to wring tears from angels and bring gods to their knees in wonder."

Aoibhe watched him as he spoke. They walked alone down the Tunnel's left-hand lane, the other traffic, the spirits and sídhe and even the occasional god, apparently deciding to keep well, well clear of them. And Aoibhe watched him, the deadly light in his eyes as he talked of music and madness and death.

"We played for three days and three nights," the Devil continued softly, lost in his own kind of peace as they walked between the pools of light and slim shadows along the Tunnel's length. "We played like madmen, like music made flesh. We played every song under the sun, every motion, every mood. We played dances to wear down a faery's iron shoes, laments to mourn the passing of worlds, marches to guide the armies of the Apocalypse to war. We played it all, that mortal madman and I. For three days and three nights he matched me, and we played the Barrow Courts to their knees."

He fell silent for six lengths of light, the Tunnel unending until the goal was reached. They would walk inside its confines until the Boundary faded and the Barrow Courts opened before them. Geography in the Otherworld was never quite the same as on the outside.

"But he was mortal," said the Devil after a moment, something maybe like grief in his eyes. Or possibly only regret, for an entertainment cut short. "He was mortal, and he was frail, and her power had burned him through before I ever arrived. He played his fingers to the bone, flayed them open unheeding before us, made fiddle strings of his own blood. He played his fiddle into dust, spun his mind and his soul up into song to try and match me, and he failed. In the end, on the third night, he failed. And having failed, he died." A small smirk, a black and bottomless expression. "And then... that was that."

Aoibhe swallowed faintly. Strength hummed through her, the endless rhythm of movement, the gift of her calling and her Patron. She listened to the pulse of her breathing, her blood, the soft chiming of her mail as she moved, the echo of her armoured boots against the Tunnel walls, the chink of her spear haft in time to her steps. Her own music, her own fealty. A loyalty that cost her in blood and bone and armour, in pain and debts and walks beneath the world and into death, with the Devil at her side. A patronage that cost her, yes, but not like that. Not ever like that. Not devoured, not turned against herself, not spun up into blood music for the pleasure of gods. Her oath took a price, yes, always. But not *that* price.

"That would horrify me," she said, at last. Carefully, very carefully, trying not to imagine being so lost in another's power that she couldn't even notice herself dying. "That *does* horrify me. But..."

She paused, thought very carefully, and as she did he turned his head to look at her, his smile gleaming blackly, a slickness in the twilight, a pale shining in the darkness. He looked at her, this Devil at her side, and she fought the sudden shudder for the end of the thought and the tactical consideration that came with it.

"But that wouldn't horrify *her*," she finished steadily, despite the tremor in her gut, the whisper of blind fear across her spine. "That wouldn't horrify the gods. That wouldn't make Manannán Mac Lir throw a draugr and a threshold across my path to keep me from guarding your way." She looked at him, glared at him through the fear he sowed in her, and rang her spear that little harder against the tarmac to break his spell. "What did you *do*, Old Scratch, that they don't want you to come back?"

Like a glacier falling still, he stopped: a slow, inevitable ceasing. The Devil stopped beneath the flickering sodium lights, painted gold and grey by the electric lighting in this Tunnel beneath the world, and met her eyes.

"Not so slow all the time, are you," he said softly, those grey-green eyes cold as wet moss on her skin. "Not so stupid, Aoibhe McCabe of the Gallóglaigh."

Aoibhe swallowed hard, her body bracing itself automatically, the spear coming across her torso and her knees flexing inside the armoured leather. The bruises from her battle with the draugr, her ribs, her hip, protested. On the rush of adrenalin, she ignored them. Beneath her hauberk, her medal flared now to heat, power flooding through her. She called on the almost berserker strength of St Christopher, who'd told the Devil he wasn't good enough all those centuries ago, and braced herself to meet that cold regard with all the power and determination she possessed.

And in the face of it, the Devil laughed, long and rich and deep, the pealing of bells, the thunder of mountains falling. He laughed until his shoulders shook with it, the violin case riding the waves of his mirth, bright tears in his eyes. The Devil looked on her defiance and he laughed.

"Oh," he breathed, one fist coming up to press against his chest, knotting in the red wool of his jumper. "Oh, I'm sorry, my dear." He grinned, now grey and worn once more, the smile human-looking once again. "I didn't mean to alarm you, Way Guardian. Of course not. Forgive me."

Aoibhe growled at him, her knees still flexed and her spear still ready. She owed him, she owed him her *life,* so she couldn't leave him now, but damned if it gave him leave for anything else. *Damned* if she let him have anything else because of it, not even the lowering of her guard.

"Give me an answer, Lord Scratch, and I might consider it," she said coldly, straightening carefully, watching him with narrow eyes. The point of her spear drifted in his direction, as much bravado as warning, but she could offer nothing less, even against the Devil. "Tell me what I want to know. What I *need* to know. And then... we'll see if we keep walking, or if Manannán might find us easier to delay than he thought."

His eyes narrowed, at that, a gold-dark gleam of warning, maybe anger, but his mouth stayed soft and crooked, his mirth still fixed on his face. He spread his hands out to the sides, his leather jacket gaping open over the redness beneath it, and Aoibhe couldn't help but wince, for all she knew it was only the wool of his jumper.

"Of course," the Devil said quietly, against the soft crackling of the lights over his head. "Certainly, Gallóglach. A toll, then. An answer to pass forward." He chuckled a little. "Apt, I think. Yes, all right. You asked why the Otherworld fears me tonight, yes? Why the Old Gods would have me delayed, and the time of my duel pass unmet. Well..."

He snarled, all the darkness of the abyss, and the electrical elementals that lighted the way screeched and juddered for a moment's shock. In the sudden, flickering obscurity as the rhythm of the night and the journey broke around her, Aoibhe bore down, and ground her spear into the road, that it might bear her up. That was the old blessing, wasn't it. *Go n'éirí an bóthar leat.* May the road rise to meet you.

For a Way Guardian, for her, it just might.

"They fear me," the Devil said, voice harsh and ringing in the stillness, "because last time, for the first time in twelve centuries, I *won*. For the first time since we began this game of duels, I beat the Leannan Sídhe. For more than a thousand years, I have paid her price each century, I have bent to her whims within the limits of our rules, I have bowed my head and called the game well played. And it *was*." He grinned, black as pitch. "It was, Gallowglass. One long con, so expertly played. Escalating century on century, the humiliations and the prices climbing inch by inch until at last, the winner could ask what they pleased. Any service, any gift of music, any opportunity. Last century, she bid a poor Devil play against her finest Champion, lose to him as he had lost to all lesser champions previously. And this time, as no other time before... the Devil *won*. The Devil won, and he demanded his price."

He was an angel now, Aoibhe thought, an angel in the dark beneath Dublin, in the Boundary around the Barrows of Meath. He was an angel, and a demon, and somewhere too a mortal man, or at least the seeming of one. He was madness and music and death. He was the gambler's friend, the thief's guardian, the musician's cheerful opponent. He was immortal and unending and *enraged*. He was smug, standing in the Tunnel in his leather jacket and his woollen jumper with his fiddle riding his shoulder. He was bright, and he was terrible, and he was laughing in the ringing stillness before her.

She had to ask. For her debt, and her blood, and the price

her oath might yet ask of her. With the web of roads spread out beneath her feet, the Way Guardian's duty and Manannán's challenge, she had to ask him.

"And what price," she murmured, slow and clear, "did the Devil ask of them? What prize did he demand for his victory?"

The rage vanished. The triumph, the thunder, the radiance, and the abyss, all of it, every last scrap, vanished in front of her, and the Devil stood before her once again as that hitchhiker he'd seemed on the N11, heading south for the ferries out of Rosslare, with his hiking boots, and the scarred case of his violin, and the coat he'd thrown in front of a Dullahan's blood. As the elementals regained their courage and the lights grew brighter, the Devil shrank before her into something smaller, and more weary, and somehow so much older.

"He asked leave to play for them," he said, softly. A glimmer of darkness still lurked in his expression, but no more than that. "He asked possession of their court, the Barrows beneath the world, for one night, the Crossing Night, All Hallows Eve. So he could play one song and have it be heard across the worlds, have it echo through all the boundaries." He grinned, the conman's grin. "Can you guess why, Aoibhe McCabe?"

She could. Of *course* she could. She was a Way Guardian, of course she understood. With the web of roads under her, and Manannán's power all around her, she could guess, oh yes.

"You'll play at the centre of the Boundary," she said quietly, watching his eyes, watching that grey-green gaze and how warm it suddenly seemed. "On the night it fades thinnest, on the night it touches most worlds and reaches into the deepest depths of the Otherworld." She faltered, a weight in her chest, a sudden knowledge. Not of his plan, but of his *reason*. Of the thread running underneath it all. "You'll play... and there will be no world you won't touch. And no God who will not hear you."

The lines spread around his eyes like the web of roads, warm creases of triumph and pain and weary delight, and he looked so ancient then. He looked so *old*, so worn, so casually wicked and unutterably tired. Not an angel, no, nor a devil either. Just... just an old man, an exile who, after all these years, wanted to send a message home.

And she was going to let him, Aoibhe realised. No matter what resulted from it, no matter what price it called down on their heads, she would help him stand in the centre of the Old Gods' power and lay open the boundary before them. She would help him challenge a judgement laid down so many aeons ago. She was going to help him play that one song, and all the gods be damned.

However...

"One more question, my lord," she said, resting her spear against the cant of her bruised hip, her mouth soft and a little crooked. "One last coin, before we pass on." She raised her eyebrows, wry and vaguely concerned. "Exactly what *kind* of song are you planning to play?"

She'd help him send the message. Oh yes, she'd guard his path through the Boundary and stand with him in the Barrow Courts, watch him send his song racing down all the roads at once, tribute and price all in one, a toll in and of itself. She would help him do that—that was already decided.

But she could stand to know, first, the *nature* of the message he'd be sending and whether she'd need to stand at least a lightning-bolt's width to the side. The Devil was still the Devil, after all, a dark and wicked thing beneath that age and that pain, and he'd won his chance with the souls of men spun to bleeding.

He paused for a second, his eyes twinkling in the yellow lights beneath the earth. He paused as his eyes lost focus, one hand creeping over his shoulder to touch the violin case, to trail delicately over it and feel the strength of the instrument cradled inside it. To touch, maybe, the threads of his inspiration, the strings spun from his own blood, mischief and pain and rage and longing, and a thousand other things besides.

"I don't know," he said at last, the map of lines creasing pained and contemplative on his face. "I haven't decided yet." He laughed, the sound of bells and dawn breaking, the sound of worlds ending. "I'll know when I set bow to strings, I think. I'll know... when I can feel Him listening. Not before."

He looked up, then. Flashed her a grin, soft and wicked, the gambler's friend that her McCabe blood recognised so very, very well. Wicked and warm, and maybe, just maybe, on your side.

"I'll make you some promises, though, if you like?" he offered, with an impressive facsimile of seriousness. "Not to smash any worlds irreparably. Not to call down an Apocalypse or anything." He smirked a little. "Though I can't make any promises on *His* behalf, you understand. I can't promise how He'll react." She raised an eyebrow, and he offered a little half-bow of demur. "Oh, all right. I can promise not to *immediately* go out of my way to offend, either. Will that do?"

Aoibhe thought it over, pursed her lips to exaggerate the moment, to make him wait. To taunt, to tease. Not at all wise, of course, but she'd had a bad night. She'd fought a draugr corpse-warrior on the coast road at Greystones. She'd been needled at by Manannán Mac Lir. She'd been roped into a millennia-long dispute by the Devil himself and threatened by him on top of it. The very least she was owed, by this stage, was the chance to needle the Devil in return. In honour of her Patron, she thought she could risk that.

And then, because there was risk and then there was stupidity, she inclined her head with only the smallest of smirks, and nodded agreement. "Good enough," she decided, and brought her spear around as she straightened, pointing the head down the Tunnel towards the light at the end, flavoured differently to the electric lights around them. The light of fires and torches and the Barrow Mounds, the end of Boundary, now that the toll had been paid.

"Good enough," she repeated, her medal of office warm beneath her motorcycle leathers. "Shall we go send your message then, my lord Scratch?"

He grinned, a thoroughly wicked creature, a monster standing at her side, and offered her a tiny bow. "I thought you'd never ask," said the Devil wryly and turned to walk beside her into the heart of the Ways.

And if, hours later, the Barrows and the Tunnel, the Boundary and the Otherworld, the owl moon over Dublin and the Light above the Silver City all rang, each and every one of them, with the vast and terrible sound of a fiddle, with rage and pain and joy and grief, with longing and hatred and adoration and love, with madness and music and death...

Well. He'd paid his toll first, hadn't he? The Ways cared not who travelled where or why. Only that they paid their dues to manage it.

LIN THORNHILL

Verisimilitude

N*o Vampires Beyond This Point.* The portable sign with its misaligned plastic letters stood off to the side of Highway 101. Ben traveled three or four hundred yards further before slamming on his brakes. He backed the SUV until the sign was clearly visible through the rhythmic swipe of rubber blades sluicing rain from the windshield. He hadn't been mistaken.

Briefly, he felt exposed; then, self-preservation overrode common sense, and his canines lengthened into fangs. He snarled, shifted the transmission to park, and opened the driver's door to step onto the asphalt.

Ben's heightened senses assessed his surroundings, the road-hugging forest beneath a gloomy cloudbank and the single building behind its attention-grabbing sign. There were two humans in the building, but he was the most lethal creature in the vicinity. No one observed the lone driver as he transformed, crouching in a fighting stance in the middle of the highway, frigid rain drenching him. The only constant between his human and wolf forms was his amber eyes glowing in the dark.

Hackles rising, Ben ducked his head, hunched his shoulders, and shook himself free of the sodden shirt before stepping from jeans and boots that no longer fit his altered form. The rain weighed his fur down, but the distance over which he could scent danger tripled when he was in wolf form. His eyes darted along the highway to the near and distant trees. The forest's regular host of animals had long since sought shelter from the downpour, and none were a threat to him.

Vampires? What purpose could there be in posting such a sign? he wondered as he peered into the distance. After several minutes, Ben finally remembered the date.

It was October, the time of fantastical ghosts and ghouls, candy and costumes. Children, teenagers, and even adults strung out on sugar highs succumbed to the irresistible urge to prank innocent bystanders and their local proprietor of the all-night minimart and tackle shop—which meant him.

Aren't you a moron, Poundstone? he derided himself mentally. There were no other supernatural beings in his territory. Not in the past decade. He had made certain of it. The tiny town of Forks, Washington was his home ground.

With practiced ease, Ben shifted back to his two-legged form. He gathered his soggy flannel shirt, jeans, and boots, wondering why he couldn't transform into something more useful. Why did he have to turn into a furry, four-legged beast when Count Dracula had been able to become a bat?

The rain slowed to a misty drizzle. Ben wrestled himself into the sodden jeans, and threw the rest of his clothing into the SUV; then he climbed back into the driver's seat. He executed a swift U-turn, returning the way he had come. He would need a change of clothes before work.

"It's seven o'clock, Ben." Christine stated the obvious when he walked through the door of Hook Line & Sinker, the bell above the door chiming to announce his arrival. "I expected you at six."

"I got caught in the rain."

"It always rains." She was clearly in a snit. "You knew I wanted to leave on time tonight."

"I had to change."

Christine's frown turned into a distressed pout. "Gary's taking me to Port Angeles for dinner if we haven't lost the reservations. It's the six-month anniversary of our first date."

Ben knew Gary but didn't particularly like him. There was nothing impressive about the former jock, and Ben kept interactions between them civil and short-lived. He reminded himself that Christine's choice of companion was not his business. "Why didn't you have Allen stay late? He may not be the liveliest lure on the hook—"

"He called in sick," she interrupted. "Actually, his mother called."

Ben rolled his eyes. It was a long-running joke as to whether Allen, the store's teenaged clerk, knew how to do anything without his mother's knowledge or consent.

Christine sniffed unhappily, and Ben angled his head to catch her attention. He stared into her dark brown eyes, watching to see if her pupils dilated. When they didn't, he sighed. Unlike others who were easy to influence mentally, she had always been resistant to his charm. "Please give Gary my apologies," he said.

"Give *Gary* your apologies? Where's *my* apology?" With jerky, angry motions, she collected her raincoat from where it had been draped across the stool behind the counter. She strode toward the front door, short skirt flirting with her thighs and her heels clicking a staccato counterpoint on the cement floor.

Just before she opened the door, Ben blurted, "I'll let you select our holiday novelties."

Her anger faded as if it had never existed. "Really?"

He glowered at her. "Don't make me regret it."

She laughed. "I won't, Boss." Just before shutting the door behind her, she said, "Apology accepted."

A month later, Ben stared at the contents of a large

cardboard box filled with new merchandise for the store, just in time for the Christmas holidays. *Forks Bites!* read the slogan on the mug, on the key chains, and on the girly tees in sizes small, medium, and large.

I regret it now, he thought while carrying the box to the neatly arranged storeroom at the back of the building. He didn't bother turning on the lights while shifting tackle and fishing line to make room for the novelty items. He could see as well, if not better, in the dark. His artfully graying hair straggled across his eyes when he shook his head. *What a ridiculous slogan,* he thought as he unloaded the key chains. Where were they going to display the souvenirs? Between the fish hooks and silicone lures?

A week later, Christine poked her head through the doorway of Ben's closet-sized office located in one corner of the storeroom. "We're out of *Forks Bites!* mugs. We need to reorder."

Ben looked up from the stack of invoices on the scarred desk he had called his own through two personae and the better part of four decades. "You're kidding?"

"Nope. They're selling faster than I can put them on display." Her grin was infectious and her excitement intoxicating. He had forgotten she had peek-a-boo dimples.

Ben had long since discovered that heightened emotional responses could trigger his own desires, both visceral and abnormal. Willing his fangs not to descend, he gritted his teeth before biting out the question, "What the hell is so special about this stuff?"

"It's that book," she said, and disappeared toward the front of the store.

"What book?" he shouted after her, but she was busy with the after-school rush. Four gossipy teenagers in need of their afternoon dose of caffeine, salt, and sugar. It was just as well, Ben thought, angrily repressing his sudden desire to taste

Christine. He had made it a policy never to drink from someone he actually liked.

It was a balmy Tuesday in April when twelve boxes of merchandise arrived at Hook Line & Sinker. *Twelve?* Ben had no idea where it would all fit. He cut into the first box and unfolded the lid. His eyes widened. Quickly, he opened the other eleven boxes. Their contents were essentially all the same.

"Christine!"

Within seconds, she skidded into the storeroom. Her curly hair bounced about her face, and her expression turned from anxiety to irritation in less than a heartbeat. Ben knew; he could hear her heart pounding in his ears.

"From your bellow," she said tartly, "I expected you to be lying prostrate on the floor."

Choosing a paperback novel from the first box he had opened, Ben waved its cover toward her. "What the hell is this?"

She sniffed. "*Dracula* is a classic."

"It was written in the nineteenth century, I'll give you that." He looked into the fourth box and made another selection. "But what then do you call this?"

"Let me see." Christine's eyes sparkled mischievously. "I'd call it *Guilty Pleasures.*" Then she turned her attention to the delivery, flipping cardboard flaps of box after box. "*Interview with a Vampire. Dead Until Dark.* Yep." She frowned then, fumbling through the stacks of books. "Where are the graphic novels?" She flipped the lid of another box, one as yet unexplored. "Ah. Here we are." She nodded in satisfaction. "*Hellsing.*"

Ben folded his arms and watched Christine browse through the sensational fiction. His expression darkened to a glower. Much of what had been written about vampires was titillating speculation, but there was enough legitimate information to make him uncomfortable at providing it on his home ground. Few people knew him well enough to draw conclusions about his perennially youthful looks, but there had been comments before.

After several minutes, he cleared his throat. "Is there a reason we're presenting the community with the most salacious collection of vampire fiction since the Victorian era?"

"It's almost summer," Christine replied.

"And?"

"I keep telling you it's because of that book." Christine huffed at his lack of comprehension. "You know, the one based here in Forks about the family of vegetarian vampires. We're famous, and I thought it would be a good idea to cash in on the tourists' interest."

"And you think its popularity will draw enough tourists to Forks—" he waved a hand to the storefront "—to order *twelve* boxes of vampire stories?"

"Oh, yes," she said fervently. "It's put our little town on the map, Ben, and it'll put money in your pocket."

"It's pandering to the lowest common denominator."

"It'll sell." From the fourth box, she removed an invoice and two stacks of a vivid turquoise paperback whose title Ben couldn't see. Her expression turned thoughtful. "Every time I order vampire merchandise you have a problem with it. You're not particularly religious, as far as I know. You aren't, are you?"

"No."

"Well, why does it bother you?"

He stared at her for a long moment, his eyes riveted to the sight of her front teeth biting her full bottom lip. He recognized the signs of her ripening uncertainty. Telling her the truth was out of the question, but Ben had become quite deft at half-truths. "You've seen the accounts, Christine. I don't have much of a profit margin, and I don't like to speculate on iffy ventures."

"We've never not sold this stuff," she replied defensively while placing the books on the shelf above two cases of *Forks Bites!* shot glasses. "Not once."

He threw up his hands and conceded. "It's your job to sort this out. Find somewhere to store this lot, and make arrangements for their display."

She picked up *Dracula* from where he had dropped it and fingered the pages. "Fine. I've already got it worked out."

"Nothing too garish, Christine," Ben said, hoping to moderate her continuing efforts to make the store *more accessible to a broader cross-section of the community*. She had said those very words to him in February while decorating with red crepe streamers and balloon bouquets for Valentine's Day. He had nixed the streamers but agreed to keep the balloons while wondering if he was insane to let her re-organize the store's layout to something more *aesthetically pleasing*. Also her phrasing.

Christine's confidence re-emerged. "Mark my words, these'll be gone before July."

He managed to nod before taking her place in the front of the store, settling on the stool behind the counter. He had to admit, if only to himself, that he enjoyed the store's generally more cheerful ambiance.

Ben's brow furrowed as he considered Christine's strategy. Time and experience had taught him that Edgar Allen Poe had been right when he wrote *The Purloined Letter*. Hiding in plain sight had kept Ben safe for more than a century. However, providing his customers with a revolving stand of clues courted potential disaster.

The bell over the front door chimed to announce a customer. A comfortably padded woman in her forties entered the store wearing a cheap version of the latest fashion. She was one of the newer residents in town and had been to Hook Line & Sinker once or twice. He hated to admit Christine was right, but there were a lot of new people in Forks. Ben nodded at the customer, and she smiled before turning toward the refrigerated cases lining the store's western wall.

While she shopped, Ben answered a phone call. According to his mother, hapless Allen would be missing another shift at work.

"You're English, aren't you?" The customer had brought a liter of soda and a bag of chips to the counter.

As they had barely exchanged a dozen words before, Ben was slightly taken aback by her comment, and he replied cautiously, "I was born there."

"I thought so," she said. "My cousin married an Englishman, and I've always loved the way he talks."

"I wasn't aware I still had an accent."

"It's not strong," she said, waving her hand as if his comment were negligible. "I've just got an ear for it."

The bell chimed as elderly Jack Newsome came through the door. "Afternoon." His voice quavered as he headed toward the display of fishing line and freshwater lures.

The woman handed Ben a ten-dollar bill, and while he made change, she asked, "How long have you been here?"

Using the cover story he had developed for this mortal lifetime, Ben let the practiced lie trip off his tongue. "My parents divorced when I was very young, and my father left the store to me when he died. I thought why not see what the States are like. I've been here ever since."

"That's kind of sad."

"Not really." He shrugged. "I hardly knew him, and it's been fifteen years."

"Fifteen? Wow." She leaned over the counter and held out her hand. "I'm Carol, by the way."

Ben took her hand, shaking gingerly. "Ebenezer Poundstone. Ben."

"Nice to meet'cha, Ben. I'll certainly be back." Carol gathered her snacks, and as she exited Ben was positive he heard her mutter, "He's definitely not *that* old."

He couldn't help but think he would never be *that old*.

As summer waxed and waned, Hook Line & Sinker welcomed a steady influx of new clientele. Situated at the less developed end of town, the store was housed in a sturdy wooden building and shared a dirt-and-gravel parking lot with the Smoke House restaurant and lounge.

Over the years, an occasional, transient morsel had stumbled into Ben's shop after leaving the bar. He had welcomed their intoxicated largesse before sending them on their way with nothing more than a vague memory of an enjoyable evening and a small cut to the wrist, neck, or thigh they couldn't remember acquiring. This summer, however, had provided something of a smorgasbord for Ben's dining pleasure.

In addition to an increase in late night snacks, Hook Line & Sinker's overall sales were higher than ever before, and Ben hired two additional employees. Rachel was tiny and enthusiastic while Lukas was strong enough to shift the heaviest boxes in the storeroom.

Christine's shrewd understanding of changing local interests bore fruit. By June fifth, the last book from the initial twelve-box order was sold. She never mentioned catching Ben reading *Interview with a Vampire* early one morning, and he pretended the incident never occurred.

In the past, the majority of the store's patrons had been grizzled fishermen sipping coffee at pre-dawn, fathers and sons embarking on bonding excursions, afterschool kids buying snacks, and the occasional teenager attempting to buy beer with a faked license. Yet the summer saw an increasing number of women, tourists and locals alike, trolling the store's aisles. Many became repeat customers, a number of them eager to chat up the Englishman who worked most nights. Business was good, and Ben relaxed into complacency.

Late one August afternoon, Ben arrived at Hook Line &

Sinker under the umbrella of a gloomy sky and persistent drizzle which threatened to develop into a downpour. He pulled into the parking lot, stopping next to Christine's pickup. He grabbed his keys and opened the driver's door without widening his senses beforehand.

A snarling hiss was his only warning as impossibly strong arms ripped him from the SUV. The acrid stench of vampire in aggressive territorial dispute assaulted Ben's nostrils. He scrambled to gain his footing and dropped his keys. He got a brief impression of yellow hair, glowing eyes and distended fangs before he was completely engaged in repelling his assailant.

"You've got a fucking goldmine here—" the other vampire grunted the words, "—and I want it."

Within seconds, Ben's feet were knocked out from under him, and he found himself flat on his back, his assailant's expression one of terrible delight.

Ben didn't waste time talking. The intruder was entirely focused on killing him and doing it quickly.

Grappling for a hold—hair, coat, shirt—Ben bent his legs, pulling his knees as tight as possible toward his chest. His opponent was in the way, snarling and brutally crushing him into the ground.

Ben's fangs elongated, and he growled, the challenge vibrating in his chest. He managed to push one hand against his rival's face, hissing when fangs sliced into his palm, but pulling back would be fatal.

The interloper shifted his weight for greater leverage.

Ben forced his feet under his assailant's hips, thrusting his legs straight and throwing the other vampire backward several yards. He landed at the edge of the parking area near a small stand of scattered trees edging the dense forest beyond.

In an instant, Ben charged his rival, slamming him against a tree trunk and momentarily stunning him. Seizing his opportunity, Ben gave no quarter. He broke his assailant's neck as easily as one might snap one of the twigs in the forest.

Ben's fangs ached to rend flesh, to drain the vermin dry. Instead, he snarled and grabbed the intruder's head, twisting it beyond the break. Blood from his wounded palm streaked the vampire's fair hair, and Ben's grip threatened to slip, but he held tight. Biceps flexing and tensing, he continued twisting until the head separated from its body. Crimson blood soaked into the damp ground.

Belatedly broadening his senses to confirm there were no other immediate threats, Ben checked that he wasn't within sight of the store or restaurant. He sighed in relief not to have drawn unwanted attention. Then, taking no chances, he scanned the area, located a slender tree branch, and shoved it through the decapitated vampire's chest. The body immediately began to decompose.

Dead, dead, and dead again.

The entire encounter had taken no more than two minutes.

That was too damned close. Ben bent double, his muscles trembling in the aftermath of the lethal confrontation. He rested his hands on his knees, his own blood soaking his jeans as he attempted to gather his wits. *Goddamn it!* He should have transformed into a wolf early in the fight, leading the interloper deeper into the woods.

In his experience, vampires were solitary hunters who marked and defended their territory aggressively. Ben had barely survived his first encounter with another vampire, shortly after he had been turned. There had been no telltale heartbeat or other warning sign, just a swift, deadly attack of bared fangs and vicious grappling holds.

It had been during that brutal fight that Ben discovered his additional ability to transform into a wolf. The unexpectedness of his skeletal structure shifting had provided him with a desperately needed advantage over a far more experienced opponent. *How could I have forgotten that lesson?*

Ben wondered and shook his head in disgust.

"Ben?" It was Christine, calling in the near distance. He could hear her heart racing, her breath coming too fast. "Ben, where are you?"

Take her! Feed now! his instincts screamed, nearly as demanding as the day he had been turned. He closed his eyes and gritted his teeth, quelling the insistent desire, willing his fangs to retract. After several seconds, he yelled, "Be right there."

Fortunately, his response prevented her coming in search of him.

He glanced at the other vampire's rapidly deliquescing body. In mere minutes, the only evidence of the intruder's presence would be his bloody clothes, and he would retrieve them later. Fire would be his best option for their disposal.

Stepping from under the tree's shelter and further from his SUV and Christine, Ben removed his tee-shirt to stand under the now steady downpour. He used the shirt to wipe his face and hair before wrapping his still-bleeding hand in it.

With some degree of control, he straightened his shoulders and walked toward the parking lot. When he emerged from the small stand of trees, Ben saw Christine's disheveled appearance, and he sprinted toward where she stood under the store's front awning. For a second he thought her skirt was soaked with blood, but then realized crimson was just the color of the fabric. "Are you hurt?" he asked urgently.

"Yes," she replied. "No. I'm not sure. I can't really remember." She rubbed her forehead as if soothing an ache.

"Look at me, Christine." Wide, trusting brown eyes looked right into his. Her pupils were dilated, clear evidence of his rival's mental tampering. She would have a vicious headache for some time. Ben ground his teeth, resisting his urge to *take her*, mark her as his, to erase the challenger's taint.

He should have prevented this, he thought. Suddenly, Ben raised his head, cocking it as if listening to a distant noise.

"Where's Rachel?"

"I sent her home earlier. It's her Mom's birthday."

Ben sighed in relief once again. His people were safe, his instincts under a veneer of control. "You have to stop making a habit of that."

"I wouldn't have wanted her to get hurt. She's such a little thing."

"I don't want you to be hurt either." Ben hugged Christine then. He had never done so before, and he worried she might be affronted. She wasn't. She clung to him, trembling like a fawn escaping a forest fire.

After several minutes she noticed his naked torso and tee-shirt wrapped hand, and she gasped. "Ben, you're hurt. What happened?"

"Just some kid hopped up on something. Ecstasy, speed, meth." He shrugged, and she stepped back, frowning.

"Maybe it was the same kid in the store," she said. "Why can't I remember?"

"Did you hit your head on anything?" He was unable to explain the most probable reason for her pain.

"Not that I remember."

Ben gently examined her skull with his uninjured hand. "There are no bumps, but that doesn't mean you didn't get hit in some fashion." He steeled himself and managed to ask, "Did he touch you?"

Christine's eyebrows rose at his tone, but she said, "I don't think so." Then she shook her head as if to clear it, but was distracted by his injury. She gestured toward the improvised bandage. "Shouldn't you have that looked at? Maybe get some stitches?"

Somehow, her reaction eased Ben's residual anger at his own laxness, dissipating the last of the adrenaline-fueled desire to fight or feed. Her honest concern reminded him that it was this closeness—this human affection—that was the reason he had remained in Forks for as long as he had. With that thought, he finally understood the reason Christine was resistant to his charm, the reason he had never been able to mentally control her. He cared for her, and it provided her with some degree of immunity.

Ben smiled, and it was both rueful and filled with affection. "It's not that serious. I'll take care of it inside."

"Okay."

"Be right back." He dashed to the parking lot, retrieved his keys from the muddy gravel, and then closed the SUV's door. He didn't look over his shoulder at the location of the dead vampire's clothes. He did look at Christine. Her skirt was a bright contrast to the aged silvery hue of Hook Line & Sinker's native wood siding.

When he returned to the storefront and a still-dazed Christine, he said, "It's a good thing I leave a change of clothes here now."

"Yeah," she said, smiling a little. "You're all wet again."

He chuckled and held the door for her. Ironically, the only damage in the store was to the carousel of vampire fiction. It had been knocked to the floor, its contents scattered across the walkway.

"I'll pick these up."

"It can wait." Ben flipped the lock on the front door, turning the Open sign to read Closed. "You need to take something for your head," he suggested.

"I have Tylenol in my bag."

He rolled his uninjured hand, gesturing in the direction of the left aisle where they offered various first aid supplies and over-the-counter remedies. "Use whatever you need."

"Thanks." Pointing her finger at his wrapped hand, Christine said, "Do you want help with that?"

"If I do, I'll ask. Thanks."

By the time Ben reached the office his wounds had begun to close. He would keep his hand bandaged for a few days, but the injury would be completely healed by the following morning.

Fifteen minutes later, Christine knocked on the office door, a mug of hot chocolate in her hand. When he opened the door, she eyed his fresh clothes. "Are you all right?" she asked.

"Fine. See." He raised his gauze-wrapped hand.

She smiled. "You'll do."

"How's your head?"

"I'm okay. I can't figure out how I got hurt. Things are a little fuzzy."

He stepped back from the doorway, and offered her a seat. "Maybe you chased him out of the store?"

She sat, sipping her chocolate. "Me?"

"Maybe he insulted your books, and you went for him."

"Oh, yeah. That's me. Defender of vampires." She giggled.

Ben was pleased to see her rally from the distressing incident. He offered her a tissue for her chocolate mustache and laughed as she wiped her mouth and stuck out her tongue at him. She took another drink of the chocolate, then licked her lips clean. The movement of her tongue was mesmerizing.

Christine bit her lip, then said, "If I did chase him, that would account for the book rack falling over."

"It would."

"Maybe he saw your SUV and panicked."

"Perhaps." In all likelihood, the other vampire had been distracted by Ben's arrival, but not for the reason Christine thought. However, Ben had no intention of enlightening her. "This situation has made me realize how inadequate our security is."

"We don't need a security guard or anything like that. Nothing like this has ever happened before. Has it?"

"Not in all the years I've been here." He leaned back in his chair, turning his wounded hand to inspect the bandage. It was pure white and unblemished; he had already stopped bleeding beneath the gauze. Ben looked at Christine. "There will be no more shifts where you're alone in the store, or alone with Rachel."

"Ben!" She sat upright, her chocolate sloshing in the mug. "That's—I can take care of myself. And I'll take care of Rachel, too."

"I don't like that you were hurt today."

Her expression softened from outrage to something unreadable. "I don't like that you were hurt either."

"I'll keep us safe," Ben declared. He would make it his business to keep them safe. He would keep them all safe.

"I know you will," she said softly.

Ben began to spend his hours off in wolf form, silently patrolling his territory like a wraith flickering into visibility at the edge of the forest, using all his senses to monitor the activity in the store. In the process, he discovered that the lamentable Allen did know how to operate independently of his mother's directives.

The pimple-faced teen backpedalled until he hit the stockroom's wall. "But—but—I—What are you going to do to me?"

"Other than fire you for stealing from me?" Ben asked, menace tainting his tone. Allen nodded vigorously, and Ben said, "I'm going to offer a suggestion."

Allen's terrified eyes flicked up to meet Ben's intense amber stare, and the boy's pupils dilated fully. He was Ben's now, whether he knew it or not. "I think you should make a donation to a worthy cause, Allen."

The hammering of the boy's heart fluttered in Ben's sensitive ears, igniting an urgent, immediate hunger demanding satisfaction. His canines responded to the prey's fear.

"What worthy cause?" Allen asked, his voice breaking mid-question.

"Me."

Allen never knew when Ben's fangs sank into his jugular, or how he got home later that night. He never remembered anything about his last night of work other than the headache which kept him bedridden for three days afterward. Allen's mother never knew what cured his acne, but she attributed it to the fact he no longer worked at the mini-market tackle shop where all that junk food had been available to her weak-willed son.

In early October, a fresh shipment of novelties arrived. Rachel and Christine unpacked and decorated the store for the season. Ben's opinion wasn't asked as everyone knew how little he liked Halloween, but he had learned his lesson and did not interfere.

As was customary on Sunday afternoons, he sat in the office and calculated the store's receipts. Ben could easily hear the conversation between the two women, but it was like white noise in the background: soothing and companionable. At one point, he tuned in to listen.

Rachel commented on the cuteness of the werewolf hats she was unpacking, and Ben choked. *Werewolf?* He didn't hear Christine's response, but his attention was piqued by Rachel's reply.

"You didn't?" Rachel's tone was awed.

"I did," Christine replied. "He's gone from my life."

"But Gary was so cute."

"Definitely eye candy, but after a while it just wasn't enough."

"What do you mean?"

Christine lowered her voice to reply. Ben didn't need to lean toward the door to hear her clearly. "It's all well and good to sleep with a *fine*-looking man—" she confided to the younger woman "—but if he's stupid, what is there to talk about in the morning?"

"Christine!" Rachel exclaimed, clearly shocked.

The bell over the front door announced a customer, and the women's conversation broke off.

In his office, Ben's lips curved in a sly smile. An hour later, he stepped into the stockroom where Christine was putting the last container of fake vampire blood on a shelf.

"Go home, Christine."

"What?" She turned toward him.

"I think you deserve an evening off to celebrate."

Her expression was puzzled. "Celebrate what?"

"Dumping the eye candy," he said, smirking. Christine's eyes widened and she blushed. Ben's smirk broadened to a grin. "Now go home and do something fun."

"If you say so." She wasted no time grabbing her heavy coat and purse. "Thanks, Ben."

"My pleasure." He watched Christine exit. Her smile was brighter and her steps lighter than they had been for some time. He said quietly to no one, "You were far too good for him."

Autumn turned to winter, and the Christmas holidays were upon them once again. The tourist trade that year had been the most profitable in Forks' history, and Ben offered no quibble to the number of trinkets Christine wanted to order for the season. He encouraged Rachel to learn from Christine, and the two women planned Hook Line & Sinker's future with happy fervor.

On Christmas Eve Ben worked alone despite two or three invitations to dine with others. He would close early, he thought, just as the bell rang above the door, and a voluptuous, dark-haired beauty entered Hook Line & Sinker.

She fingered a display of flies and bobbers intended for salmon and steelhead fishing near the counter. After two or three minutes, she asked, "Are you married?"

Ben looked up from the newest Charlaine Harris book Christine had ordered. "I beg your pardon?"

The audacious young woman leaned across the counter. At eleven-thirty at night, it wasn't fish she was attempting to lure. "Married?" she asked, her eyes wide and expression intent. "Are you married?"

Suddenly, Ben felt like prey. It was not a role he particularly enjoyed, so he turned the tables. He smiled, arched an eyebrow, and caught her attention. "Does it matter?"

When her pupils dilated, he knew he had hooked his dinner.

On New Year's Day, Ben noticed the new town sign for the first time. The old one had been so weathered the white paint had faded and blurred until it was barely legible.

City of Forks. Population 3,175. Vampires 8.5.

Unlike the first vampire sign he had read more than a year before, he understood the reference. Stephenie Meyer's fictional vampires had certainly made a lasting impact on the town.

Ben chuckled as he drove north on Highway 101.

JAE EYNON

Nothing But The Best

Mr Big likes his food. Anyone unlucky enough to meet Mr Big in person can see that Mr Big likes his food, though it's perhaps the wiser course of action not to say anything about it and not to let the eye be drawn to the, shall we say, *embonpoint* that is, to the uninitiated, Mr Big's most salient feature. Of course, that's like asking a passing asteroid not to be sucked into a black hole, but there you are. Try to keep your eyes on his face, unpleasant though the vista may be.

Yes, Mr Big does like his food. A person inexperienced in the ways of characters like Mr Big might assume that *quantity* is Mr Big's chief interest in the matter—to be fair, the evidence does point that way. But to venture out loud an opinion of this sort in Mr Big's hearing would provoke a reaction of such wounded delicacy, such a widening of the eyes and fluttering of the hands, such a tearing-off of heads and limbs, that, well, perhaps it's just better to keep your trap shut.

You see, Mr Big thinks of himself as quite the *bon viveur*. Where other experts are mere artisans of the table, he is an *artist*. His culinary concepts go quite beyond the everyday, embracing the extraordinary, the esoteric, even the abstract. To be invited to dine with Mr Big is to have your life transformed. The dishes that previously filled you with delight—even your grandmother's lemon meringue pie—will taste like dust in comparison.

Mr Big says that the trick is not so much in the cooking itself, though naturally any faults in the kitchen will have the *direst* consequences, and Mr Big's cooks live in a state of perpetual terror (which Mr Big considers a subtle and necessary condiment). No, the real skill comes in the preparation of the ingredients before they even cross the threshold of the kitchen. It's all very well, for example, to serve your guests a perfectly fine mermaid-fin soup, but why be satisfied with so half-hearted an offering? Mermaid fins taste far better when stripped directly from the living mermaid at the apogee of her leap from the waves under a full moon. Unicorn liver is plain fare without the piquancy lent by being served in a bowl fashioned from the hands of the virgin in whose lap the unicorn has laid its foolish head. And why would one even bother with fairies' tongues unless they are torn from the fairies' throats as they sing honeyed praises to the flower goddess?

Mr Big devotes a significant proportion of his time to the creation of each culinary masterpiece. Once the initial concept has come to fruition in his mind, he summons his procurers and presents them with their task. Often, the procurers will frown and puzzle and discuss the difficulty involved—for Mr Big's orders are seldom easy to fulfil—but they have learned never to tell Mr Big that what he wants cannot be had. One recent demonstration of the fact that even procurers can be made into something exquisite and delicious has proved sufficient argument that, while the job may take some time, nothing is actually impossible.

Lately, Mr Big has been turning his attention to humans. In the classical repertoire, humans are considered an adequate and nutritious day-to-day diet, but essentially uninteresting. To most of Mr Big's kind, to say, "It tastes like human," is a way of saying that it will keep the stomach away from the backbone, but little more. Human is *never* served at important events. However, Mr Big is something of a trail blazer, an innovator, a questioner of inherited culinary truths, and Mr Big intends to show his fellow ogres that even human can be a delicacy—if sufficient attention is given to its preparation.

"More flowers for you, Ange!" sings Colin, mincing across the foyer with a swing of his skinny hips and a flutter of mascaraed lashes. He's not even gay—just puny and effeminate and frantic for significance. Most of the gay guys she knows could play prop forward for England. Actually, one of them does.

She checks the card nestled in the tasteful bouquet of lilies and makes a moue of distaste. "Bin them," she orders Colin.

He makes an exaggerated "Oh!" of shock and clutches the flowers against his concave chest. "Well, if you don't want them..." he says, stepping away.

Which of the editors does he imagine he's going to woo this time, she wonders.

"They're mine, Colin. Just do what I tell you." It's obvious he's not going to, so she grabs the flowers and shoves them head downwards in the nearest bin.

Colin clearly wants to tell her she's a bitch, but she's valuable and he's not, and a word would have him off research duties and back in the filing room or worse, so he settles for folding his arms and cocking a hip. "Must be nice to have so many admirers you can afford to stick them in the trash," he says cattily.

"Trying to talk American doesn't make you look any bigger or cleverer," she says over her shoulder.

The door swings shut, and she puts Colin out of her mind. She runs the gauntlet of good mornings and reaches the haven of her office, where she hangs her coat carefully and sets her bag on the desk next to the stack of papers that await her attention. She cranks up the computer and slips into the adjoining dressing room to wash the smell of lilies off her hands. Admirers wouldn't be altogether unwelcome, but it's not admirers that she's got. What she's got is stalkers.

She shakes water from her hands and dries them carefully. She rubs in precisely the right amount of lotion before settling her bracelet and rings back where they belong. She checks the mirror to make sure her make-up is perfect and not a hair is out of place, then turns to the full-length glass to assess her outfit. Today, she has opted for sexy-conservative, outlining without clinging, scooping without revealing, hinting but giving away nothing. The colours are sober, the fabric exquisite—if you know what you're looking at, then you'll know she buys the best. Satisfied, she returns to her office, where Pauline is arranging coffee and a plate of sliced fruit just so on the desk and admiring the Gucci bag enviously. Pauline knows better than to touch, but her eyes are all over it like a pervert's tongue.

"Thank you, Pauline," she says.

"Morning, Angie," Pauline replies. "Angie" is one step up from "Ange", but it's still repellent. Angela thins her lips, but Pauline doesn't notice. "You look smashing as always. Oh... my... God! Your shoes!"

Angela is very pleased with her shoes and pleased that they have drawn comment. They were very expensive—not surprising, considering where the leather came from. They are also extremely flattering to her slender feet and elegant ankles. However, she ignores the compliment and sits at her desk, pulling the daily papers towards her. They will start by skimming the tabloids and then move on to the broadsheets; Pauline will already have emailed the links to breaking news and anything important in the international press. Once they've caught up with that, she will start to prepare the day's major interviews. She glances sideways at the computer screen, angled so only she can see it. HotRocks has sent her another indecent poem on Facebook, and BigBoyBertrand thinks she should follow the link to his online album, which she knows is a pictorial ode to his own genitalia. As if familiarity makes a penis any less ridiculous.

The tabloids are full of the usual rubbish, though she tells Pauline to follow up on the interest they are all taking in the inner city werewolves and the spread of STDs. Privately, she thinks the do-gooders would be better off giving their attention to the run-down schools and hospitals that are failing the weres and humans alike. Or addressing the hybrid rat-fish problem in the sewer system. The government is being entirely too quiet about the involvement of its scientists in that little debacle—and with public toilets now too dangerous to use even in direst need, the streets are becoming a health hazard.

She sips her coffee and spears a piece of mango.

"Who do we have on the list today?"

"You've got the PM at two, the Minister for Social Affairs live in the studio this evening, and the head of the UN live via satellite after him."

"Okay, I'll prep them in that order."

"I don't think anyone else does the amount of work you do, Angie," says Pauline. It's half admiration and half complaint, because Pauline is there to make it all possible. But you don't get to be Angela Philips, the face of network news, without putting in a great deal of effort. Pauline thinks she could do the job better, but Angela knows Pauline will never occupy her position.

Gerry elbows the door open. He has an armful of post. "Morning, ladies," he says. Gerry is fifty, running slightly to fat, wears tweed, and makes a good job of disguising his lust as paternal interest. Pauline's cheeks flush. Interesting. So Gerry's managed to have her at last. Angela raises an eyebrow and Pauline glares.

"You've got another one for 'Angel' Philips," he says.

Angela motions him to take the post over to the coffee table, where she keeps a high-sided tray ready for fannish offerings. He sets the pile of envelopes next to it and scratches his palms.

"Time of the month?" enquires Angela as she approaches the table with some reluctance.

He nods. "Harvest moon, too," he says. "They're always the worst."

She notes that his reddish hair is looking thick and lustrous.

"Could you open it for me, Gerry?" she asks. "I got a stain on my dress last time."

Today's gift is a small, fake-jewelled pot full of a recognisable bodily fluid.

"Have it sent to the police for DNA analysis," she tells Gerry.

"I keep telling you to stay away from social media," Pauline says. "It's a sure-fire way to attract the crazies."

BB the procurer is a professional. He's at the top of his game, the best in Mr Big's force. He's ruthless, inventive, and very, very patient. Mr Big knows that if BB is on the job, then he'll get exactly what he wants. BB is proud of his work, and because he is proud of it, he pays great attention to every detail, including the way he dresses. BB's mother always said that looking the part gets your head in the right place, so BB takes care to be smart. It's important to step out of the door looking smart, even if you come back messy. And BB usually comes back messy.

BB wears a black suit, black shirt, and, generally, a black tie—though today he is in the mood for a spot of colour and opts for the dark red of venous blood. His shoes are black, too, and very nice in a conventional way. But BB had them made specially out of dragon hide. Even the soles are of hide: the scales give exceptional grip—but angle your feet the right way and you can slide like you're on ice. Over the top of this ensemble, BB likes to wear a trench coat in the usual fawn colour with an unusual number of useful pockets. He takes care not to overload the pockets because he doesn't want to drag the coat out of shape, but pockets are necessary for the tools of his trade. BB's broad-brimmed hat is also both stylish and practical. It keeps the rain and the sun off his head and shadows his face, should he be careless enough to let anyone see him. He's never been careless, but accidents can happen and BB doesn't take chances. Last and best are BB's gloves. They're the most expensive thing he owns. Genuine infant selkie skin. It's supple, durable, allows full sensitivity, and never, ever takes a stain. In BB's line of work, that's important.

Last of all, BB picks up his muzzle and chains his jaws shut. It's got quick release catches at the back of his head, just in case the appropriate tool for the task should happen to be a double row of jagged iron teeth, but in general, BB leaves it on, or he couldn't do his job at all. BB has this little problem. He finds it embarrassing, but he's learned to accept that it's a feature of who he is and that, with a little effort, it's manageable. BB can't stop talking, you see, and that's not great when you have to be stealthy for a living. Worse than that, when he talks, he says the vilest things. By nature, he's rather sweet, and it upsets him to hear the dreadful stuff that comes out of his mouth, so he wears his muzzle with gratitude. He still remembers fondly how his mother sat back smiling, all breathless and sweaty after wrestling him into his first one on his fifth birthday. She'd ruffled his hair. *If you can't say anything nice, don't say anything at all* was her motto.

BB checks that he can't move his jaw at all and tugs the brim of his hat down. He looks at his watch. Time to go. Number Three is ripe. BB's been dosing him with his own infectious spit, just a drop or two in every pint of cheap lager, for a few weeks now, and the filth Number Three's been spewing online is ready to spill into action.

BB's timing is spot on, as usual. His target is just swinging her legs out of the taxi. She has such elegant calves and ankles, thinks BB. He's not sure he's supposed to think about her, as such, but he doesn't think it's wrong to admire something pretty—especially when she has such good taste in shoes. Today, they're simple high-heeled pumps in fine dark blue leather that catches the light with a green shimmer. It's as pretty as a well-cured chimera tailskin, and he might even think it was genuine if the target wasn't human. The target pays the taxi driver and shakes her head at something he says. The taxi drives off and she looks around, then darts into the delicatessen where she buys most of her evening meals. She doesn't see BB in his patch of deep shadow high above. A movement at the street corner catches his eye. Good. Number Three is waiting, fidgeting, even drooling. BB shakes his head. Disgusting.

The target comes back out of the shop with a paper carrier dangling from one hand. She only has a hundred yards to her front door, but in those heels she won't be able to run if she has to, and the paving stones are uneven in places. She leaves the safety of the light spilling from the shop windows. Number Three waits a few moments, then rounds the corner and follows slowly. The target hears Number Three's footsteps and her own falter, then quicken. Her shoulders are stiff. BB can hear her breath coming fast and shallow.

BB takes a flying leap from his rooftop to the one on their side of the street. He lands neatly and takes time to check his pockets are closed before slithering head first down the side of the building into a narrow alley that smells of rat and urine. As he slides over a window, aware of the TV blaring within, he remembers the time, very early on, when one of his implements fell out of a pocket and landed with a clatter. His prey nearly got away, and he'd had to finish the job with no finesse at all. But BB never makes the same mistake twice, and he alights in good order. He listens. The target is moving at a tottering run, her heels clacking. Number Three has lengthened his stride and breaks out of a walk just at the alley mouth—which swallows him.

BB makes sure there's a bit of noise. He can work quietly when he wants to, of course, but noise is all part of his plan this time. He allows Number Three a groan as he lets just enough blood into the windpipe to produce a gurgle on the last breath. It's perfect. He drops the body, slicing off a trophy as it falls.

The target's footsteps have stopped, but BB can hear her panting. Then, slowly, she turns and approaches the alley. BB retreats into the shadows as she comes into view. She is trembling as she peers into the darkness. Her hair has come loose, soft brown curls tumbling to her shoulders, a diamond stud earring winking through. She's clutching her lapels together. BB tosses the severed finger forward. It rolls to a stop at her feet. This time, she doesn't look surprised. This time, she whispers, "Thank you."

Mr Big does not take well to delay. Patience has never been his strongest suit, and were it anyone else on whose pleasure he was waiting, he would long since have made a flamboyant and colourful (well, mostly red) demonstration of his strength of feeling on the matter. But, since it is his best procurer who is causing him his current distress, he contrives—for the present—to contain his ire. When the creature that calls itself BB says a thing will take time, then it will take time. Mr Big has come to understand that BB's judgement of such matters is sound, and that, ultimately, waiting for BB to produce the goods will be less irksome than early delivery of a less-than-perfect product by someone else.

Currently, Mr Big is waiting for something he believes will be very special indeed. He's so excited about it that he's quite off his food, and this doesn't make him any sweeter to be around. The kitchen staff are all in hiding until BB comes back. They tried their utmost best to make Mr Big the most fabulous things from their repertoire, they really did, but it's hard to cook when the head chef's just been eviscerated into his own stock pot.

And now Mr Big's even more annoyed, because Mr Wart and Mr Gurgle have come to see him and they've got some rather unpleasant things to say. Mr Wart says his brother, Mr Wart minor, has gone missing. Mr Wart says that there are rumours that Mr Big's been searching for some very special ingredients. Mr Wart suspects that Mr Big might be turning to.... Oh, the very thought is an affront to poor Mr Big, who vomits on the spot when he hears it. Mr Wart thinks Mr Big has taken up *cannibalism*. Mr Gurgle agrees with anything that Mr Wart says, though he can't help thinking that if Mr Wart gave it a moment's consideration, he'd be glad to rid himself of his little brother, and indeed that Mr Wart has plenty of incentive for doing so. Mr Gurgle is standing at Mr Wart's shoulder and wondering how much of a reward there would be if he turned Mr Wart in to the authorities for the little trifle of fratricide.

In the meantime, Mr Big is demonstrating how loose his skin has become—it's not a pretty sight—since he conceived his newest dish. How could he *possibly* have eaten anything as large, not to mention unappetising, as Mr Wart minor and lost this much weight? Mr Wart isn't altogether convinced. He knows that some meats have to be hung for a very long time before being eaten, and he thinks that Mr Big might be waiting for Mr Wart minor to become sufficiently gamey. Mr Big wonders whether Mr Wart has any idea what the word "delicacy" means, and if he has, then how he could even dream that Mr Wart minor would fit into that category.

Mr Gurgle confesses to a soupçon of curiosity as to what it is that Mr Big is waiting for, if it's not for Mr Wart minor to rot off the rope he's hanging from.

Mr Big is affronted at their scepticism. He is, he declares, in the process of preparing something extraordinary—something revolutionary. He is preparing... a *human*. Mr Wart and Mr Gurgle are beginning to think that Mr Big has lost his marbles, which isn't a very reassuring thought, all things considered. But Mr Big is not interested in the looks they are exchanging, for Mr Big has started to rhapsodise about turning *human* into something *divine*, something *exponentially* better than stop-gap fast food. Mr Big has come to realise that what might make human an appetising dish is the emotional state of the specimen at the moment of slaughter. Brain chemistry, you see—it's all about the spicing.

Angela has been given a few days off to calm her nerves. She spends the whole weekend talking to the police, who are very nice to her but want to be extra specially sure she didn't hear or see anything of the gruesome murder that took place just twenty feet from her front door. A sweet little DC with an unfortunate taste for polyester brings her endless cups of tea and keeps apologising for the inconvenience. They leave her alone on Sunday evening, convinced at last that she must have got home before anything occurred and that her double glazing is so thick, she can hear nothing from the street. Detective Inspector Jones advises her to keep her house locked up tight and never go anywhere by herself because she's probably in more danger from her protector than from the stalkers he's killing.

So Pauline is quite surprised to push the office door open on Monday and find Angela sitting behind her desk, thumbing through the *Telegraph*.

"Oh!" she says.

She's never seen Angela so casually dressed, but she makes even jeans and a crisp cotton shirt look fantastic. There's a soft grey leather coat slung over the back of Angela's chair that she thinks is new. It looks utterly touchable.

Angela looks up. She knows Pauline is in here to try out the desk for size. "The world doesn't stop just because I'm not telling it it's still spinning," she says. "I have to keep up."

"How *are* you, Angie? It must have been *awful!*" Pauline does an excellent job of faking concern.

"I'm fine. Why should I be less fine than I was before this happened? I didn't see a thing."

"Oh, but Angie—"

Angela doesn't really want to talk to Pauline about it. Her thoughts on the matter are her own. She takes an exquisitely wrapped parcel out of her desk drawer and offers it to Pauline.

"Happy birthday. I hope I got the right day."

Pauline is overwhelmed. She wasn't expecting anything this soft-hearted from Angela. There's a spark of something like devotion in her eye as she carefully negotiates the wrapping to reveal a short jacket in the same grey as the coat on Angela's chair. Angela watches as Pauline discovers the lissome perfection of leather that moulds to her like a second skin. Angela forestalls Pauline's effusions with a raised hand.

"You work very hard for me; I thought it was about time you got some recognition. Now—shall we see what's happening in the world?"

It's at least an hour before the door bangs open, but today it's Colin who has the armful of post, which he dumps unceremoniously on the desk.

"This isn't my job!" he whines.

"Where's Gerry?" says Angela.

"The lazy fat git never showed up this morning!" says Colin. He notices Pauline's jacket and pouts.

Angela looks at Pauline, who frowns back. "Didn't he phone in?" asks Pauline. "He always phones if it's been a bad moon and he's ill."

"Don't know, don't care," says Colin. "But I'm not going to cart letters round the building like some glorified errand boy forever!" He flounces back out.

"We should send him round to Gerry's to check on him," says Pauline. "After moonrise."

"Gerry has better taste than to bite *that*," replies Angela, but she smirks.

There's a new complicity to their work today, but Angela calls a halt early. Pauline's worried about Gerry, and Angela is a little abstracted, too.

She opens her email. There's one from the DI to say the murder victim has been positively identified as Wayne Hopkins, aka HotRocks. She shrugs a little. A part of her will miss his flights of inventive obscenity. Her Facebook page has developed an air of nervous propriety. Not surprising, really. Since all this went public, the stalking brigade have kept their heads down. As she scrolls through the doings of acquaintances, she reflects on the less-welcome consequences of being beautiful, authoritative, and in the public eye. She stops at a new name. The Sperminator—*really?*—wants to do, well, the usual sort of thing to her. She imagines that the police will already be drawing up outside some suburban semi to haul a spotty teenager called Malcolm over the coals while his mother, a far worse prospect, waits for her turn. The real stalkers are cleverer than that.

She calls reception to tell them she wants her car. The network will pay to keep her safe for a while, at least. The driver waits outside the deli while she pops in for the smoked salmon, blinis, sour cream and champagne she wants tonight, then drives her the short distance to her door. He won't leave until she's safely inside and the lock has clicked.

She looks into the alley as they drive past. It's never as dark as it was on Friday evening, when something very dangerous saved her for the third time. She's still a little disgusted by the finger, but it is, she supposes, the thought that counts. It's quite thrilling to have a protector, even one like this—more perilous than all the remaining stalkers put together. She wonders when BigBoyBertrand and the others are going to get back on duty. It's certain they will, because fear simply adds spice to obsession. She stands at the window, looking out onto the empty street. She knows she's being watched and senses she's being watched over.

Even BB is avoiding Mr Big now. The enthusiasm of the police has been a nuisance, and it's taken him a whole month to bring Number Four to the point of action. Mr Big gets very angry when BB explains the problem and won't listen to reason at all when BB points out that had Mr Big been less specific in his demands, it would be easier to get him what he wanted. Mr Big even complains about BB's swearing and cursing and calumny—and he's never done that before. He knows BB has a problem, and it's at his insistence that BB takes the muzzle off at all. BB feels quite angry at that and has to go away for Mr Big's own safety. *Don't bite the hand that feeds you,* BB's mother always said, so BB goes away—never mind the fact that the thought of biting Mr Big makes him feel quite ill.

BB considers Mr Big's checklist: *human, female, mature but fairly young, beautiful according to human tastes, confident, worldly.* BB is to *invoke in the target a sense of generalised fear spiked with episodes of specific, localised terror, and at the same time generate some sort of romantic hero worship,* which Mr Big claims will add an accent of rich sweetness to the earthy and acidic notes. None of it makes much sense to BB, but then Mr Big's appetites never make much sense to him. BB likes much simpler things to eat. (Right now, he has an egg-and-cress sandwich in his lunch box.) So BB found the best possible target and feels just a tad resentful that Mr Big is complaining. If he'd chosen something of inferior quality, *then* Mr Big would have something to complain about.

So BB spends a month dosing Number Four and encouraging him to be brave. He wonders whether Number Four's family know what kind of man he is and whether they will miss him when he's gone, but that's beside the point. Police vigilance has been relaxed, and Number Four is impatient, now he's on the point of action. He isn't the brightest of sparks, so BB has prepared the way, and Number Four is excited almost to the point of climax when he discovers the back door is unlocked. He doesn't notice BB following him into the house. BB can be very unobtrusive when he wants. He could pick your pockets, steal your trousers, and slit your throat, and you'd never know he was there.

BB likes the target's house. It's simply and elegantly furnished. The colour scheme is neutral, very peaceful, with ornaments or paintings that add vivid accents. Everything is perfectly clean and orderly. BB approves of this—it satisfies his way of thinking. He resolves to get rid of Number Four in such a way as will ensure no staining. Number Four, meanwhile, has gained the living room door and has his debased and sweaty palm on the handle. BB waits for the right note of alarm to enter the target's voice. It takes longer than expected for terror to outweigh outrage in her tone—the target is unexpectedly tough in some ways—but as soon as BB judges the situation ripe, he bursts into the room, plucks Number Four off the struggling woman, breaks his neck and hurls him out into the hall, where the tiled floor will not be harmed by any incidental bodily evacuations.

BB takes a moment to straighten his coat and draw the shadows more deeply around his face under the brim of his hat, then turns back to the target. She is getting to her feet, a hand on the wall by the fireplace to steady her. She is trembling. He can see the tremors passing through her body, outlined by the thin wrap of numinous Japanese fairy silk she is wearing. One shoulder has been exposed in the attack, and BB can see a bruise blooming on it. *Clumsy,* he thinks. Number Four probably got a thrill out of damaging the target. Mr Big won't be pleased, though. He wants the goods unblemished, and now he'll have to wait until the bruise has gone. BB hopes the target has some arnica gel to speed the process.

BB glances round the room while he reviews his mental

order sheet. Here, too, the décor is pale with accents of colour. The target is steady on her feet now and is warily approaching, her bare toes sinking into a russet brown wolf skin spread across the white carpet. BB has to nurture the target's feelings of gratitude and make sure they are flavoured with attraction and romance. It's not an onerous task—the target is the most pleasing example he could find. Perfect skin, wavy brown hair, sapphire-blue eyes, and a mouth like rose petals make proximity no trouble. She smells nice, too, he notes as she comes closer still. She peers up, trying to see his face. He reaches out and ghosts his fingers over the bruise. He lets her catch his hand and watches her eyes widen at the touch of his selkie gloves. She rests her cheek in his palm, rubbing her skin against the supple, iridescent hide. He brushes her hair back with his other hand then turns to leave, but she holds on to him.

"I hope you're not intending to leave..." says the target. She takes a slow, shuddering breath as she steps closer still. "I hope you're not intending to leave that thing cluttering up my hallway."

Mr Big is very excited today. He has received word from his procurer that the thing which has been so very, very long in the preparation is, at long last, ready for delivery. Just as well, really. Poor Mr Big is in a parlous state. He has worked himself up into such high dudgeon, such excesses of miff, such frenzies of justification, that he has stopped eating *entirely* until such time as his special dish should be ready. This course of action has had such a detrimental effect on Mr Big's nature that his closest friends—had he any friends at all—would have abandoned him long since. His most constant companions are Mr Wart, still unconvinced that Mr Big is not responsible for the disappearance of Mr Wart minor, Mr Gurgle, who has developed a degree of curiosity about Mr Big's doings, and a flea-bitten satyr sent by the authorities weeks ago to verify the truth of Mr Big's absurd claims of innocence.

Poor Mr Big is looking terrible—a shadow of his former self. He can fit himself into his massive couch with barely an inch of overflow; his skin is loose on his once impressive bulk. And—oh, here is the saddest thing of all—he's lost his colour. He used to be such a lovely dark mottled grey, shaded with an attractive algal bloom here and there, but now... Poor Mr Big has faded so much he can be described as nothing other than... beige. Or perhaps ecru, if one were feeling generous. Even the algae have lost heart, and there sits poor monochrome Mr Big, starving himself for a dish which will surely serve only to rob him of any reputation that still remains and, quite possibly, leave him dyspeptic to boot.

But none of this troubles Mr Big at the moment, for he is on the verge of being proved the foremost visionary of his age. He has ordered his procurer to bring the offering to him in public, unharmed, so that all those present (all three of them) might witness his triumph. He will even let them taste the finished dish, he decides—how else will word of his brilliance get out? A chirp from Mr Big's mobile alerts him to a message: BB is at the door and is about to bring in the prepared human. Mr Big wriggles in anticipation. It is all he can do not to clap his hands.

The procurer, it seems, has an appropriate sense of ceremony, for he has left his ubiquitous hat and coat off and chosen to pace on all fours as nature intended a creature of his ilk to move. The suit, with its custom tailoring that allows the procurer's tail the freedom to lash fiercely, ought really to look ridiculous, but somehow attention is diverted by his luminous crimson eyes and what little can be observed of his over-endowment of teeth inside the restrictive muzzle. The human, a comparatively puny thing, walks a little ahead of the procurer, encouraged forward every few steps by a sharp nudge to the small of its back. It is wearing a stylish grey leather coat that causes Mr Wart some consternation. The satyr makes a mark on his clip-board and leaves. He has no interest in cooking—but he really, really needs a drink. Mr Gurgle reflects that being on the wrong end of a sewing machine has worked a considerable improvement in the looks of Mr Wart minor.

The procurer allows the human to stop walking only when they are very close to Mr Big. This is correct, for Mr Big wishes to verify its condition before it graces his gastric tract. The human's eyes are very wide as it surveys Mr Big. He wonders how they will taste when cooked or whether he should take them in the *simplest* way, raw. He still gets a child-like pleasure from popping eyeballs on his tusks. He leans forward to take a sniff. The smell is fresh. The heartbeat is swift, and he can hear the rush of blood round the body. His stomach rumbles. He directs the human to strip, for it is more than his sensibilities will allow to touch blemished food. The human is reluctant, but a glance from the procurer seems to change its mind. It drops the oddly familiar grey coat and swiftly gets rid of its other wrappings. Mr Big is very pleased indeed. This will be worth the wait. He directs his procurer to proceed.

The procurer surges up on his hind legs and draws a long, elegant blade from a pocket sewn into the side of his trousers. He puts a gloved hand to the back of the human's neck and draws it towards him. A strange expression crosses the human's face, which Mr Big supposes must be surprise and betrayal. Oddly, it stretches its mouth in what he would, in a normal species, interpret as a smile.

"Go on, BB, sweetheart," it says. "Proceed."

Angela's return to the public eye is hailed as an act of great bravery and an example to women everywhere. She still gets bothered by crazies in the social media, but she ignores them and carries on with her life and career as if nothing untoward has ever happened. She continues to enjoy her reputation as one of the toughest and most knowledgeable interviewers around, as well as one of the best-dressed.

Nevertheless, Angela spends a little less time in the office now, entrusting some of the work to Pauline, who has become something of a disciple in matters professional and sartorial. Angela is finding her home life more rewarding than she used to.

BB is a perfect companion. He is quiet, clean, polite and protective. She doesn't mind the awful things he says when he needs to remove his muzzle. If anything, she finds his remarks amusing. Sometimes, *she* wears the muzzle, because it's such a turn-on for them both. BB likes living with her because he's an uncomplicated fellow who enjoys simple meals and likes to have his work appreciated. He shares Angela's taste in fabrics and décor and likes to feel he's contributing.

Angela smiles and turns a page of her book. BB is stretched out on Gerry in front of the fire, dozing. Angela fingers the polished elf-bone necklace he gave her when he moved in. She looks around her living room, considering that it is, at long last, exactly as she wanted it, and nestles back contentedly into the soft, off-white, hide-covered cushions of her Big new sofa.

LIBBY WEBER

Seeking Single Human Male, No Stakers

Sophie usually considered the vampire community's preferred epithet 'children of the night' to be a bit of a misnomer, since most of the vampires who lived in Southern California were so ancient and tough that they were nearly impervious to sunlight. Thus, she was surprised when the vampire friend of Emily's who had requested a noon meeting appeared to be a young woman barely into her twenties. Still, the vampire's well-tailored clothes and expensive accessories suggested that she was older than her flawless skin implied.

Acutely aware of the office's secondhand furniture, Sophie stood and extended her hand. "Violet Tran? I'm Mrs. Warren. Any friend of Emily's is a friend of mine."

"Pleased to meet you, Mrs. Warren," Violet replied. Her voice was warm and pleasant with only the slightest sibilance to suggest the presence of fangs concealed behind perfect, even veneers. She took Sophie's hand and shook it firmly.

Violet's skin felt creamy to the touch, which made Sophie suspect she'd been to the spa in La Jolla that catered to vampires by offering long-lasting, full-body sunscreen treatments. The service was too expensive for your average vampire, but clearly not for someone who wore this season's Louboutins on a work day. Violet's application listed a large solar energy company as her employer, so clearly the investment she made protecting herself from the sun had paid dividends.

Since Emily had already vouched for Violet, Sophie handed her the business card she reserved for her most trusted clients. It had *Mrs. Warren's Professional Services* embossed in pewter foil, but the phone number listed was the cell phone she carried with her at all times. Not even the law firms she consulted for had that number.

"Please, sit," said Sophie, indicating the worn leather armchair opposite her desk. "Would you like anything to drink?"

"No, thank you," said Violet, smoothing her hands over her thighs as she sat. The nervous gesture made Sophie smile to herself. Apparently even senior engineers got nervous when discussing their private lives with strangers. Violet's reticence made Sophie even more curious about her background and exactly how she knew Emily. But first things first.

"I've reviewed your application," she said. "You're looking for an exclusive, long-term relationship with a human male, is that correct?"

"Yes, that's right."

"Before we get into details," said Sophie, "I have some concerns about your request."

Violet crossed her arms. "Mrs. Warren, when I indicated that I wanted a hot-blooded male, I meant only that I was looking for a passionate relationship, not that I wanted a one-time dinner date. As I noted in my application, I'm a mycotarian— I don't drink blood. I prefer to subsist on yeast cultures. Surely if I were simply seeking sustenance, there would be far less expensive and suspicious ways of obtaining it."

"True," said Sophie, regarding her with a bemused expression. "Is it fair to say that you're not interested in dating another vampire?"

"In my experience, they take the presence of other vampires as an excuse to behave badly. The community arranges all sorts of singles events where it's *de rigeur* to wear one's undeath on one's sleeve, and frankly, all the blood-letting and fang-flaunting disgusts me."

Interesting. "Are you opposed to werewolves?"

Violet looked as though she was about to object when a thoughtful look crossed her face. "I really couldn't say," she said at last. "I don't have much of a social circle outside work and my volunteer work with Emily at Allway House, so I've never met one, at least that I know of."

Sophie scribbled a note in the margin of Violet's application and tried not to let her confusion show. A third of Allway House's transient residents were werewolves, but Violet had never met one? Something wasn't adding up. She cleared her throat. "So you've dated exclusively humans?"

"'Dated' is too strong a word," said Violet. "I've met the odd co-worker for drinks, but I never felt that any of them were liberal-minded enough to see past the vampire stigma. Besides, my industry is cutthroat. I've worked very hard to get where I am today, and having my status disclosed would raise questions about whether or not I could do the work, despite the fact that I've never shied away from the potentially dangerous aspects of the job."

"What about meeting people online?"

"I haven't had much luck. The biggest dating sites are out of the question for privacy reasons, and the smaller, allegedly exclusive ones only seem interested in screening out those who can't pay."

"Understood," said Sophie. "As far as discretion goes, I've vetted all my clients personally and performed extensive background checks. What's more, should you agree to retain my services, you will be signing a confidentiality policy and nondisclosure agreement that some would call restrictive and others would call paranoid."

Violet gave her a small smile, and Sophie continued. "Now, have you done much exploration of the human Goth communities? They're vampire-friendly."

"Not those pathetic hangers-on! They have all sorts of stupid ideas about what it means to be one of us, and all they really want is to be turned."

Sophie was slightly taken aback by the vehemence of Violet's dislike, but merely checked a 'no' box on her client evaluation form. "What about blood play fetishists? They're not always easy to locate, but they do have a presence online."

"Definitely not. I'd be at too high a risk of turning them accidentally, and I really can't stand blood."

Sophie blinked in surprise. She knew of vampires who eschewed human blood for ethical reasons, but this was the first one she'd met who outright disliked it. "If you don't like blood, why insist on dating a human? Why not go for someone bloodless, like the walking dead? They have truly marvelous preservation techniques nowadays. They're virtually indistinguishable from humans except that some of the older ones have a slight odor of disinfectant."

Violet's thumbs rubbed nervous arcs on her thighs. "I really don't know."

Sophie knew that Violet was lying about something, or at least not telling the whole truth. Time to shake the tree a bit.

"What about a ghoul? There's an enclave in Carlsbad that consumes only free-range corpses that died of natural causes."

"Ugh, no!"

Sophie checked another box. "Right. As for meeting human men, have you tried fan conventions? Comic-Con alone attracts tens of thousands of fans of supernatural television shows, books, and films."

"Fanboys are like Goths minus the self-respect," said Violet, wrinkling her nose. "As if any of them would know what to do with a real vampire." She looked at Sophie quizzically. "Not that I'm complaining, but I assumed you'd have me retain your services before giving me advice on how to meet people."

"Ms. Tran, in order to help you, I need to fully understand where you're coming from and exactly what you're willing to try. And in order for me to be confident about your tastes, I also need you to be honest with me. Now, have you ever been intimate with a human male?"

"A few times," she said, guardedly.

Aha. She was getting closer to the source of Violet's strong opinions. "Any kinks, fetishes, or special needs that I should be aware of? Even if I can't match someone completely to your taste, I can at least ensure that he might be open to your desired activity or activities."

Violet straightened in her chair, fingers clutching the hem of her skirt. "Yes. I— I'd like to be allowed to perform oral sex at least once a week."

Sophie managed to suppress a snort as she realized why Violet only wanted to consider human males. In retrospect, it was odd that more vampires didn't seek consensual harvest from such an immediately renewable source of vibrantly living fluid. "I doubt that will be a problem for most men. In fact, you wouldn't need my services at all if you were able to communicate that to potential dates."

"I wish I shared your confidence."

"You will," said Sophie, smiling. For every supernatural being who wanted a human lover, there were at least ten humans seeking the supernatural. Add Violet's dietary preferences to the mix and she would have dozens of candidates to choose from. Sophie made a mental note to send Emily a thank-you card for referring Violet to her. "Now, before I hand you a mountain of forms to sign, there is one last thing I must ask, and I apologize for the intrusive question. Is there anything about your sexual past or dating history that I should know? Any domestic violence, bad break-ups, or psychiatric conditions?"

Violet's dark-lashed eyes widened, and Sophie suspected she was about to lie. But instead of delivering what surely would have been a fabrication, she lowered her eyes to her knees and began to speak in a quiet voice.

"I had a very bad experience with a necrophile who lives in Riverside. We really hit it off in our chats, and we decided to meet. He was even more handsome and charming in person. I thought I'd found the one, until we got back to his place. After a nightcap, I tried to make the first move, but he refused to touch me unless I agreed to act out a scene from *Dracula*. I've never been so humiliated in either of my lives."

Sophie knew that vampires couldn't cry but offered her guest a tissue anyway. Violet took it gratefully and dabbed at her eyes.

"He sounds like a manipulative piece of shit who pulled the worst kind of bait-and-switch."

Violet blew her nose. "You must think I'm pathetic."

"Hardly. You had a terrible experience, but you're getting back on the horse. That's no easy thing. Now," she said in a brisk voice, "just to clarify, would you be willing to consider occasional clichéd vamp play with a partner, provided you were already in a relationship and the encounters occurred within previously agreed-upon rules?"

Violet paused for a moment before answering. "Perhaps, but only on rare occasions. I don't want someone who's only in it for the fangs."

Sophie made a note in the margin of her form. "I know it's frustrating that an accident of rebirth landed you in a community of vampires with whom you have little in common. But as you yourself prove, there are exceptional people in any group, and I make it my business to represent only exceptional people. If you'd like to retain my services, I'll send you a list of possible candidates for you to evaluate. Based on the feedback you give me, I can refine the search. When you find someone you're interested in meeting, I'll arrange a lunch date in a neutral setting. Should you decide against further contact, all you need to do is let me know, and I'll find someone else for you to meet."

Violet nodded slowly. "All right," she said. "Where do I sign?"

Sophie beamed at her. "You won't be sorry." She reached across her desk and picked up the pile of new client forms she'd prepared for Violet's visit. "I'm afraid the first part involves a lot of paperwork," she said, laying the forms on the edge of the desk closest to Violet. "There's a general waiver saying you won't sue us if things don't work out well. This release form gives me permission to run a background check. These others are standard—restricted permission to distribute your photograph, fee agreement, liability release, that sort of thing. Oh, you won't need the reference contact sheet because Emily referred you."

"How do you know Emily?" asked Violet, thumbing through the documents.

"Her philanthropic work, mostly," said Sophie noncommittally.

"Do you volunteer at Allway House?"

"I consult on certain matters germane to my areas of expertise."

"Legal expertise?"

Sophie blinked in surprise. "How did you know?"

Violet smiled, the first unguarded expression Sophie had seen on her face. "The forms and disclaimers gave you away."

Sophie allowed herself to smile in return. "What about you? Emily usually sends me pro bono cases, not paying clients for my matchmaking sideline."

Violet gave her a measuring look. "But this isn't your only sideline, is it?"

They were straying into dangerous territory. Not all of Emily's enterprises were strictly above-board, and Sophie suspected both of them knew it. Sophie had just opened her mouth to change the subject when the door burst open and David, Sophie's secretary, ran breathlessly into the room. He was so worked up that his fangs were extended, and he glanced quickly from Violet to Sophie before letting his story come out in a rush.

"So this guy called," he said, "and says he heard from another vampire who heard from someone's relative, I don't know, maybe a cousin's half-brother or something, that he saw this ugly ho turning tricks on El Cajon Boulevard, and she looked real green like maybe she was sick or something, and he's a nice guy, right? So he offers to take her to the hospital if she'll get in his car, and she sort of moans at him and bites the guy! Right on the hand!"

"Okay," said Sophie, hoping that the point would be reached sooner rather than later.

"So then he drives to the hospital and has to get it cleaned out and it don't look real good, so they keep him overnight. But the next day, his hand's all swelled up and red, and they thought it was some kind of flesh-eating bacteria or something, and they had to cut his hand off!"

"Sounds unpleasant." Sophie's quelling look was lost on David, and he continued at high speed.

"So I'm thinking the guy's a liar. I mean, what kind of girl would bite a guy trying to help her? He was probably trying to pull her into the car. But if she was sort of green, I thought she might be a zombie or something, and since none of the girls on the Boulevard work for themselves, I thought there might be another, you know, bunch of bad guys to take out."

The lead would probably come to nothing, but any rumor, no matter how unlikely, was worth investigating. "Why don't you call Emily and tell her?"

"You got it!" he said, heading back to the front desk. "I probably should have done that first, huh?"

"Probably," said Sophie, shaking her head.

When Sophie had closed the door that he'd left open, Violet asked, "New guy?"

"Yeah. David's organized, detail-oriented, and puts people

at ease, but apparently his sense of timing and discretion could use some work."

"Don't be too hard on him," said Violet. "We've met before."

Several things fell into place at Violet's seemingly nonchalant admission, but the most important was that Violet wasn't just an occasional volunteer at the halfway house that Emily ran for supernatural beings. She was deeply involved in the vigilante aspects of Emily's work.

"I'm surprised you recognized him," said Sophie, remembering David's gaunt face and hollow gaze the day Emily had brought him in to interview for the secretary position.

"I took a special interest," said Violet.

Sophie knew it was probably a bad idea to ask, but she did anyway. "Was it the Bloods?"

Violet nodded grimly. "It was a stark reminder that there are worse predators out there than vampires. They had three of them locked in a foreclosed mansion. They fed them doped blood and made them turn tricks done up as Angel, Edward, and Lestat."

"Oh my God," said Sophie softly.

Violet's face was grim. "You knew, though."

"I suspected. I know in general what Emily and Allway House are up against. I just rarely hear about it in detail. It's best that way, actually."

Violet gave her a small smile. "I know. The contracts you wrote for the tactical teams were quite specific."

Sophie stared at her for a minute as she processed Violet's comment. "You're Ms. T," she said at last. "Tactical. Alpha Squad."

"I can neither confirm nor deny that," said Violet, smiling broadly.

Sophie sat back in her chair, shaking her head in amazement. Now all of Violet's idiosyncrasies made sense: the difficulty meeting people, her obsession with privacy, her avoidance of the vampire community, and her disdain for people who idolized vampires. It seemed Sophie wasn't the only one with an unusual hobby. In her spare time, Violet rescued newly turned vampires from trafficking rings run by cross-border gangs.

Resolved, Sophie gestured for Violet to put the forms back on the desk, which she did.

"I'm afraid I can't take you on as a client at this point in time," said Sophie, stacking the papers neatly.

Violet was about to protest, but Sophie held up her hand to forestall her. "However," she said, unlocking her client drawer and placing a file on the desk in front of Violet, "I'm going to turn around and face the wall for about a minute."

Sophie wasn't surprised to see a look of understanding cross Violet's face before she turned her chair around and covered her ears. She hummed tunelessly for good measure, and when she had counted to sixty, she spun her chair around and folded her hands demurely in front of her. The file was where she had left it, but Violet's eyes were dancing with mirth.

"If one were so inclined," Sophie said, "one might go to O'Brien's Pub on Convoy some Thursday evening. They have an exquisite beer list—dozens of bottle-conditioned options, all containing different strains of live yeast. Just the thing for a mycotarian such as yourself. I think you'll find the clientele quite friendly."

"Might one expect to see you there, as well?" asked Violet.

Sophie handed Violet another business card, this one containing Sophie's real name, law firm, and contact information. "One might," she said. "Of course, if things don't work out, Mrs. Warren will be happy to take you on as a client. I must say, it has been an unmitigated pleasure meeting you, Ms. Tran."

Violet rose and shook Sophie's hand. "And you, Mrs.

Warren."

"Please call me Sophie."

Violet smiled. "Perhaps I'll see you at Allway House, Sophie."

"Anything can happen," said Sophie, "and it often does."

When Violet had gone, Sophie pulled the client file back and opened it. She smiled at the picture inside. "Oh, Matthew," she said softly, "you're not going to know what hit you."

She was confident that he would be able to handle it. After all, Matthew was Violet's counterpart on Emily's Beta Squad.

CAIREANN SHANNON

Little Monsters

The poster caught her eye right in the middle of one of Poppy's meltdowns.
"Poppy, stop it. Stop it right this minute!" Helen hissed, flashing the old lady behind the cash register an apologetic smile.
"Deary me!" the woman said, raising a grey eyebrow.
"Waaaagh!" wailed Poppy.
Helen reached down and took her five-year-old by the arm. "Poppy, I mean it! Mummy is getting very angry."
Poppy didn't reply. She just opened her mouth and screamed again. Helen knew there was nothing to be done but wait until the madness had passed. Poppy had gone rigid; she had that far-away look in her big blue eyes that Helen had seen too many times before. She was used to the tantrums by now, but why did it have to happen here, in the middle of the shop? At least at home she could just shut the windows before one of the nosy neighbours called the police on suspicion of murder.
A man at the magazine rack turned and frowned; a woman with a beautifully behaved baby shook her head in disapproval. Helen blushed with embarrassment and bent over her still-roaring daughter. She had an almost uncontrollable urge to start screaming herself.
"Poppy, stop it! Enough. You're wailing like a... like a..." Helen straightened and put her hand over her mouth as if to

stop the word escaping. She wouldn't say it; she wouldn't say the name her useless boyfriend had said before he'd walked out on her when she was seven months pregnant.

Just then, as she stared over her daughter's head, she saw the poster. Taped clumsily to the back of the shop door, it was almost eclipsed by the pictures of missing dogs and the handwritten For Sale signs. It stood out from the rest, written in elegant black script on velvety red paper:

> Finding it hard to control your
> LITTLE MONSTERS?
> Support group for struggling parents of
> troublesome tots.
> Meets each Tuesday at 10am
> Room 23 at the Town Hall
> All welcome.

Helen stared at it, oblivious, for a moment, to Poppy's tantrum. It was as if it had appeared out of nowhere in her moment of need. *Little Monsters*, she read. That's what Poppy had become: a little monster; a troublesome tot. The doctor didn't understand; the so-called counsellor at the school didn't understand. Maybe these other struggling parents would know what she was going through.

When she finally tore her gaze from the poster, the noise had stopped. The man at the magazine rack was still frowning; the perfect mother with the perfect baby was still shaking her head. But Poppy was quiet, and the little old lady with the grey hair was kneeling before her, holding out a lollipop.

"There, that's done the trick," said the woman, beaming.

"Thank you very much. Strawberry's my favourite," Poppy said prettily, as if the recently screaming child had been replaced by an angel.

The old lady patted Poppy's cheek. "Oh, they all have their moments, don't they?" she said, smiling up at Helen.

"Yes, they certainly do," Helen said with a sigh. With one last glance at the red poster, she dragged her little monster through the door. The perfect mother was still shaking her head. Helen left before the temptation to punch her perfect face became too much.

The brass number plate that read *Room 23* was so highly polished that Helen could see her own reflection staring back at her. She ran a hand through the chaos that was her long brown hair and wished she hadn't overslept. She'd *meant* to hunt out the hair straightener, and the concealer, and her pretty red cardigan. But the morning had disappeared in the usual flurry of toast and cereal and hunting for the car keys, and here she was, looking like something the cat had dragged in. In fact, her cat had altogether better taste; the dead rats and rabbits he often brought home were better groomed than Helen.

She reached for the doorknob but didn't turn it. She could hear voices inside, laughter and the clink of teacups on saucers. What if they all had flawless make-up? What if they had impeccable figures and tidy houses and they weren't struggling at all? Maybe their problems were limited to things like whether to choose a Mercedes or a BMW, or which doctor gave the best Botox. They'd make her feel even worse about herself.

Dropping her hand, she turned to go and almost ran into a man with a wrinkled jacket and shadows under his eyes.

"Sorry," he said, stepping aside with a small smile. "Are you here for the support group?"

"I... well..." She looked uncertainly at the door and then back at the man again. He was a few years older than her, she thought. He looked tired, and his slightly-too-long hair was a mess. He definitely hadn't had Botox. "Maybe..."

"Maybe? Come on... You look like you'll fit right in. And don't worry, we don't bite. Unless there's a full moon, of course." He laughed and threw open the door.

"A full moon?"

He shrugged. "Bad joke. Sorry." He gestured for her to go ahead of him.

With a deep breath, she stepped through the open door. There weren't many people inside, and the room was small, with a circle of chairs in the middle. Helen had hoped for a bigger crowd so she could make a discreet escape if it wasn't for her, but the man with the wrinkled jacket closed the door behind him, and that was it. She was trapped.

"Jack!" said a woman with lank, black hair.

The woman hurried over from a table in the corner that held cups, a kettle, and two laden plates of biscuits. She was the palest person Helen had ever seen, and she was glad she wasn't the only one who hadn't got around to slapping on some make-up that morning.

"It's good to see you," the woman said, patting the man on the arm. She turned to Helen. "We have a new member! Are you a friend of Jack's?"

"No, I... I don't know anyone. I saw your poster in the shop."

"We just met outside the door," said Jack.

"Well, you're very welcome. I'm Clare," said the woman, holding out her hand.

"I'm Helen. Nice to meet you," Helen said, trying not to wince as she shook Clare's hand. Her skin was like ice.

"Have a seat, Helen. I can get you a tea or a coffee, if your condition allows?" Clare said with a smile.

"My condition?" Helen asked. Maybe she was at the wrong group. Maybe this was for people with allergies, or something. She looked down at her slightly flabby tummy. Maybe the woman thought she was pregnant.

"Your hand is warm, so I'm assuming you're okay with

liquids. Biscuit?"

"I... No. Er, just a coffee, please. Milk, no sugar," Helen said, confused. What had her hands got to do with anything?

"I'll get it," said Jack. "Clare can introduce you."

"Thanks," Helen muttered, wishing she was anywhere else. It was like being the new kid at school.

Clare steered her towards the circle of chairs with one of her cold hands. "It's nice to have someone new. Livens things up a bit."

Helen allowed Clare to press her into the nearest chair, and the next minute or two passed by in a blur of introductions. A small woman called Raya had a foreign accent and a face covered in bandages. Her hands were bandaged too, and Helen tried not to stare. The poor thing had clearly been badly burned. A younger woman called Suzanne was built like a tank and had an eye patch over her left eye; a man called Frank had multiple piercings and a silver bolt running through the back of his neck. Maureen looked heart-breakingly sad and wore far too much make-up; Karen was covered in cuts and bruises and clearly had an abusive spouse; Stella was so dark-haired and pale that Helen was sure she must be related to Clare.

In fact, with the exception of a perfectly normal-looking woman called Chris, they were the most bizarre group of people Helen had ever met. She'd never felt more ordinary in her life.

"Here you go," Jack said, handing her a steaming cup of coffee.

"Thanks," she said. He took the seat next to her and balanced a plate of chocolate biscuits on his knee.

"Biscuit?" he asked.

"No, thanks." She looked around at the others and whispered, "I am in the right place, aren't I? Little monsters?"

Jack chuckled. "Yes, you're definitely in the right place. How many kids do you have?"

"Just the one. Poppy. She's five."

"My daughter is six," he said. "What's the problem with Poppy?"

"She just ... Well, she *wails*. Really loudly."

Jack nodded. "My Hannah howls. The neighbours hate us."

Helen gasped. "Our neighbours have complained too!" She really was in the right place, after all. Maybe these strange people *would* understand.

"Right, let's begin," said Clare, clapping her hands. "We'd like to welcome Helen to the group today, and—"

"Sorry I'm late, everyone!" said a woman in a ridiculously short skirt, breezing through the door.

Helen couldn't help but gape. The woman's miniskirt was teamed with a hot pink, lacy blouse, and she wore garish red lipstick and glittery eye shadow.

"Morning, Cherry," Clare said with a roll of her dark eyes. "Busy night?"

"Yes. Gotta keep the clients happy," Cherry said with a yawn as she poured herself a coffee.

Helen's cheeks grew warm. Busy night? Clients? She sincerely hoped Cherry was just a night nurse whose taste in clothes was a little on the risqué side.

"Okay. Who'd like to start? Suzanne, maybe? I know your little Bobbie was starting Montessori this week."

"Yes," said Suzanne, the woman with the eye patch. "He started yesterday, and so far, so good. The other kids think he's a pirate, and thanks to Disney, pirates are all the rage right now."

Everyone in the group laughed.

"Obviously, he wears a patch, like me," Suzanne explained to Helen. "But you know how it is: People see only what they want to see, so they all think he's playing at being a pirate. No harm in that, really. At least he fits in!"

"Right. Yes, of course," Helen said. Suzanne's son had clearly inherited some kind of eye problem from his mother.

"We've had an awful week," said Chris, the one who Helen thought looked by far the most normal.

"Has Alex been getting teased at school again?" asked Jack.

Chris nodded. "He decided to be female last week, so he wore a skirt. The staff were very supportive. His teacher, Mr Kelly, even wore a pink bow in his hair to try to show the kids that it's okay to experiment. They all assume he has transgender issues, of course, and I know it's hard for a bunch of ten-year-olds to understand, but it's still upsetting when he comes home from school in tears. They tried to chuck him out of the soccer squad." She gave a loud sniff, and the man called Frank patted her awkwardly on the shoulder.

Helen remembered reading something like this in the paper: children who felt they were the wrong gender from a really young age. Chris dissolved into tears, and Clare gave her a hug.

"Anyone have any behaviour issues this week?" Clare asked when Chris's crying fit had passed.

"Yes. Really, I'm on the verge of having my two adopted," said Stella with a frown. "We're going to have to move house again if I can't control them. It's only a matter of time before the neighbours complain."

Helen sat up straighter. She knew all about problems with the neighbours.

"Oh, Stella. Not again?" said Clare. "What was it this time?"

"Next-door's cat."

"No! They... they took Mr Fluffykins?"

Stella nodded miserably. "I loved that cat. Not the way Jack loves chocolate biscuits..."

They all laughed, and Helen looked at the empty plate on Jack's knee. "You ate them all?" she whispered.

Jack grinned. "Fast metabolism."

Stella continued, "He was just such a friendly cat, Mr Fluffykins, but you know what the twins are like, and they're having a growth spurt. They said they were thirsty."

Helen frowned. What had that got to do with the cat?

"What had they had for supper?" asked Clare.

"Two hamsters and a rabbit each."

Helen gaped and then shook her head. Stella clearly meant animal-shaped biscuits or something. Or maybe her husband was foreign and they had really strange taste in meat. Lots of people ate rabbit, after all. But hamsters?

"That should have been enough," Stella went on, wringing her hands. "But I just suppose the scent was too much for them."

"How did you find out?" Karen, the woman with the cuts and bruises, asked in a gravelly voice.

"It was horrible. I was cleaning out their room while they were at school. I reached under Tim's bed and pulled out what I assumed was a cuddly toy, but it was Mr Fluffykins," Stella finished with a sniff.

"Oh, honey," said Clare, patting her hand.

"He was all desiccated. Not a single drop of blood left. They'd sucked him completely dry!"

Helen had thought *she* had problems, but what was a little wailing compared to twins who murdered a cat and drank its blood? Stella's children were obviously deeply disturbed. She gasped and put a hand over her mouth. Most of the group turned to look at her and she flushed.

"I… I'm sorry," Helen said to Stella. "It's just I've never heard anything like it!"

"Not to worry," Stella said, waving a hand. "You've probably never been around our kind before. It's a shock, I'd imagine."

"Well, yes," Helen said. The others didn't seem surprised at all. Maybe they were used to Stella's twins by now.

"I'm glad you weren't here last year, when my youngest almost drank his full-human cousin!" Clare said with a laugh.

"Or last month, when my Stephanie ate half a pony at her horse riding lesson," said Karen matter-of-factly, as if pony-eating was an everyday occurrence. "We've changed to basketball. Much safer."

A few of the group sniggered, and Helen gave a nervous laugh. What was going on? Who were these crazy people? She glanced at the door. Maybe she should make her escape now. The others started to chat among themselves, and Jack gave her a sympathetic smile.

"You haven't been around vampires much, then?" he asked.

"What? I..." She didn't know what to say. He was obviously pulling her leg. Vampires? "No, I haven't been... around... vampires."

"They're not all sparkly, as you can see. No super-human strength, either, despite what some novelists would have you believe," he said with a grin. "Silly, isn't it?"

"Yes! Sparkly vampires. Silly, really," Helen said, her gaze moving again to the door.

"Do you mind if I ask what your condition is?" Jack asked.

There it was again. The word condition. Helen met his gaze and frowned. "Well, I'm not pregnant, if that's what you mean."

"Pregnant? No, that's not what I meant, sorry. Look, I didn't mean to pry or anything... I know it's your first time here...." He shifted awkwardly in his seat. "I can tell you about some of the others first, if you'd like?"

"Tell me what?"

"About their conditions. I mean, Raya's obviously a mummy."

"Well, all of the women are, or they wouldn't be here," Helen said.

Jack rolled his eyes and laughed. "I'm sure she's never heard that one before. Some of the others are undead too: Karen is, as you've probably guessed, a zombie; Frank is your straightforward, brought-back-to-life monster; and Maureen is a ghost," Jack said, nodding at the miserable-looking woman with the heavy make-up. He leaned closer and whispered, "I feel really bad about eating in front of her, actually. She misses food."

"I... see..." Helen said. She looked around, examining the ceiling for hidden cameras or something. This was clearly a stupid TV prank. Or maybe a bizarre dream.

"Cherry is a succubus, which makes her fully supernatural. Then Suzanne, Chris, and I are living."

Helen looked at Suzanne with the eye patch. "So, you're going to tell me that Suzanne is a Cyclops, or something?"

"Yes! Well done!" Jack said. "And I'm obviously a werewolf."

"Obviously," Helen said, sipping at her now cold coffee. Maybe this was some kind of dramatic society, or a role playing club. Some of the sci-fi people had been into stuff like that at college. "Look, Jack, everyone here seems perfectly nice," she said. It wasn't a lie, they did seem nice. Just not quite normal. "But I'm not sure I... fit in."

"Oh, don't give up so soon," he said, looking disappointed. "Give it a few weeks. You're bound to fit in. You saw the poster, didn't you?"

"Yes, but I—"

"You can only see the poster if you have need of it. Cherry arranged it that way; she's the only one of us who has power like that."

"Right," Helen said, more confused than ever.

"Come along next week. Please. You don't have to speak or anything if you don't want to. Sometimes, just listening to other people's problems makes your own seem more bearable. One more week?" he said with a pleading look.

"Well, okay," she said, giving him what she hoped was a convincing smile.

No way was she coming back.

The following Tuesday she parked outside the Town Hall and stared at the front doors. They were clearly crazy, the people at the *Little Monsters* meeting, but there was something about them, all the same. They were different; they were quirky. And for the first time in her life, Helen felt like she actually fitted in, just as Jack had said. Maybe that made her crazy, too. Or maybe Jack, with his easy grin and his mop of sandy hair, was the only reason she'd come back. With a sigh, she switched off the ignition and took her handbag from the passenger seat. One more week. She'd give it one more week and then decide.

Helen gave them all a shy smile as she slipped through the door of Room 23 and took one of the empty seats. Clare gave her a cup of coffee just the way she liked it, and Jack took the chair next to her with a smile, his chocolate biscuits balanced on one knee again. She thought he looked better this week. Less tired, somehow; less lined around the eyes.

Maureen, the woman with the miserable expression, was dabbing at her eyes with a handkerchief.

"Is there anything you can do? Forge a doctor's certificate to say that Alice has a... I don't know..." Stella said, frowning. "A problem with growth hormones or something?"

Maureen shook her head. "They already have one. They're just getting suspicious. It's not just that Alice never grows or looks any older, it's other things, too. She can't go swimming with her class, because it would wash away the makeup; I have to keep her home when it rains for the same reason. And they've noticed that she never eats. They want to send a social worker round to the house. We'll have to move again. I know it. Just when we'd settled!"

"Oh, Maureen! I wish I could give you a hug," Clare said.

Maureen sobbed louder. "Oh, how I miss human contact. And food, of course..."

Helen met Jack's gaze. He raised his eyebrows and then subtly moved his plate of biscuits under his chair, out of sight.

"Why can't Clare give her a hug?" Helen whispered.

"Well, Maureen doesn't have corporeal form, does she?

The clothes hide it, but there's nothing underneath. She's one-hundred percent spirit," Jack explained. "She can move things, touch things, but she can't feel them. She has no sensation."

"Oh, look, I've made a mess of my makeup!" Maureen cried, looking at her foundation-smeared handkerchief.

Helen moved her gaze to Maureen's face and stared. Beneath the smeared make-up, there was nothing. Nothing at all, as if the light from the window behind shone through her cheek. It was like a fancy special effect from a movie.

"Oh, goodness! My hand, too!" Maureen said miserably, holding it up.

Helen's heart started to beat faster. There was no doubting it now. Part of Maureen's hand had disappeared. After a moment, she realised Jack was watching her with an amused smile.

"You look like you've seen a ghost," he whispered. "Get it?"

"A ghost…" she repeated, still staring at Maureen's hand. This couldn't be real. She was imagining things, surely. She looked around at the others. None of them seemed shocked; none of them were staring at the woman's hand or her face, trying to figure out what was going on.

Jack was watching her with a frown. "Wow. You *really* haven't been around other monsters much, have you?"

Maureen had taken a tube of foundation from her bag and was starting to dab it onto her see-through hand. Her heart pounding, Helen looked around at the circle of parents again. She remembered the cold touch of Clare's hand, and sure enough, none of the people Jack had described as undead were holding cups of tea or coffee. Could it really be true? Could Clare really be a vampire? Were some of the group actually, truly unable to eat or drink?

Then, as she watched, Suzanne removed her eye patch with a grimace and started to scratch at the skin beneath.

"I think I'm reacting to the material in this patch," Suzanne said to Raya, who was next to her. "It's itching like crazy!"

Helen gaped. Last week, she'd assumed Suzanne must have a problem with her left eye. But there was nothing wrong with Suzanne's left eye. She didn't *have* a left eye beneath the patch. There was nothing: no empty socket, no eyebrow. Just skin; just a continuation of her forehead. She really *was* a Cyclops.

Helen gripped the armrests on her chair, her knuckles whitening. There were monsters, real monsters, sitting here, in this very room. They weren't crazy sci-fi nerds or eccentric actors from a drama group. They were real, live monsters. Or *not* live, in some cases.

"You must be mostly human, then?" Jack said, still frowning at her.

"Human... yes..." Helen managed. Her heart was thudding painfully against her ribs, her breath coming in short, staccato gasps. She had to get out. She was hyperventilating.

She looked across the room to the door. There were only two vampires, a mummy, a Cyclops, a zombie, and a werewolf between her and freedom. She gave a slightly hysterical laugh and clenched her teeth, trying to choke back that familiar urge to scream.

"Here, I think you need another coffee," Jack said, taking her empty cup from her lap.

Helen shook her head, as if it could get rid of the people, the monsters, in the room. She closed her eyes and counted to ten, but when she opened them, they were all still there. What's more, Stella was smiling at her as if they'd been friends for years. Frank gave her a wide grin, showing black teeth beneath his bluish lips.

Then Cherry came over and took Jack's vacant seat, and Helen was enveloped in a cloud of sweet perfume.

"So, honey, how's it going?" Cherry said as she rearranged her indecently short red skirt. She was wearing fish-net stockings today, and shiny stilettoes that were more like stilts than shoes.

"It's... great," said Helen, giving her a brittle smile. She took a deep breath and tried to slow her racing heart.

Cherry flicked her mane of auburn hair over her shoulder and said, "How's your little monster doing?"

"Not too bad. She's been fine this past week, thanks. How about yours?" Helen asked, wishing she could remember what Jack had told her about Cherry. Cherry certainly didn't look like a monster. With her vibrant hair, glittery make-up, and pink bra showing through her sheer white blouse, she looked more like... well...

"Oh, she's finding it tough at the moment. Her name is Candy. It's been fine up to now, but she's thirteen, just hitting puberty, and it's all so difficult for her, you know, given my line of work," Cherry said with a sigh, pursing her cerise lips.

"Yes, of course. And what is your, ah... line of work," Helen asked.

Cherry raised a pencilled eyebrow. "I'm a succubus. Sorry, I thought you knew."

"A what?"

"A succubus. You haven't been around monsters much, have you, darling?"

"No, I haven't, I'm afraid."

"Were both your parents full humans? Sometimes these things skip a generation, don't they?" Cherry said with a sympathetic smile. "Well, never mind. I'm a succubus. Basically I'm a supernatural entity." She looked around and dropped her voice to a whisper. "It's my duty to seduce men. In fact, just like Clare and Stella, I have to drink to stay alive. They drink blood; I drain men of their sexual energy. But like the vampires, we succubi have tried to blend into modern society. Clare and Stella only drink the blood of animals, and I never visit the same man twice. It's bad for their health if I do. I'm too much for them," she said with a giggle and a wink.

Helen gave a nervous laugh. "Yes, I can tell you would be."

Jack came back with her coffee, and while Stella was

relating the most recent exploits of her blood-sucking twins, a man in a neat suit arrived.

"Sorry I'm late, everyone," he said, grabbing a tea before he took the last seat.

Helen frowned. He looked vaguely familiar, and not at all like a monster. "Who's that? He wasn't here last time," Helen whispered to Jack.

"You've met him before, remember? That's Chris."

"No, you and Frank were the only men here last week," she said. "There was a woman called Chris here, though. I remember her... Her kid was the one who was getting bullied at school because he wanted to wear a dress."

Jack laughed. "Chris was a woman last week, Helen. Chris is a shape shifter. He, or she, can be whatever gender he wants."

Helen stared at the man in the suit. She could see it now. "No way! That's amazing." Chris's face had hardly changed at all, apart from the faint stubble on his chin. But the effect wasn't like a woman dressed in a suit, this was a man. Gone were the breasts, the narrow shoulders, and the curved hips. Even the voice had changed.

While the meeting went on, Helen examined the others, one by one. Her heart had stopped beating so fast now, and even though she could hardly believe that she was in a room surrounded by actual, real monsters, she felt at ease among them. Much more at ease than she normally would have in a group of parents.

"Okay, thank you for coming, everyone," Clare said when they'd finished. "I've left some leaflets at the door. There's a talk at Trinity College next month by Professor Reginald Green, that goblin from California. It's called *Monsters and Modern Society*, and it should be full of useful information about how to fit in. I'll be going, if anyone fancies a lift. We can talk about it next week. See you all then!"

Helen picked up one of the leaflets as she made her way

through the door. There was a list of monsters on the back. All the ones from the *Little Monsters* group were there, and others like demons and goblins and mermaids. Then there were a few she'd never heard of before: harpies and furies; jinns and kelpies.

Feeling numb, she tucked the leaflet into her bag and slid behind the wheel of her car. Monsters. Real monsters, living all around her. It was madness.

Madness or not, she still came back. She came back the next week, and the week after that, and the week after that. In the evenings, when Poppy had gone to bed, she even took to looking their conditions up on Wikipedia. Now she knew that Clare's hands were cold because no blood ran through her veins. She knew that Raya would disintegrate into dust if her bandages were removed. She'd noticed that Jack was at his most handsome just before the full moon and looked haggard for a few days afterwards.

And Jack had been right: Just listening to everyone else's problems had made her own feel so much more insignificant. Poppy was still having her wailing fits, but when they happened, Helen took a deep breath and thought about the others. She remembered Mr Fluffykins; she remembered Chris's poor, bullied son and how Karen's daughter had eaten half a pony. It made her sad to think about Maureen's little Alice, who would never again eat or drink or feel the touch of another human. So every time Poppy threw one of her tantrums, Helen just held her close until it passed and silently rode the wave of her own urge to wail out loud, knowing her own troubles were comparatively easy to manage.

The *Little Monsters* group was the best thing she'd ever done, but it had added a new worry to her list of troubles. She *felt* like she fit in, but she didn't. Some accident, some malfunction had made that poster visible to her on that day in the corner shop. Jack had said you could only see it when you had need of it. And she *had* needed it. But she wasn't a monster. She didn't have a condition like all the rest of them, and as soon as they found out, that would be the end of it. She'd have to leave the group.

But she didn't want to. They were such nice, caring people. So far, they hadn't pressed her to share her own problems, or even to talk about herself. That wouldn't last forever, she knew. The day was coming when they would learn the truth, and then they would ask her to leave.

Helen put it from her mind. She would attend the *Little Monsters* meetings for as long as she could, until her time was up.

"I was called in to see the principal last week," Jack said with a deep sigh. He took another biscuit from the plate on his knee and shook his head. "Hannah bit a boy in her class."

"*Bit* him?" said Chris, who had become a woman again. "That doesn't mean..."

"No, he won't become a werewolf, don't worry. That's only if we bite when we're in wolf form," Jack said.

"And why do you think she bit him?" Helen asked, fascinated.

"She says he stole her new pencil case. I told her that's no excuse, and that it was a very, very bad thing to do. But it was a few days before the full moon, and she can get quite, well... feral. I think she might be missing her mum, too. I know she doesn't really remember her, but the *lack* of a mother must be hard. Or maybe it's just my fault," he said, his shoulders slumping.

The others made soothing noises, and Helen looked at Jack's ringless hand. She'd guessed he didn't have a wife, and it didn't sound like he had a girlfriend, either. Trying to appear casual, she waited until the others were chatting amongst themselves and then leaned over to Jack, who, as always, had sat next to her.

"I know what it feels like, you know," she said, hoping she wasn't blushing.

"What, to have your pencil case nicked?" he said, his smile returning.

She laughed. "No. To have to do it all on your own; to have to cope with a problem child without much support."

"Oh. I... Right. Are you... Are you single too?" Jack asked, looking suddenly flustered.

Helen nodded. "It's been just me and Poppy since she was born. My boyfriend walked out on me when I was seven months pregnant."

"Silly man," Jack said, his cheeks faintly pink. "My wife and I divorced when Hannah was two. It was all too much for her, I think. She'd assumed our child would be fully human, like her, but after a few months it was clear that Hannah had my condition. A werewolf husband was bad enough, but two was too much for her. I'm not sure that human/monster relationships really work."

"Yes, maybe not," Helen said, disappointed, worrying what he might think of her when he found out the truth. It was strange, sitting in a room full of monsters and being the odd one out. It was stranger still to wish she was a monster so that she could stay.

"And then the nurse actually had the gall to ask me if I was on drugs," said Frank, balling his hands into fists. "She said that my piercings and my colouring fit the profile of a druggie."

"You should make a complaint," said Jack.

"Oh, what's the point," said Frank with a defeated sigh. "Maybe I should have just taken the bolt out of my neck and let my head fall off. Little Miss Perfect Nurse wouldn't have been so smug then, would she? Don't know what I'm supposed to do about the greenish skin, though. Borrow Maureen's make-up or something."

Maureen gave him one of her sad smiles.

Frank continued, "My youngest, little Seán, has been getting comments at school, too. His classmates have called me a weirdo. Poor little fella. He's fully human, of course. All three of the boys were born before I was brought back to life. We said we wouldn't tell them until they were twelve, but it's hard hiding it from Seán. He's only nine, but we might have to tell him sooner. No kid likes finding out that their dad is reanimated."

"Tell me about it!" said Karen the zombie, with a roll of her eyes. "Our in-laws won't have anything to do with us, now that we're undead."

"Snobs!" said Cherry with a sniff.

"Sounds like you're better off without them," said Helen, sipping her coffee. "And Frank, why don't you wear a scarf to hide the bolt? Just until you break the news to Seán."

"I do, in winter. But what about the summer?" asked Frank.

"Why not get one of those light, linen ones. I've seen lots of men wearing them with t-shirts. They're all the rage," Helen said.

"Ooh, yes!" said Chris. "I've got lots of them. You can borrow one of mine, Frank. I've a few that are sure to go with your green skin-tone."

"Yeah, I might try that. Thanks, Helen," Frank said with one of his black-toothed smiles.

Helen smiled back.

"You've been so helpful, these past few weeks, Helen," said Clare. "I would never have thought of breeding my own rabbits for snacks, and Maureen's looking better than ever, thanks to that make-up you recommended."

Maureen gave her one of her sorrowful smiles, and Helen blushed. "Oh, it's nothing!"

"No, really, you've been fantastic," Cherry said, exchanging a glance with Stella. "And we, well… we wanted to help you out, in return.…"

Helen put down her mug, her pulse starting to race. This was it. She could tell by the way they were looking at one another and by the nervous cough Jack gave to her left. They'd probably wondered about her for ages, speculating why she hadn't told them anything about her own life. For weeks and weeks they hadn't asked, but now her time had run out. She'd known it wouldn't last forever.

"Help me out?" she asked in a small voice.

"You can only see the posters I put up if you have need of them, Helen," Cherry said kindly. "So we'd like to help you with whatever problems you might be having. You know… with your little monster."

Helen gulped. Would they be angry when they found out? "Well, my daughter is five, and she… she's called Poppy. I mean, it's nothing too bad, really. No bullying at school, or being undead or murdering cats or anything…"

They all laughed.

"She just… It's a bit like Jack's problem, I suppose, with Hannah's howling. Poppy has these sudden tantrums. She goes rigid, you see, and she gets this far-away look in her eyes, and then she just… wails. Really loudly. And when it's passed, she can't seem to remember it."

"Well, it's to be expected, isn't it?" said Clare.

"Is it? Is that normal for a five-year-old?" Helen asked.

"Well, it's perfectly normal for your kind," Stella said. "She's so young. I mean, it's easy for you to repress it, as an adult, but Poppy's only five."

"For *me* to repress it? What do you mean?" Helen asked with a frown.

"Well, aren't there times when you have the urge to wail?" Cherry asked.

Helen shook her head, confused. Yes, there were times when she wanted to scream for no apparent reason, but didn't everyone?

"And didn't you say you live in Oldtown Road? Isn't that

near the hospital?" Jack asked. "Surely that makes it worse?"

"Near the hospital? I'm sorry... I don't follow you..." Helen said. "What has the hospital got to do with anything?"

"And was it your mum, too, or did it skip a generation? Was your grandmother the last one? Is that why you haven't been around other monsters?" Clare asked.

Helen moved her gaze from one face to the next. They were all looking at her expectantly, interested and sympathetic as they always were. With a deep sigh, she shook her head and looked at the floor. "Look, guys, I think the time has come to tell you the truth. I'm sorry I didn't say anything sooner, but to be honest, you're all so nice, and I knew that once you found out, you'd ask me to leave."

"Ask you to leave?" Clare said. "Why would we do that?"

Helen raised her gaze, and with another sigh she said, "Because I'm not a monster. I'm not one of you."

There was silence for a few seconds, and then Cherry laughed. "Helen, honey, you saw the poster. I designed it myself. In order to see it, you have to be a monster, and to have need of this group."

"It must have been a mistake," Helen insisted.

"There's no mistake, honey."

"Helen, you're among friends here. We hide our natures from the rest of the world, but you don't have to hide it in here. It's okay. Really," said Clare.

"But there's nothing to hide! I'm just a human," Helen said.

"Helen," Jack said, putting down his biscuits. "I've known since the first time you mentioned Poppy's wailing. It's okay, you know. Banshees are as welcome as anyone else."

Helen turned to look at him, feeling her face drain of colour until she was sure she must be as white as Clare. "What did you just say?"

"You're obviously a banshee. So is Poppy," he said.

"It's great, really," Stella said. "Such a manageable condition!"

"But I'm not a... a..." Helen stammered, rising from her seat. It was hard to breathe, and she felt dizzy.

"Helen, it's okay. It explains everything about Poppy," said Raya. "And there are so many of them here in Ireland."

"Nothing wrong with a bit of wailing! Better than sucking the blood of your neighbours' pets," Stella said.

Jack nodded and said, "There are much worse things than being a banshee."

"Don't call me that!" Helen yelled, covering her ears with her hands, her heart thumping with anger. That's what he'd said, her no-good boyfriend, right before he'd walked out. Then he'd left, slamming the door behind him. And now Jack, whom she liked so very much, had called her the same thing, and the people she'd thought were her new friends were nodding in agreement.

"Helen, what's the matter?" Cherry asked, reaching out to touch her.

"I am *not* a banshee! And neither is my daughter," Helen said through gritted teeth, forcing back the screech that was threatening to break free. She turned and fled to the door, slamming it behind her the way her ex had. Shaking her head, she raced down the steps and out onto the street.

She ran all the way to the park and didn't stop until she got to the bench opposite the duck pond. Sitting down, she put her head in her hands, her chest heaving. The word banshee went round and round in her head like a drum beat.

From nowhere, memories came at her like a montage in a movie: standing on a hill in Connemara with her grandmother, both of them wailing as loud as they could, smiling at one another when they were done; sitting on her grandmother's knee, listening to stories in Irish about the fairy women who wailed when someone died; screaming at the top of her lungs when she was seven years old because she knew, minutes before the phone call even came, that her grandmother had passed away.

"No, I can't be. It's not possible," she whispered to herself.

There were other memories, too: Waking in the middle of the night, trying to muffle her cries with a pillow; wanting to scream in the middle of a geography lesson and not knowing why; and Poppy as a toddler, with that look in her eyes, wailing as loud as her little lungs would allow.

She jumped when she felt the hand on her shoulder and turned to find Jack on the bench beside her.

"Helen, I'm so sorry. We... We thought you knew," he said, frowning at her in concern. "We've never met someone who didn't know about their own condition before."

She held his gaze for a moment and then looked out over the pond. "I'm sorry I reacted like that, Jack. It's just... that's what my ex-boyfriend, Poppy's father, called me before he walked out on us. He said he couldn't take it any more... the wailing... I hadn't even realised I was doing it."

"It's more difficult for monsters to control their natures when they're hormonal. It's harder for teenagers... for pregnant women."

Helen shook her head. She felt calmer now. For the first time in her life, everything made sense. "All this time, and I never saw it..." She looked at Jack again.

He smiled and said, "Your parents never said anything?"

"No. They... I don't think they knew. They thought I was having tantrums, like Poppy. Later they blamed it on bad dreams, and then I learned to keep it all in. My dentist says I grind my teeth. I think that's why: I clench my teeth to stop from wailing."

"So your mother wasn't a banshee?" he asked.

"No. I'm certain of it. My grandmother, though... My father's mother. She must have been. She had five sons, and it's only women who are banshees, isn't it?"

"Yes," Jack said. "That's what ban, or *bean* means in Irish. Woman."

"Fairy woman... The fairy women who keen and wail with

grief when they sense someone has died. She told me stories about them all the time, my grandmother from Galway." Helen laughed and shook her head again. "She was trying to let me know, wasn't she? But she fell sick when I was only six, and then, the year after, she died before she could tell me the truth. It's all so obvious now…. That's what you meant about the hospital, isn't it? People die there, and Poppy can sense it."

"Yes, that's exactly what I meant." He reached out and took her hand. "I meant the other things I said, too. There are much worse things than being a banshee, Helen. You can lead an almost-normal life. You can eat and drink; you can feel human warmth and touch, and the wailing is easily explained away… tantrums, behaviour disorders, bad dreams…"

"I suppose it could be worse. Eating cats; shape-shifting; working nights like Cherry and having to do all kinds of—"

"I'd rather not think about the things Cherry has to do," Jack said.

"Yeah, me neither."

They both laughed.

"I'm sorry, Helen, that you had to find out like this. It must be a shock."

"Yes, it is." She drew in a long, slow breath, then let it out all at once. "But in a way, it's a relief. It explains things about me and about Poppy. And for weeks now, I've been dreading you all finding out that I wasn't a monster. I thought I'd have to leave the group, and to be honest, it's the first time I've ever felt I belonged to something like that."

"You *do* belong."

"Yes, I know that now," she said, smiling.

They fell silent, watching the ducks on the pond, until Helen looked down at their entwined fingers and said, "Jack, are you holding my hand?"

"I, eh… Yes. I am. Do you want me to let go?"

"No. It's quite nice," she said, suddenly shy. Her heart was thumping again, but for a very different reason, this time.

"I was wondering if, um... Would you and Poppy like to come over for dinner? I'm sure Poppy and Hannah would get on well."

"We'd love to," Helen said shyly.

"I've spent a bloody fortune having the house soundproofed, so we can scream and howl as much as we like."

Helen raised an eyebrow, and Jack blushed.

"Well, I didn't mean, you know... *that* kind of screaming and howling..."

Helen giggled. "It's been a long time since I did any of that kind of screaming and howling."

Jack laughed. "Yeah, me too."

"But dinner would be lovely."

"Friday night at seven?" he asked.

"Yes. Thank you."

"Come on," he said, getting up and pulling Helen to her feet. "The others are worried about you. I promised I'd bring you back."

Helen held his hand all the way back to the Town Hall, back to her new friends, where she fit in, happier than she'd been for ages. Finding out she was a monster was the best thing that had happened to her for a very, very long time. She and Poppy would be just fine. She had a hot date with a werewolf. And for the first time since she'd stood on that Connemara hill with her grandmother, she felt the urge to scream for joy.

M.R. GLASS

Grace Abounding

When I was a little kid, I used to imagine I would grow up to be a ballerina. With a name like 'Grace', I figured it must be required. It didn't hurt that my mother loved to dance. I have a vivid memory of her feet. On a stage, I think, or maybe in a studio in front of a huge mirror. She was wearing a giant tulle skirt, and I have the clearest picture in my mind of her, spinning. I was too young when she died for that memory to be real. That's what Dad always says. It's just someone else's version of her playing in my head, like most of my memories of Mom.

It's a good thing I haven't got much physical grace. Not like my mother. If I had shown any signs of coordination, I probably would have spent years shuttled to and from dance classes until the painfully obvious limits to my physical agility became clear even to my father.

What I can't do with my body, though, I can do with words. Weaving pictures, building stories. It makes my heart sing in ways dancing never would have. I don't imagine Dad ever really thought I had a future in dance, but he's not exactly thrilled I'm a writer, either. No, wait. That's not right. He doesn't care if I'm a writer as long as I also get a 'real job.' You know, one with a salary and benefits. I know he means well. He's had to work doubly hard to raise us since Mom died. All he wants is for us to be happy.

"Self-sufficient would be good, too," he says.

I just need some time to show him, you know? To find the stories. To write them. And then, to share them.

It's probably too late to be cutting through the park, but I don't feel like walking all the way around. I've done it a thousand times, and it's never as exciting as everyone tells me it's going to be one day. No muggers, no rapists, no gangs. Nothing. Not that I want any of that, you know, but still. It's pretty tame around here.

What's not tame is the sight of someone leaning over a body under the old oak tree just off the bike path. There's no good reason for anyone to be lying on the ground in the middle of winter. The streetlights need fixing, but the one just behind them casts enough of a glow that, from this distance, I can just make out their silhouettes under the flickering light.

Flash.

Light bathes them both for a moment. The person leaning over reaches out an arm to stroke the prone one's head. It's a tender gesture. My stomach clenches.

The light stutters, and it feels like I'm watching old film on a projector. Choppy and far away.

"Hey!" I shout. "Do you need some help?"

If anything, the crouching figure curls in on itself even more. That's not the usual response to an offer of help. I pat my pockets, looking for my cell phone.

Not there, dammit.

The lamp goes out again and all I can see is the anemic pool of light thrown on the pitted pavement by the streetlamp across the street.

"Hey!" I shout.

Every self-defense teacher I've ever had is screaming in my head, telling me to run in the other direction instead of right at them, but there's somebody hurt or sick lying on the ground, and I'm the only other person here.

"What are you doing?" The words are out of my mouth before I can process what I'm looking at.

The figure lifts its head—her head. The lamp has come on again as if to help me out, and I wish it hadn't. Longish hair, streaked with grey, slight figure, full mouth. Bile rises to my throat, and I'm afraid I'm going to pass out. Her lips are wet and crimson, and for a second, it looks like her eyes are red. She blinks, and her eyes are normal again, but now I can see that her mouth is red because it's smeared with blood.

Oh, God.

I'm on my hands and knees, vomiting. She'll be gone by the time I can lift my head again, but at least I'll be able to get help for the guy, if he's not already dead.

But when I finally sit up, she's just standing there, looking at me as if I'm the one who's got blood dripping from my mouth. My phone must be in my backpack, which is currently, inconveniently, still on my back. My whole body is shaking, but I try to slip the bag down my shoulders.

The woman's got her arms crossed, and she looks furious, but, oddly enough, not murderous.

"What are you doing here?" she asks, which is not exactly what I expected her to say.

I've managed to pull my backpack off and am fumbling with the zipper. My cell phone is in here, somewhere. (Yes, obviously I'm an idiot for not keeping it handy. I already have my father's voice harping on at me inside my head.)

I'm still digging through the bag when she glances at the body on the ground. Now that I'm sitting down, I'm close enough to see him, too. It doesn't matter that the streetlamp is still flickering.

I recognize him right before I realize he's dead—eyes staring, body limp with no hope of ever moving again. Charlie. She's covered him with his tattered coat, and my stomach churns again. It's Charlie, the homeless guy who lives in the park—as much as he can, at least, between sweeps when the cops drag him and the other vagrants down to the station. I can tell that they sort of like Charlie, though, because when it gets really cold, they don't bother booking him. They take him right to St. Francis Hospital. Usually, he just gets admitted to the psych unit for a few days for a shower and some hot food.

He was gentle. He never hurt anyone, and now he's dead.

My chest is tight, but I'm not about to cry in front of this woman.

"Why did you do that to Charlie?"

She looks confused. "Aren't his memories as important as anybody else's?"

Her words are defiant, and I really, really need to get some help. Murderous and crazy is a bad combination.

"What do you mean, his memories?" I'm fumbling with the phone. "You *killed* him."

She looks horrified, and I actually stop dialing.

"What do you mean, I killed him? I didn't *kill* him!" She takes a step back into the shadows. "You're not a vampire." As if accusing me of not being a murderous mythical creature makes any sense while standing over an actual, *real* dead body.

"No," I say, scooting backwards on the frozen ground. "I'm not." I wonder how fast she can run. I may not be graceful, but I'm quick.

Run. Call the cops. Get the hell out of here.

"Wait!"

Yeah, right.

I nearly trip trying to stand up because my right foot has fallen asleep. This hampers my speed quite a bit, and I'm half-running, half limping when she calls out again.

"Please! Wait!" Now she sounds desperate.

I turn around, and she's sitting on the ground. Her arms are wrapped around herself and she's shivering.

Oh, wait.

She's crying.

There's no way I'm getting any closer, but I don't move

farther away, either.

"What do you want?" My voice is raspy and I realize I'm crying, too.

"You can see me."

I'm starting to feel almost as bad for her as I do for poor Charlie.

"Obviously."

"You shouldn't have been able to see me," she says. "I was cloaked."

She must be able to tell I'm about to run away again because now she's talking really quickly.

"No, don't go. Please. I know this must be difficult to understand, but this isn't what it looks like." She inclines her head to the body on the ground.

"You mean, you didn't just rip out Charlie's throat and kill him in cold blood?" I ask, and I sound crazy even to myself. "Because that's exactly what it looks like."

"No. Well, I..." She glances back at Charlie and then at me. "Not exactly."

She stands up. She's smaller than I thought. I've got to be at least a head taller and have broader shoulders. I can't imagine how she overpowered Charlie. He was a big guy, even if he was sort of confused sometimes.

"'Not exactly' isn't reassuring," I tell her. I wave my cell phone. "I've dialed the police. I'm just going to back away, now, and if you make any sudden moves, I'll call."

She'll probably be long gone by the time they get here, but then again, so will I.

"Please," she says, and she reaches towards me but doesn't move closer. "I just want to talk with you. We can go somewhere public."

"I'm not leaving Charlie here like this," I tell her, horrified.

"No, no, of course not," she agrees. "Go ahead and call. You'll see. The cause of death won't be from blood loss."

She stands there with me, calm as can be, while I call for

help. We wait together, silent. Maybe I expected her to be aloof. Smug. But there's something almost reverent in the way she looks at his body, the way she stands. It doesn't make any sense, but it feels right, to me. Keeping vigil, here, for Charlie.

I tell the EMTs and the coroner that we found him here. I tell them I know his name, and they nod like they've seen a thousand homeless guys frozen to the cold winter ground. The tall one, Murphy, is gentle with the body. He knew Charlie, I think.

"Natural causes," the coroner tells us when he's completed his assessment. "Murphy says he discharged himself AMA last time they took him in."

I look at the woman. She looks at the ground.

"So, he didn't bleed to death?" I ask.

"What gave you that idea?" He looks confused. "There's no sign of bleeding on the body. Skin intact, no external sign of hemorrhage."

Skin intact?

I don't know what to do, so I say, "Thank you."

I watch them take him away, and then I'm alone with a woman who still has flecks of Charlie's blood on her skin. Nobody else seemed to notice.

Fine. I'd like to know what the hell is going on, and I expect the only way is going to be by talking to her.

"Is that diner around the corner still open?" asks the woman.

"Yeah," I say. "The coffee is atrocious."

We sigh the sighs of people surviving bad news in the middle of the night.

And that's how I end up having coffee at midnight with a vampire.

Seriously, you can't make this stuff up.

The coffee is worse than atrocious, but at this point, I don't care. The diner is empty apart from shift-workers on break and a couple of high-school kids whose parents think they're in bed. It's too bright in here; I hate fluorescent light, but at 2 a.m., when it feels as if the world should be painted in shadow, it's a crime.

We haven't said a word since we sat down across from one another, pretending to drink. The woman—I still don't know her name—isn't even trying anymore. She's just circling the rim of her cup with her fingertip.

"What's your name?" I finally ask.

She looks up, and I check out her eyes. They aren't red, unless bloodshot counts. I was sure they were red, at least from that first glimpse I had of them.

"Anna," she says. "You're Grace, right?" She'd heard me introduce myself to the ambulance drivers and the coroner.

I nod.

"Are you going to explain what happened out there?" I ask.

"Yes." The finger circling the coffee cup drops to the table. "But it would be easier to show you."

I don't have time to say anything before she reaches for my hand and grips it with a strength that belies her size. I twist my hand, but I can't pull free and now I'm scared again. There's still blood on her fingers, but before I can even argue, my head is filled with noise.

"Just notice," she whispers, and I don't want to pull my hand away anymore.

At first, there is nothing to notice except irritation. There's rustling in the background, the sound of my own breathing, and I'm waiting with half an ear for my cell phone to ring.

There's a sudden flash in my peripheral vision (if one can be said to have peripheral vision with eyes closed). My eyes move beneath my lids, and now it's like watching flickers of film.

Oh! It's me. Must have been last summer, because I'm wearing that old tee-shirt with Grumpy the dwarf on it that

Dad made me get rid of. I'm in the food pantry at the shelter where I volunteer, and I'm handing out boxes, but I'm watching through someone else's eyes—it's disorienting. I can see myself and the other volunteers, but I can't tell who's doing the seeing.

Hands reach out to take the box, and I hear Charlie's voice, rough and joking, come out of my mouth.

"Thank you kindly, Grace. This'll do me for a few weeks."

I remember this. I remember this conversation with Charlie.

"If you'd stay in the shelter, you could have hot food every day, Charlie," I say. I don't have much hope he'll listen. We have this conversation every time he comes in for supplies or medicine.

"Nah," he says. "I appreciate the offer, but I gotta be free. You know?"

I did know. He says the same thing every single time.

It was the last time I saw Charlie alive.

I'm about to yank my hand away when the woman begins to shiver and the scene in my mind changes.

I feel a wave of ambivalence and confusion that doesn't belong to me.

All I know is I must *hurry* because the hunger is so strong. The streets are empty and the moon is a splotch of white in a puddle of ink.

These aren't my memories. Not mine...

She's me and I'm her, and I can't tell where I end and she begins.

All we know is loneliness.

The hunger pushes us forward until we round a corner and find what we are looking for. There's a leap in our chest as the sound of raspy breathing seeps out from behind layers of wood and plaster. We press our ear against the front door of a tiny brick house and listen.

A woman is dying behind that door. We already know this

(how do we know this?), but the knowing is slippery and then it's gone.

We can feel a soft rush of air against our skin, and we know that nobody can see us now. We know without knowing how that this is freedom and imprisonment all at the same time.

The front door opens at the turn of the knob. The bedroom door is ajar and we slip inside, willing ourself not to look at the husband, the man who will soon wake to a cold body and a hole in his heart.

It never gets easier, we think; it's not meant to. Our whole body aches, not just from the hunger.

The dying woman is breathing rapidly now, gasping, and her fingers are hot where they brush against our skin.

"I'm here," we tell the woman in the bed and press a hand to her forehead. "It'll be over in just a minute."

Her eyes are wide and bright. We don't want to look, we can't look. We have to look.

"You'll feel better soon." We hope it's true.

Feverish eyes close, and we crouch alongside the bed and tilt the woman's head back (gently, gently) just as she takes in one last breath.

Our teeth sink into the sick woman's neck. We feel shame and revulsion both, familiar and new.

A lifetime of memory flows through our veins. Blood and memory. Memory, and love, and life, all flowing from the heart and soul and body of the woman dying on the bed.

It feels like forever, but it's probably only a moment until we lift our mouth from the other woman's skin and reposition her body.

There's a sound from behind the door, and we startle.

In the hallway, curled into a ball on the floor, is a child, whimpering in her sleep. Big Bird nightgown and a head full of curls. She's resting her cheek on a brown stuffed bear, the nap on its ears flattened from wear.

So tiny.

She can't be more than three years old.

The child hiccoughs as if she's been crying.

"Mama?"

The cloaking falls away. We are no longer hidden.

The child watches us. Solemn. Waiting.

There is rustling from the bedroom. The child's father is waking.

"Gracie, honey?" His voice is blurry with sleep.

We are in agony. It tears through us as we look at the little girl with the big brown eyes calling for her mother. We can't bear it. Can't bear to leave this child with nothing of her mother. Empty.

We crouch down next to the little girl—*me, it's me*—and reach out our hand.

"Hello, little one," we whisper.

I hear her voice in our two memories, combined. The words echo, doubled.

We trace our fingertip along the soft curve of a baby cheek. "Here you go," we say.

It's not explicitly forbidden, we think. It isn't.

Just a few memories, we think. Important ones. The child must remember her mother (*I want my mother. Where is my mother?*) and is too young for her own memories to suffice.

We can spare a few, we think.

Just this once.

I yank my hand away. My whole body is shaking.

"That's not... That wasn't..."

I can hardly speak. That sensation. Someone else's memories weaving themselves into my own. Tendrils of impressions and feelings that aren't mine, but now they are.

I know this feeling. I've felt it before.

She's watching me.

"What did you do?" I'm shivering, but I don't want to let

her see.

She looks shaken, too.

"I meant to give you a memory from Charlie. One I took when he died." She pauses. "But I think I gave you more than that."

I can't speak.

"I've seen you before." Her voice is so low, I can hardly hear it.

My eyes are blurry, and I blink and blink, trying to shake the images of my mother, and Charlie, and of me, a child of three, layered one over the other like a triple-exposed photograph.

I already know what it's like to feel someone's else's memories wind their way into my own. I experienced it seventeen years ago.

The night my mother died.

There's no sign of the diner staff, and the place is deserted now. So I lie down on the bench seat, because the thought of sitting up like a regular person who hasn't had someone else's memories in her head—for the second time—is just too much right now.

Anna sits on the floor right next to me like it's no big deal, and to be honest, I'm a little disappointed. I guess part of me wanted to make her uncomfortable, too, even if it was just physically.

"So," she says. "You're Gracie."

Gracie. Nobody calls me that anymore.

"I thought I dreamed you," I say. A hooded figure, a soft voice, and a touch that brought vivid images of me with my mother. "Nobody believed me when I used to tell them I remembered her. Not just vague impressions. I mean things that we did together, like that time in the park when we flew a dragon kite and she pretended to make it roar."

I'd been too young to remember something so detailed.

They all said so. They always insisted those memories couldn't possibly be mine. I guess they were right. "You did that, didn't you?"

She nods.

"So is that what you do? Take memories from the dying and deposit them in their relatives?" Confusing them. Making them think they remember their mother when, really, she's just a blur of skin and laughter, and picture albums, and other people's stories.

Where are the rest of them, then? My mother's memories. With a surge of resentment I know I want them. Desperately. She shouldn't have them; they belong to me.

"No, no," she says. "I'd never done anything like that before, or since. It's just that you reminded me—" She shakes her head. "Sharing memories isn't part of the process. You were an exception."

I sit up.

"Why me?"

She's silent. Just looks at me for the longest time.

"It always hurts," she says eventually. "Every single time. The curse was designed that way, I think." I want to ask her what she means, but the silence of her pause feels fragile, and I don't want to shatter it with words.

"But that night, it hurt differently," she continues. "I didn't only feel guilt and remorse and obligation the way I usually do. You were there, and your mother had just died, and there was nothing I could do about that. But I could give you something to help you remember her. I just wanted to do something for you."

"After you took my mother's memories?"

She nods.

I think about the pressure of having Charlie there in my mind and remember the sensation of my mother's memories weaving into my own, when I was too small to know the difference. I try to imagine taking in my mother's whole life.

The smell of my father's cologne on her pillow. The burn in her muscles when she danced. The sensation of holding me, newborn, in her arms. I shiver, and I don't know whether it's from anticipation or terror.

"How can you stand it?" I ask. She looks puzzled. "All those memories."

For a moment, I see the shadow of hundreds of people, thousands, hundreds of thousands of them, pass over her face.

"It's not meant to be easy."

She rubs at the speck of blood on her sleeve.

I suppress a wave of nausea and remember the blood dripping from her mouth in the park.

"How do you take them?" I want her to say it.

She's looking wary again.

"You already know," she says. "Why are you—"

"Just tell me," I say, and I can feel the hysteria rising in my chest. I don't want to think about it, but I have to know what she did to my mother. "Are you a blood-sucking monster?"

She winces, but she answers.

"Not blood sucking," she says. "Memory sucking. At the point of death, we take memories—hold them, preserve them. Bear witness to them."

She's still not telling me the whole story.

"So why were you covered in Charlie's blood?" *And my mother's blood*, but I don't say that part out loud.

She raises her fingertips to her lips.

"That's how we extract them," she says. "Through the blood. It doesn't even leave a mark," she adds, as if that matters.

"Through the blood." I'm woozy again. I slide off the bench to plop down on the grubby floor next to her and put my head between my knees. "That counts as 'blood-sucking', Anna," I mutter.

"Only once they're gone. We don't kill them, Grace. But memory—it's held in the blood. We haven't got a choice."

We.

I manage to lift up my head without passing out.

"There are more of you?"

"Not so many, anymore, if the rumors are true," she says. "The curse... We are dying out slowly."

She looks so sad. Lonely.

My God. I'm feeling sorry for a vampire.

"That's the second time you said something about a curse."

Anna nods and stares at the linoleum floor. She just looks so alone, I can't help myself. I reach out to her, careful not to touch her skin. When I put my hand on her shoulder, she sighs.

"It happened in Prague," says Anna, finally. "More than five hundred years ago... I was twenty-two years old."

She reaches for my hand but waits—for permission? That's new. Twice before she's done this without hesitating. Twice, she's given me memories that she thought I needed, that helped me, even though they hurt. With a jolt, I realize that I'm grateful. Because of her, because she felt compassion for me when I was just a child, I have memories of my mother that I never would have known. I can't just ignore that.

I look at her hand; it's trembling a little. Her lids are lowered, and it occurs to me that sharing this memory might unburden her. I can only imagine what she has been carrying for all these years. It makes my heart lurch to think that I might relieve some of her pain.

I move my hand forward and nod. She lets out the breath she's been holding. The tear that falls to the floor as she wraps her hand around mine is all the thanks I need.

My eyes are burning when she lets go of my hand. The bonfire spitting flames and billowing smoke exists only in our joint memory, now, but my eyes don't appear to have gotten the memo. After what I've seen, the furniture and décor of the diner seem like a plastic set for a play.

"I always thought those were fairy tales," I tell her. "Just legends."

"Most people do," says Anna. "The Golem of Prague is a great story, but it actually happened. So did the pogroms and blood libels."

My high school history class had covered that period, and I vaguely remembered the claims—false allegations—that religious minorities used children's blood in religious rituals. I'd learned about the brutal attacks driven by frightened villagers who didn't understand that the Jews didn't cause the plague, despite being largely untouched by it. It was said that the chief rabbi of Prague fashioned a creature out of clay and used ritualistic magic to bring it to life to defend the innocent.

I'd filed it all away under the general brutality and superstition of the Middle Ages and mostly forgotten about it.

Those stories were nothing, nothing to the memories Anna just shared. I think the images of wailing mothers, the stench of plague, and the brutality of murder in broad daylight are burned into my mind. They won't ever fade.

I'm not sure I want them to.

"So when the Golem failed to stop the massacre of the Jews, the men and women who had been making false accusations—you—were... cursed?"

The town square, full of the wronged, the enraged, and the bereaved. The Golem, towering above them all, and his creator, wielding a magic nobody had known he possessed:

> *"...false stories told, lives' stories stolen*
> *my judgment rendered:*
> *wander alone, o caretakers of memory*
> *thralldom without end..."*

"The punishment fit the crime," says Anna softly. "We were afraid. We fabricated lies in the service of our prejudice and fear, and people died. Our penance is to live alone forever, our only human contact to bear witness to people's lives, their stories, no matter their race or religion." She pauses. "At best, it's unbearable; at times of war, especially the last World War—"

She swallows and just shakes her head.

Horrific, I'd imagine.

Poetic justice at its grimmest.

"So, you don't go around biting people at random?"

"Grace, unless you're *dying*, you're at no risk of being bitten," says Anna with a touch of impatience.

"Okay." I'm trying really hard to think. "You take memories from the dying. Through their blood." In remembrance of the blood they had spilled, she'd said, and the false accusations that this blood had been ritually used.

"Only rogue vampires take blood and memories from the living," she explains. "They like creating 'Undead'. They find it entertaining." She looks disgusted.

I can't help myself. It's bizarre. It's completely overwhelming, but it's interesting.

"Umm. 'Undead'?"

Anna purses her lips. Undead are clearly not entertaining to her.

"I told you, we don't take memories for fun," she says. "We have no choice. I can go for a few days without it, but then the hunger comes back. We take the memories because it's our curse. It's our responsibility."

I don't say so, but I think it. *What a crappy job.*

"But I suppose every culture has its outliers," she says. "There are some of us who don't take their penance seriously. They harvest memories from the living and leave their victims... empty."

"Dead?"

"Not exactly," she says. "Physically alive, but without any capacity to feel. They live to feed. They become another sort of vampire, the sort you probably think about when you hear the word. They gorge on memories and discard them. They don't respect them any more than the vampires who made them did."

I shudder. That's a whole other kind of blood lust. Gobbling up people's histories as if they were nothing more than delicacies for their own enjoyment.

"Isn't there anything you can do about it? You and the other vampires, I mean."

She looks confused for a moment. "You act as if we have some sort of organized community. Remember the curse. We're scattered. Each vampire to him- or herself. We can't stand being near each other. It's part of the legacy we carry for ripping apart innocent families. It's at the heart of our punishment, don't you understand?"

"You're all alone?"

She nods.

"What about humans, then? Can you be near humans without wanting to... you know?"

Anna sighs. "Unless you're dying—"

"Right, right," I interrupt. "You're no danger to me if I'm not dying. Got it." I smile, but it feels sort of lopsided. "So do you at least have human friends, then?"

"No friends, Gracie. Cursed, remember?"

What's funny, though, is that she seems kind of regular, to me. Blood-sucking aside, I mean. Like a youngish woman with the marks of living on her face and a few grey streaks of stress in her hair.

Huh.

"How old did you say you were when you were cursed?" I ask. "Aren't vampires supposed to stop aging, or is that another fairy story?"

"We don't age," she says. "I was born more than five hundred years ago."

"So why are you going grey? Not to be insulting, or anything, but you don't exactly look twenty-two."

She stares at me blankly. "I can't see myself in reflective surfaces," she says. "I have no idea how I look."

Oh, right. I guess some of the vampire myths are true. Apart from the really big one. The one that changes everything.

"Probably doesn't matter." I fail to suppress an enormous yawn.

We sip lukewarm coffee, and I get back up onto the bench because it's relatively soft and I've finally gotten to the point where I'm so tired, I'm about to keel over. I lie back down and fall asleep halfway through telling her about my ambition to be a writer, to tell the stories that sing in my blood.

Dreams come quickly and are filled with the chaos of people shouting, searching for help, moaning with lost hope. Children search for parents, scream in fear, sob with relief. Young voices blend with older ones, no single one distinct enough to be understood. Together, though, they're nearly loud enough to drown out the sound of a dragon, shooting fire from its mouth and roaring.

It's barely light outside when I wake. Anna is sitting on the bench opposite me, a fresh cup of coffee on the table in front of her. Before she notices that I'm up, I reach for my jacket and pull out my notebook. I have to capture the threads of my dream before they slip away. There's a story here, and I'm compelled to write it down.

Images and characters and events flow together— memories, dream images, tales told to me long ago and recently. They are all part of one another, I realize, and they tell a story. Perhaps more than one.

I feel lighter as I write. My mind is clearer.

When I put down my pen, I notice her watching me.

"May I see?" she asks.

I hesitate only for a moment. Part of this story is hers, after all.

She bows her head over the notebook, hair shielding her

face as she reads.

"It's still rough," I say, nervous. "First draft. It's not done yet."

She ignores me until she's finished. Even then, she sits, notebook closed, with her head down for what feels like forever.

"Thank you," she says softly. Her skin is blotchy, and tears cling to her lashes.

I understand, even though she doesn't explain. I feel it, too. The weight is lessened now, through the sharing. Anna's body bows with the weight of the memories she still carries. I reach out my hand, and she gives me the notebook.

It's not as if I make the decision on purpose. All at once, it's just *there*, and I can't turn back.

I put down the notebook and extend my hand again. Anna looks at it for a long time, and then at me.

I nod and hold my hand steady. She knows what I'm offering. After five hundred years of bearing the burden alone, I figure I can give her a moment to decide.

The door closes behind me. The grandchildren have gone to sleep for the night. Their parents are probably cleaning up the last of the evening meal, and I'm here to check on her.

I adjust her pillows and dab her lips with a wet washcloth. My skin is wrinkled now, and my hair is completely white. So is hers, actually.

Old age has finally taken its toll, and her body is worn and tired. We're doing all we can to keep her comfortable, and my children and grandchildren have come this week to visit her.

She told me once that it has all been far more than she believed she deserved.

"What can I get you?" I ask.

"Just your company."

I sit next to the bed and turn towards her. My body creaks with age.

It took ten more years for her to realize that my assessment of her graying hair was the result of more than the inexperienced eye of youth. Our best guess is that her body began to age again the night my mother died, the night she shared my mother's memories with me. None of the vampires we eventually persuaded to meet with us could explain the phenomenon, though they admitted that the scattered stories of the cursed beginning to age and ultimately dying of natural causes sounded similar to what had happened to Anna.

She told me once that she didn't long for death anymore, the way she had in the lonely years, before we became friends. When she'd been by herself, cut off from vampire and human alike, she lived alone with only her guilt and grief along with the histories of the men, women, and children whose deaths she'd witnessed as companion. But then I brought her into my family—my father was wary at first, but ultimately welcoming—and, eventually, into the family I created. My children and grandchildren. My husband, while he lived. My family is hers, now, and she theirs.

We made memories together.

There's a book on her side table. It's one of mine. Short stories set in the sixteenth century. At first, I thought she wouldn't read those, but actually, they have always been Anna's favorite. Finally, after centuries of guilt, unable to change what she had done or what she had failed to prevent, she could at least share the stories of those who had died. Others would know them through my writing.

One day, I'd hoped, she would share her own story with me, and I could relieve the weight of it, finally. She never did. Never got around to it with so many others to tell.

Those histories are woven together in this volume and in the other books I have written over my long career. Anna couldn't share every memory she harvested over five centuries, but she shared a fair few. After a while, she said once, their edges softened and she couldn't remember where they'd each originated, only that the weight of carrying them all had lessened, and her heart had grown lighter.

Tonight, though, she's having trouble breathing. The pain is clearly worse, but she is refusing medication.

"I want to be clear-headed at the end," she'd said.

I wonder what it's like, after centuries of anticipating the hour of other peoples' deaths, to be counting down the minutes until her own.

Her eyes shut, and she begins to whisper. I lean in more closely, and the image of Anna, the night I saw her in the park, rushes back to me. Her body, leaning over Charlie. She was listening, just as I am now. In her own way.

"I miss them," she whispers. "Anya. Hans." She tries to swallow and I dab her lips again. "I loved them."

So long ago.

"I am so, so sorry." Her voice breaks.

She has been sorry for more than five hundred years. I wonder if it's enough; is it ever enough?

I reach for her hand, and for a moment, she looks confused.

"Let me," I say softly.

"What?"

"Show me, and I'll remember. I'll write it down. For you."

The tightness in her face relaxes, and she takes the first full breath I've seen in days. I take her hand and it's warm against my cool skin.

We both close our eyes.

It is time.

MICHAELA VALLAGEAS

Cold Cuts

"We were so lucky to get this lovely flat," said Mum, laying another strand of golden tinsel over the tip of the tree's lowest branch. "It was so nice of the council lady to bump us to the top of the list and set us up in a brand new building."

"I know my rights," said Dad, and he folded up his newspaper, tapping his knee with the roll the way he used to tap on Rex's nose to stop him whimpering when Huggy petted him. "I would have gone over her head to the mayor if she had refused. Special needs families have priority over the others, it says so in the law."

"Oh, she wouldn't have refused," said Mum, taking a step back from the tree to admire the decoration. "Not when she lived in the flat just underneath ours. She knew how cramped it was, and how much we needed something bigger for the children. It's so good to have a room for each of them and a real living room too, and there's a lot of sunlight for our Huggy..."

"Call him Hugo, pet," said Dad. He put the newspaper down on the coffee table and stood up. "He's a big boy now, or he will be, in—" he looked at his watch "—less than nine hours."

"Seven years," said Mum, and her voice trembled a little as she hung one more bauble in the Christmas tree. It was a real Christmas tree, very big and it smelled good, not like the little plastic one we had in the old flat, but I loved the angel on top of the old tree. It had a blue dress and a shiny silver star in its hands and I was sad when my little brother stuck it on the top of Rex's head and Dad took Rex to the vet and he didn't come back, I mean Rex, but when I asked about the angel my Dad said not to ask stupid questions so I think the vet threw it out too when he sent Rex to dog heaven.

"I know," said Dad. "It's been seven years since we've been blessed. I made sure to look at my watch at the exact moment you gave birth, love. Our Hugo will be seven years old at midnight."

Mum screwed her eyes up as she does every time when Dad speaks about That Night, and she turned to him and burrowed her face into his shoulder because of the happy memories.

"Now, now, love," said Dad, patting her back. "It's our first Christmas in our new home and it's going to be a wonderful evening."

Mum pulled away from his arms, sniffling, and dabbed her eyes with the sleeve of the pink angora jumper Grandma gave her last Christmas just before the accident when Grandpa pushed her wheelchair into the lift without looking because he was waving back with the bottle of brandy he had got from Dad, but the belt of his coat was tangled in the wheels so he fell too when Grandma screamed so loud all the way down, and Dad says that's when he 'applied decisive pressure to get us the new home' as they say on the TV, though I don't know why he had to do that because Grandma was already flat enough.

"I hope the mince pies will be ready in time for Doctor Jollyhead. It's so nice of him to take the time to come to see Hug- Hugo, on a day when he certainly wants to be with his family."

I know that Mum wanted to say Huggy, but she did it for Dad, and Dad knew too and smiled at her with pride and joy, but I'll always think Huggy because he's my little brother even if he's got so big and heavy now.

"He's almost family, dear," said Dad. "When all is said and done, we could have lost our son if Doctor Jollyhead hadn't taken over when the midwife fainted, and remember, he's always been kind to us and interested in how Hugo is developing and all the progress he's making. Jasmine," he said, turning to me, "go and help your mother."

"But Dad," I said, because he had taken out the box he brought home from Asda with the pretty pictures on it, and I knew Dad was going to put up the fairy lights and the Electrical Reindeer because that's a man's work. We've never had Electrical Reindeer before, it would have been against health and safety in our old flat, but now we were going to have a proper Christmas as a family, and it was only a pity that Grandma and Grandpa couldn't see it as Dad told Uncle Kevin when Mum couldn't hear because it would make her cry.

"I don't need help, dear," said Mum with a hand on the kitchen doorknob, "let Jasmine look after her brother, I'm sure she misses him."

"You heard your mother," said Dad, without looking at me because he had knelt down on the genuine acrylic heavy duty wall-to-wall carpet which is going to last at least six months if everything goes well as the nice fitter said, and he was struggling to unwind the cables while squinting at the user instructions.

I looked up at Mum, but it was no use, she had already closed the kitchen door behind her as she always does because Hugo shouldn't get into the kitchen as it's not a boy's place. I mean Huggy— that's what I'll always call him in my head.

So I slipped into my brother's room and quietly closed the door behind me because Huggy was sleeping.

I knew he was sleeping, because he was in his wheelchair by the window and the sun was falling right in his face as we had a fine winter day and the nice doctor had yet to come at sunset to fit the new cap on my brother so we can spend a good Christmas Eve all of us together as a family round a real tree with the fairy lights. All the same, I tiptoed from behind and checked his eyes were shut, especially the big one under the skin on his forehead which the doctor says won't open yet only sometimes it opens, just a little. But Huggy was sleeping really well with all his eyes shut and also he had a bit of clear yellow drool like honey at the left corner of his mouth, and he was making his happy whistle of when he dreams nice things like petting Rex's soft fur.

So I went to look out of the window and it was so beautiful out there with all the bright fresh snow that had fallen last night all over the tracks of the old railway station, so thick and white and soft above that broken car with just a little red showing through like my rabbit's fur when I had a rabbit, but now I've got a little brother so that's all right. It was also sitting in neat white caps on the black railings of the iron bridge across the tracks, and on the cabin of the excavator the workers just left there on a cloudy day when Huggy got to the window and his eye opened a tiny bit, because, as Mum says, it's lucky they've given up building on this side because it's looking to the south and this way nothing blocks the sun from shining into Huggy's room and helping him sleep soundly which is best for him without pills or injections, except when it's cloudy which is not as good.

When it's cloudy I'm supposed to stay in my room on the other side of the flat, while Mum and Dad take care of Huggy with the little red pills down his throat or the little injections if he's almost awake but it's not yet time to put him in the new cupboard with the chains when Mum and Dad go to bed, because the doctor said that family life is important for my brother and with patience and love everything is possible.

I'm lucky to have got a room of my own though I'm normal, but my window is much smaller and there's nothing much to look at except the car park and there's only our car there since everyone else in the building left but as Dad says we're well shot of them because they were just jealous. So at night when I can't sleep and Huggy is moaning in the cupboard I get up quietly to look at the moon from his window when it shines so clear and bright over the black iron bridge.

But I like it even better in the day when the sun is warm and after I have a good look at the bridge across the railway and think how it could be on the other side, I can stand behind Huggy's wheelchair while he sleeps so well and the little soft fingers come out of his head and wriggle slowly in the light from yellow to green and to yellow again like the pretty weeds in the sea when I hadn't got a little brother yet and Uncle Kevin and Aunt Vanessa took us once to the beach. Dad says to call them tentacles, that's their scientific name. I know what tentacles are, I saw them on the TV when they showed jellyfish because people complain how their holidays are ruined and Dad says he'd give them something to complain about. I still think they're fingers because when Huggy dreams about nice things like now and I put my hands very gently on his head, they curl around my fingers and it's like we hold hands and I can hear my brother's thoughts but that's our secret.

So I was standing behind Huggy, with my hands in his hair like a sister, and I was wondering if Dad had finished wrapping the presents and if I'd get a doll this year who speaks and walks and blinks because Mum said a rabbit is too much bother, when I heard something big fall in the living room and Dad swear and Mum say "Dear, oh dear" which means there's trouble because someone rang at the door and I knew it was Doctor Jollyhead because the postman doesn't come any more. So I took my hands off Huggy's head just in time before the door banged open because our Doctor is always in a hurry with his big strides and his black leather bag, and Mum was right behind him wringing her hands in her apron because the mince pies weren't even half baked yet and Dad through the door was still standing up the Christmas tree from where it had fallen when the bell made Dad jump, but the golden strands were all right even if the baubles had broken.

"Never mind the mince pies," said Doctor Jollyhead, and he put his big black leather bag on the new white chenille bedspread on Huggy's bed which Mum and Dad bought because with patience and love you never know when it might come in handy. "I've come earlier because I have another interesting case just after this and my wife wants me back in time for, you know, Christmas Eve and all that—" He winked at Dad who had propped up the tree with a big box wrapped in green paper with a red ribbon which I'm sure is for Huggy because I never get something that big as I'm a girl and also I'm normal. "So no need to fuss over me, I'm in a hurry. By the way, could you sign these papers?"

"What's that?" said Dad.

"Just so we can file a patent on all products designed for or from or related to your son as well as all relevant genetic material," said the Doctor, rummaging in his bag. "Your name is going to be famous, Mr. Percer."

So Dad signed because Doctor Jollyhead was like family and he even put in a word with the council to help us get the new flat and he got us the Special Needs allowance so that Dad could stay home to give Huggy his little injections and Mum could buy the new stove and the new wall-to-wall carpet and the candlestick on the dresser.

"But, Doctor," said Mum, "do you think we'll be on the TV?"

"Certainly, Mrs. Percer," said Doctor Jollyhead who was checking Huggy's big eye with a mirror on a handle like the dentist. "Everyone ready, now?"

Mum and Dad nodded because Doctor Jollyhead had already put on his Huggy gloves and was taking something round and shiny out of his leather bag.

It was a big silver helmet like the one on Magneto only bigger and better because it had a lot of coloured buttons and lights and little screens like Aunt Vanessa's new rice cooker. Huggy was still sleeping but the little fingers on his head were moving faster and beginning to hiss, so Doctor Jollyhead plopped the helmet quickly on his head, clicked the lock closed under his chin and stepped back. Huggy woke up with a start and began to thrash and I was very afraid because he is very strong. All the red lights lit at once and began to whirr, the screens flashed really quick and the plug on the top whistled, but the steel straps around the wheelchair held fast so he only foamed at the mouth and lost his rubber slippers and his jumper broke at the seams and his feathers came out a bit, but Doctor Jollyhead pushed them back quickly and he didn't get cut because he had the gloves and anyway he says they're not real brass yet, maybe later when he's fully grown up.

I was clutching Mum's skirt and Mum was clutching Dad's arm very hard and Dad was a bit white but Doctor Jollyhead really knows his stuff so after a moment the helmet stopped whistling, the little lights turned to orange and Huggy stopped thrashing so much. The doctor checked the lock under the chin, tapped on the top plug and turned a few buttons.

Then all the lights turned green and the screens filled with nice little figures, so the doctor got out his black notebook and wrote them down before he took a sample of blood from Huggy as he always does. When he finished I could see he was really happy, because he was humming a tune while he put the notebook and the little bottle back into his bag. "Very interesting," he said. "Really fascinating. He's maturing faster than we thought. I bet that idiot Breckinridge-Watson will be stunned when we publish all the data."

Mum let go of Dad's arm and straightened up a bit. "Our Hugo is exceptional."

"Well, he is," said Doctor Jollyhead. "There are only three other known cases, and they're very poorly documented."

"Dear, oh dear," said Mum in a hurt voice, and her lips pursed. "Hugo's not the only one?"

"Oh, he is, certainly. All the others were girls and they only had two eyes."

Mum sagged with relief. "What happened to them?" she asked politely.

"I'm afraid one of them died and we've kind of lost track of the other two. Now those were very different cases, a long time ago, who didn't get the right medical attention at the right moment and as a result could never be properly studied and integrated into society. Your son, on the other hand, thanks to your love and patience, has made extraordinary progress and now, with the help of this new technology, he'll be able to share the life of his family every evening, without any medication."

"Without the red pills, doctor? But..."

"Without pills, without injections, my dear Mrs. Percer. Oh, maybe an injection now and then if he gets too agitated, but mostly without."

"But, Doctor," said Dad, "they won't cut our Special Needs allowance, will they?"

"In fact I'll get you a Disability Living benefit on top of that," said Doctor Jollyhead, pulling off the Huggy gloves. "I'll sign off the certificate just after Boxing Day."

"And for Jasmine, Doctor?"

"Not a chance, I'm afraid. Now come here to see how it works; Mrs. Percer, you too."

So Mum and Dad tiptoed up to the wheel chair and the Doctor explained how the helmet would stop the tentacles growing too much and coming out of Huggy's head, so his thoughts would stay inside and wouldn't hurt, and he showed them how to operate the lock under the chin and the little buttons and, most important, how they should adjust the front flap over the big eye in the middle of Huggy's forehead which is how he makes pigeons fall when they come to the window ledge to look for crumbs and the eye opens a little which doesn't happen very often but that's how he got the workers at the railway station and it could open a lot more when he's an adult who will make us proud, and how to take the helmet off for cleaning only when my brother sleeps soundly under the sunlight and to watch out for the clouds which I could have told them but nobody minded me because I'm normal and only a girl, but Mum and Dad were happy listening to the Doctor and the sun was already setting and Huggy stirred up.

"He'll wake up any time now," said Doctor Jollyhead, looking at his watch, "and you'll be able to enjoy your Christmas Eve as a family gathered around the tree. Anyway, here are the instructions, and if there's a snag you just give him a little injection then you call me. If you can't get hold of me immediately just give him another shot and maybe three red pills as usual but whatever you do, don't call Breckinridge-Watson. He may fancy himself a specialist but he's a bungler. Have a nice Christmas!"

So he snapped his bag closed and left with big strides with Mum and Dad thanking him all along the corridor, but as he went out he bumped into Uncle Kevin who was just coming in with his arms full of boxes because Dad had forgotten to close the door.

"Dear, oh dear," said Mum with both her hands at her mouth when Doctor Jollyhead sprawled on the new carpet. "Oh dear, dear!"

"There's no harm, Susan," said Uncle Kevin who hadn't dropped the boxes because he's a big man who's served in the army and can change a track on a tank all by himself as he always tells Dad after the third whisky, "I'll pick him up," but Doctor Jollyhead had already got up and left because he's always in a hurry.

"Nice chap for a doctor, pity he's a bit of a lightweight," said Uncle Kevin. Susan, I'll put the boxes under the tree, right?" So Mum and Dad moved back into the living room to make room for Uncle Kevin to puff along the corridor because he's always a bit red in the face but he'll outlive all of us whatever the cardiologist says, and when he put the boxes down Mum frowned because Aunt Vanessa behind him was carrying a lot of shopping bags. Aunt Vanessa was supposed to bring the slices of raw liver and brains for Huggy because they have to be very fresh and there's no butcher around here, but I knew Mum had prepared a real Christmas dinner for our new flat and Uncle Kevin is Dad's brother but Aunt Vanessa is only his wife so she's not really family though she's a teacher and knows a lot of things.

"Here is the special food for our Hugo, Susan," said Aunt Vanessa, holding out the bags to Mum, "and I've bought quite a few other things for us because I thought it would be actually nicer for Hugo if everyone has a cold cuts dinner. It can't be comfortable for him when the rest of us at the table are having a hot meal which he can't enjoy."

"But…" said Mum.

"Anyway, I hate the idea of anyone having to slave over the stove on Christmas Eve, it would be such a pity, don't you think? Really not worth it. I've brought cold cuts, potato salad, cucumbers and jellied salmon because the cardiologist said Kevin should eat more fish, isn't that so, darling? There's also sushi for us ladies, and then some food for Hu Ling."

"Who's that?" said Mum without taking the bags, so Aunt Vanessa dropped them on the table with the pretty red and green tablecloth and turned towards the corridor.

There was a girl standing there, smaller than me, in a blue anorak, and she looked a bit like Mrs. Chang's daughter who lived across the street from our old place, with her glossy black hair around her pale yellow face like the moon, and black eyes that looked straight in front of her like there was no one there.

"Hu Ling's mother is our new neighbour on the landing. She got hospitalized today. I just couldn't leave the girl alone." She lowered her voice. "Monoparental family, you know."

"But," said Mum, "what's happened to her mum?"

"She's got some kind of Asiatic flu," said Uncle Kevin who was helping Dad fix up the last fairy lights and plug in the Electrical Reindeer. "Nasty stuff, if you ask me – all the paramedics had the masks and gloves on."

"Goodness gracious, Kevin, how can you be so insensitive? That is only a sensible safety precaution, nothing to do with Mrs. Sayaw. Also, the girl can hear you."

"Of course the girl can hear me," said Uncle Kevin, righting up the pile of boxes under the tree. "She may be blind, but she plays that violin at every hour of day and night, so I know she's not deaf. The point is, she doesn't speak English."

"You can't be sure, Kevin. I think she's just shy."

"But, but," said Mum. "She can't see?"

"She's visually challenged, that's all," snapped Aunt Vanessa.

"But, but, *the flu?*"

"Oh, for heaven's sake, Susan, stop making a fuss about nothing. Of all people, I thought you'd understand you can't exclude someone just because they're different. Anyway, Caring at Christmas wouldn't have her, they're such bigots."

"I think," said Dad a bit loudly, "the children should all get in the living room and we'll sit like a family around the tree. Jasmine, get Hu Ling in and lay one more place at the table for her; Kevin is going to help me get Hugo."

So Uncle Kevin helped Dad lift up Huggy's wheelchair which was a good thing because that way the carpet doesn't get any more grooves and maybe it will last six months after all, and they set the wheelchair down on the other side of the table from the Electrical Reindeer because Huggy was beginning to wake up as he does every evening when the sun is away, only this time it was going to be better as Dr. Jollyhead had promised.

Uncle Kevin wiped his brow after they put the wheelchair down because it's really heavy, and took a step back to have a better look at Huggy's helmet, and whistled between his teeth: "Nice contraption you've got here, boy. How does it work?" Dad began to explain the lights and the buttons and how they were going to make things much better, so he took the straps off my brother's ankles and wrists. Huggy waved happily at the shinies in the tree and stamped his feet with joy on the foot rest but it didn't make a lot of noise because of the rubber slippers, and then Dad explained about the flap on the forehead and how it had to stay pulled down now that Huggy was almost seven years old, except of course when Doctor Jollyhead wants to check his big eye with a mirror.

"Oh, stop goggling at the poor boy as if he were an animal," said Aunt Vanessa. "And you, Jasmine, don't just stand there, now be a good girl and do as your father told you."

So I went to get Hu Ling who was still standing in the doorway like she didn't know where to go. Her hand was small and cold, and she smiled at me like Mrs. Chang's daughter did when we played cat's cradle in her shop, so I thought maybe I'll have a friend again, but Dad said to make her sit at Huggy's right to keep him company and Uncle Kevin would sit on his left side just in case, which was a good idea because when I helped Hu Ling get seated Huggy looked at her with puppy eyes like he used to look at Rex and he said "Hhgghnn…"

"Yes," said Aunt Vanessa, "this is Hu Ling. Hu Ling, this is my nephew Hugo."

"Hhhu… llnng," said Huggy, and everyone clapped their hands because the helmet worked so well, except Hu Ling because I was just helping her get off her anorak and Huggy tried to grab her arm but he only got the sleeve and Hu Ling's hand brushed against the nice helmet.

"Hu… go?" She smiled with her lips.

"Hu-go," said Aunt Vanessa. "Hugo."

"Hugo," said Hu Ling, and I held my breath because her little hands were running all over the helmet light and quick like spiders and I was afraid she'd touch the wrong button but Huggy didn't thrash or even grab and when her fingers moved down his cheeks he said "Hhh...llnng" again but very softly and when she took her hands away he just kept looking at her.

"That's all well and good," said Uncle Kevin, "but I feel rather peckish."

Then Mum asked me to help set the table so I was very busy with the cutlery and the glasses while Mum and Aunt Vanessa got the best trays out of the dresser. Huggy was still looking at Hu Ling, so Uncle Kevin got up and helped get the plastic food boxes out of the bags and lay the food on the trays, and Dad got out the wine bottle for the Special Occasions, only the corkscrew broke at the first attempt but Dad didn't really put his eye out and Uncle Kevin managed to get the cork out with his Swiss Army knife.

While Mum and Aunt Vanessa were fussing with Dad's eye, Uncle Kevin tried to snatch a sausage, but Aunt Vanessa told him off and served him some nice jellied salmon with cold boiled rice and cucumbers, then she pushed the special dish for Huggy in front of him with the nice slices of raw liver and chunks of brains because it's good for him and she rummaged at the bottom of the shopping bag and brought out a small brown pot which she put on Hu Ling's plate.

"What's that?" said Mum, squinting at the pot.

"That's what we found in Mrs. Sayaw's fridge, she pointed at the fridge then at Hu Ling while the paramedics were putting her on the stretcher, so I thought she had prepared it for the girl. Has to be a traditional dish, they're Chinese Filipinos."

"Are those bits of eel?" said Mum, still squinting. "Grandma used to cook that for Grandpa, with mashed potatoes."

"I think it's snake."

"As long as it's not jellyfish," said Uncle Kevin who was still scowling at his salmon. "Or that kind of mess."

"Kevin! Don't be disgusting!"

Dad quickly poured wine in Uncle Kevin's glass so he stopped scowling, I got myself some potato salad, Aunt Vanessa had all the sushi to herself as Mum always says after she's left, and Mum and Dad got the ham and the sausages. Huggy ate his slices of liver and brains very quickly and I think he tried not to make noises but it was difficult because he likes them so much and they were very juicy. Then he looked at Hu Ling who was eating so quietly with her black eyes looking at nowhere, and he said "Hghnn…" very softly. I don't think Mum and Dad heard, because Uncle Kevin had given up on the salmon and was already telling once again how he had changed that tank's track all by himself, but Hu Ling piled two bits of snake on her fork, put them in Huggy's bowl without letting fall a single drop of sauce, and Huggy ate them with the black skin and the bones but nobody noticed because Mum was busy putting more bread in the baskets and Dad was getting out the whisky.

When Aunt Vanessa had finished her sushi at last, Dad got up and lit the tea candles on the coffee table and the tall red candles on the dresser because it was more magical. Uncle Kevin served himself another glass of whisky, leaned back in his chair and asked if there was some pudding.

"Of course there is," said Dad who was lighting the last of the red stick candles in the chandelier. "Susan made some mince pies, didn't you, love?"

Aunt Vanessa said not to bother because sugar isn't healthy as she told us so many times, but Uncle Kevin perked up and helped Mum clear the table for the dessert. Then Mum went to the kitchen but she forgot to close the door because it was a magical evening, so we all heard when she opened the oven door and screeched, so Dad went to see what was the matter, and Aunt Vanessa of course, and Uncle Kevin last so I went too.

Mum was crying with her apron over her eyes because the mince pies were all mushy and white and the stew she had left simmering on the brand new stove for a real Christmas dinner and we could have eaten it the next day was cold.

So Dad took Mum in his arms and patted her back, and Uncle Kevin touched the heater and it was cold too so he went to check the boiler. "Doesn't work either," he said.

"Thought it was getting a bit cool in your living room," said Aunt Vanessa.

"Drat, they've cut the gas again," said Dad.

"Did you pay the bills?" asked Aunt Vanessa.

Mum sobbed harder and Dad held her tight in his arms.

"Of course I did," he snapped. "It's their damn repairs, they say they have to renovate the pipeline, don't know what is wrong with it. Every time they forget to turn the gas back on and when I call they say they thought the building was empty. Don't even say sorry or anything."

"Then call the company now," said Aunt Vanessa. "They can't leave people without heating in the middle of winter, who do they think they are?"

"Our Huggy is going to catch his death," wailed Mum. "I so hoped we'd have a nice Christmas!"

"It's Friday night and Christmas Eve," said Dad. "Who do you think is going to answer the phone?"

"Not to worry," said Uncle Kevin. "I'll just go to the basement and turn it on."

Mum wailed louder.

"Are you sure?" said Dad, still holding Mum.

"Positive," said Uncle Kevin. "Done much more difficult stuff when I was with the army."

I think Dad didn't want to hear the story about the tank track again, because he let go of Mum and he got a screwdriver and a torch for Uncle Kevin and Aunt Vanessa said Uncle Kevin should take his pills first but he said he'd be back in a jiffy and Dad said he'd go with him so both of them set off and Aunt Vanessa was left holding Mum who was still crying.

"Let's go to the bathroom," she said, "you look a fright. Jasmine, you look after Huggy."

"But, Aunt Vanessa," I said, because I was afraid Huggy would be upset after all that hubbub as Dad sometimes says and I didn't want to be alone with him, not in the evening when he hadn't had his little injections.

"Do as you're told," she said, holding the bathroom door open with one hand and pushing Mum inside who was still wailing.

So I went back to the living room and Huggy wasn't upset after all, he was still looking at Hu Ling with his two eyes and holding her small hand in his big one and she was smiling her little smile and looking straight through the Christmas tree because of course she couldn't see how pretty it was, and she was kind of humming under her breath so I thought maybe I could have a quick look at the gifts just to see if there was anything for me.

I had to move the Electrical Reindeer first because Dad had set it in front of the gifts so I pushed it to the side and took the first box but that one was marked HUGGY with the golden marker because it was the biggest, and the second too, and the third was for Mum and the fourth for Dad and the fifth for Huggy again, so I had to move all the boxes around and I knew that Mum and Aunt Vanessa would be in the bathroom for quite a while because Aunt Vanessa would first get Mum to take her little white pills and wait until she'd calmed down before getting her to wash her face in the sink and comb her hair flat because it stands up when Mum's upset; but still I wasn't sure I could put the boxes back so that nobody would notice. In the end I found a box at the bottom marked 'Jasmine', and that's me, so I listened to the bathroom and Mum was still sobbing so I pulled the pink string and unwrapped the paper just a little bit to have a look inside.

There was something black and silky like Hu Ling's hair, so I pulled the paper a bit more and it was the head of my doll and when I stood her upright to have a better look she opened her blue eyes and said 'Hi, I'm Cindy. Nice to meet you!' so I couldn't stop peeling all the paper off and taking her out of the box. She had a soft blue jumper and when I took her in my arms she giggled like my friend Jennie back when I still went to school before we got the new flat, because it's too far though they promised to build a new school where the old railway station is, but that was before Huggy looked at the workers.

So I rocked Cindy in my arms and I was showing her the nice fairy lights in the tree when I felt someone tug at my blouse from behind and when I turned Huggy yanked Cindy from me and put her on Hu Ling's lap. I tried to snatch her back, but Huggy had turned his wheelchair sideways and thrust his arm out in front of Hu Ling, so I just caught an arm and a leg and when I pulled I heard a crack and the wheelchair overturned and Huggy fell head first on the Electrical Reindeer.

It was a good thing the lights went out, even the fairy lights and everything except the candles, because that way Mum and Aunt Vanessa were in the dark in the bathroom at the end of the bathroom corridor and they couldn't see the sparks and the firebolt when Huggy bellowed in pain, but I could see the helmet was smoking and all the red lights on it were flashing, so quickly quickly I kneeled behind my brother and opened the lock under the chin and the helmet came off with a sizzling noise and Huggy bellowed again.

"Shh," I said in his ear like I do when Dad is late with the little injection, "shh, Huggy, be quiet," but the little fingers on his head were much thicker and thrashing a lot, and it hurt so much to hear his thoughts when the eye on his forehead burned through the skin. I think it must have opened quite a bit because when Aunt Vanessa reached the living room to see what was the matter Huggy looked straight at her and Aunt Vanessa keeled over like a stone, but that was a good thing too because Mum who was right behind stumbled over her and knocked herself out before she could look at us.

    Huggy had stopped bellowing and he turned to bury his head in Hu Ling's lap and moan, and she put her arms around him with the doll on top and Huggy's head fingers clasped over her hands over and around the doll. So I thought it was safe to go and have a look at Mum because she was beginning to stir, so I pulled the apron over her eyes and told her not to move, that I would put out the candles and then she'd be safe, at least from the eye, and not to worry because Dad and Uncle Kevin would get back soon to give Huggy his little injection, but Mum groaned and said I should open the windows really quick, and that's when I noticed the gas smell.

    I ran to the door to see if Dad and Uncle Kevin were coming back already, but the smell was much worse on the landing. I was so afraid the thoughts boiled out of my head so I slammed the door shut and ran to open the window in Huggy's room then I ran back to get Huggy but he had got up by himself with Hu Ling in his arms and she was holding tight on his neck. It was a full moon and the moonlight was flooding the room, so I put my hands over my eyes and watched just a tiny bit between my fingers, but Huggy wasn't looking at me anyway, he clambered on the window sill and I was so afraid they would fall, but then his wings burst through the clothes on his back and they shone like brass, so I knew I shouldn't worry and I ran back to get Mum too, but that's when I felt someone was pushing me hard in the back like flying, then everything went bang and everything went dark.

    It's very cold where I'm lying on my back in the snow with the dust falling in my face and I wish I could get up to look for Mum and Dad and Uncle Kevin because I don't think Aunt Vanessa made it, only I can't move my legs, but it doesn't hurt at all even with the stove on top of them. There's something warm trickling from my forehead into my eyes but if I blink hard enough the red veil goes away and with the full moon behind the railway station I can see Huggy on the old iron bridge with Hu Ling in his arms, turning round slowly again and again like a dance. Her head is falling back like she's happy and he's holding her so tight I'm not sure she can breathe but I'm glad for them even if I wanted so bad to get a friend. Then my ears stop ringing and I hear someone whimper "dear dear oh dear" from under the rubble, so I know Mum's alive and it feels like everything's all right, but as I close my eyes I do wonder what Doctor Jollyhead is going to say.

JAE EYNON

Learning Curve

"After all this time, and all the resources I've provided, the best the vampires can come up with is Seductive and Dangerous with a side order of Romantic and Misunderstood?" said the Lord Apollyon, Angel of the Abyss and Ruler of the City of Destruction.

Seated to the left of his Lordship, usually a highly sought-after place of dishonour at board meetings, the Count and the Sheriff exchanged an uncomfortable glance. The creature Renfield, having once again weaselled his way in on the hem of the Count's cloak, sat inconspicuously, fussy little snack pack of bugs in hand. He simply faded into the background and picked his nose, apparently oblivious to everything but the squirming bluebottle he'd accidentally inserted up one nostril.

The Sheriff ran a hand through his floppy blond fringe. "I think you'll find, my Lord, that with certain notable exceptions, we have recently been trending back towards the—"

At his Lordship's gesture, a section of wall slid open to reveal a multitude of shelves crammed full of gaudy paperbacks. The Sheriff blushed a darker white.

"As I said. Seductive, Dangerous, Romantic, Misunderstood." His Lordship counted off the items on his fingers. "Ticky box after ticky box, gentlemen. Arse-kicking ninja skills and the odd growly fit do not disguise the fact that you have failed to move on from the tired old methodology laid down by Marlowe, Milton, and—bless his little cotton socks—Stoker."

He got to his feet with a metallic rustle and leaned forward, hands on the glass table top, claws tapping an uncomfortable rhythm while he surveyed the six hundred and sixty-six board members with an air of mild impatience.

"Gentlemen—"

"Ahem."

"… and Ladies—do excuse me, my dear, we are of course an equal opportunities organisation."

"Ahem."

"And Things." There was a testy pause. "Any other entity-specific honorifics I need to include?"

"Transdimensional Ectoplasmic Duo-Demonic Incubi and Succubi, my lord, newly unionised. We prefer to be called by our acronym, as it saves time," called something round and furry but oddly alluring from halfway down the table.

"Very well. Gentlemen, Ladies, Things, and TEDDIS… Teddies? Really?"

"It keeps people off their guard, my Lord."

"Ah. Jolly good. Where was I?" His Lordship took a sip from a bejewelled horn and began to pace, his pads making no noise on the plush carpet.

"The Project has stalled. I am…" He turned his back to them and let his feathers droop before, not above a little drama, he whirled round with wings suddenly at full extension. "… disappointed."

There was a thud and a patter as plaster crumbled to the floor. His Lordship's secretary slipped in from the office dimensions to lend a discreet talon. Always so embarrassing when a wingtip got embedded in the wall.

"Yes. Disappointed."

The Count raised an elegant hand. "If I may, my Lord?" He

rose smoothly to his feet, his silk cloak a black waterfall from his shoulders. "I don't know about the other Departments, but we, my esteemed colleague and his associates and I—" He coughed modestly. "—*have* been recruiting."

Through the smatter of applause, a sulky voice at the other side of the table snarled, "So have we."

"But with so much less style, my hairy friend, so much less style."

"Recruiting," his Lordship said flatly.

"As you say, my Lord," replied the Count, resuming his seat with a satisfied inclination of his head.

"And has anyone else been... recruiting?"

A large demon with smoky breath and a somewhat ruddy complexion hove eagerly to his hooves, knocking the table and spilling goblets of liquid which variously oozed, flowed, dribbled, or ate right through the glass and into unsuspecting neighbour universes.

"We," he rumbled, "are successfully growing demonic possession as a project-vital methodological strategy. Year-on-year improvement lies at thirteen percent, and costs are down as we recruit a younger, less qualified but still largely effective workforce while encouraging older workers to seek alternative employment—"

"Yeah, right," said someone from the pointy-hatted part of the assembly.

"—and we are leveraging investment through a bid—"

"Hostile takeover!"

"—to subsume the departments of witchcraft and sorcery in order to—"

"Oh, dear God," growled his Lordship.

The obscenity rang in the air.

"To think I could be wasting time with a handful of nubile brunettes in my nice, comfortable abyss, and yet I come here in the hope..." His Lordship savoured the general cringe at his salacious choice of words. "In the hope that we might have managed to come up with something other than the same tired old conventions dressed up in ghastly management speak." He fixed the big red demon with a fiery eye. "My dear chap, whatever we may be, whatever disgusting, deliquescent, putrefying, delightfully corrupt regions of the nether world call themselves our homes, let us at least maintain our regard for the language. There is such a thing as standards."

The unfortunate demon opened and closed his maw a few times. "As head of the Department of—"

"Careful, now," said His Lordship.

"—I can categorically state that, statistically speaking—"

His Lordship sucked air noisily and gave a sad shake of the head. "Sit, dear boy, be seated. Allow me to help you all with a summary of matters as they stand." Careless of the risk to the two fingers he stuck between his dripping fangs, he gave a piercing whistle. His secretary rematerialized with an armful of files.

"A new trick, my Lord?" the secretary said blandly.

"There are some collateral benefits to be gained from stirring up trouble at football matches, Baal, my friend. You like it?"

"Not especially, my Lord. It makes you drool. Here are the figures you requested."

Baal laid out the documents and stepped back, nimbly whisking his tail to the side to avoid entanglement with the legs of his Lordship's executive throne. His master clawed open the folders and gave a moment's consideration to the contents of each one before passing to the next. He resumed his seat, leaned back, and gave a judicious nod.

"Yes," he said. "Yes, you have all been working very hard—I can see that. Possession, hexing, haunting, perversion, conversion, reversion, inversion… Inversion? We have a Department of Inversion?"

From below the far end of the table, where a pair of stout, hairy legs was waving in the air, a slightly muffled voice spoke up cheerfully. "Yes, my lord! We turn things upside down. And sometimes back-to-front. Or even inside out. Cups, vehicles, underpants, arguments, logic. It's unbelievably annoying."

"I can imagine. As I was saying, you have all clearly been working very hard. Vampires in particular have made significant population gains, though the werebeasts seem to be doing their best to keep up. Is there a betting pool?" he asked Baal.

"Yes, sir. I have ninety souls on the vampires coming out ahead by the end of the year, and a further twenty that the new wave bloodsuckers beat the traditionalists."

The Count showed fang, at which the Sheriff grinned toothily.

"Belial's running the book?" his Lordship asked.

"Of course," replied Baal.

"Tell him I'll have a hundred on the weres."

Both of the vampires frowned across at the grinning werewolves.

"However," resumed his Lordship, "we have a problem." One pewter-coloured claw poked the files, emphasising his words. "None of you thinks on a large scale, and more importantly, none of you considers the consequences of your actions."

"But, my Lord," exclaimed the Count, heading up the general hubbub of protest. "We strive for the spread of evil! We dedicate ourselves to the suborning of human souls!"

"When you're not just wallowing in hedonism," muttered Renfield through a large spider.

"Quiet, minion!" snapped the Count.

Renfield gave an infinitesimal shrug and folded his empty packet of bugs neatly into a pocket.

His Lordship closed his eyes, briefly lowering the temperature of the room by a few degrees. He shook his head.

"No, no, no." He sighed. "Let me use very simple words.

We have two problems. Firstly, you are going at the project one human at a time. One by one by one. Attrition doesn't work when the creatures breed like cockroaches. Do, as they say, the maths. Secondly, I think that perhaps the Department of Inversion has been overstepping its remit just a little."

An unabashed snigger came from below the table.

"I see you are unconvinced. Behold the evidence."

His Lordship clapped his hands, and the wall that had revealed the shelves of gaudy paperbacks opened further, exposing a seemingly endless array of books, pictures, films, clothes, jewels, and every conceivable representation of the demonic, vampiric, witch, and were.

"Well," said the Count, smoothing an eyebrow with a delicate digit. "Haven't we been productive boys and girls? And things. And teddies."

His Lordship thunked his forehead against the table, his wings a dismal hump of feathers.

"You really don't get it, do you?" he muttered from underneath. "You are supposed." His voice grew louder. "To be." And louder. "Destroying them." A violent tremble ran through the razor-sharp pinions. "And yet, you *inspire* them! Bugger." He yanked his wingtip out of the plaster again and blasted a hole through the wall with a glare. *'Is nobody here capable of lateral thinking?'* he roared.

"… outside the box," mumbled the big red demon.

A voice inserted itself between the gusts of his Lordship's irate breath.

"I believe I may be able to offer something that pushes the boundaries as required by the project manifesto."

Seeking the owner of the voice, his Lordship's gaze came to rest at last on the individual who always seemed to squat unobtrusively in the Count's shadow. This individual, of indeterminate species, medium height, average build, and moderate ugliness, ought to have stood out in such a flamboyant crowd. Instead, the eye—no matter how fiery—

tended to slide away, and the brain wearily block out a voice which in every respect matched the appearance of the point whence it issued.

His Lordship, concentrating hard, said, "And you are?"

"Renfield. From bookkeeping, sir."

"We're not that much over budget," protested the Sheriff.

Renfield peered over his perfectly ordinary spectacles. "We can discuss that later, if you like, but I fear the stakeholders would disagree."

"I thought you worked for me!" said the Count.

"So you did, Master. There is," continued Renfield without missing a beat, "as your Lordship points out and my esteemed red colleague remarks, a need to think outside the box."

"Though some of us might not want to be outside the box when the stakeholders are around," said a werewolf, *sotto voce*.

Renfield resumed. "Statistical analysis shows—"

His Lordship suppressed a yawn.

"—that indeed the project is failing to meet its targets. Current projections calculate that the rate of subornation and spiritual erosion of the human race is falling far behind the levels of inspiration and, dare I say it, 'fun' that are deriving from the activities of the board members here present and of their departments. The board is in denial, sir. And what makes all of this the more distressingly ironic is the ease with which our goals might be accomplished for minimum expenditure by keeping our eyes firmly on the big picture."

Renfield waited a moment and then, perceiving from the slightly glazed expression on his Lordship's face that while encouragement was unlikely to be forthcoming, so too was obliteration, he continued.

"Our operatives have been observing for some time that the majority of soul-antithetical techniques have quite rightly targeted the appetites and desires, be they physical, emotional, or intellectual, of the human creature."

"And it's so much more amusing when they think they're

resisting," put in the Count, to a general murmur of agreement.

"Perhaps," Renfield said. "Speaking as your erstwhile minion, however, I have never seen the amusement value of your activities." Once more, he peered over his glasses through colourless eyes. "In any case, 'amusement' should not be our goal. In your pursuit—your expensive pursuit, I might add—of choice entertainment, you neglect to pluck the low-hanging fruit on your every side."

"And they complain about the way I talk," said the big red demon.

"You are incentivising yourselves with process when, at the end of the day, it is the bottom line that counts."

"What is he talking about?" said his Lordship. "Baal, can you understand a word the fellow says? Baal, wake up!"

"Perhaps," Renfield said, "I should simply cut to the chase."

"Do the what to the what?" Baal said, jerking back to consciousness.

"Spiritual destruction for minimal cost, sir. Low effort-to-soul ratio. Your other departments having so obligingly provided much of the material that is ours to use, I can now illustrate the way we will move forward into a new age. The approach must be two-fold."

Renfield snapped his fingers, and a screen unrolled from the ceiling, showing a pyramid schematic, one stick figure at the apex, multiplying to a crowd at the bottom. "Suppose," he said, "I give to one human... a book." With the press of a button, a small picture of a book appeared next to the figure. "It is deemed to be a 'good' book. The reader recommends it to a few friends, they to their friends, and so on." Books popped up all over the pyramid. "The book may inspire, educate, please, comfort, amuse.... Whatever its effects, they usually end up working counter to our aims. Now let me show you a short film made by one of our undercover operatives."

The diagram disappeared, replaced by a grainy moving

picture shot from a strange angle. In a train carriage, a person in grey took the vacant seat next to a woman reading. The grey person struck up a conversation. The woman responded eagerly, but was quickly persuaded that her book was dull, worthy, difficult, and generally not worth reading. She closed it and turned to stare disconsolately out of the window.

"That's not what I call spectacular," remarked the Count.

The Sheriff looked up from his smartphone long enough to nod.

"Indeed," his Lordship growled. "You will not beguile many humans with boredom. You try my patience, demon."

Unperturbed, Renfield continued.

"This retroactive work, addressing already-extant media content, represents the lesser part of our load, and indeed these pleasure-drainage exercises provide solid and virtually cost-free entry-level experience for our trainees. The greater thrust lies at the other end of the creative endeavour." He crossed to the gaudy bookcases and extracted a volume. "Behold," he said, "this book. Note the striking cover design with the biblical allusion to Eve and the apple."

"Thossssse were the dayssssss," moaned a disconsolate voice in the middle distance.

"This book, if you will allow me, is incredibly popular. It has sold millions of copies. It has even been made into a film."

"And how is this not part of the problem?" his Lordship enquired.

"Observe," said Renfield, "the author of this book, who is our most successful subject to date." He flicked open a dimensional window to a sunlit study where a writer was tapping away at a computer. Every so often, she paused, and in those pauses a colourless presence perched unobtrusively on her shoulder bent to whisper in her ear.

"Nice use of the classical trope," said the Sheriff.

"Not really," objected a dark elf. "Where's the angel?"

"If you observe carefully..." said Renfield.

"Oh, I see it," said the elf. "Is that whisky in its hands? It looks completely shitfaced."

"Ladies present."

"The angel," said Renfield, "has been convinced of the pointlessness of its efforts."

"I still don't get it," complained the Count.

"My Lord?" Renfield ceded precedence to the Chair.

His Lordship was nodding slowly.

"I see, I see. You subvert the writer's inspiration in order to perpetuate a story so lacking in spine, spirit, ideas, intelligence, integrity, moral courage...."

"We extract all of that from the book at source while leaving the sparkly, addictive elements in place. All the fat, none of the vitamins, so to speak."

"Which in turn..."

"Drains the end users of knowledge, creativity and thought, until all that remains is a husk containing only ignorance, greed and apathy. Our cleverer demons are particularly adept at making nothing look like something, as you might see from a perusal of the more serious journals and literary shortlists. As a by-the-by, we outsource editorial and proofreading abominations to graduates of the current human education systems, a move which has dramatically improved our cost-benefit ratios in the last year."

There was a slight pause.

"We call this the 20/20 Moral Engineering Paradigm," Renfield said with a modest smirk. "It functions equally well through all media."

"Nihilism wrapped in cheap showmanship," snarled the Count. "Unacceptable. You suck everything meaningful from our endeavour."

"Rather than just the blood, yes," said Renfield. "It is very up-to-date."

His Lordship sat back with a frown. "Are you saying that we... that I... am obsolete?"

Renfield took on the air of a demon negotiating tricky lava.

"I would say that, while you display a certain old-world charm, sir, today's human is more likely to find scales, fangs, talons, bear's feet and so on more, shall we say, appealing than otherwise. Looked at judiciously, I would say that our conventional approaches still carry some small merit, but that a gradual cutting of ties to the more traditional departments, while representing a steep learning curve for us all, will at the end of the day positively impact our un-lives going forward."

"That is what you would say, is it?"

"Indeed, sir."

His Lordship rested his cheek on a scaly fist.

"Your use of language is an affront, your presence a blight, your methods a canker—and not in a good way. If you can rot my brain to this extent, I shudder to think what you are doing to the human race. And no, it's not a compliment. It goes against my worst nature to adopt your policies."

A relieved stir passed round the table.

"See the fangs, cretin," the Count sneered, baring his own. "This is how we make a point."

"However," continued his Lordship.

Renfield nodded as though expecting the 'however'.

"Despite the fact that you run counter to the spirit and traditions of the project, you seem to be... effective. We shall place your methods on probation for the next century, and I shall expect the other departments to descend to the challenge. Meeting adjourned. Run along, now."

In the vacant boardroom, the Lord Apollyon sat silently for a few minutes.

"Fetch the scorpion-horses and my chariot, Baal. I need some smog under my feathers."

"Under the circumstances, sir, don't you think...?"

Apollyon sighed.

"The Bentley, then. And..."

Baal held up a conservatively cut grey suit.

"And I'm hungry. Bring me a dish of beating hearts in acid."

Mournfully, Baal pointed to a fresh packet of bugs left behind on the table.

Apollyon's fists closed with a sound like screeching metal.

"A steep learning curve indeed."

MURPHY MCCALL

The Freakshow File

For the next three months, Dr. Heather Ballou, Egyptologist and assistant curator of the Antiquities Division of the Southwest Museum of Art, had only one assignment: superintending the examination and cataloging of every item in the Pike Family Collection.

The rich Texas industrialist, Lamar Pike, had died and left to the museum a magnificent collection of pieces ranging from drawings and paintings, to antique furnishings, to ancient Egyptian artifacts. It was common knowledge that the old man had exhibited no more than half of what he owned, and urban legend said he'd had a massive underground bunker that housed the pieces for which he could not prove lawful ownership—not to the exacting standards of the post-imperial twenty-first century. When he died, his heirs quickly unloaded the pieces of doubtful provenance, trusting that the museum would, if necessary, return them to their rightful owners.

Though many of the pieces would therefore one day pass completely out of her sphere, for the remainder of her three-month assignment, *all* of it was available to Heather. The paintings, drawings, and antique furnishings she relinquished gladly to the relevant experts on the curatorial staff, but the ancient Egyptian artifacts she kept for herself and jealously hoarded like a dog with a bone. She chose to call it responsible custodianship, but some of the underlings at the museum stigmatized her behind her back as 'unprofessional' and 'academically desperate'.

Heather didn't mind the whispers. She knew they were wrong. She needed to keep her dealings with the mummy private. And she was quite certain that the mummy wanted it that way, too.

Days at the museum were busy and often chaotic, with constant interruptions, both legitimate and not. If it wasn't the ringing telephone, or the mail clerk hand-delivering test results, it was chatty co-workers. Heather quickly realized the atmosphere was all wrong for her work. She needed quietness and empty spaces and solitude to concentrate upon her task—so she began coming to the museum after it closed and working through the long spring nights, enjoying the seclusion.

It was on the night of the spring equinox that Heather performed the preliminary physical examination, the neon hue of her nitrile gloves seeming garish and wrong against the ivory-to-rust colors of the funeral wrappings. The sarcophagus had been opened in the distant past, and the body within was in a state of deterioration, its wrappings loose and frayed. The solidified layers of the epiphyses and the good condition of the teeth as revealed in the CT scan showed the mummy to be that of a relatively young man. With meticulous care, Heather made note of every detail, and afterwards, with his body still upon her table, she sat upon her high stool, laptop on her knees, refreshing her memory about the late Eighteenth Dynasty, talking aloud, as if he could hear her.

"The writing on your sarcophagus indicates that you were a priest magician," she informed the mummy. "You may have been of royal blood—a cousin, perhaps, of your king—and the digital reconstruction of your face shows you were a hottie, weren't you?"

Peeling away her gloves, she took up the high-resolution photographs of the pages from the *Book of the Dead* that had been buried with her mummy. She frowned as she read the introduction, a variation on words she'd read many times before, but the second page... she reached blindly for the next photograph, inadvertently sliding the tip of her finger along its edge.

"Ouch!"

The paper cut went right across her fingertip, and she put it thoughtlessly between her lips to clean the blood away. She couldn't be bothered with something as inconsequential as a paper cut when she was engrossed by her reading.

"I've looked through all my resources, and none of them have anything like this spell," she told the mummy. "The first two parts are quite typical, but the last section—I've never seen it before."

She took time to consider the English translation she'd made, then read it aloud in the ancient tongue.

"I have come unto you, O great sovereign rulers who dwell in heaven and in earth and in the underworld, and I have brought unto you Ra-Bes Shai. He hath not sinned against any of the gods. Grant ye that he may be with you for all time.

"Thy Father Amun hath woven for thee a beautiful chaplet of victory to be placed on thy living brow, O thou who lovest the gods, and thou shalt live forever. The whole of the northern and southern parts of the heavens and every god and goddess who are in heaven and who are upon earth ordain the victory of Ra-Bes Shai over his enemies.

"Bring ye forth Ra-Bes Shai, who lovest the gods, that he may live thy glory in thy sight unto the end of days."

The floor beneath her chair trembled, setting all the equipment and instruments on the worktables to rattling. Heather's laptop fell to the floor, its lid slapping closed. Earthquakes weren't unknown in north Texas, but they weren't usually strong enough to knock things over.

"I hope nothing's broken," she said, retrieving the computer and putting it safely aside. She did a quick survey of the room, but nothing appeared to be damaged. "We'll have to thank your gods for that, won't we, Shai?"

She smiled fondly at the linen-shrouded figure and laid her hand fleetingly upon its fraying wrappings. When she realized she was still bleeding, she guiltily snatched her hand back, content for the moment to simply gaze at him.

Heather adjusted the high-powered lamp on her office worktable and bent to more closely inspect the intricately made shabti fashioned of Egyptian faience, an ancient ceramic. With mute reverence, she studied the hieroglyphs etched along the figurine, which promised that this shabti would work on behalf of its master in the afterlife.

She typed notes into her laptop and saved them, then stretched to the sky, straightening the kinks from her back. It was past midnight on Easter, but the hours until dawn stretched before her with infinite possibility, and she was thankful, once again, to be alone as she worked.

She swallowed water from her bottle and pinned up her long hair again, securing the strands that had come loose. She hated the hairnets because they made her scalp sweat, and she only wore them when it was absolutely necessary.

Cataloging the shabti had been her goal for this work session; once she had examined it, compared it with the standard characteristics, and recorded her findings, she was finished with her reportable work for the night. Her boss would say she ought to go home now that her work was complete. He often spoke to her about the necessity of a healthy work/life balance.

Heather smirked and turned away from the worktable. The truth was that she had little 'life' aside from work. Becoming an Egyptologist had been an enduring dream—true, one that had been dreamt for her by her father, the high school science teacher who had never carried through with his fantasy of following in the footsteps of Howard Carter. His underlying unhappiness had been apparent to his hyper-sensitive, only child. The powerful combination of his passion and his disappointment had inspired Heather to persevere through the years of school, training, and fieldwork, and along the way, she had fallen in love with the life. She had grown accustomed to the absorbing toil among fellow enthusiasts, but as the years went by, she had begun to hope for a different sort of existence, one day. She thought she had found it when she had been hired by the museum, but this last year of attempting to live outside of academia had been strangely unfulfilling.

She was sure being thirty-five and still single had nothing to do with it.

Heather slipped on a fresh pair of clean, white gloves, then she slid her identity card through the reader and entered the climate-controlled conservation room, only to be confronted with an unwelcome sight.

"What are you doing here?" she said, unable to keep the hostility from her voice.

Noah Boyce, assistant curator of the conservation department, looked up from his microscope with raised brows. He was short and stout, with dark, curly hair that made him look like a hobbit. The extremely thick glasses he wore distorted his eyes, making them seem unnaturally small in his round face.

"I could ask you the same question, Dr. Ballou," Boyce replied. "It's after midnight on a holiday, so you shouldn't be here. I was instructed to come in at a time when I wouldn't disrupt your work."

It was a lie. Everyone on the museum staff knew—and marveled at—her peculiar work hours. Struggling to contain her temper, Heather frowned at him. "Instructed by whom?"

"The head curator of conservation, of course. We've got

our tasks to complete too, you know."

Boyce was standing over the polarized light microscope, his museum-issued laptop open beside him. When Heather saw the canopic jar on his worktable, she started towards him, suddenly flooded with an adrenaline-powered urge to knock him down.

"What are you doing with that? I haven't cataloged it yet!"

Boyce moved two steps away from her, a coward whose answer to confrontation was flight. "That can't be right!" he answered shrilly. "You had the CT scan results weeks ago."

Heather continued forward, gently picking up and cradling the jackal-headed jar representing the god Duamutef, which held the mummy's embalmed stomach. She knew she was behaving impetuously, but she could not *bear* to see anyone else handle these things.

Making a terrific effort to sound rational, she said, "Please follow the established protocol, Dr. Boyce. The master register lists the items I have fully cataloged—the items *you* may work with. Do not deviate from procedure." She held his gaze and dealt the low blow. "I would hate to have to speak with your boss about this—or with mine, for that matter."

She turned away from him, glad to hear the whoosh of air as he flounced from the conservation room. She opened the canopic chest, intent upon replacing Duamutef in his proper place with the three other containers—but it occurred to her the jar seemed strangely light, as if it were empty—and she knew that was not the case. As the annoying Boyce had said, the jars had been scanned. None of them was empty.

Gingerly, she lifted the falcon-headed god Qebhsenuef, guardian of the intestines, then the baboon-headed god Hapy, guardian of the lungs—too light! It was the jar depicting the god Imsety, the human-headed guardian of the liver, which she carried to her worktable.

Modern-day sensibilities dictated that the scientist disturb the ancient artifacts as little as possible, but Heather could not just send these jars back for another computerized tomography scan—she had to know *now* if...

She pulled on a blue smock, settled safety goggles over her eyes, and placed the Imsety jar on her worktable. She knew from her first examination that the seal on this one was the least stable—it was entirely possible that it might have become damaged as it was handled and x-rayed—not that she would put any blame on the CT-lab...

Staring into the empty container, Heather was awash with emotion, each new feeling rolling into the volatile mix until confusion, rage, and fear propelled her from the room. Boyce had been meddling with the jars—he had corrupted the artifacts—but she would be held responsible. She rushed down the corridor, knowing even as she went that she was too late—Boyce was surely already gone—but the compulsion to challenge him and place the blame overrode everything else.

She entered the employee lounge, pausing to glance around the room, hoping for a sight of Boyce, but he was not there. She continued toward the door to the parking lot, but something was under her feet, and she stumbled, feeling a sharp pain in her leg. She cried out, her voice reverberating loudly in the deserted building.

A large, tawny cat head-butted her shin and meowed, looking up at her with limpid silvery-green eyes, as if he had not just scratched her leg.

The driving urgency to find Boyce faded and died.

"What are you doing here?" she said, bending to stroke the cat's soft fur.

Living animals did not belong in a museum—there was too great a chance of contamination. But hadn't Dr. Mason mentioned something to her about an infestation of rodents the extermination company had been unable to eradicate?

The head curator's notion of pest-control wound between her ankles, purring loudly. She laughed and gave him another pat before she turned back to her workroom. "Go exterminate some mice!" she told him.

The scribble on the cover said 'The Freakshow.'

Most of the folders were meticulously filed in alphabetical order, labels color-coded based on case type (red for sexual assault, yellow for stalking, blue for cold case), but this file bore no label—just a scrawled note where the label should be.

Detective Paul Vasquez of the Dallas Special Investigations Unit removed his glasses, meaning to polish them, but he was too eager to review the forensic reports again. Squinting, he opened the file, his glasses forgotten.

Riffling through, he noted that the first two of the five cases had no fluids or trace reported, other than the usual bath products, pet hair, and clothing fibers. It wasn't until the third victim was found that a sharp female uniform had noticed the... residue on the victim's feet. The rape kits from then on had included swabs from the tops and bottoms of the feet and between the toes.

Vasquez wrinkled his nose in disgust. To each his own and all, but what sort of freakshow wanted to forcibly do *that* to a person's feet?

He filed the new report, settled his glasses on his nose, and left the deserted Special Investigations office, flipping the light switch as he went. It was after ten at night, but it wasn't as if anyone was waiting for him at home. Forty-three, fat and divorced, Vasquez didn't consider himself in the market for romance. Besides, he was married to his work. And next week, if not sooner, he'd have DNA test results to run through the national data base.

Then the freakshow might acquire a name.

The next night, Heather brought a resealable packet of cat treats to work. She tucked them in the pocket of her lab coat, just in case visitations from the museum's new mouser were going to be a regular occurrence. She felt a peculiar affection for the creature. She had never particularly liked cats before.

Quickly immersed in her work, she spent several hours examining and documenting some of the many amulets and pieces of gold jewelry that had been bound up in Shai's wrappings at the time of his mummification. Dr. Mason had been dissatisfied with her progress in the beginning, frequently leaving notes for her indicating that she needed to speed things up if she hoped to complete the job on time. He did not understand—in fact, she hoped he would never know—about the hours she spent simply sitting with Shai, delving ever deeper into her research of his identity. So she would rush through her reportable work to make time for the far more important opportunity... to be alone with Shai.

Online resources were invaluable for her research, but she had also requisitioned numerous volumes from the university library system. Heather read aloud the most interesting passages she found to her silent companion, and she strongly felt that Shai *heard* her—and furthermore, that he approved of her devotion.

"I wonder if you were part of the court of Pharaoh Akhenaten?" she murmured. "He moved the capital to another city and instituted monotheism... Not all of the priests accepted the new religion. Were you one of those? You must have been, judging by your burial prayer."

She continued to read aloud, her mind filled with her image of Shai as a surreptitiously dissenting priest-magician in the court of Pharaoh Akhenaten and his wife, Queen Nefertiti. It was as if she could feel the relentless burning sun and the scorching desert sand, smell the fennel in the baking bread, and hear the plucked strings of the lyre and the rattle of the sistrum from within the holy temple.

"There were legends about a priest whose magic rituals and transformations rivaled those of any other servant of the god Amen-Re in all of Thebes." Heather heaved another hefty book onto her lap and opened it to a page she'd marked with a sticky note. "The story's given here. This priest pretended to reform his ways, embracing the royal decree that all Egyptians would worship only the god Aten—but in reality, this powerful magician secretly continued to perform ritual magic for the other gods, and the pharaoh, who feared him, had him killed."

She put that book aside and took up another, older tome, its binding cracked and tattered. "But this historian, who recounts the same legend, disputes the reason for the magician's assassination. He insists that the writings of the Chief Servant of the God Aten in Amarna indicate that the powerful magician priest had transgressed against one—or more—of the pharaoh's daughters. The reason given for having the magician killed—that he was disobeying by worshiping an outlawed god—was a fabrication meant to protect the honor of the princess."

She looked up then, cocking her head to one side as if she were listening to another voice. "Of course you would never do harm to the royal princess... but I'm on the right track, aren't I?"

Near dawn, she put away her research and bade Shai goodnight. Seconds after she exited the climate-controlled conservation room, the mouser streaked down the hallway, looking like a miniature version of a big cat in the wild. He wasted no time, but rose on his back legs, front paws planted upon her thigh as he meowed at her.

"Yes, I brought treats for you," she told him, kneeling to pet his ocher fur. She brought out the packet of treats, and the cat's cries became more insistent. She held a tidbit out to him, and he snatched it from her greedily. "You should be getting plenty of mice to eat," she murmured, stroking his soft pelt, allowing her fingertips to pass gently beneath his tail, confirming her assessment that he was an unaltered tomcat. The cat turned quickly, batting at the offending fingers, leaving a shallow scratch on the back of her hand.

"You'd better be nice," she scolded, and in the next moment, the big-eared cat head-butted the injured hand, purring. She dropped the next treat to the floor, not trusting his sharp teeth this time. Everyone knew a tomcat was more aggressive than a neutered cat—besides, most toms were unfit as indoor pets because they were likely to spray walls and furniture...

"For the boss to have let you in, you must have had a very good CV for mouse-catching," she told the purring tom, offering another treat. "I'll call you Am—it means 'the devourer'."

The next morning, Detective Vasquez stood in the middle of a bedroom in suburban Dallas—a three-bedroom ranch-style house in a decent neighborhood. The victim had been taken to the hospital, but the pantyhose that had tied her arms to the bedstead were still in place.

Vasquez saw a photograph hanging on the wall, and he studied the happy woman posing on the deck of a cruise ship—pretty, with long, blonde hair. Vasquez had five photographs in the freakshow file of women who could be *this* one's sisters.

"She says she didn't see anything?" he asked Detective Xuân Nguyen, who lived closer than he did and had arrived at the scene before the victim was removed.

Nguyen shook her head. "She didn't see anything, doesn't remember anything—has no idea how she ended up tied to her bed. Says she woke up that way."

"Did you see her feet?" Vasquez asked, and Nguyen's expression of distaste as she nodded confirmed his suspicions. He gestured towards the men's clothing hanging in the open walk-in closet. "What about the husband?"

"He found her this way," Nguyen said, flipping through her notebook. "He works the nightshift at the GM plant. They don't have kids. He went with her to the hospital."

"Call the plant and see if anyone can confirm what time he

left," he told her, but he knew it was pointless. This scene was identical to the others.

Nguyen didn't make a note of his words; she knew her job. She just stared at him until he met her eyes. "It's time to go to the public for help, Paul," she said firmly. "Even you can't deny we have a serial on our hands, and he could have done *anything* to these women. If he begins to escalate..."

He paced through the house to the kitchen and stood for a moment in the middle of the stereotypical American home: a few unwashed dishes in the sink, coffee-maker on the counter ready to go, boxes of cereal on top of the fridge, pet bowls on the floor. He rubbed his face and turned to Nguyen, who waited in the doorway, pen in hand. "If he begins to escalate, then we're holding the bag for not having done something to warn the public before now. All right. We don't have to keep all the fun to ourselves. Set up a meeting with Community Outreach—let's ruin everybody's day."

As Heather typed feverishly on her laptop, meticulously arranging the information she had accumulated about Shai—well, about his time period, the mummies already identified from that era, the similarities and differences—she was buoyed with a mood of academic excitement she hadn't felt in years. Her fondest childhood memories were those of her dad sitting on the side of her bed, smelling of pipe smoke and Old Spice, reading her bedtime stories. When other little girls were hearing tales of princesses and damsels in distress, Heather's dad was showing her colorful illustrations from a picture book as he told her tales of ancient Egypt—and of the scientists and adventurers who had unearthed the mummies thousands of years later, revealing the glory of those ancient times to the modern world.

If she identified Shai—known now as the Pike Mummy, although in Egypt he would be assigned a number—her name as an Egyptologist of note would be *made*.

All she had to do was complete her paper, have it accepted by the International Alliance of Egyptologists for publication in their quarterly journal, and the success she had hungered for—ever since her father began to fill her head with stories of ancient Egypt in her cradle—would become reality.

Her only regret was that her dad had not lived long enough to share in her impending success. She snatched up a Kleenex and impatiently wiped the tears from her cheeks, wondering when she would cease to feel his loss so acutely. After all, he'd been gone now for nearly a year.

When she was satisfied with her writing, she sat back in her office chair, rubbing tiredly at her eyes. Working at night gave her fewer distractions because she didn't have to pretend to be sociable with her co-workers. And she could spend time alone with Shai—although as the volume of her research increased, she spent less time with the mummified body in the climate-controlled conservation room and more time with the image she carried of him in her mind...

The overhead light of her office was suddenly flipped on, and Heather spun around in her swivel chair, momentarily confused by the sight of him—of *Shai*—standing in the doorway. The man was tall—over six feet—with light green eyes so riveting she could scarcely look away from him. His sandalwood brown hair fell to his shoulders, shorter strands curling about a lightly-stubbled face so exquisitely formed that Michelangelo would have begged to sculpt it. He wore a tight black tee-shirt, snug over his muscular chest, and fitted jeans above work-boots. It wasn't until Heather noticed the denim shirt hanging open over the tee—with the name 'Bubba' embroidered in red letters over the pocket—that she became aware of the fact that she was gape-mouthed and staring.

I've got to sleep more, she thought, as she struggled to clear her thoughts. *I have to be more tired than I realized to see this man and immediately think he's Shai.*

The young man—surely he was five or ten years her

junior—seemed unperturbed by her inability to formulate words, for he entered the room carrying a large toolbox and closed the door behind him, producing a screwdriver from his back pocket.

"Broken shelf?" he said in accented English.

Heather gathered her wits and stood uncertainly. It was nearly five o'clock in the morning—hours before the museum staff would begin to arrive—and although she had muttered about the shelf that had fallen, leaving books scattered over the floor, she did not recall reporting the problem to Facilities for repair.

Seeing her confusion, the man put the toolbox on the floor and pulled a paper from his pocket. "Hathor?" he said, reading from the triplicate form.

"Heather," she corrected him, charmed by his accent and trying unsuccessfully to place it. The Metroplex was a popular destination for immigrants from all over the world, but she couldn't identify his origins from his voice. She could ask, but it would seem rude.

The man from Facilities smiled, revealing a mouthful of beautiful white teeth. "Hathor," he said again, taking one step closer. "Pretty."

He was close enough for her to feel the warmth radiating from his body and to smell the light musk of his sweat. Attraction warred with an instinct for self-preservation that helped her find her voice, even if she still did not move away from him.

"Dr. Ballou," she said more firmly. A Facilities worker did not go around calling the curators by their first names—even if said worker mangled the pronunciation, giving her instead the name of the Egyptian goddess of motherhood, joy, and feminine love.

"Hathor," he repeated proudly, as if he were imitating her exactly, and Heather was once again caught by his remarkable eyes.

Then he did something amazing and very, very wrong. He plucked the clip from her hair, and the golden-blonde mass tumbled to her shoulders. The action was overly familiar—in this enclosed space, at this time of night, it might even be termed harassment—but he was so very beautiful, and Heather was disinclined to make a fuss. He was so tall she had to look up at him, a fairly rare occurrence for her. The sharp angle of his jaw, the cleft of his strong chin, the notch of the clavicle at the base of his throat—every detail of his appearance was like a physical blow to her, creating an exquisite ache. And the way he looked at her, as if he saw through to her very soul with those mesmerizing eyes, filled her with a sensation of breathless anticipation.

He reached for her hair as if he would stroke it, and Heather put up a hand to intercept him—any excuse to touch him! she thought wildly. He captured her fingers and raised them to his lips. She had a crazy, fleeting vision of them sweeping her desktop clean and ripping each other's clothes away. But instead of kissing the back of her hand—as an old-world gentleman might do—his lips closed over the skin marred by numerous claw marks, sucking with such sudden violence that it felt as if each of the scratches opened and began to bleed again.

Suddenly free of the madness that threatened to engulf her, she struggled to get away from him, but he was pulling her closer—and then she was just... gone.

Heather opened her eyes to a crystal sky and bright sunshine: a perfect Texas spring day. But her entire body ached, as if she had spent too much time on the elliptical machine at the gym—and then the face of her boss, Dr. Milton Mason, appeared over her, staring down.

"Dr. Ballou!" he said. "What happened? Were you robbed?"

Heather looked away from Dr. Mason's face and saw she was lying upon an asphalt surface—right beside her car. Why was she on the ground in the museum parking lot?

"I... I don't know," she answered Dr. Mason. "What time is it?"

Dr. Mason gave a distracted glance at his wristwatch. "It's seven-thirty—I came in early this morning to prepare for a meeting with the board of directors and found you like this."

Heather struggled to sit up, but suddenly there was a young Asian woman with short, shiny black hair and a badge of some sort in her hand who knelt down and placed a hand on her shoulder.

"I'm Detective Nguyen, Dallas Police," she said, displaying her badge for Dr. Mason even as she smiled down at Heather. "The paramedics are right behind me, ma'am, if you wouldn't mind waiting for them before you try to get up."

Heather looked in some confusion from Nguyen to Mason. "You called the cops?" she asked him.

Nguyen answered her. "He called the paramedics, and I was nearby, so I came, too. He thought perhaps you had been mugged."

Heather moved restlessly, wanting to get up from the ground. "I'm fine," she insisted, hoping it was true. "I was just working late, and I... I must have passed out or something."

Nguyen produced a small notebook and pen. "What time did you finish your work?" she asked.

Heather considered. The last time she had looked at her watch was two and a half hours ago—why didn't she remember anything else?

Before she could answer Nguyen's question, the ambulance pulled up with lights flashing, though thankfully, there was no siren. Then she had two paramedics working her over, talking to her in short, incomplete sentences. They were diligent, but they found nothing wrong with her—not even a bump on the head. They assisted her to stand, and even though she was sore, she felt perfectly able to drive herself home.

Her car keys were found in her purse, and Dr. Mason

unlocked her car, his glances at his wristwatch becoming more frequent with each passing moment. "I'll be fine, sir," she assured him, sitting thankfully in the driver's seat. "Please don't let me make you late for your meeting."

At that he finally went away, and Heather had only the detective to contend with.

"Dr. Ballou," the detective said carefully, "there have been some... attacks in this part of town. That's why I came when I heard the report over the radio."

Heather hooked her hair behind an ear, wondering why it was loose down her back. "What kind of attacks?" she said, then before the woman could answer, she added, "Wouldn't I know if I'd been attacked?"

Nguyen squatted on her haunches so Heather wouldn't have to look up at her. "You might not remember," she said carefully. "And you have a physical resemblance to the other women who've been assaulted." Assuming an almost nonchalant air, the detective added, "I was just wondering—what happened to your shoes?"

Greatly puzzled, Heather stared down at her bare feet.

The incident in the parking lot put an end to Heather's ability to come and go as she pleased. The museum employed security guards, and when the second shift ended at 11 PM, Heather was expected to be out of the building.

Heather found she was no longer able to sleep at night, and she spent the long hours before dawn wandering through her small house, trying and failing to distract herself with books or cable television, succumbing to slumber only when the rose of dawn touched the eastern horizon. She was restless and distracted when she was at the museum, forced to share space again with the other curators, including Noah Boyce of the conservation department, whose smug self-satisfaction irritated her beyond reason.

Boyce made a habit of stopping by her desk daily to

provide her with information about his department's plans for conservation on the Pike Family pieces—not that she wasn't interested in those things, but she would prefer by far to read his reports than to see him infesting her office.

If her work had been going well, she might not have been so aware of the annoyances, but it was not. Because no matter how determinedly she sought, she was unable to find the zone she'd been in with her research and cataloging of the Pike Family Collection before the... disruption. And she missed Am, who never seemed to visit her anymore, now that she was a day worker—and somehow, the presence of the museum mouser had become as much a part of her productive nights of work as were the artifacts themselves.

The saddest thing of all was losing the feeling of connection—of *intimacy*—she had shared for so long with the mummy. Before, her energy and imagination had fed on the nightly visits to the climate-controlled room. But now that her visits were made during the day, with the bustle of the museum staff all around, the magical quality of the visits was gone. She felt as desolate and barren as the empty canopic jar.

Why had Shai deserted her?

Vasquez went by the laboratory after lunch on Monday, on the off-chance that they had the DNA testing on the samples collected from the victims' feet completed. Fifteen minutes later, he was back in his battered, unmarked car, on his way to the Southwest Museum of Art. If you stuck a pin in a city map at every scene the freakshow had hit—as Vasquez had done on his office wall—the museum was right at the center of the pins. He wasn't sure what that meant, but he intended to find out.

In the office waiting room of the museum's head curator, Vasquez realized he had carried in the test results with his notepad, and he hastily folded the paper and stuck it between the pages of his notebook—he wanted to look as organized and professional as the people who ran this place were. He stole a glance in the mirror on the wall. His swarthy face was clean-shaven, his close-cropped black hair was tidy, and he wore his second best suit, a lightweight tobacco brown number his sister had nagged him into buying, with a white shirt and striped maroon tie. To a criminal, his look probably screamed *"Cop!"* but Vasquez thought he looked his best. The suit coat even camouflaged the middle-aged paunch he was developing.

Dr. Mason led him from the public areas into the hidden labyrinth of offices, workrooms, and storage areas where the work of the museum was actually done and pointed him in the direction of the Egyptologist's door.

"Dr. Ballou? I'm Detective Paul Vasquez of the Special Investigations Unit, Dallas PD. May I speak with you?"

The woman who stood at the worktable was lovely—just Vasquez's type, for all the good that would do him. She had a swathe of blonde hair piled on her head, with little strands of it escaping to curl on her long neck, and eyes of a remarkable, aquamarine blue. He had a quick impression of a womanly body beneath the lab coat, but he couldn't really tell. The last thing a policeman needed to do was check out a crime victim.

She motioned him into the room, and as he came closer, he saw that she was not as young as he had first thought; the lines at the corner of her blue eyes indicated that she was near his age—and the best news was, no wedding ring.

"Do you work with Detective Nguyen?" the woman asked.

"She's my partner," Vasquez admitted, his attention caught by the object on her worktable. "Hey, is that a miniature sarcophagus?"

Heather Ballou smiled at him, and his mouth was suddenly very dry. Maybe when the case was over he could...

"It's part of the Pike Family Collection," she said. "Shall I tell you about it?"

Vasquez ditched his notebook on her desktop and gave her his attention, listening as she explained about the hammered gold and the inlaid, multi-colored glass. Her hair smelled of peaches, and Vasquez knew it must be her shampoo, but he couldn't shake the idea that the scent nestled in the hollow of her throat. She talked with great enthusiasm about the ancient artifact, but Vasquez had trouble concentrating on her words.

Finally, she said, "But you didn't come for an Egyptology lesson, did you, Detective? How can I help you?"

Vasquez took a step away from her, noting that her eyes were exactly on level with his, and he felt the impulse to kiss her. She gazed calmly back at him, guileless and undisturbed... perhaps even curious.

Forcing himself to concentrate, Vasquez swallowed and thought about the freakshow file folder, stacked with photographs of women who looked a lot like this one. "I have some questions about the incident last week, ma'am. Can I buy you a cup of coffee or something and talk to you about it?"

The doc peeled her gloves off with a rueful smile and turned to hang her lab coat on a hook, confirming his first impression of her body—tight, with curves in all the right places.

He had to *focus*.

"I don't remember how I ended up passed out in the parking lot, Detective. And I don't know how much I can tell you—but let's go into the staff lounge. There's a soda machine there." She glanced over her shoulder at him with a smile that strained his determination to keep his mind on his work. "I wouldn't recommend you drink the coffee, though—I believe it's been sitting in the pot since King Tut was a kid."

Vasquez grabbed his notebook as they passed her desk, so busy not checking out her derriere that he didn't notice the lab report slip out and tumble to the floor.

Nothing would prevent Vasquez from completing this investigation—but he watched Dr. Ballou with a burgeoning urge he hadn't experienced in a long time—the inclination to pursue.

Noah Boyce, assistant curator of the conservation department, watched Heather walk from her office in deep conversation with the rumpled Hispanic man. Did she ever pay that much attention to anything he said to her? No, she did not. Even though they were close to the same age and had similar passions—for their work—she had never shown the least inclination to... socialize with him. He slipped into her office, his eyes darting around the room. She had left the coffinette on her worktable, unattended—a clear violation of museum policy. What if someone were to report her many improper procedures—would she be disciplined by the head curator? Might she lose her job?

Boyce felt a grim satisfaction at that idea and indulged for a moment in letting the scene play out in his mind. But as pathetic as he might be in his interactions with women, he wasn't stupid. He could see little benefit in having Heather fired from her position if what he really wanted was for her to pay... attention... to him.

He deposited the folder containing the DNA testing on the Pike Mummy in Heather's inbox, noting with a sour twist of his lips that she had yet to review the last two reports he had delivered to her—but what was this? He glanced quickly over his shoulder for bystanders, then picked up the folded paper and opened it. It was a laboratory result for a DNA test. Was she going behind his back to do his job? He felt a rush of rage, but the anger didn't distract him. He surveyed the entire report with focus sharpened by anger. To verify his conclusion, he flipped open the folder he had just left in Heather's inbox and compared the results, his lips compressing to a straight, implacable line.

Identical.

Noah snatched all of his reports from Heather's inbox and stuffed her test results into his file, as well. He wasn't sure what he was going to do, but whatever it was, she wasn't going to like it.

Vasquez arrived back at his office just before five o'clock, when most of the place emptied out. He had not learned anything new from Heather Ballou, but he could understand Nguyen's gut feeling that the Egyptologist's incident was inextricably tied to the freakshow assaults: she was a physical ringer for the victims, she had been barefoot when they found her, and she didn't remember a thing.

He also had her cell phone number now, but it was simply to complete her witness profile—not so he could ask her out. Definitely not.

Not yet, anyway.

When he failed to find his lab report amongst the pages of his notebook, he called the lab and asked for the results to be faxed ASAP.

Nguyen came in as he was retrieving the fax from the machine in the corner.

"I've got the DNA," he told her, waving the sheet.

She collapsed in her chair and kicked off her pumps, bending to massage her feet.

"And I've got something from the trace lab," Nguyen said. She took her notebook from her purse. "You know how all the victims had animal fur on them?"

"Yeah, they had pets, right?"

Nguyen made a 'sorta' gesture with one hand. "All of them had doggie doors. Three had dogs, two had cats, and one had just euthanized her pet. But get this, Paul. All of the pet hair trace from the scenes? It was from an Abyssinian cat."

Vasquez frowned at her. "An A-B what?"

Nguyen tapped on her computer keyboard and sent him an Instant Message link. "Abyssinians. They're purebred cats, not all that common. So I called the entire list of victims. None of them owns an Abyssinian."

Vasquez clicked on the link and stared at the big-eared cat

that appeared on his screen. "It looks like a miniature puma with stupid ears."

Nguyen shrugged. "According to Wikipedia, legend says Abyssinians are descended from the ancient Egyptian cats—the ones worshiped as gods."

Vasquez sat back, rubbing a hand over his bristly black crew-cut. "I was at the museum today, talking to the Egyptologist. She's working now on the mummy that rich guy left to them. Egypt keeps popping up in all this, but I can't figure out why."

Nguyen pulled a pair of bright red Chucks from her bag and put them on. "Well, let's talk about it over dinner. I'm starving."

Vasquez put the DNA report in the growing freakshow file and stuffed it in his backpack. "I need a drink," he muttered, following her to the door.

She snorted. "What did you think I meant by 'dinner'?"

Just past nine o'clock that night, Noah Boyce crept past Heather's office, pausing for only a moment to peek around the doorframe and watch her pecking away at her laptop. The sight of her used to make him feel happy, but he was pleased to note that now it made him feel nothing. She was just another fickle woman.

He turned from her door. The security guards made rounds every two hours, and Mack, the old guy, had just finished patrolling the office area. Boyce would have all the time he needed to go behind Heather's back and check up on her work.

Boyce realized that Heather Ballou was out of his league, but the knowledge had done nothing to staunch his yearning. He had always fallen for the smart, pretty girls, and now, with age forty looming ever nearer, he was too humiliated to admit—even to himself—that he had never so much as had a date with any of the women he had idolized. Only the intelligent, unattractive women would give him a second glance—only with them did his intellect trump his appearance.

Even in his professional life, Boyce had found it was the pretty people who were hired, who got the promotions, who walked all over those of their colleagues doing the real work. In the past, the undeserving had stolen accolades from Noah Boyce, but never more than once. Exceptional as he was in his own work, Boyce was equally brilliant at searching out mediocrity in others. And disclosing it to those in power.

It had brought him this far in his career, hadn't it?

He logged into the catalog file on his museum laptop and began methodically removing artifacts from their storage boxes, reassessing each piece she claimed to have completed work on. Time ticked by as he double-checked her work, but the only discrepancy he found was in the canopic jars. The weight of each was off by a few grams—scarcely a glaring error, but precision was everything in science.

He typed notes on the inconsistency in his computer and checked the time. He had fifteen minutes before the guard would be back, so he hurriedly carded into the climate-controlled environment and made his way to the back corner of the room, where the sarcophagus lay upon a trestle. It was a relic of such power and splendor that Boyce was momentarily reminded of why he had wanted to do this job. Conscientiously, he donned white cotton gloves and lifted the sterile sheet that shielded the mummy within.

For several moments, he was frozen, one hand still holding the covering aloft—and then with his free hand, he reached into the sarcophagus and fingered the fragile strips of ancient linen heaped together in the space where the mummy ought to be.

Heather did a final read-through of her proposal for the International Alliance of Egyptologists' quarterly journal. If it was found to be acceptable, she would be asked to send the full article—and if the Alliance chose to publish the article, her name would be made. She would have job offers then—from places more prestigious than this museum—and she might even choose to go back into fieldwork.

And somehow, somewhere, her dad would know of her triumph—and be proud.

She hit 'send.'

"Dr. Ballou?"

The detective from earlier that day was standing in her doorway with two Starbucks cups in his hands. The ugly suit had been discarded in favor of jeans and a denim jacket, which made him more approachable but also rather discomfiting. Heather knew Paul Vasquez was attracted to her. He was nice enough, if you went for the rumpled type. And he was here, and solid, and real—but there was no danger in his gaze, no rush of magic in his presence.

Was this the most she could hope for?

"Back so soon, Detective?" she said.

He came in and placed one of the cups on her desk. "I hope you like lattes," he said. "I made it decaf."

Heather accepted the cup and watched as Vasquez perched one hip on the edge of her desk.

"I don't want to bother you," Vasquez began, "but I have to tell you—this case I'm investigating keeps bringing up references to ancient Egypt, and I can't understand why that is."

Heather felt a faint echo of anxiety, and she hid it by taking a drink of coffee. "What sorts of things link your case to Egypt?" she asked.

He set his coffee aside and pulled a folded paper from his pocket. "All of our victims had pet hair adhering to their bedding or their skin," he said, "and the weird thing about the fur is that it all comes from one breed of cat—maybe even the same cat, so we're doing DNA testing on it—but that will take a while."

"What breed is it?" Heather asked, the sensation of foreboding increasing.

"It's an unusual one," Vasquez began, but he was not destined to complete his thought.

In a blur of hissing movement, Am bounded into the room and leapt past Vasquez onto the desk, spilling the abandoned cup of hot coffee all over the detective's jeans.

"Holy crap!" Vasquez swore, moving away from the desk and rubbing at an angry, bloody scratch on his wrist.

Heather blinked at Am, who stood defensively before her on the desktop, his fur bristling, a low, threatening snarl issuing from his throat.

"Hey, what's that cat doing here?"

Heather gathered Am gently against her breasts before she even looked at the security guard hovering in her doorway.

"He's the museum mouser," Heather explained shortly, suddenly feeling there were far too many people in her office.

"There's not supposed to be a cat in this building," the guard said flatly, giving Vasquez a glance and noting his visitor's pass. "There shouldn't be any visitors in here this late at night, either." He started forward, and Am hissed from the safety of Heather's arms. That seemed to make the guard reconsider. "Keep that cat shut up in this room," he instructed her, "and I'll call Animal Control to pick it up in the morning."

After admonishing Heather not to let the cat escape, the security guard ushered Vasquez out, closed the door firmly behind him and left. Am head-butted Heather's chin and kneaded her shoulder with his front paws, his sharp claws easily penetrating the fabric of her shirt, leaving stinging scratches on her skin.

"Ouch!" she said, reaching to detach him from her clothing. "Stop that!"

He mewled piteously, looking up at her with bright, intelligent eyes. Unexpected sympathy came to the fore, and as Am purred and nuzzled her ear, Heather stroked his fur, murmuring softly.

"I've missed you. Where have you been hiding yourself? Has anyone been leaving food and water out for you?" A thought occurred to her, and in mere seconds progressed from possibility to firm decision. If the museum no longer had use for Am, she would be responsible for finding him a home.

She stood with Am in her arms and headed for the door.

She had forgotten Vasquez was even in the building.

Vasquez rubbed at the nasty scratch on his wrist, trying to remember what they had been discussing before her cat jumped on the desk and spilled coffee all over his one clean pair of jeans. He had the nagging suspicion it had been something important, but his mind had gone completely blank on the subject.

He was still attempting to gather his thoughts when Heather Ballou walked past him with the cat in her arms. He said, "Are you leaving? Can I walk you to your car?"

"If you like," she agreed indifferently.

Unheeded, Vasquez trailed her down the hallway towards the parking lot, and Dr. Ballou spoke to the animal without giving Vasquez another glance.

"You're coming home with me," she said into one of its big, stupid-looking ears.

Am was a good passenger, making the journey in Heather's lap, occasionally rising to put his paws on the window as if he were looking out at the dark streets, but that made it hard for her to steer. Fortunately, she did not live far from the museum, and when she reached her home, he allowed her to carry him inside.

Heather went through the house, from the living room to the bedroom to the kitchen, switching on lamps and talking to Am, who managed to stay beneath her feet the entire time, nearly tripping her. She picked him up again, laughing.

"Do you want me to break my neck?" she scolded. "Then who would open a can of tuna for you?"

She dumped the contents of a can of Starkist into a bowl and put it on the floor with a second bowl full of water.

"Tomorrow I'll pick up some cat food," she promised him, walking out of the kitchen as she unbuttoned her blouse.

She ran a warm bath, tilting sweet-smelling salts into the water, and hummed to herself as she pinned her hair on top of her head. For some reason, she felt less restless and more relaxed than she had in days. She shed her clothes and immersed herself in the water up to her chin, sighing with contentment.

She soaked in the tub, allowing her mind to wander as it would, and she found herself thinking again of Shai, imagining his image, seeing him in ceremonial dress, standing in the presence of his pharaoh. When she opened her eyes again, Am stood on his hind legs, paws planted on the side of the tub, watching her with silvery-green eyes.

She wrapped herself in a bath sheet and padded into her bedroom, feeling sleepy. Eschewing her usual sleep shirt, she slipped naked between the sheets. As she was drifting to sleep, Am leapt onto her bed and curled up at her feet.

Heather floated free in a cocoon of pure, undulating arousal. The embers were low in her belly, banked and waiting. The accelerants were silken touch, provocative lips, and a wicked, devastating tongue. The stirring began slowly, fingertips ghosting over touch-deprived flesh, soft, drugging kisses, tongue against tongue, and the almost-forgotten glory of a man's body upon hers—a welcome weight.

Her eyes opened slowly to the ambient light of the streetlamp through the sheer curtains at the window. Shai was there, his very real hair tickling her cheek as he looked down at her, his body poised above hers, held up by gorgeously muscled arms. She reached to touch him, but she could not.

Her wrists were restrained.

Then she was fully awake, her body still riding the waves of pleasure, while her brain struggled to focus on the things he had made her forget.

A *mouser* in the museum? *Really?* How could she have been duped by something so fundamentally wrong? Dr. Mason would never have permitted a cat to have full run of the museum—Shai had made her believe it.

The empty canopic jars! She had discovered the absence of the mummy's internal organs—and she had found the pile of linen strips in the sarcophagus—but he had taken the memory from her. And he had come to her in human guise—the breathtakingly beautiful form he inhabited now—wearing a shirt inscribed *Bubba*, of all ridiculous names. Bubba was the Facilities guy who took care of the grounds and parking lot—gray, shambling, and wracked with a smoker's cough—how could she have forgotten that? Wearing Bubba's shirt, he had loosed her hair and seduced her body, inducing a rush of euphoria so overwhelming she had scarcely noticed when he completed the act by making love to her feet.

Then he had stolen her shoes and left her lying in the parking lot like an abandoned plaything.

"Hathor," he murmured, beginning to kiss his way down her body.

"Stop!" she tried to say, but she found she was unable to speak, and the lethargy of passion overtook her body.

Working his will on her, he lingered at the apex of her thighs, and in a blinding rush of pleasure, the bothersome memories were washed away from her consciousness, leaving her docile and somnolent once again.

She was *his*. She belonged to him. She had always belonged to him, though for years and years she had not known his name.

Shai.

The Missing Persons Squad of the Dallas Police Department was assigned to investigate the disappearances of Heather Ballou and Noah Boyce. Detective Paul Vasquez found himself strangely bereft when the freakshow attacks stopped as suddenly as they'd begun, and he pestered the detective in charge of the missing persons investigations until his colleague took pity on him and shared the case files.

Vasquez stared in disbelief at the photograph of the linen-wrapped figure nestled in the sarcophagus. The wrapping had been carelessly done, and gaps between linen strips showed modern-day clothing rather than desiccated mummy flesh.

At chest level, off to one side, a pair of eyeglasses slipped through the wrappings, like sunglasses hanging jauntily by one earpiece from a shirt pocket.

Noah Boyce had been found in the sarcophagus only when his semi-mummified body had begun to putrefy and stink. Oddly enough, the ancient coffin was the last place anyone had thought to look for him.

The Homicide Squad had stepped in immediately and upgraded the case from Missing Persons to Murder. The autopsy had not proved a cause of death. There was no external trauma to the body, and the tox screens were negative. He was simply a healthy thirty-eight year old man whose cause of death was 'undetermined.'

No one wanted to acknowledge the decaying body organs arranged around Boyce's body like a pundit's mockery of the mummification process. The liver was stuffed in a mostly empty Folgers coffee can, the lungs in a sugar-specked Krispy Kreme donuts box, and the intestines and stomach were in matching Tupperware containers still smeared with tomato sauce from the decaying lasagna found dumped out beneath the hedge bordering the museum parking lot. No disease process was found in the organs, and DNA testing proved they belonged to Boyce.

Not a single clue was ever found in the disappearance of

Dr. Heather Ballou. The International Alliance of Egyptologists had responded favorably to Heather's paper proposal, but in the absence of the Pike Mummy, the Alliance's interest waned.

Ballou's bank accounts were cleaned out, which Vasquez felt was indicative of a criminal going on the lam. Museum employees had reported it was common knowledge that Boyce had nourished an unrequited passion for Ballou. Perhaps she had killed her unwanted admirer and put his body in the sarcophagus.

But Vasquez wasn't really satisfied with that scenario—it didn't fit his impressions of Heather Ballou—and none of the evidence explained what had become of the Pike Collection Mummy.

In the end, it was time to relegate the case file to the open/unsolved category and let it go.

That worked for a while, until he was alone in the office one night, dolefully remembering Heather Ballou and her intriguing, aquamarine eyes. Like a gateway drug, the temptation to retrieve the folder and see her face led to a fruitless night of reviewing every detail of the case again, his tenacious detective's mind searching for an answer to the many puzzles presented by the freakshow file.

When he gave it up at 3:00 A.M. to go home, he hid Heather's photograph beneath the box of emergency Twinkies in his drawer.

But lying alone on his lumpy mattress—he would have to dig the sheets out of the dryer and put them on the bed tomorrow—he had a moment of panic, imagining Nguyen going into his desk to filch a snack and finding his rather pathetic souvenir.

She would rag him about it until the end of time.

So he would return the photograph to the file. Soon.

The next morning, he met his partner—wearing the

Chucks she would exchange for more appropriate footwear at her desk—in the elevator, and they exchanged desultory greetings. It wasn't until they entered the Special Investigations Unit that they saw the pristine new file folder resting in their inbox.

Vasquez was flooded with new purpose.

"Get your shoes on, Detective," he said as he dropped his backpack on his desktop. "We've got work to do."

A young man lounged beneath a beach umbrella, a frosted glass adorned with festively speared fruit slices at his elbow. His skin was golden, his hair a shoulder-length tawny brown, his eyes silvery green and arresting. Those eyes, after three thousand years, looked once more upon the gentle tide as waves creamed upon the white sand beach, and the world, for all its age, was new again.

It was obvious that he found the scantily clad ladies of interest as they paraded past him—particularly the blondes—but he did not respond to their overtures. Instead, he turned reassuringly to his companion, their eyes meeting, soul-deep communication achieved without the use of ungainly words.

Although the ladies were disappointed not to pique his interest, they could almost understand his unflagging devotion. Seldom had they seen such a mystical bond as seemed to exist between a person and his pet—an Abyssinian with eyes of the clearest aquamarine blue and fur as golden as the sun.

WENDY WORTHINGTON

Morrigan Mine

The first time I saw the cat, she was trying to Friend me on Facebook. I ignored her request, and she didn't try again. The second time, or maybe it was the third, she emerged from the bushes a hundred yards away, saw me, and turned back quickly in a flurry of grey. The next time, she was disguised as a lady in Costco, wearing a hairnet and offering samples of cheese ravioli in little paper medicine cups, and the time after that, she was back in cat form but playing drums behind a rowdy rock band in a bar I had never visited before. I stopped keeping track, but I was always aware of her presence, somewhere on the edge of wherever I happened to be at the time.

The first time I heard her singing, it weirded me out. But nothing happened, not to me, anyway, and I started to think I might be special, though I never had been before. I had been born into an ordinary family with ordinary looks and ordinary friends. I had grown up in a middle class world with a middle class education that had led to a run-of-the-mill job that didn't really qualify as a career but paid the bills. I had never even won the lottery, not even the two-dollar scratch-off. Until the damn cat had marched into my life, nothing really notable had ever happened to me.

I found it hard to believe that I had been chosen for anything out of the ordinary. Maybe other people were able to see and hear her strangeness, too, but they just weren't willing to admit it. I asked a few of them, and every one of them just frowned at my question, so eventually I stopped. But whoever she was, she wouldn't let me go.

Danny O'Brien was the first one she sang to me about. The first I noticed, anyway. The more I thought about it, the more I realized she might have been around a lot longer, and she might have been singing, too, but I just hadn't noticed. Life is like that, you know. Things happen, strange things even, but you're too busy doing the laundry or watching *American Idol* to pay attention, especially when you aren't used to being singled out by fate or the universe or whatever it was that was stalking me. She might have been there from the beginning, and I was just too preoccupied to know it.

But I noticed with Danny. He'd told me once, over a plate of calamari and way too many beers, that the O'Briens were one of the five chosen Irish families that the Morrigan was supposed to sing a mourning song for when one of them died.

"Morrigan?" I asked. "I thought those were Banshees."

"Hardly," he huffed indignantly.

I spread my arms at him. "Isn't it the same thing?"

He sat back in his chair, nearly knocking himself to the floor in the process. "Banshees are your bog-standard fairy women. They'll scream for anybody. Anybody can have a Banshee." His voice was thick with contempt. "But the O'Briens are royalty. We get our own special harbinger. The Morrigan is powerful. And she can actually sing."

"Well, excuse me for living," I muttered into my third beer, but I was secretly glad that Danny was special. I had been sweet on him for the first ten minutes I'd known him, but I had gotten over that fast. It turned out to be just as well, because he made a much better friend than he did something more fleeting and complicated. I felt closer to him than I probably would have if he had taken me up on my amateur attempt to bring him home one night after yoga class. He turned me down, rather nicely, managing to keep me from feeling humiliated by one more failed attempt to make a romantic connection with someone. We laughed about it later.

So when the Morrigan sang to me, I somehow knew that the text saying he was stuck in a thunderstorm on the 405 was the last thing I would ever hear from him. Her song made me feel a hole in my life where Danny had been.

She was in cat form that day, and she let me see her clearly. She was dark grey, with huge green eyes, and she stood outside my kitchen window on top of the concrete block wall between my apartment building and the Hendersons' bungalow. It felt like she had been waiting for me to look up after dumping another coffee cup in the sink without even rinsing it. She held my eye for a moment, and then she sang. She had a clear, high voice, and there were no words. It was not the voice of a cat.

She finished the song, closed her mouth, maintained eye contact for one more moment, and then raised her tail and leapt out of view. I did not hear the clatter she must have made landing on the Hendersons' trash cans on the other side of the wall. I was too stunned by the sound of her song.

I stayed at the sink, waiting. I'm not sure if I expected her to pop her head back up over the wall, but of course she did not. She had delivered her message. I only had to wait for the human communication chain to catch up. I saw the helicopter shots on the news later that day and spotted the mangled bit of bright orange metal that used to be Danny's dumb little Chevrolet Tracker in the middle of that whole mess. Sandra sent a confirming tweet, and Bijon left an unending phone message that seemed to revel in every gory detail he had managed to put together from his online sources. But I didn't need to hear from them. I knew Danny was dead. It hurt like hell, more than it would have if I had just been one of his old girlfriends.

Danny's funeral was a week later. I think I expected to see the cat somewhere around when we put him in the cold, cold ground. She did not make it, of course. Cats don't attend funerals. They are too cool for that. And they certainly don't attend after they have already sung to you about it. They've mourned and moved on.

We raised a glass in Danny's honor at a pub near the cemetery, and each of us said a few words. Sandra was the weepiest, but that's just how she is. It wasn't like Danny was deeply special to her—she would have been like that for anybody. Evan was the most eloquent, though I still think that quote from Tennyson was pushing it. We'd all seen the movie he got it from, and Judi Dench had delivered the lines better.

I stood there at the bar, staring down into my glass and hearing them say nice things, and I realized all at once that these were really Danny's friends. They weren't mine. They were just some people we used to have in common. Even Sandra, who by this time was soppy drunk and a little snotty from crying, even she had been more Danny's friend than mine. He had loaned her to me for a while, but it wasn't going to last.

I didn't see the cat at all for the rest of the month, and I started to think that maybe she had been either a figment of my imagination or that she had discharged her sole duty regarding me with Danny O'Brien. I should have known better. The Morrigan was just getting warmed up.

The confirmation that it wasn't just my imagination came from my landlord, Mr. Roehmer, the farthest thing possible from an Irishman and the least superstitious person you will ever meet. I ran into him by the mailboxes one morning, and he stuck his big canned-ham face in front of me. "You're gonna hafta get rid of it," he announced.

I leaned back, trying to get out of range of his bad breath. "Get rid of what?" My mind ticked through the possibilities, including the 'Free Tibet' t-shirt I was wearing. I knew Mr.

Roehmer was politically backward, but I didn't think he had the right to dictate what I wore, even if I was wearing it on his property.

He eyed me and my t-shirt, but for once kept his political stupidity to himself. "Yer cat," he snapped.

I stared at him. "I don't have a cat."

"I seen it. Sittin' in the window. Lease says no pets. At all."

"You're seeing things, Mr. Roehmer," I said as politely as I could, but a shudder ran up my spine. "Come in right now, you can look."

His eyes narrowed. "Them things hide. It'll hear me comin' and hide."

"Then look for a litter box or food bowls. I don't have a cat."

He seemed to be considering whether it was worth it to be invited inside. He hadn't been through my door since the flood in Mrs. Duncan's bathroom next door. That hadn't gone in his favor. Maybe he could find something to complain about and fine me for, to recoup a little from the bathtub thing. I could see him thinking exactly that as he watched me.

In the end, though, he simply shrugged. "Better not see it again, that's all I'm sayin'." He lumbered away, and I turned to look up at my front window. It stood open and empty, the thin curtains framing it awkwardly at either side and flapping a little in the breeze from the ceiling fan. There was no sign of the cat, but that didn't mean she hadn't figured out a way to get in when I wasn't looking. I willed her to stay hidden. If she got me evicted, I was taking her to small claims court, even if she was a supernatural being.

She didn't show her furry face again for a while.

But she called me a few times on my landline, hanging up when I answered. I started picking up the phone even when I didn't recognize the number, just to hear the soft 'click' on the other end that I knew had to be her. The whole business made me nervous.

She left a few text messages on my cellphone, too, though she pretended they were to tell me I had won contests I had never entered. But the problem with getting texts from a creature without opposable thumbs is that she couldn't seem to leave a complete callback number, so I could never verify that those were from her.

I did some research. I found out she wasn't supposed to be showing up as a cat, but I guess the eel, wolf, and cow forms were a little too old-school and rural for her, and the crow was simply a cliché. Cats are cooler, and she wasn't always a cat anyway, so I decided that maybe it was just a personal choice. Even monsters can make personal choices, right? I mean, what's the point of being a monster if you can't have some say in what you look like once in a while? She didn't have to stick to tradition any more than anybody else. If vampires can suddenly decide they want to sparkle and walk around in the daylight after hundreds of years of being creatures of the night, I guess the Morrigan can turn into a cat instead of an eel. It's the twenty-first century, after all.

I started to convince myself that, no matter what Wikipedia said, the Morrigan wasn't a real monster at all. She was just a freaky messenger service. It wasn't like she was *causing* any of the deaths, after all. She was just giving advance word that they had happened. When she sang about Danny, he was already lying in a mangled heap underneath a couple of tons of steel, beyond help or hope. She wasn't trying to tell me that I had time to run out into the middle of the freeway and save him. She was just singing a goodbye in his honor. What was so monstrous about that?

She did, after all, have a crummy job, and I was an authority. Anybody who knew what she was about was just going to run the minute they heard her. It's not like you could escape what she was trying to tell you, of course, but you could stretch denial out for a very long time before you had to use it as the first step in the grieving process.

She was at least nice enough to stay out of my landlord's sight for most of November, but there was more than one time when I came home and found her staring down at me from my living room window. She was always gone by the time I opened my front door, but she made sure I knew she hadn't forgotten me.

Late one day shortly after Christmas, just after I got home from work, the phone rang, and the ID said it was from somebody named 'Kavanagh'. I couldn't think of anybody I knew named Kavanagh, and I was starting to get tired of her little game. I didn't answer.

But this time she left a message. The flashing light on the phone base mocked me for a couple of minutes before I screwed up my courage to listen to it.

I dialed in my access code. There was a moment's pause. And then the singing started. I think it was a different song than the one she sang for Danny, but I couldn't be sure. It was slow and mournful, and it made me shiver.

I saved it, and later I made Sandra listen to it, but she just frowned and gave the phone back to me without saying anything. I'm not sure what that meant. The fact that she didn't say anything might just be Sandra being succinct. But maybe the Morrigan had rendered her even dumber than usual.

"It's the Morrigan," I told her. "She's a monster who sings when someone royal and Irish has died," but Sandra just gave me a kind of blank stare like she'd never heard of monsters before, so I didn't press the issue. Maybe Sandra doesn't think monsters exist anymore, like they're old-fashioned or something. She once tried to convince me that people don't get polio these days, and she was serious. So monsters may not be part of her version of the modern universe, I don't know.

But they're part of mine. And this night, before I tried to make Sandra understand that there really still are monsters in the world, I just listened to my own monster singing the song a couple of times, pressing the keys to make it replay and wondering who it was for this time. "You better not be singing for me, cat," I murmured into the dead mouthpiece the third time through.

I gave up after a few more times through and turned on the TV to get my mind off the message, and we were right back where we started. Between the horror film fest on one channel and the disaster movie on the next one, there was no escaping monsters or monstrous stuff. I flipped off the set. (What *is* the point of paying for three hundred channels, anyway?) I walked over to the front window and stared down into the darkness.

Of course, in a city, it's never really very dark, and the halogen streetlight made the sidewalk outside my window brighter and greener than it was during the day. It certainly made it easy to see the person leaning against the lamppost. I couldn't tell whether it was a man or a woman. The long, dark trench coat had the buttons on the man's side, but that means so little these days. The shoes were dark and nondescript. It was hard to see the hair under the baseball cap, and the brim wasn't helping to make the face any more visible.

At least the face wasn't pointed up toward me. Maybe whoever was down there was just waiting for somebody to come out of one of the neighboring apartments, and the fact that he or she was standing outside my window was just a coincidence.

But there was something about the figure, something about the way it was standing or the ambiguity of it, something that played into my thoughts about monsters and the Morrigan and the premonition of death and all that junk—something that made my stomach feel cold. I stepped back from the window. I didn't want to find out if it was all connected. A coincidence felt like a safer answer.

The phone rang again. I picked it up without looking at the readout, prepared now to hear a sorrowful song and dreading it.

"What?" I demanded into the mouthpiece.

"Hey," said Sandra, and I realized that maybe I wasn't going to get more singing but was instead about to hear what the singing had been about, but it turned out that she just wanted to find out if Abby was going to be in town for dim sum on Sunday, and she hung up as soon as she got her answer (which was "no", by the way). It was enough to change the atmosphere in the room, though, because by the time I went back to the window, the figure was gone, the street looked normal, and my stomach didn't feel cold anymore. And I realized I hadn't turned on most of the lights in the apartment, so I dispersed the gloom with the simple click of a switch. Still, I kept thinking I had missed something important.

The darkness came and went for the rest of the week and into the new year. Life at work continued to be miserable, and a lot of little things kept going wrong. You know how you sometimes have days you think you should have bought a lottery ticket? These weren't those kind of days. All the technology in my life decided it hated me—my computer stopped talking to my printer for a couple of days, my cellphone battery died even after I remembered to recharge it, and my GPS sent me to an address that didn't exist when I tried to meet the gang for a drink after work at a new bar, and not one of them ever asked why I never showed up. I lost my mailbox key for a whole twenty-four hours, and then it turned up in one of the places I had looked at least three times. I never did find my favorite pair of socks again, they just vanished into an alternate universe. I think the Morrigan took them. I made a mental note to see if she was wearing them the next time I saw her in human form.

Billy Dean, the asshole who has the cubicle right next to mine, spent the whole week being even more of a dick than usual. I found myself starting to hope the Morrigan had been singing for him, but then I remembered that she only sings for people who are already dead, so there went that happy thought. Still, I wondered if maybe I could put in a special request. "Cat," I muttered under my breath, "please take Billy Dean." She didn't, of course, and I would have felt guilty if she had, but it was kind of fun thinking it.

"Come on, Morrigan," I said out loud as I left work on Friday night, "if my life is suddenly going to take a turn for the unusual, couldn't it be because I turned out to be the Princess of Denovia or became an international movie star or something?" But I discovered as I reached my block that a party at the Hendersons had filled every close parking spot. I ended up finding one space in front of a creepy house with a wooden windmill in the front garden. I trudged the two blocks home muttering bad things about Molly Henderson and her damn parties.

I needed something light and happy for Saturday to start things off on the right note. I thought I'd found it when I set out to go looking for garage sale bargains that morning, but the universe doused me with another bucket of cold stuff. My car decided to make only a horrifying and agonized noise when I turned the key. I was left sitting at the curb, cursing.

I walked slowly back to my apartment, wondering if it was worth calling the auto club. Maybe my car would just heal itself. Maybe it just hadn't felt like going anywhere on a Saturday morning. And then of course I wondered whether the Morrigan had been singing for my car. Can mystical creatures foretell the death of inanimate objects? Of course, the car had still been alive for a few days when 'Kavanagh' had called, so that probably wasn't it, either.

I checked the mailbox out of habit, but it was empty. And then, when I glanced up at my front window, she was staring down at me. A line of goosebumps ran up both my arms. She was in cat form again today, but somehow in this light, she didn't quite look right. She looked like a person, like she hadn't fully committed to being a cat this time.

I can't really describe it very well. I couldn't see whether her pupils had the vertical slit they should have if she was trying to look feline, but something was off with her face. This cat looked nearly human. It was creepy. And she was maintaining eye contact with me, which was very unlike a cat. Most times, they'll stare at you for a moment or two and then look away, like it's not worth their time to connect with you for very long. This one was almost daring me to be the first to give in.

"Shame about Molly Henderson," said a loud voice at my elbow.

I swung around, nearly knocking Mr. Roehmer into the bougainvillea. He had appeared out of nowhere, holding a green garden hose and being unusually quiet. I shot a surreptitious glance back up at the window, but the cat was gone now, and I muttered a silent thank you for small favors.

Then I registered what Mr. Roehmer had said. "What do you mean?" I asked. "Is Molly still hung over from her party last night?"

He gave me an odd look. "That'd be one helluva hangover. She died Tuesday. Last night was a wake, or whatever you call them things. Mostly an excuse for the Micks to get drunk." He snorted. "Like they need one."

"Tuesday," I repeated, wondering if I had the last asshole landlord in Los Angeles. When had the Morrigan called? And why would she tell me about Molly? I had barely known the woman. *But you did know her name,* I reminded myself. *And you knew her on sight. She was the first neighbor you met when you moved in.*

Mr. Roehmer started spraying the bougainvillea with the hose. "Least they didn't go hog wild till the end of the week," he muttered. "Guess that's something. Probably felt like they hadda wait for her family to get here."

"Where were they coming in from?"

"God knows." He shot a spray of water across the driveway,

toward the scraggly patch of blackberry bushes that separated our driveway from the Hendersons. "Can barely understand the father. Sounds like a stupid soap commercial. Like that guy who played Lincoln really sounds. You ever hear him? Got some foreigner to play our greatest President, what were they thinkin'?"

I stared at him for a minute. "Wait," I said at last, "you mean her family is from Ireland?"

He shrugged. "Guess so. 'Magically delicious.'" His attempt at an Irish accent was atrocious. If I hadn't recognized the reference, I could have just as easily suspected that Molly Henderson had been Lithuanian or something.

"That's not a commercial for soap," I murmured, but I tried not to say it loud enough to offend him. I shifted my attention to the garishly painted bungalow on the other side of the bushes. I had never given Molly's ancestry any thought before. Hell, I had barely given the woman herself any thought before, just waved at her across the driveway and exchanged a few empty pleasantries over the blackberry bushes. I really knew nothing about her. If the Morrigan had indeed been calling to tell me that Molly was no more, I had no idea why. Unless, of course, she had called everyone on the block.

I looked back at Mr. Roehmer, who had abandoned his desultory attempt at watering and was now frowning into the dumpster.

"Mr. Roehmer, how did you hear about Molly?" I asked carefully. I held my breath, not sure if I wanted to find out that his phone had rung, too.

He looked up. "What? Oh, Brian told me." He pointed into the bin. "You throw out all these phone books? They go in recycling." He reached in and pulled out a couple of thick telephone directories and waved them in my general direction.

I shook my head. Telephone books. They were as antiquated these days as Sandra's ideas about monsters. "Not mine," I assured him. Then I had a thought. "But, hey, give me one."

He handed it over. "What, you need a doorstop or something?" He sniggered at his own stupid joke. When I didn't join him in giggling, he went back to fishing more phone books out of the trash bin.

I glanced at the cover. "Greater Los Angeles," it read. I flipped it to 'K.' I was suddenly curious about whether there was any listing for Kavanagh. I didn't actually expect to find one, but why not look? My finger stopped abruptly at 'Kavanagh, M.'

The address was right next door. Did the Hendersons have a tenant? Someone named Kavanagh? Would the phone number match the number on my voicemail?

I reread it a few times, sure that I must be seeing it wrong. Finally, I stepped to Mr. Roehmer's side, close enough to hear him panting as he tried to snag the last phone book from inside the dumpster. "Um," I said. It wasn't as eloquent as I hoped to be. "Um, Mr. Roehmer, who's this?"

It took him a moment to pull his head out of the dumpster and another to realize that I was voluntarily standing closer to him. He followed my finger and squinted at the line I was pointing at. Then he looked at the house where it said M. Kavanagh lived. The Hendersons' house. "Huh," he said. "Musta kept her maiden name in the phone book."

"Who?"

"Molly. Henderson. Didn't think you knew her that well. Didja know her when she was still Kavanagh?" He insisted on pronouncing the 'gh' and mangling the name in the process. He really was a dope. "I forgot that was her name before. Weird, huh? You ladies get to change your whole identity. Dunno if I could do that. I'm too used to my name. Not sure I could just give it up like that."

Privately, I thought that maybe it would have been the perfect opportunity for someone like him to leave the husk of who he was behind and try for full humanity this time around.

But I was still shaking from the idea that the Morrigan had been able to manipulate caller ID. She had told me who her song was for. I just hadn't known Molly's real name.

I went back up to my apartment and ransacked my pantry for a suitable offering to express my bereavement. My mother taught me that you don't visit the house of someone who has passed on without bringing food. I couldn't just bang on the dead neighbor's door empty-handed.

I ended up baking some cookies. They weren't anything that would win a Betty Crocker Bake-Off, but they were sufficient to the task. I balanced the plastic-wrapped paper plate laden with my humble contribution in one hand as I knocked on the Hendersons' front door early that afternoon.

The man who came to the door was tall and lean, and his eyes were red-rimmed, set in a careworn face. The knees of his dark khaki trousers were darkened as though he had been kneeling in the dirt.

"Hi," I said, as he peered uncertainly at me through the screen door. "I'm Mary Margaret from next door. You must be Mr. Kavanagh. I just heard about Molly. I'm so sorry."

"Oh. Come in, come in," he replied, opening the door wide, "that's very sweet of ye." I found his gentle lilt perfectly understandable. I had no idea what Mr. Roehmer had been on about.

"I didn't know that was Molly's maiden name until this morning," I murmured as he ushered me inside. "I didn't know she was from one of the five families. She never told me much about her background."

I realized he had frozen in the doorway and was staring at me intently. He stood there for a moment, then he asked, very softly, "So, ye heard it, then?"

"Heard what?" I replied breezily, but my blood froze at his question. Except for my abortive attempt to tell Sandra, I had been surprisingly reticent in mentioning my indefinable companion. Maybe I had been afraid that talking about her would make her more real.

He continued to stare at me, and I recognized that playing dumb was cruel to a grieving father. I set the cookies on the coffee table and took a deep breath. "I heard her," I admitted. "I just didn't know she was singing about Molly. But the Kavanaghs are one of the five families, aren't they? I remember seeing their name on the list in one of the references I read. My friend Danny O'Brien told me the story. And then she sang for him."

He had sagged a little, leaning against the front door frame. "There's no escapin'," he said softly. "I suppose it's an honor and all, but it sure doesn't seem like it, havin' your family business announced to the world like that."

I tried to convey my sympathy. "It's not like she was responsible for Molly dying. She just told some people about it after it happened."

He raised his head and fixed me with a wary gaze. "That's what they say, all right, but I've wondered many a time. Does she sing after it's all said and done, or is it a warnin' that you could actually do somethin' about?"

I frowned at him. "I thought she always sang afterwards."

"Ah, but do ye know that for sure? Do ye remember when ye heard her singin' fer me Molly?"

"Tuesday. In the evening. When did she die?"

He nodded sadly. "Earlier that day. So ye got the message after." He sighed. "Yer sure about the time?"

"Yes," I said. Then I straightened up. "Wait, I saved it."

He cocked his head at me. "Saved it? What are ye talkin' about?"

"It's on my phone. She called me. The caller ID said 'Kavanagh.' That's how I finally figured it out. When I found out that was Molly's name, this morning."

"The Morrigan *called* ye? On the tellyphone? How in blue blazes did she do that?"

I shrugged. "I have no idea. She's very talented, I'm

discovering. She seems to have no problems with modern technology."

Mr. Kavanagh's expression was completely skeptical now. "Lass, are ye sure this is the Morrigan yer talkin' about? And not just some practical joker friend of yers, havin' a laugh?"

I thought about it. Maybe Danny's original story had developed in my brain into something all by itself. After all, what had I really seen or heard? I shook my head. "I'm not sure of anything, Mr. Kavanagh. If you'd like to come next door and listen to the message, maybe you can tell me what you think about all this. It's very peculiar, I have to admit."

He studied me for a moment. Frankly, I wouldn't have blamed him if he had decided I was just some crazy American caught up in the mysterious tragedy of an Irish folktale. I could as easily believe it myself. After all, the alternative was believing that a cat had chosen me to sing to. I wasn't sure that was better.

In the end, he agreed to come along and listen. He did take the precaution of telling Molly's husband where he was off to, though he had the decency not to reveal why until he had more evidence about my sanity or lack thereof. I let him into my living room, half expecting to find the cat herself perched in the window or lurking outside on the sidewalk, but she was nowhere to be found. I offered Mr. Kavanagh tea.

He shook his head. "I've had a gallon already."

I gestured him to a seat on the couch and fetched the phone receiver, dialing in my access code before handing it over to him to listen to the message.

I watched him as it replayed. His face went a little pale and the sadness in his eyes deepened. At the end, he handed it back to me without a word. I saved it once more and then put the phone back. I wondered how long I could hang onto that mournful song. Would it become a conversation piece? *"Hey, you wanna hear a supernatural phone message from beyond the grave? I happen to have one on my machine. Doesn't everybody?"*

Mr. Kavanagh was staring at my rug.

"So?" I asked at last.

He raised his eyes to meet mine. "Who are ye?" he asked quietly. His face had a haunted look.

"What do you mean?" I asked. "I'm Mary Margaret from next door."

"Are ye, now?"

"What's that supposed to mean?"

"It means, why is she singin' to ye, lass? Ye didn't know me Molly, not well enough to know her family name, at least. So why do ye get to hear the Morrigan's song?"

I shook my head. "I have no idea. Is it the same one you heard? I think maybe she sang something different for my friend, Danny, but I can't be sure."

His face collapsed. "She didn't sing to me, lass. I never heard her mournin'. Who are ye, that the Queen should pass over her own Da?"

"I have no idea. I'm not even Irish."

"Sure ye are, lass. Everybody is, deep down." He was smiling now, but his eyes were glistening, and he almost seemed serious.

I smirked. "Well, maybe on weekends." I remembered a song I had heard a few times that made the argument sound plausible. "But, really, I'm not Irish, not even a little bit."

He cocked an eyebrow at me. "Are ye sure? And ye with the name of Mary Margaret and all."

"I think that was just my mother's idea of a joke. A stick in the eye to my dad's side of the family." It had taken me years to understand my shiksa mother's attempt at a joke. Still, I was pretty sure neither side of my family was secretly Irish. "And I have no idea why the Morrigan would sing to me, even for my friend Danny. Maybe her singing to me about Molly was a mistake."

He shook his head. "The Morrigan doesn't make mistakes like that, lass. There's a reason ye were the one who heard it."

I frowned at him. "What do you mean, 'the one'? Surely lots of people hear the songs. I just happened to be one of them. Maybe she thought we were closer. Or maybe she was just warning me there'd be a funeral last night so I'd get home earlier and be able to find a better parking spot."

He was staring at me again. "There's just one song for each passin'. And you got to hear it. She sang it to ye. That must mean somethin'."

"Well, maybe she sang to me because she knew I'd record it and then *you'd* have the chance to hear it. Maybe she was just being lazy." I was beginning to be annoyed. I hadn't known Molly Kavanagh Henderson well enough to have to deal with all these complications. I wondered how I could make a copy of the song for her father and pass it along to him and be done with the whole business. I suddenly wanted to have a private conversation with the damn cat. She needed to find somebody else to haunt and annoy and sing her stupid songs to. I had better things to do with my time.

Mr. Kavanagh rose from the sofa. "Calm yerself," he said quietly. "It will all come out right in the end. I thank ye for lettin' me listen. It was a privilege, I can tell ye. And whatever her reasons, it was a privilege to meet ye, as well. Irish or not." He smiled. "Though I do think ye should investigate yer family tree. Ye might find a thing or two that would surprise ye."

I smiled back at him. "Hey, it'd be worth it just to annoy Nana Epstein. Though I think my mother might have told me already if we had a right to the wearing of the green. I'm pretty sure she just liked the name Mary Margaret and knew it would piss off her mother-in-law."

Mr. Kavanagh's words stayed with me, though, and I started to obsess about why the Morrigan had chosen me. I asked her the next time I glimpsed her, but she simply gave me what passed for an enigmatic smile on a cat and leapt over the wall without even pretending to consider my question.

She didn't try to contact me again for quite a while. Maybe

she had realized her mistake or decided I was just too thick to figure out what she was going on about. I stared at a lot of strangers through most of the winter, and all I got for my pains was a sneer and a couple of nonverbal 'Fuck you's.'

By the time the rainy season had petered out, signaling the early days of spring, I was actually thinking about erasing her message. I hadn't let anyone else hear it, but I listened to it a lot, mostly late at night when I was feeling maudlin. By then, I had it completely memorized.

That final Thursday was particularly miserable. The boss was out sick, which Billy Dean always took as permission to act like an even bigger jerk than usual. He had been pelting me with spitballs over the top of our shared cubicle wall regularly since lunch. His barrage was especially unwelcome during a protracted phone call from an unhappy customer, a man who began by impugning the legitimacy of my birth and who then proceeded to question my intelligence, the company's integrity, and the strength of my patience. I did my best to stay cool, but it was a near thing.

By the time we finally ended our tiresome little conversation, I had quite a nice sized heap of Billy Dean's spit mixed with crumbled soggy paper detritus scattered around my chair, and my last nerve was about ready to snap. With an exasperated sigh, I stood up, pushing my chair back through the slippery trail of soggy paper wads, ready to tell Billy Dean just what he could do with all his saliva.

As I stood, I happened to look across the office, toward the plate glass window that was all that separated us from the unwashed masses passing through the building's lobby. Standing just outside the glass, staring in at me, was a figure in a baseball hat and trench coat. I still couldn't tell its gender, but I recognized the eyes, even at this distance. I froze, feeling that cold sensation flood into my gut once more.

I took a deep breath and started toward the main door. Out of the corner of my eye, I saw Billy Dean flinch and dive under his desk, fearing retribution. He staggered back up in confusion as I walked past him without giving him a second glance. I didn't dare look away from the figure at the door. I suddenly wanted answers, and I was not about to let her get away this time.

But just before I had cleared the last cubicle and rounded the bend for a straight shot at the door, Billy Dean caught up to me and began tugging at my sleeve. "Hey, MM, what's up?" he demanded in that screechy whine of his, and he forced me to take my eyes off my goal for a brief moment, and by the time I looked back, the figure was gone.

"Let go of me!" I bawled, shaking loose from his grasp.

I pushed past him and shoved open the glass door into the lobby, then struggled through the gaggle of people waiting for the elevator and out the open doors onto Wilshire Boulevard. Most of the surrounding offices were letting out for the day, and I found myself in a crush of office workers hurrying toward the bus stop and threading their way toward the parking garage. I scanned the crowd, looking for a trench coat and baseball cap but finding nothing.

"Damn!" I murmured. In my pocket, my cellphone began to vibrate. I pulled it out, checking the reading, half expecting to see 'Morrigan' on its face, but instead it read, 'Private.' I cursed and tapped the reply key, raising it to my ear and bracing myself for another round of otherworldly music. "What do you want?" I snapped, and there was a moment's pause.

"Mary Margaret?" asked the voice on the other end.

"Yes?"

"Hey, it's Sandra."

I frowned hard enough to send my confusion across the phone connection. "What line are you using? The readout says, 'Private'."

"Oh, I'm calling from work. Doesn't it register?"

"No, Sandra, that's why I asked." She really could be remarkably thick. "What do you need?"

"Oh," she began, and I wondered if she had already forgotten why she was calling. It wouldn't be the first time. But suddenly the line stuttered, and the ambient sounds tamped down as though the air around me had been muffled in cotton, and the damn singing started. And it was indeed a different song, I knew it for sure this time. Similar, yes, but a slower rhythm, the chords more desolate, the vocalizations more indefinite, as though precise words weren't the point.

"Sandra?" I called, but I knew she wasn't on the other end of this. "Morrigan? What the hell do you *want?*" I scrutinized the people on the sidewalk around me, searching for the figure in the baseball cap or for anyone singing into a cellphone, but strangers pushed past me. No one was paying me any heed at all. A large man shoved into me with an audible huff, annoyed only by the fact that I was in his obviously important way. Everyone else ignored me entirely.

I swung back to face the open door from which I had emerged, realizing that even Billy Dean had abandoned me. In my ear, the singing continued, oblivious to my distress. It reached its mournful end, trailing off into silence. For a moment, the whole world remained strangely muffled.

Then, with a roar, the sound rushed back—the click of heels on pavement, the rumble of passing cars, a distant siren, the chatter of unarticulated conversations, the thunder of ordinary life. Even Sandra was back, though she didn't seem to realize she had ever been gone. "Look, I forget what I wanted, it was probably nothing, sorry, I'll call you if I remember," she sputtered, and she hung up, forgetting me along with whatever she thought she'd wanted to say. Typical.

I lowered the phone from my ear and looked at the readout again, thumbing my way through to the 'Call History' listing. There was Sandra's 'Private' number. But it wasn't the last number on the list. And the final number wasn't some mysterious Irish surname, either. It read, 'Schwartz, Irene.' I was fairly sure I didn't know her. The Morrigan had started singing to me about strangers, strangers who weren't even Irish.

I didn't bother thumbing my way back to the main menu. I let my hand drop to my side and scanned the crowd once more but without any real hope of seeing the face of my tormentor. The world around me looked completely, boringly ordinary, but now I felt its underlying menace. The bald man crossing my line of vision, clutching his briefcase in one hand and adjusting his sunglasses with the other, was either carrying out the same routine he did every Thursday and would every Thursday for the rest of his natural life or he was hurtling toward disaster, about to be smashed into the grill of the Metro bus that was pulling out from the curb more or less into his line of travel. The young Latina digging through her backpack to his left was either searching for the wallet buried somewhere within or for a loaded .45 so she could start spraying the crowd with hot lead. The scruffy couple leaning against the wall, intent only on one another, were either busy making dinner plans or were on the point of stabbing one another viciously with a scream of fury and a homicidal rage drawn from the depths of their dysfunctional relationship. All around me, banality or violence threatened and warred with one another. I felt certain that the slightest shift in the wind could send things in either direction.

And someone's song had just been sung. Someone connected to me in some way I could not yet determine was already gone from the world, leaving behind nothing but a musical whisper. Someone's life was already over, and it was entirely possible that, at this exact second, only an unearthly creature and I knew about it.

I spun back toward the office, bursting through the glass doors off the lobby and hurtling onward to my drab little cubicle. I felt rather than actually saw Billy Dean hovering behind me, torn between ridicule and running. I surveyed my abandoned swivel chair in its circle of spitballs, the empty desk, the forlorn cork-lined half walls, the nothingness that delineated the place where I had reported every day for more than three years in order to finance my pointless existence. It looked as abandoned as a grave. I had always assumed this would just be a temporary position, a job I would hold until I found something I actually liked doing, and in the interim it had become a bad habit I couldn't afford to break.

I opened the bottom drawer of the cold metal desk and retrieved the only thing it ever held, my purse. I slung it over my shoulder, fishing within it for my car keys as I headed for the front door once more. I ignored the whine that was Billy Dean's belated attempt to find out where I was going. I didn't have an actual answer, and I wouldn't have told him even if I had known.

I found my car in the parking garage where I had left it, wedged into a spot next to the dumpster. The sour smell of garbage permeated the air. I squeezed into the driver's seat and turned the key, fumbling with the seat belt.

Out on Wilshire, the traffic was as awful as always, but I barely registered the jangled rumble of mechanized chaos. I needed to get home, though as I articulated the thought, I suddenly realized that 'home' wasn't the right word anymore for where I was headed. 'Home' had once meant refuge and comfort and independence. Now it just meant the place I went at the end of the day, the place that my drab little job paid for. It was a shelter from the storm, but only barely. It held a lot of things, but none of them were warm memories. But where else did I have to go?

There was, amazingly, a parking spot open right in front of my apartment, and I thanked the gods of parking for being kind to me when no one else was. I didn't even bother checking the mailbox. I didn't want to see even more evidence of the meaningless obligations of my life. But I did stop and look up at my front window. It was dark and empty, just like everything else around me.

Up the stairs, I unlocked my front door into the gloom. The living room was cold, but there was more than that to make me tremble. It took me a moment. Then I saw her, in the dark space between the living room and the kitchen. At first glance, she could have been just a shadow, but there was something deeper, something palpable about her darkness.

I stood very still for a moment, absorbing her presence in my apartment, trying to decide if I had finally lost my grip on whatever mundane reality I was used to occupying. I wanted—needed—to ask why she was here, but I almost knew already, and I knew as well that words weren't any more important than they had been in any of the songs she had sung to me.

I asked anyway.

"Why do you sing to me?"

I could barely make her out, but I could see that she had cocked her head at me. I wondered suddenly if she was capable of actual speech, or if music was her only means of communicating across the divide. I tensed, expecting another melodic torrent.

All I heard was the sound of her breath.

Her breath.

If she could breathe—hell, if she *needed* to breathe—maybe she wasn't who I thought she was at all, and my hand slid into my pocket, groping for my cellphone and wondering if it was time to dial 911 for the first time in my life. Funny, but the possibility of being confronted with a living human being inside my own apartment was almost more terrifying than being faced with something from beyond the grave.

But the more I listened to the sound of her breathing, the less it sounded like air moving in and out of corporeal lungs. Instead, it started to sound like leaves rustling in the woods, like the distant ripple of the wind, like a suggestion or a promise or something I had known once and nearly forgotten. I pulled my hand out back of my pocket and opened the empty palm toward her. It became a plea.

"Why do you sing?" I murmured. "To me?"

The whispered inhalation of air, of breath, of wind, took on a tone and a color, too, if I'm being perfectly honest. It was silver turned into a current of air that lifted itself into music. It wasn't a coherent answer to my question, but it suggested the start of a response. I still wasn't sure why she was singing, or why she was singing to me, but it began to make some kind of inexplicable sense.

And in the quiet between her breaths, I could just barely begin to hear the music of her song, as though several far away voices were vocalizing the notes together. As it had been with every tune, there were no words. The notes drifted in through the open cracks in the physical barriers of the world, slithering through the fissures in my apartment walls and around the thin curtains that framed my front window, teasing the ceiling fan, and tempting it to start spinning slowly in the opposite direction.

And as that thought occurred to me, I started to understand why she was here, why she had chosen me, why she had begun to sing to me, and what she wanted. Like the song she sang, there weren't words, exactly, but I understood her. She sang because she believed in me. No one else ever had.

To my lightened heart, her song suddenly sounded less like a forlorn dirge and more like assurance. It embraced the inevitable end without the expectation of inevitable sadness. It simply was. And the rhythm of her breath, her song, her assertion began to invite me along, urging me to match it and join it and, yes, to sing with her.

She had come for me when no one else had bothered. Her song was not finality. It was possibility. It was intention. It was something important to do. I could learn this song. Hell, I had learned this song, and it was the first thing in a very long time that had made any real sense to me.

I stretched my hand out toward the shadow. It was no longer a plea but acceptance. I could taste the question in the air between us. *Are you certain?*

Of course not, I answered. *But I will come with you anyway. I can do this. I want to.*

I don't know what they found when they unlocked my empty apartment or how they got Mr. Roehmer to use his key to let them in. And I never did get to meet Irene Schwartz. But the rest, the rest is part of the story someone tells about me. Mary Margaret the Morrigan. It has a nice ring, don't you think?

ANTIOCH GREY

The Proper Task of Life

"It's all a bit of a cliché, I'm afraid." Gerald leaned on the balcony and gestured to the garden below, the setting sun etching deep shadows across the lawn. "The cypresses are interesting, I suppose, with the strong verticals, and the long line of their shadows breaking up the acid green where the last of the sun hits. That dark patch has the most fascinating mix of purple tones in it."

Gerald turned and looked back across his shoulder. "Sorry. Artist's shop talk. It's very dull if you're not in the trade."

"No, no, it's fascinating. Do go on." Susan settled against the balustrade next to him and peered down the sudden drop, along the line his finger had been pointing. "I can't see any purple there—just brown and black."

"Oh no, the trunk, there, that's brown, lots of different browns, but that patch of shade is very definitely purple."

"Which is why you're the famous artist," she said. "And I am a journalist. I can paint pretty pictures with words, but not see the depths of tone and shade before me."

Gerald examined her with hooded eyes. "And are you going to paint a pretty picture of me?"

"A truthful one, I hope."

"Ah, much more dangerous." Gerald grinned. "I only hope I can withstand the scrutiny." He propelled himself upright with a wince, pushing against the sun-bleached stone. "Tea? Which is something of a cliché in itself, I suppose. The ex-pat clinging to the old forms and ceremonies..."

"Thank you, tea would be lovely."

Susan followed Gerald through the French windows into the drawing room. Its décor merited the term—the rioting gilt cherubs surmounting panels painted to look like Sienna marble could be called nothing less. In the corner, unevenly stacked canvases faced the wall, tucked behind an easel that held one, dark painting.

"Is it all right if I look?" Susan asked.

"Help yourself," Gerald said, waving a hand in general permission. "I'll just fetch the tea from the kitchen. I won't be long."

He paused at the door to flick the light switch, bringing a soft, warm glow to the room, chasing away the gathering gloom.

From afar, the picture looked black. Close to, the details slowly resolved—patches of dark and darker shifting into blocks of colour, then identifiable shapes, the forms of the trees, a lawn, and a huddle of fallen pillars, eventually revealing the view she had just been looking at from the terrace, but painted at night.

Susan leaned closer to the picture, tracing the shadows with a finger a short distance from the paint, almost but not quite touching—there, deep in the darkest corner, was a long shape that could be a human figure, but with a grotesque twist that made it threatening.

Gerald returned, teapot in hand, muffled in a ridiculous frilly tea-cosy. He grinned ruefully and wiggled the pot at her. "Not in the best taste, is it?"

"Not really." Susan smiled. "But it won't affect the tea."

Gerald busied himself with the ritual of tea, milk and sugar, and biscuits, Susan already mentally composing the paragraph contrasting his suburban habits with the avant garde nature of his work. The tea was good, a strong blend, sharp and hot on the tongue.

Cup in hand, she moved back to look at the picture.

"It's amazing," she said. "I can see what you mean about the purple, I think. This seems to be nothing else, just different shades of purple, layered on each other to give this... this depth of darkness. I've never seen anything like it."

"You won't have."

"Is this new work of yours?"

"I didn't paint it. A friend of mine did. It's interesting, don't you think?"

"I do. It's very different from your work. More representational."

"You mean you can tell what it is?" Gerald moved to stand by her. "Or you think you can. David does work in an old-fashioned idiom, but he gives it a fresh life, a new meaning. It's really rather beautiful, and utterly unexpected."

"You sound half in love with the work."

"A little." Gerald reached out to the picture, his hands touching the frame gently. "And bitterly envious of all the time he has before him to refine his skills."

He stood there, hand to art, then gave it a final pat, like a much loved pet.

"Shall we get on with the interview?" he said.

"By all means."

Evening had settled into night by the time they had made their way through half the questions on her list.

"So that takes us up to your move to New York," she said. "In the eighties."

"God, yes. That was a mistake, in retrospect. I did some of my worst work at that time, but it sold for really good prices." Gerald shrugged. "What can you say about that? It's enough to make you cry, though I will be honest— the money does help. If you're going to sell yourself, you should sell yourself high."

"You stayed there five years," Susan said. "Until Mark...."

"I won't talk about that."

"I wasn't going to ask," she said.

Gerald snorted. "You'll be the first reporter who didn't want to know the details."

"Perhaps the others hadn't read the cuttings file." Susan checked the tape recorder with one eye, and flipped to a clean page in her notebook. "After you came back to the UK, you didn't paint anything for a couple of years."

"It didn't feel right." Gerald knotted his hands together, shifting his thumbs over each other restlessly. "All the dealers were watching, looking at my pictures to see if there was any evidence of my great tragedy. And it turned out there were limits to how much of myself—and Mark—I was prepared to sell. It was bad enough he was dead, without prostituting his memory."

"I interviewed Haret, after the death of his wife. He said he did nothing but paint her over and over again for a year, and then one day he just stopped. He decided to paint something else. He's never painted another woman, but he managed to keep working. He's turned to those lovely landscapes."

"I didn't know that. It wasn't in your interview."

Susan shook her head. "It was strictly off the record. Until he dies, anyway."

"I couldn't paint Mark. I tried. I couldn't paint anything real, just swirls of black. It was all so trite. I burned all the canvases."

Susan nodded encouragingly. "I know I'm not in your league, but when my brother died, I couldn't write for a long time. It all seemed so worthless and banal. I did a bit of investigative journalism for a while, but there was too much pressure on me to make up stories, to make them more interesting. So I went back to this. Trying to get into others' skins."

"Giving them some sort of immortality?" Gerald asked.

"I suppose," Susan said. "Something like that."

"What did your brother die of, if you don't mind me

asking?"

"Drugs. It was all such a bloody waste."

"Ah," Gerald said, on a long breath out. "So you do understand. About Mark, I mean."

"If you mean how you feel angry that someone has died doing something so bloody stupid...?" Susan sighed, fingers twitching round her pen. "Oh, I understand that all right. And the way you think they'll walk through the door at any moment, laughing and joking, and teasing you about how stupid you were to fall for that prank."

Gerald nodded. "God, yes. That too. I had to leave my flat, sell up, and come here. Here, where there are no memories unless I allow them in. No reminders of time together—the little clock he bought me in Prague on a whim, the shoes he always wore, scuffed at the heel, all the flotsam and jetsam of a life."

He took another long shuddering breath. "I burned them all."

"I wrapped them up in a box and put them in the attic. I couldn't bear to part with them," Susan said softly.

"I think that it would be worse to lose a brother than a lover." Gerald leaned back in his chair, smoothing his hands down his thighs. "It's not that you can replace a particular lover, but there is always the possibility of meeting someone else, of having another relationship. There is never another brother."

"Did you meet someone else? David?"

"Oh, God, no. He's very definitely not my type. There's a sweet young man in the local town who knows absolutely nothing about art, but has a thing for older men. It's not serious, but it's fun. And there was long time when I thought I would never have fun again." He looked at her kindly. "And you?"

Susan took a deep, sharp breath. "I ... One day, I might write his story, though it's ordinary enough."

"There's power in the everyday. If you know how to look for it," Gerald said. "You just have to draw it out. I'm sure you'll do a good job."

"I hope so."

A silence settled on the room, both occupants lost in their pasts.

"More tea?" Gerald said.

Susan gave a small huff of laughter. "Indeed. More tea."

They left the drawing room, heading to the kitchen in search of clean cups, fresh hot water and some more tea.

"I don't know about you, but I could do with a snack," he said. "There's some cheese in the fridge, and some ham. And there's some bread, fresh from the village. I... er, went down there earlier today."

"Does your young man work in the bakery?" Susan opened the fridge, and took out several carefully wrapped pieces of cheese, and a plate of thinly sliced ham.

Gerald put rolls on two rustic plates on the table, and a pottery dish holding butter, with a knife stuck in it at a jaunty angle.

"Off the record?" he said, his eyes crinkling with amusement.

"Entirely."

"Actually he works in the café across the road, but it doesn't do to be obvious."

Susan laughed. "But is the coffee any good?"

"Absolutely delectable."

They filled the rolls haphazardly, with the cheese in slabs and the ham hanging out of the sides, so they could only eat by coming at the food from below, with a hand cupped beneath to catch crumbs.

"My mother would be shocked to see my table manners," Susan said. "But these are good. Do you think there might be a delectable baker for me?"

"He's fifty, if he's a day, and his wife might have something to say about that," Gerald said. "No, you should try the bookshop if you're looking for a little romance. Face like an angel and an arse you could bounce... well anything off. David painted him a while back."

"Sounds good. I'll be sure to look for him." She brushed the last of the crumbs from her shirt, and looked round for a cloth to wipe her hands on. "Is David around? I'd like to meet him."

Gerald stiffened. "I'm not sure that's wise."

"Oh, I'm sorry. I didn't mean to pry."

"It's not that. He's just terribly shy and something of a recluse."

"It's not something that has to be in the article, and you do have final say on that anyway." Susan shrugged. "I'd just like to meet the artist who produced work like that."

"I'll see what I can do—will you be around tomorrow evening?"

Susan nodded. "I was going to wander round the village tomorrow. Take some pictures of the landscape, and just soak up the atmosphere."

"I'll call you, if David agrees."

The town converged on the square at its heart, which was flanked by butcher, baker, small café and the bookshop of an angel. Unlike the other buildings, the bookshop was flamboyantly modern, yet the sparse lines of the newer building blended with the classical proportions of the older shops. It looked like it belonged there, as if the building next door had pupped, and the family resemblance deep in the bones could be seen.

It also, in the best traditions of bookshops, did not open until 11 am.

She settled in the café with an espresso and her notes from the night before, annotating the margins with comments to remind her of expressions, stresses and emphases, all the modulations of an interview that revealed the subject to her readers.

The place was empty but for the single waiter who plied her with coffee and biscotti, and seemed to be constantly on the edge of saying something. Susan wondered whether he was Gerald's lover, full of news and questions, or simply a waiter curious about the only new person in town for months. There seemed no easy way to ask, so she sat and drank another cup and waited for him to make the first move.

A shadow fell across her page, and she looked up into the face of one of the most beautiful men she had ever seen. His nose was strong, his eyebrows perfectly arched, his lustrous hair fell in artful disarray, and his eyes were soft, brown, and fringed with the longest lashes she had ever seen on a man.

It was the sort of face that belonged in a Florentine portrait of the Renaissance.

"No wonder David wanted to paint you," she said.

The man turned sharply to her. "You know David?"

"You know English?" she said. "Sorry, of course you do."

When the man moved closer, his imperfections became apparent. His eyes were shadowed and bruised; his clothes seemed to hang off his frame, and his long, elegant fingers trembled slightly.

"You know David?" he said again, urgently.

"No, I know of him," she said. "I'd like to know more about him."

"I'm not here to satisfy your curiosity," he replied, and turned to leave.

She caught him by the sleeve. "I need to know more about him, I should say."

He looked at her, long and hard, then seemed to find whatever it was he needed in her eyes because he sat down at her table and ordered a coffee from the watching waiter.

"I'm Susan," she said, and held her hand out.

"Ferdie," he replied. His hand was hot, and his fingers had no flesh on them.

"And why do you need to know?" he asked.

"I had a brother, once...."

"Had?"

She nodded. "If someone had believed him when he told his story..."

She let the words hang there between them, and then after a long pause he said, "What do you want to know about David?"

"Everything there is to know." Susan folded up her notebook and slipped it back into her handbag, the pen following after.

He shook his head. "You won't believe me."

"You'll be surprised by what I'll believe," she said. "Try me."

He paused whilst the waiter delivered his coffee, considering what to say. The waiter moved away, staying within earshot, cleaning a table for the second time. Ferdie added three sugars to his drink, stirred it well, then tapped the spoon on the side of the cup to ease off the last drips of coffee.

"Gerald used to come into my bookshop a fair bit," he said. "He liked books on travel, the idea of places he could go to and change his life. This is... was odd. He had the money to travel himself. He didn't need to imagine he could change his life, he had that power anyway. Or so I supposed."

"He'd already tried that once," she murmured, not wanting to break into his flow.

"Yes. There is that." Ferdie took a sip of coffee, and grimaced at the over-sweetness. "But still he came, and still he bought books, and we talked. Finally, one day, he said he had a friend who was looking for a model, a man."

"He suggested you?"

"Not at first. I think he was, what is the expression, testing the waters?"

Susan nodded.

"So, finding I was agreeable, he invited me up to the villa to meet David." Ferdie's hand shook as he put the cup down with a clatter. "I was flattered. Who wouldn't be? An artist wants to paint you. That doesn't happen to most people, and it certainly doesn't happen to people in small towns in Italy."

"What did you think when you met him?"

"I..." Ferdie shook his head. "I didn't think anything, not at first. He was tall, good looking, but a bit pale, and he didn't say much. He wanted to paint me nude, and by candlelight. I didn't want to pose nude, so he did a few sketches of my face, and showed them to me. They were amazing. I looked... it looked like me, but a better me than I had ever seen."

"And so you agreed to pose nude."

"I did."

"I don't think anyone can resist the lure of a really good portrait," Susan said. "And there's nothing wrong with a tasteful nude anyway. I have several on the walls at home."

Ferdie smiled a little. "He promised it would be tasteful, nothing on show, if you know what I mean, but I spent the first few sessions feeling cold and self-conscious, and trying not to scratch every itch or breathe too deeply, so before long I had forgotten I had no clothes on."

He looked at her, large eyes fringed with long lashes. "It is very hard to keep still for longer than a few minutes. Hard, and tiring."

"So, naturally, you felt drained after each session."

He nodded. "And I would tell people it was hard work and they would not believe me, so I stopped telling them about it." He took a deep breath, and let it out slowly. "But after a while I noticed I was getting more and more tired, that it wasn't getting easier. I lost weight, I couldn't eat, and I couldn't sleep. I would fall asleep when posing, or I thought I did.... It's hard to say now, but I started to lose hours at a time. I would go there to sit for David, and the next thing I knew, it was time to leave."

"And then you realised?"

Ferdie snorted. "Not really. There aren't any words to

describe what was happening. Not ones you use in the daylight anyway. But David couldn't help gloating, dropping little hints here and there." Ferdie's voice dropped to a whisper. "He started telling me about an article he'd read about some cultures thinking a photograph could steal your soul."

Ferdie ran his fingers through his hair, tugging an errant curl behind his ear, and stared at his coffee as if it held all the answers. When he looked up again, his face was haunted. "And all the while he was laughing at how stupid anyone would look who believed such nonsense, how we'd moved beyond such primitive beliefs, and how, if you really wanted to steal someone's soul, there would be other ways of doing it that would be far more successful. And all the while his paint brush flicked backwards and forwards across the page, and I knew what he was doing, but I knew that I was powerless to stay away."

He breathed out in a long sigh. "I can't tell you the horror of it. His terrible, pointed smile, and the way he looked at me, the way you look at some piece of meat, a thing to be consumed. It's nothing you can explain: to know that you're prey, and that you're a fly struggling on a web, and the more that you struggle, the more the spider is excited."

Susan reached out and touched Ferdie's arm gently, like stroking a wild animal.

He flinched, balanced on the edge of a half pleasure at a sign of their commonality, but woven through with the apprehension of something alien, as if what he had passed through had stolen his humanity and they were on opposite sides of an impermeable barrier, as if they were already separated by life and death.

His breath came in short gasps, like a man in pain, then his hand closed round hers in a convulsive grip. "He told me because he wanted me to know, to know and not to be able to stop him. It made it sweeter for him."

She held Ferdie's hand, as much for her comfort as his, and

waited for him to gather himself, and continue. "It's sickening," she said softly.

He nodded, beyond words. Another cup of coffee arrived in front of Ferdie, and the waiter squeezed his shoulder as he left.

"Gerald's boyfriend?" she asked.

Ferdie nodded, his expression easing. "He misses him. Gerald doesn't come down to the village that much these days."

"Do you think Gerald knows?"

"Yes. Yes, he does. And he doesn't care." Ferdie swallowed hard, his Adam's apple bobbing. "For him, it's all about the art."

A rapid flood of Italian came from behind Susan's shoulder, prompting Ferdie to shrug. "Angelo wants me to tell you how I got out of there. He wants me to tell you how Gerald saved me."

"And did he?"

"I was fixed there, with the spider coming closer and closer, as the portrait neared completion. As it ended, so would I, I was sure of it. He would not need to keep me alive once it had finished, and yet I couldn't move. His eyes were fixed on mine. He didn't even need to see where he was moving his brush, so sure was he of the ending."

Susan shivered.

Ferdie's lips twisted in a grimace. "I felt weaker and weaker, until I was at the point of fainting like a woman." He caught Susan's expression, and his grimace turned to more of a grin. "Not a modern woman, a woman from the past, before they were so brave. And so prickly."

Susan grinned back.

"So," he said. "I nearly fainted, like a woman from out of history, and then there were voices. David was arguing with someone, so it must have been Gerald. I couldn't follow it all; they were speaking so quickly, but..."

Angelo said something else.

"*Si,*" Ferdie hissed. "Yes, yes, Gerald said something about me feeling unwell, and David should stop, he'd worked me too hard, and then Gerald called a taxi to take me home. And home I went.

"I've never been back."

"That seems very sensible," she said.

"I see his eyes whenever I try to sleep." The simple words contained a world of terror. "I'll never be free of them."

A note was waiting for Susan when she went back to the hotel. She was to come to the house at sunset to be introduced to David, who was intrigued by the news of a reporter. She was not to write about him, of course, but he would be happy to share some of his work with her.

She had enough time to bathe, to dress and eat an early dinner before the taxi arrived to take her up to the gates at the end of the drive.

There was, she thought, something of the horror film cliché about the whole trip. The arrival of the young, innocent woman at the castle gates just as the sun set, abandoned by the nervous peasant who drove off at speed into the night to leave her to her fate.

It was only faintly undermined by the driver leaving her his mobile number to call when she was ready to be picked up, and the loud blare of his car stereo as he raced away down the road.

She passed through the gates and into the grounds.

The last of the summer sun gilded the trees that led up to the house, leaving dark shadows tinged with orange clawing across the path. A stone archway was barred by a rusted iron gate which resisted her push, but eventually gave way to let her through to the back garden. She threaded her way through the low box hedges of the knot garden to the terrace, and then up to the open French doors.

She coughed.

"How very polite of you."

Susan turned sharply to find a stranger draped elegantly over a stone bench, deep in the shadows.

"How very posed of you," she replied. "You must be David."

"And you must be Susan," he said, copying her tone perfectly in conscious irony.

"Yes, I really must."

He pushed himself up from the bench, still careful to stay in the darkness. "I can see we're going to get on."

"Like the proverbial house on fire," she replied.

Gerald appeared at the door, looking like an anxious mother watching her child take his first steps in the world. "Er, I can see I'm too late to make introductions."

"But not too late to offer us a drink," David said easily. "I've a real thirst."

Gerald stumbled, and put out a hand to steady himself on the sofa. "I suppose you'll want red wine?"

"Of course," David said.

"Is that all right with you, Susan?" Gerald picked up a bottle of wine from the side table and waggled it at her. "It's been breathing for an hour or two. I could get some white, if you'd prefer."

"How could she prefer white?" David sauntered into the room with all the conscious grace of a cat. "Insipid stuff. You can barely taste the blood of the wine."

"Red will be fine," Susan said.

Gerald waved her into a seat and passed her a large glass half-full of wine.

David arranged his long limbs on the arm chair opposite, carefully laying down his book on the table to the side before taking his glass from Gerald. "Do sit down. You're making the place look untidy."

Gerald poured himself a drink, fuller than the others, almost touching the rim of the glass, and sat next to Susan on the sofa. "Cheers!"

"What are you reading, if you don't mind me asking?" Susan said.

"Dorian Grey," David replied, smiling archly. "You may have heard of it. I find it interesting from an artist's perspective, this fear that having your likeness captured means that something of your self has been caught."

"It's just a primitive belief," Gerald said, then took a long swallow of his wine.

"Oh we always have this argument. It may be primitive, but it's no less profound for that," David replied. "The really deep fears are primitive. They're what motivate people—fear…"

"Love," said Susan.

"Oh let's not give things pretty names to give them a better colour. Lust," said David. "Hunger. *Revenge.*"

"Had some bad reviews recently?" Susan said. "It's my experience that artists get convinced of the ineluctable cruelties of human nature just about the time they get a review calling their work derivative."

Gerald laughed. "Oh that's very true. It's amazing how very much that sours your view of humanity."

"Humanity is nothing more than a collection of primitive urges," David straightened in his chair and leaned forward, prodding the air to emphasise his words. "Pretty window dressing won't change that."

"And you're so very different?" Susan asked.

"Well, now, there's a question." David leaned back in his chair gain, a smile playing on his lips. "What do you think?"

"Oh I think you're projecting," she returned coolly. "It's not humanity, but yourself that you're talking about. People are more than appetites. They are rich, confusing, puzzling bundles of contradictions, and not to be fitted into your casual pigeonholes."

"Ah, you would say that, you're only human." David

gestured impatiently.

"And you're not?" Susan said.

Gerald made a small, choked noise from the side of her.

"Of course not." David twisted his mouth in a smile, his eyes still hard and cold. "I'm an artist. We're a breed apart, aren't we Gerald?"

"Er, yes." Gerald nodded his head, eyes wild. "Something like that anyway."

"Are you really an artist though, if people don't see your work?" Susan asked. "Aren't you just a painter?"

"Just a painter?" David leaned forward again, mouth open to continue the argument.

"It's an interesting question," Gerald said, smoothly interrupting the brewing tirade. "Even if there were such a thing as just a painter, the difference between being a painter and an artist isn't the presence of an audience, but whether it's something you enjoy doing or something you need to do. Like breathing."

"Or feeding," Susan said

David closed his mouth with a snap.

"But you said that David was the better painter," Susan continued.

"I did." Gerald took a long drink from his glass, brow furrowed. "He is. It's just... I wonder how much of that is hollow. It's practice and longevity, not from the heart and soul." He shook his head, as if trying to clear it of troubling thoughts. "In the end, is that enough?"

"It's hard to say." Susan swirled the wine round in her glass, watching David's expression out of the corner of her eyes. "There's many a talented draughtsman who is missing the special something that makes a great artist—too much concentration on detail, without the ability to stand back and see the wider picture."

"What would you know about that, Gerald?" David said, his voice low and hard. "You've not painted anything for years."

Gerald went white, his fingers tightening round his glass, almost to the point of snapping the stem. "I've painted things."

"One thing," David said. "Over and over again. That doesn't smack to me of distance."

"I...." Gerald put his glass down, and folded his arms across his body. "I have painted some very fine landscapes."

David made a dismissive noise. "You've copied some very fine landscapes."

Gerald sucked in a breath. "We may have worked together on some aspects of my work, nothing more."

David laughed bitterly. "Why don't we let Susan be the judge of that?"

"But..." Gerald said.

"This is strictly off the record," Susan put in. "No one would believe me anyway."

"You assume that we will let you leave here alive," David said, in the same sort of tone he had used to discuss his reading habits.

"This is the point where I mention the sealed envelope," Susan said. "Left with someone reliable to pass on if I don't return."

"As you said, no one would believe you," David said, impatiently twirling his glass.

"I wasn't stupid enough to say I suspect you of being a vampire," Susan replied. "I'm not an idiot."

Gerald gave a bark of laughter, on the cusp of hysteria. "If you came here, knowing what you know, you really are an idiot."

Susan shrugged. "I'm a reporter. In the same way you need to paint, I need to know."

"Then know you shall." David waved towards the doorway. "Come into my... lair, I suppose you could call it."

Gerald swore under his breath, then levered himself unsteadily out of the sofa, clearly well on the way to being drunk before Susan's arrival had interrupted his evening. "Yes, do come and see the studio. You won't see it at its best at night, of course. It has fabulous light in the morning, not that you'd know about that, David."

Susan followed them through the door, and along a low-ceilinged passage to the front of the house. A faded blue door was half open, showing a hint of the room beyond.

David pushed it fully open with a dramatic flourish and gestured for Susan to go through first. "Manners are so important, don't you think? It's what separates us from the animals."

Susan stared at his face, with its sharp edges and fierce eyes, and shuddered. David gave an odd hissing laugh, then followed her through the door. Susan's hair stood up on end at the thought of him behind her, like a rabbit knowing it was being watched by something inimical and cruel.

The room had bare floorboards, smeared with paint. A drying rack at the far end held a series of paintings, there was a row of canvases along one wall in various stages of stretching and priming, and a bucket stuffed with paint brushes giving off a strong smell of turps.

In the centre of the room, an easel held a canvas, flanked by two battered wooden stools. An artist's palette covered in oils was resting on one stool, and a jar of turps and some old rags on the other.

"Those in the racks, those are Gerald's landscapes, poor things that they are. You will see that there is only one easel set up," David said. "Mine."

Susan moved away from David and further into the room, peering at the painting. "Ferdie's portrait," she said.

"Oh, you heard about that, did you?" David's smile grew wider and more cruel. "It's not finished, but you knew that."

Susan nodded. It was a fine piece of work, full of rich colours, warmth and life, until you looked closely at Ferdie's face. The eyes were fixed and glazed, hardly aware, and he looked tired and drawn. His left arm was draped over the side of the sofa, and dangled limply, almost as if he was dead already.

And there, on his neck, were two faint marks, and the barest smudge of red.

"I'll never be able to show it," David said. "But it is a masterpiece."

"It's horrible," Gerald said.

"But powerful," David replied. "Art shouldn't always be about beauty and life."

"It rarely is these days," Susan said dryly. "There's been a competition going since the 1960s to see who can make the ugliest piece of art, it's just no one's told the viewing public about it."

Gerald snorted, and then flinched back from David's glare as it if had been a blow.

"You sound like a philistine, Susan," David said. "Are you a philistine? And here I was thinking you were all cultured, being an arts reporter."

"Oh I am cultured," she said. "Which is why I can recognise this for meretricious nonsense. Oh the brushwork is good enough, but the subject matter is banal and uninspiring. You show us nothing about the subject of the work. The object, I should say. You reduce Ferdie, all his hopes and dreams, to nothing more than a block of meat. Dinner. And that tells us a lot about you, and nothing about him."

"All portraits tell you more about the artist than the sitter," Gerald said, shifting his weight from one leg to another uneasily, torn between going and staying.

"But this tells us nothing we didn't know before," Susan said. "Nothing we couldn't tell from looking at David himself. He's a parasite, living off others."

"I really don't think that's fair," said Gerald. "He gives something back. To me, at least. I can't paint without him...."

"Shut up." David put his hand up, palm upright, to silence

him. "Don't interrupt Susan, she's just getting started."

Susan moved closer to the painting, resting her fingers on the jar of turps. "There's not a lot more to say. It's just not interesting enough to move me to words."

David straightened, his whole body stiff with outrage. "Are you calling me boring?"

"I am." Susan looked at him through hooded eyes. "Boring. Banal. Evil so often is. It lacks… greatness."

Gerald put a hand out to restrain David, who shook it off and stepped forward.

The air seemed to have left the room. Susan's chest was tight with fear and fury, and determination to see this monster buried. She shoved her hand in her pocket, bringing out a lighter. Her other hand clasped the turps jar, and in one swift movement she emptied the contents over the painting and held the lighter close to the canvas until the fluid caught alight.

There was a whoomph of noise as the fire expanded, rippling over the surface of the canvas, turning it dark.

"You bitch," snarled David.

"I think that's your cue to say something about how I'll pay for that," Susan replied, edging towards the corner of the room.

The lights in the studio fractured in the heat, and the room darkened, lit only be the fading, flickering bonfire of David's art.

"If you think that's going to save Ferdie…" David advanced on her, growing taller and more monstrous with each step, seeming to have wings of darkness streaming out behind him, his teeth glowing white and sharp. "It's not the portrait you have to worry about, you stupid woman."

"Never thought it would…" Susan replied, backing further away.

Gerald rushed forward, dabbing ineffectually at the painting with a cloth, trying to put the flames out. David turned his head, distracted by the movement, and Susan seized her chance. Her fingers closed round the handle of the bucket of turps. She hefted it upwards in a swinging motion, and let go.

The bucket rose high and wide, describing a perfect arc, then connected with David's outstretched arm, put out to defend himself against the attack. Turps splashed along his arms and torso, and the bucket fell to the floor at his feet with a thump.

"Missed," he said. He tilted his head on one side, like some wild animal contemplating the kill, and smiled.

"Christ, David, watch out!" Gerald cried. "The fire…"

David turned sharply, spraying turps still more widely. The air, saturated with turps vapour, ignited with a sharp crack, engulfing him in flames. He turned back to Susan, took three shaky steps forward, and then fell face down on the floor.

There was another rush of fire as he toppled, which spread out across the room in search of more fuel. The flames licked at the canvases, then leaped up to the curtains, which caught light. Other tendrils of fire sought out the oil paints, which exploded with a pop. The canvases in the drying rack were soon ablaze, making a ring of fire around the David's prone body which lay still and unmoving in the centre of the room.

Susan moved to the other wall, coughing and spluttering. Her eyes were watering from the smoke which had quickly filled the room, making it hard to see. She was vaguely aware of another shape moving around in the partial darkness as she groped her way to the door.

There was a terrible wailing coming from the centre of the room, and it took her a couple of minutes to realise it was Gerald, screaming. "My work, my paintings, all gone."

"For God's sake, leave it," she shouted.

At first she thought he'd listened to her, but as he loomed up at her through the billowing fumes he swung at her.

"You killed him," he shouted. "And now I'll never paint

anything again."

"Of course you will. Who do you think was stopping you from painting?" she shrieked, ducking back from his fist. "Now, let's get out of here. That stuff about art being more important than life? It's just bollocks. Unless you really want to die for your art."

Susan had a moment of panic, wondering whether he would see sense now that David's influence was ended, or whether he'd lost his reason completely.

"The fire's reached the door," he said. "We can't get out that way."

"Windows?" she said.

"It's worth a try," he replied.

They placed their backs against the wall to orient themselves in the room, then struck out blindly for the other side, ducking down low in an attempt to avoid the worst of the smoke. Stumbling and slipping, they managed to reach the far wall, and paused to catch their breath.

Gerald rattled the window, which refused to move.

"It's bloody locked," he said. "And I don't know where the key is."

Susan reached down, groping in the darkness to find something, anything, heavy enough to break the window. Her fingers closed round something hefty, and she grasped hold of a piece of wood. She swung at the window and fractured it in a shower of glass, then swung again to clear as much of the remaining glass as possible. Fresh air came flooding through the hole, giving them a welcome respite, but also adding oxygen to the fire, which flared higher.

"I'll give you a leg up," Gerald said. "Then you can pull me through."

He made a cradle with his hands, and she stepped into it. He straightened up with a grunt of effort, and she managed to get herself halfway through the window. She shuffled along, balancing her weight on her hands, then scrambled up, swinging a leg over the windowsill to leave her perched halfway to freedom.

She looked down at Gerald.

His face was streaked with tear tracks through the smuts. She could feel her lips curling back in a snarl, furious that he had sheltered David.

"Please," he said.

For a moment she sat there, scratched and dripping blood, and thought how easy it would be to leave him there, and everything went still and quiet. This, then, was how it felt to be David, to think you had the right to hold others' lives in your palm.

And then the world came back in an avalanche of sensation and she held out her hand.

She braced herself against Gerald's weight. He put his foot on the wall and scrabbled for purchase, once, twice, and then finally came up with a rush as Susan leaned further out. His momentum carried them forward, and they both fell out of the window onto the gravel path beneath.

Susan heaved herself on all fours and coughed.

Gerald flopped on his back and put an arm across his face, wiping the smoke from his eyes. A long gash marked his forearm, and his shirt was torn to ribbons, showing the scratched flesh beneath. From the distance, a siren could be heard getting closer and closer.

"Shit," said Gerald. "How the hell am I going to explain this?"

"Accident in the studio," Susan said, and coughed again. Her hands had been scoured by the gravel, and they looked like they had been sandpapered.

"And they're going to believe that?" Gerald said, his face still covered.

"Well, it's a better story than a flaming vampire."

"True."

Gerald turned onto his stomach, wincing as his cuts made

contact with the earth, and eyed Susan warily. "You were tempted to leave me in there, weren't you?"

Susan nodded. "I was."

"Why didn't you?"

"Because David would have done."

Gerald closed his eyes, his face contorted in some terrible expression caught on the cusp of pain and relief. "Yes, he would."

They said nothing more as the sirens came closer then stopped. The sound of rushing feet heralded the arrival of the firemen. The chief shouted orders at his men, who busied themselves with hoses, and water, and putting out the fire.

"You're all right," a fireman said. "There's no one else inside?"

"No, there's no one," Gerald said. "It's just some bloody paintings, nothing important."

There was a seat in the garden, just away from all the fuss of the firemen. Susan and Gerald settled there to watch the comings and goings of the fire crew. They were bound together by a common experience and terrible knowledge, even though they were—had been, Susan supposed—on opposite sides.

"If this was England," Gerald said. "Someone would have offered us a cup of tea by now."

"I could kill for a cup of tea," Susan said, and then laughed. "Kill. I should have asked David for a cup then."

"He wasn't very domestic," Gerald said. "I don't think he knew where the kitchen was."

"I can't believe you think that's an appropriate thing to say, after all this," Susan replied, waving at the studio where the last of the fire was being dampened down.

"You brought up the tea."

Susan could find nothing to say to that. It was true, and utterly irrelevant.

"Do you really think that I'll be able to paint again?" Gerald asked.

"Is that all you care about?" Susan twisted in her seat to stare at him.

"Mostly. It's all there is. Art."

"You never asked me my brother's name," Susan said.

Gerald stared at her, face pale.

"It was Mark," she said. "You knew him rather well once."

LIBBY WEBER

The Skin of My Teeth

I'm not going to say that Greg Samsa was a good guy. Too much water under that particular bridge. But when you've spent as much time on and in the Pacific Ocean as I have, you know words like good and bad are fluid, because there's no controlling nature. Now, you can perform experiments and collect data and be prepared for anything that's ever happened to anybody else. That's prudent. That's smart. But you can never eliminate all the variables, and that's a lesson that Greg had to learn the hard way.

It all started one rainy Tuesday night. Larry and I were at Harvey's place. The game was euchre, and the stakes were high: a bottle of orange liqueur and dinner at Tako Sushi to the winning couple, not to mention bragging rights. Harvey and Frances led by five points, and Larry, the knucklehead, had chosen to play my weak suit. I had the left bower, but Frances forced me to play it early on by trumping Larry's ace. It wasn't looking good.

Harvey stopped the game to visit the little boys' room, and when he came back, he refilled my peach schnapps and put a specimen bottle containing a single shark's tooth on the table in front of me. The tooth had clearly seen better days, since the mesial edge had been sheared off, but the compound comb shape made IDing the shark easy. Bluntnose sixgill: deep water dweller, rises to the surface at night to hunt. Ignores people for the most part—only one provoked attack in centuries. And yet, the bottle had the medical examiner's address and a case number stamped on the lid, which meant Harvey had probably found the tooth embedded in someone's remains. Odd. A mystery, even.

"Had an interesting day of beachcombing?" I asked, leading with my highest trump.

"I take it you heard about the shark attack at Royston Cove," said Harvey, heartlessly taking the trick.

"Yeah, I heard about it." Of course I had. I'd provided sound bites for two network affiliates that were covering the story as a great white attack. I ought to have known a high-profile case like that would go directly to Harvey.

Frances clicked her tongue sympathetically, for all that she was practically trembling in anticipation of the win. "Such a tragedy," she said. "The poor man was in training for Ironman Lake Tahoe, and then this happens. He had three children."

"The shark that left this tooth behind didn't kill him," I said. "If I had to guess, I'd say it's from an average-sized *Hexanchus griseus*, a bluntnose sixgill shark. They've never caused a human fatality."

"Until now," said Larry, surprising everybody by successfully taking a trick with a low trump.

"That remains to be seen," said Harvey. At this, he laid down the rest of his cards, which contained enough high cards to take all the rest of the tricks.

"Well done, darling!" exclaimed Frances. She and Harvey only needed two more points to win, and she pantomimed barn doors opening with particular relish. The way their luck was running, they would probably win on the next deal.

Harvey began to shuffle the cards. "The tooth was embedded in the victim's left leg, but it wasn't that bite that killed him. There was a prior strike that severed the femoral artery of the right leg, which caused fatal blood loss. But the muscle tissue of the leg where the tooth was found was partially eaten."

It was my turn to frown. I'd heard of cases where sixgills were suspects when shark-bite victims had been blundering about in a school of prey fish, but this was entirely different.

"Don't killer sharks usually eat people?" asked Larry, declining to cut the shuffled cards that Harvey offered him. He still had his pride, after all.

"They don't generally like how humans taste, sweetcheeks," I said, accepting my new cards and sorting them by suit. "Attacks on humans are usually a case of mistaken identity. Unfortunately, with larger sharks, a curious nibble can be fatal to the nibblee."

"And you're positive this tooth didn't come from a white shark?" asked Harvey.

"Suit, dear?" prompted Frances.

Harvey flipped over the top card. "Ten of clubs."

"Order up, Harv," I said. "And yes, I'm certain. I'll be happy to come in tomorrow and make it official."

Harvey nodded and put the ten of clubs into his hand. "Good. When can I expect you?"

"I'm giving a presentation for the AP Bio class at Del Mar High from ten to noon," I said. "Not a glamorous gig, but it pays the bills between grants and Shark Weeks. I'll swing by in the early afternoon."

"Thanks, Megan," said Harvey. "Your play."

I slapped down the right bower and took the trick. "What little expertise I have is always at your disposal."

I often dream of sharks. Learning what makes them tick is my life's work. But that night, I dreamed I was playing euchre with a shortfin mako, a white shark, and a bluntnose sixgill. The sixgill and I won, but then the white shark slapped the table with its caudal fin, bit the sixgill's head, and shook it violently until it stopped thrashing.

Maybe I shouldn't have hit the peach schnapps quite so

hard.

I drove to Royston Cove after meeting with Harvey. Examination of the body had confirmed my suspicions: the damage done by the sixgill had been post-mortem. Our killer shark was, in fact, the usual suspect: *Carcharodon carcharias*, aka, the "great" white. The bite circumference pointed at an individual somewhere north of fourteen feet long, which narrowed our list of suspects considerably, and an eyewitness statement from one of the lifeguards confirmed the appearance and hunting behavior of a white shark. At least we had a cause of death to give the widow and children, but I knew that wasn't the whole story. Harvey didn't care—additional gnawing by a shark or sharks unknown wasn't relevant to his work. Thankfully, he knew that it was highly relevant to mine and summarized his postmortem notes for me while I thumbed through the police report. All of this sat very oddly with me, and I knew I had to visit the scene of the attack to see if I could figure out what we'd both missed.

The weather at the cove was perfect: low 80s, not a cloud in the sky, but the parking lot was practically empty, thanks to a slew of yellow and red signs announcing that the beach was closed due to a shark attack. I followed the signs down to a short, broad wedge of sand at the base of the Linda Beach bluffs. It's quiet. Secluded. A few offshore sand bars and small reefs, so decent for surfing. All but cut off from the rest of the shoreline at high tide. The lifeguard station was flying a red flag to announce the beach closure to boats offshore.

As my feet hit the sand, I heard the sound of guitar music. It wasn't a song I recognized, but I knew it was being played well. To my surprise, the music was coming from the lifeguard station, where a young man in red board shorts and a white T-shirt sat absently plucking the strings, even as his eyes scanned the empty swells.

Now, I've lived by the sea my whole life and can usually

take or leave a beach bum, but there was something about the guy, with those long, golden legs, sun-streaked blond hair, and nimble fingers that made my mouth go dry. Before I knew it, I was standing at the foot of the ramp that led up to where he sat. He fixed startlingly green eyes on me.

"The beach is closed," he said. "A great white's been active in the neighborhood."

"I know," I said, finding my voice at last and handing him my card. "Megan Doyle. Shark Research Association."

"Lifeguard Lieutenant Greg Samsa," he said, setting his guitar aside and reaching down to shake my hand. "What can I do for you?"

I smiled at my luck—his name had been on the police report as the primary witness on the scene. "I"d like to ask you a few questions about the day Perry de Nardo was killed."

"I've already spoken with the medical examiner and the police."

"My organization tracks data on shark attacks. We're trying to better understand shark behavior and predict which places are likely to see multiple attacks," I said. "The medical examiner thinks the victim died from a white shark bite."

He nodded. "That's pretty much what I told them. So, what would you like to know?"

I handed him a map of the cove and asked him to identify the approximate location of the attack and the water conditions. I already knew the latter from the tide tables and surf reports, but it was good to have the information corroborated or any inconsistencies noted. Part of me was disappointed that Greg was very thorough and that he even pointed out a feature of my map that was out of date after a big storm last winter.

He made me uneasy, despite his helpfulness. At first, I attributed this to his looks. It's easier to deal with beautiful people when they have obvious personality flaws. In retrospect, I know it wasn't just his proportions and startling green eyes that were so attractive. Even now that I know what he was, thinking about him still gives me a disconcerting sense of warmth and security, an undeniable sense that the shore was his natural habitat and that I was welcome there.

But long story short: I liked the guy's looks, he was smart enough, and he seemed to be in a helpful mood, so I pressed him on the detail that was troubling me. In general terms, I asked if he'd seen any other kind of shark in the area. I didn't mention the sixgill for fear of influencing his recollection.

"Sure," he said, stretching his arms over his head, which pulled his shirt sleeves tight against his gently swelling biceps. "We get inundated with leopard sharks during pupping season."

I reluctantly tore my eyes away from his arms and gazed out at the water. "Any others?" I asked.

He looked thoughtful. "I suppose it's possible that we get other deep water visitors besides the great whites," he said. "In fact, I'd wager that of the handful of sightings we get around this time of year, most are probably something else. But the only shark I saw that day was the great white. Besides, if you were a smaller shark, would you be out in the open when there's a great white nearby?"

"I suppose not," I said, trying not to show my disappointment. "It was pretty brave of you to go in after Perry de Nardo."

He ran a hand up and down the side of his neck before the easy smile returned. "I wasn't really in danger because I was on a personal watercraft," he said, jerking his head towards a nearby trailer that held an orange-and-white jet ski. "The great white would have gotten a mouthful of gasoline for his trouble if he'd attacked me. Besides, even if it was brave, it was all for nothing. Perry de Nardo is still dead, and that's something I have to live with."

"Don't beat yourself up," I said. "People die."

"Not on my watch," he said. "I've been a lifeguard for a long time, and I've never had to deal with a fatality before. We've had some close calls, sure, but never a death."

I tried not to imagine him running out of the ocean with rivulets of seawater running down his pectorals. I failed. "You do good work," I said. "It's not easy to save people from their own stupidity."

He gave me a sad smile. "Don't I know it."

"Do you mind if I have a look around?" I asked.

"As long as you stay out of the water, go for it," he said, taking up his guitar once more. "I don't want that great white to think Royston Cove is a buffet."

His music followed me down the steps to the beach. Despite not knowing the song, I found myself humming along as I strolled along the shore, careful not to let my good teaching shoes come in contact with the water.

I walked south until I came to the cliff face that marked the edge of the cove and gazed out at the water, where the sun danced on the crests of the waves and shone through them in the moment before they broke. Nothing unusual above the water, and having reviewed seafloor maps of the cove, I knew there was nothing unusual under it, either. I sighed and headed back to the steps, fully intending to leave.

But as I put my foot on the first step, I heard a voice on the wind and realized that Greg was singing. I'm no expert, but I know what I like, and whatever he was singing, I liked it. I liked it a whole lot. I liked it so much I froze in my tracks to listen. I couldn't hear the words, but his voice rose and fell like the tides, carrying with it all the flotsam and jetsam of a life filled with heartbreak.

I glanced over my shoulder at the sea, and to my surprise, the waves seemed to part, as if inviting me in. Fascinated, I walked toward the surf, and as I stepped between the waves, foam danced around me, caressing my arms and legs before withdrawing into the walls of water. The gulls' crying sounded like voices raised in a song of joy and welcome. A path of shining sand stretched out in front of me, welcoming, beckoning, and the ocean closed in behind me, enveloping me in a safe cocoon of sunlit seawater. Up until that point, I thought there was little the Pacific could do to surprise me. But walking through the parted waves at Royston Cove like Moses through the Red Sea was the weirdest, most beautiful thing I've ever done.

But then the music stopped, and the walls of water rushed in on me with a dull roar.

Now, as you may have guessed, I'm a fair swimmer. I'm strong. I know the ocean. That's why I immediately knew that the powerful rip current I was in couldn't be fought. I moved my arms and legs only enough to keep my head above the cresting waves and let the current pull me out past the surf zone. Once I was beyond it, I knew I could swim parallel to the beach until it was safe to cut shore-ward, provided a certain large cartilaginous fish didn't decide to pay a call.

Thoughts of the white shark had no sooner flooded my bloodstream with adrenaline than I heard an engine buzz and saw Greg Samsa approaching on the jet ski. He tossed me a red rescue float that was leashed to his bare torso. I couldn't help but admire the view.

"Grab hold!" he shouted. "You can't fight the rip current!"

"I figured," I said, trying to sound nonchalant and failing.

He towed me over to him and helped me clamber aboard. He looked disapprovingly at my feet. "You didn't kick off your shoes?"

"I'm not going to lose my best work shoes on account of a bit of a rip current," I said.

"Are you completely insane?"

"Not usually," I said. "Did you see what the water did just now?"

His expression was so bewildered that I double-checked my own memory of the incident to ensure that I hadn't made it up. "Did you hit your head on something?" he asked.

I was about to press the issue further, but the more I thought about the welcoming waters, the crazier I knew I would sound. "You didn't need to come all this way, sweetheart," I said. "I'd have been fine. I know how to deal with a rip current."

"And I'm sure you'd have been able to swim around it after having your leg bitten off by a shark," he said shortly as he started up the jet ski's engine. I gotta admit, it was pretty humiliating having to be rescued like some useless damsel, especially when a pair of beach joggers stopped and applauded as Greg pulled parallel to shore.

Greg wrapped his arms around my waist and pulled me off the jet ski, and as the circle of his arms closed around me, my embarrassment and confusion crystallized into panic.

My body gave a jerk even as I tried to suppress the irrational urge to fight him, realizing belatedly whose arms Greg reminded me of. My heart was beating so hard it felt like it was going to break through my ribcage, and black patches swam in my peripheral vision. As I clung to consciousness, I repeated my mantra: Conan is dead. Conan is dead.

Thankfully, the terror began to subside when Greg released me and gestured for me to follow him back to the lifeguard station. I gave myself a mental shake and wrapped my arms around myself so he wouldn't see my shaking hands. I'd felt sudden spikes in emotion like that before, but not for a long time.

Once we were back at the lifeguard station, Greg handed me a towel. "What the hell were you thinking going into the water like that?"

"I wasn't," I admitted. I didn't like how my voice trembled, but there was nothing I could do about that. "I don't know exactly what happened."

"I ought to cite you for failing to follow official signage and lifeguard instructions," he said.

I shoved my hands into my wet pockets. "Sounds about

right."

He let me go with a slap on the wrist. Part of me was hoping for a reproachful "Don't ever scare me like that again." Still, most of me was relieved to be away from him and away from the water. My hands shook for hours.

Larry wasn't amused when I told him about what had happened. Said I was stupid and it'd have served me right if I'd been eaten by a shark. I thought about trying to explain how the weird music had enticed me into the water, but I decided against it. Larry's a bright kid, but more than a bit skeptical about the supernatural, which is just how I like them. So I let him fuss and mix me a tequila sunrise.

Larry stayed with me that night, but after he had gone to sleep, I went into the spare bedroom and opened the closet. Beneath the assorted sporting equipment was a shoebox containing a pair of old boots that needed to be resoled. Inside the left boot was my cuff bracelet.

I pulled it out and buried my fingers in the velvety, spotted fur. The skin inside was still impossibly soft, as if it hadn't been decades since I'd touched it. I usually avoided the feelings that the cuff aroused in me, but today they were a comfort.

I sank to the floor, cradling the cuff in my hands. I could hear the sea singing a song of home. But even as I let my memory wander corridors I'd closed off ages ago, a pair of green eyes glowed malevolently in the distance, and I jerked back to the present.

I cursed myself for not realizing it sooner: there was something of the fey in Greg Samsa, and I didn't like it. I didn't leave Ireland all those years ago for my health.

I turned the cuff inside-out so the dangerous sealskin was facing outward and slid it onto my wrist. Now that I had been taken unawares at least once, I knew I should be prepared for anything.

The next day, I called my friend Bonnie at Linda Beach

Parks and Rec about shark sightings and the frequency of lifeguard rescues, which confirmed one of my suspicions, after which I called Harvey to talk about what I'd found. He gave me a hard time when I told him I'd ended up in the drink at Royston Cove. Told me I should wear a life vest at all times if that's the sort of thing that happens to me. He's a real kidder, Harvey. But his ribbing gave me an idea.

The president of the Shark Research Association owns a 21-foot Bayliner called *Once Bitten, Twice Shy* that's equipped with a pretty pricey GPS sonar fish finder. Says it's a decent commercial option for tracking sharks and prey species, but the only species I've known him to track with it are yellowtail, bluefin, and bigeye on fishing trips with the SRA's biggest private donors. Fortunately, the president was off looking for whale sharks near Antarctica, the office was deserted, and the boat key was in the top drawer of his desk.

It was mostly sunny, but there was a stiff breeze on the water that made it feel unseasonably cool. It reminded me a bit of home, for all that I wished it didn't. I knew that if I had half a brain, I wouldn't be going anywhere near Royston Cove or Greg Samsa. But curiosity, scientific and otherwise, overpowered my sense of self-preservation, despite the previous day's unpleasantness.

If I could catch that bluntnose sixgill in the act of hunting during the daytime, there would probably be a paper in it for me, and papers about weird behavior got us donors and spots on Shark Week. And if the sixgill was long gone, at least I had evidence of its presence, which would be valuable to the association. As I motored northward through choppy water, I couldn't suppress the excitement that was building in my gut, despite my misgivings.

The water wasn't all that deep, but a storm far offshore had kicked up the surf, so visibility was poor. The fish finder was a godsend. Besides having a GPS to help hold position over the site of the attack, it was the nicest bit of recreational sonar I'd ever seen. The screen lit up like a Christmas tree when a school of herring brushed the edge of its range. If my sixgill was anywhere to be found, I'd find it.

I dropped anchor about a hundred yards off Royston Cove, where the depth was about forty feet. I took a glance through my binoculars back at the shore and saw the red flag still flying from the lifeguard station and Greg strumming his guitar, staring out at the sea. There were now dozens of signs about the beach closure stuck on posts in the sand, just in case anybody was considering a repeat of my performance yesterday. Chagrined, I put down my binoculars, grabbed my clipboard, and hunched over the fish finder's screen. I had a bucket of bait fish to attract larger predators, but I wanted to get a baseline of local fish activity before doing so.

It was pleasantly mind-numbing work, and I'd been taking notes for about twenty minutes before the radio crackled to life.

"*Once Bitten, Twice Shy,* this is lifeguard station fourteen, do you copy?"

Uh oh. "Affirmative, station fourteen. This is *Once Bitten, Twice Shy.* I read you loud and clear."

"Megan, is that you? It's Greg."

"Affirmative, Greg," I said, trying to sound breezy and nonchalant. "Fancy meeting you here."

"You're not planning to go for another swim, are you?" he asked. "The beach is still closed, and I will cite you this time."

"Not to worry, station fourteen," I said. "Today's mission is exploratory and boring."

"Fishing for calico?"

"No, I'm in search of larger quarry today."

"The great white."

"No," I said. "His accomplice."

"Accomplice? There was only one shark."

"That you saw," I said, "but a second one left a calling card on the body in the form of a tooth. I wouldn't have credited finding a bluntnose sixgill hunting the shallows, especially during the day, but that's what the evidence indicates. Besides, it's a nice day, my boss is out of town, and I don't have any other pressing engagements."

There was a prolonged silence over the radio, and I glanced through my binoculars at the shore. I didn't see Greg. I figured he'd gone in to where the radio was. "You still with me, station fourteen?"

"Sorry, *Once Bitten, Twice Shy*, emergency up at the breaks. Stay out of the water. I repeat, stay out of the water."

"Roger that," I said, hoping the emergency wasn't another white shark attack. "You don't have to tell me twice. Over and out."

Through my binoculars, I watched Greg shed his shirt, wheel his personal watercraft to the shore, then buzz away to the north, where he disappeared around the far side of the point.

I was more than a bit relieved that Greg was out of the picture. Just the memory of what yesterday had kicked up in me made me feel sick to my stomach. I bent over the fish finder screen once more and took note of what was below my boat for the next half hour: some wrasse lurking near a lonely pile of rocks, a huge black sea bass sunning itself nearby, a couple schools of anchovies that a flock of pelicans was dive bombing. Suddenly my screen lit up as something large appeared at two points to starboard at the edge of my sonar's range, and then it was gone. It was too small to be a white shark, and too big to be a leopard shark.

I got out my camera and tossed some of the bait overboard in hopes of bringing the large fish closer. I waited, keeping an eye on the fish finder and my camera aimed at the bait, which was sinking slowly into the water.

There it was! The sonar confirmed my size estimate, and I saw it approach the boat at a stately pace—they're not called cow sharks for nothing. Olive gray, about ten feet long. It fit the specs, but I needed to document the number of gill slits to be sure. I had to get it to break the surface. I tossed another handful of bait into the water and was rewarded by a dramatic swish of the caudal fin, which gave me a shot of the shark's small dorsal fin. Another positive sign. I kept taking pictures, the artificial shutter sound clicking every few seconds as the shark hunted for the fish that I was tossing overboard with my other hand.

Finally, the thrashing shark's side broke the surface of the water, and I saw the rounded snout, an electric green ovoid eye, and six large gill slits that positively identified my quarry. My heart nearly stopped. Had I managed to get a money shot of the gills? I tore my eyes away from the feeding shark, looked at my most recent shot, and there it was: unmistakably a bluntnose sixgill feeding in broad daylight. I let out a whoop and tossed the rest of my bait into the water before taking my soundings once more for the official record.

And then I saw it: a huge shape approaching from the southwest, headed directly toward the boat. I cursed my stupidity. I had meant to attract the bluntnose sixgill, but I'd also managed to lead one of the sixgill's few predators directly to him. The sixgill was still nosing around for bait fish. The poor slow bastard didn't have a chance.

For the second time in as many days, I didn't think. I just reacted.

I ripped off my clothes and dove into the water a few feet away from the sixgill, and then I did something I promised myself I'd never do again after leaving Ireland. I twisted my sealskin cuff so the skin side was touching my human skin and transformed.

Now, let me tell you one thing about being a human in seal's clothing: it's not nearly as great as it sounds. Sure, you have all the advantages of a seal in the water, and nothing tastes as good as fish you've caught with your own teeth, but you've still got all the hang-ups of a human, and every major predator has it in for you, humans included. At least real seals have the benefit of the Marine Mammal Protection Act. Immortal-yet-vulnerable creatures that masquerade as them, not so much. And when you're ashore, you want to lie around in the sun all day, and poor Larry knows I do that enough in human form. However, aquatic agility and tastiness to white sharks were exactly what I was counting on to save the sixgill.

Visibility was poor under the surface, but if I extended my whiskers just so, I could feel the subtle movements of the water that gave the big shark away. It was circling, as I expected. It'd do so a time or two to see what we were up to, and if it determined one of us was food, snap.

The sixgill had stopped chomping mindlessly on the snacks I'd provided and was staring at me in an uncanny, unsharklike way.

That's when I knew what I was dealing with.

If I'd had a human mouth at the time, I would have been swearing furiously. Since I didn't, I bared my teeth at the sixgill, who approached me curiously. I gave his snout a warning swipe with my claw, and he acquiesced to being herded next to the boat. Confident that he wouldn't do anything stupid, I swam out to where the white shark could see me silhouetted against the surface of the water and waited for it to make its move.

As many times as I've seen it in nature films, I'm always surprised by how sudden and powerful the first strike is. Even though I knew the attack was coming, even though I could feel him coming, I admit: I voided my bowels when I saw the enormous head of my greatest foe materialize in the murky water. Fortunately, this had an effect similar to an octopus spewing ink, and the shark's enormous jaws closed on the cloud of excrement where I had been a split-second before. But instead of savoring the near miss, I lashed out with my hind flippers and nailed the white shark right on the gill slits, all the while scratching and biting at its nose.

The white shark flailed, and its powerful tail connected with me, tossing me clear out of the water. I swam for my life and launched myself onto the deck of the fishing boat and transformed back, naked, dripping, and probably with a few badly bruised or cracked ribs.

I limped over to the fish finder and watched the white shark flee the scene with more than a bit of satisfaction.

The sixgill was still floating dumbly next to the boat. I considered taking more pictures, but I knew I couldn't publish my findings now that I knew it wasn't really a shark.

"Get back to the station, you knucklehead," I said to him as I pulled my clothes back on. "There's no fish left, anyway."

I thought he'd taken my advice, but there was a wet thump on the back of the boat, and I turned to see Greg Samsa, naked as the day he was born, standing on the deck.

I tossed him a towel with only a twinge of regret. Cold water rarely shows men to their best advantage.

"What's a selkie doing so far from Ireland?" he asked.

"Probably the same thing a siren is doing so far from the Mediterranean," I said.

"Half-siren."

No need to ask what the other half was. Sirens have weird taste, but this was the first time I'd heard of one that had a shark boyfriend.

"It's a pretty neat racket you've got," I said. "Sing 'em into the water, then save 'em. No harm done, and plenty of job security for you since your rescue numbers are the highest of any beach in the county."

He wrapped the towel more firmly around his hips, and he suddenly looked very alone.

"Don't worry, kid," I said. "Why would I tell anybody? And even if I did, who would believe it?"

He was quiet for a moment, thinking. "You weren't wearing that yesterday," he said, gesturing at my sealskin cuff.

"I wasn't planning to take a dip yesterday," I said. "Not that

I usually wear it. I haven't used it in over twenty years."

"Me, neither," said Greg. "I mean, I don't change much. It complicates things."

I sighed. Understatement of the year. "That it does."

"So why did you?" he asked.

"Because I thought my big, dumb, valuable research subject was about to get eaten by a larger predator," I said. "I know sharks. What I don't know is sirens. Now, your turn: why did you eat Perry de Nardo's leg?"

He shrugged. "There was blood in the water. When I saw he was already dead, I couldn't waste all that meat."

"You seem remarkably blasé about it."

"Dead meat is dead meat," he said, "be it human, dolphin, or seal. No offense."

I wrinkled my nose. "Typical shark."

"You would know," he said with a small smile.

"More than you would," I shot back. "So now that my dream of a paper in *Nature* has been dashed, I'd best return my boss's boat. Need a ride back to wherever you stashed your jet ski and your swim trunks?"

"Thanks," he said absently. "It's tied to some rocks just around the point."

He was silent as I turned on the capstan to weigh anchor and switched the fish finder into navigational mode. I caught his eye. "Penny for them."

He sighed. "I'm trying to figure you out."

"Smarter folks than either of us have tried and failed," I said.

"Why become an expert in something that would eat you if given half a chance?"

"Haven't you heard the expression 'know thy enemy'?" I asked, turning the key in the ignition. "Besides, a shark once did me the favor of eating a pernicious suitor. I wanted to return the favor. Before long, I was hooked. You're pretty fascinating and sexy creatures, even without the siren half."

He gave me the look that you see beautiful women give schlubby men in bars. "Are you flirting with me?"

"Sorry, sweetie, you're not at all my type," I lied, motoring off towards the point. I expected him to smile, but his eyes were gazing back toward Royston Cove and stayed fixed in that direction, even after we rounded the point. I brought the boat to a stop about twenty feet from the rocks.

"You okay?" I asked.

"I can't stop thinking about Perry de Nardo," he said, coming up behind me.

My heart went out to him a little bit. It's no easy thing to eke out an existence among mortals, but it beats an eternity alone. "You can't help what you are."

"It's not that," he said softly. I could feel his warm breath on the junction of my neck and shoulder, and goose bumps rippled over my wet skin.

"What is it, then?"

"It's just that he was the most delicious thing I've ever tasted."

His whisper sent a shiver through me, so it took me a split second to understand the message hidden in the husky sibilants. I caught sight of his face reflected in the windshield and saw the corners of his mouth stretch downward in a grotesque arc. I jerked my elbow up and caught him right in his namesake gills.

"You fecking idjit!" I shouted, reverting to my native patois as I balled my fist and delivered another jab to the gills. He wheezed through his saw-like teeth and hit the deck with a hollow thump.

He started to sit up and I kicked his supporting hand out from under him, placed my foot in the center of his neck, and pressed down with enough pressure to make his gill slits flare.

"Let me make myself very clear," I said. "You will forget what Perry de Nardo tasted like. And if I ever hear of anybody disappearing or turning up with chunks bitten out of them, I will find you, and I will kill you. Are we clear?"

He transformed back and dropped his gaze in sulky acquiescence, so I grudgingly removed my foot.

"Good boy," I said. "Now get the hell off my boat."

Despite the fact that the idiot had actually tried to eat me, I couldn't help but admire Greg's posterior as he discarded my towel and dove into the water, as well as his graceful efficiency as he swam over to the jet ski. He clambered onto the rocks, and if I'd been smart, I would have started up the engine and headed off before he had the chance to think. But instead of untethering his jet ski, he stood on the rock and met my gaze.

I swallowed hard as he ran the fingers of his left hand through his wet hair and allowed his right thumb to brush lingering drops of water from his chest. The kid was good looking, all right, and he clearly knew it. But he was dangerous. So why couldn't I look away?

It was then that I realized that his lips were moving. A tiny part of my brain began to howl in protest, but it was drowned out as an indescribable wave of lust swept over me. You know the feeling you get when you've locked eyes with someone who makes your belly warm and everything below even warmer? When your invitation to come up for a nightcap hasn't been spoiled by the guy opening his mouth? Well, multiply that by about ten thousand, and that's what being called by a siren feels like. All right, maybe it was only five thousand since Greg was only half siren, but you get the picture.

His voice was urging me to the water, and at his sweet suggestion I turned my sealskin cuff once more. I didn't try to resist, because I knew something that he didn't. Sure, lust in seal form is simple and irresistible. You just want to find something warm and chew on its neck until it scratches you in all the right places. But it's just dumb instinct, and it can be superseded.

Still, as I wriggled my way off the boat and into the water, I understood how Greg thought this would look to my nearest and dearest. They'd find the pile of my clothes on the *Once Bitten, Twice Shy,* just off the closed beach that they knew I'd imprudently entered the day before, ostensibly in search of a shark. They'd know there was no body to find, even if they mistook the reason why.

As my body moved me mechanically toward the siren on the rocks, I growled at myself for yet again underestimating a brain just because it was attached to a pretty face, even after the miserable years with Conan before I was able to steal my cuff back from him. I watched with an odd, detached clarity as Greg drew a diver's knife from one of the equipment bags on the jet ski.

Clearly, the plan was to sing me onto the rocks in seal form, stab me, then cut the skin off my left arm to return me to tasty human form just before I expired. Hell, he might just bite it off to see which was tastier, seal-me or human-me. Cold-blooded, but what do you expect from a shark? Smart, though. It's what I'd do. Don't give the victim any opportunity to escape. I was, as my kin would say, well and truly buggered.

Greg's song pulled me up on the rocks and rolled me over onto my back in a grotesque parody of a woman about to receive her lover. He was still singing something wordless—a good choice, since "Let Me Call You Sweetheart" would have lisped ridiculously through the pointed teeth that were pushing up through his gums.

But in that moment of facing death at the hands of another lucky predator, my heart began to pound out of time with the pulsing lust that Greg's song aroused in me. I recognized this feeling. It was like the night terrors that had plagued me for years after escaping Conan, and like the all-consuming panic I'd felt when Greg pulled me out of the water yesterday, only this was fury in a shade I'd never felt before. This was a seal's primal survival instinct coupled with the uncontrollable emotions of a human who has survived the unimaginable and still bears the scars.

I lashed out with my claws and raked them deeply across his calf. He shouted in pain, and the song that had clouded my brain evaporated, leaving only my rage in its wake. They say nature is red in tooth and claw. They are not wrong.

I won't bore you with the gory details other than to say that if there actually is a real bluntnose sixgill shark in the area, it's going to eat very well tonight.

ANTIOCH GREY

The Devil Makes Work for Idle Hands

"Is it your first time?" Smudger asked.

He sidled over to his companion and nudged him in the ribs. Smudger looked small and shabby next to the elegant figure in a sharp, grey suit, with a precise inch of white shirt cuff showing. Cuff links in the shape of ornate snakes curved back on themselves. They seemed to move when looked at from the corner of Smudger's eye.

"If it is your first time, I can help you out. We're supposed to do that these days, now that we are working in a mutually supportive environment as a team," he said, and spat, his saliva hissing and spitting on the hot floor.

"I could help you a bit," he said. "I wouldn't want to.... Well, it's unnatural for a demon to offer to help anyone, let alone another a demon. What is Hell coming to, I ask you?"

"Not," he added swiftly, seeing the frown his comments had provoked, "that you look like a bloke who needs any advice."

The frown did not diminish.

"Or lady bloke. Blokess?" Smudger suggested.

The frown was joined by a raised eyebrow.

"Well, I notice that you do have lovely long hair, and I just want you to know that I'm very broad minded if you swing both ways, it's just I've never met an actual succubus before—you are an incubus, aren't you?" Smudger asked.

The eyebrow settled back into its usual resting place, framing the coldest blue eyes that Smudger had ever seen. They looked through you, and about two feet behind, as if there was someone better and more interesting to talk to, just out of your eye line.

Smudger shuffled his feet uneasily, aware of how scruffy his jeans and t-shirt combination was, which had seemed perfectly acceptable until now.

"I've always stayed as an incubus. It's a lot less trouble that way."

His companion looked at him, and Smudger flinched.

It was worse than being ignored, Smudger thought, having that fierce attention focused on you. Making you feel like a small blob under a microscope, and about as important. This one wouldn't be like Smudger and his mates, sneaking out through the back door of Hell to see what mischief they could get up.

No, he probably had a True Name and everything, just so he could be Summoned. Not like Smudger, who'd had to choose his own Use Name fresh out of the pit, and had a habit of turning up somewhere without waiting for an invitation.

"The bits work easier, if you know what I mean. The trick is getting them to stop working half the time. It's like being possessed, sometimes, the way it's out there, bobbing, taking an interest in all the humans," Smudger added, gesturing vaguely towards his crotch. He was aware he was babbling but he was powerless to stop the nonsense leaking out of his mouth.

"I'm Smudger, by the way."

The frown eased, and, encouraged, he put out his hand.

"Lucy." The other demon took the proffered hand with a faint air of condescension.

Smudger shook hands, his little finger raised delicately in the air, to show he had class and style too, even if he was dealing with one of the demonic bigwigs.

Lucy wouldn't be his True Name, just a Use Name. Rumour had it that the True Names had been given by God before the Fall, and was now both title and chain, holding the fallen angels to their new tasks as demons.

Best not to ask about that: not now, not ever.

They could be a bit touchy about those sorts of questions, and you didn't want to find yourself hanging over a fiery pit, suspended by your own intestines until you managed to scrabble free. It took ages to get them back on the inside, and you would always be left with a funny pink bit at the end, that you couldn't find a home for.

The cave they were in was short of fiery pits, being dull and grey, only enlivened by a nondescript blue door at one end, and a shadowed cleft at the other leading back into the warmer regions of Hell where the screams of the tormented dead could be faintly heard. The blue door had none of the grandeur of the front entrance, with its blackened and carved figures writhing in agony, but no one who used this door needed to have a preview of what Hell was like. They knew; they lived here. Been there, bought the t-shirt smelling of brimstone.

A chill ran down Smudger's back, despite the heat.

It made you wonder what one of his sort was doing, hanging round the back door, but Smudger was damned if he was going to ask. It could be a dark plot, which was fair enough, but it could be something worse, something to do with these new rules.

He shivered again. The last person who had objected to the new rules had been forced to do a presentation to his fellow demons on the benefits of being open to new experiences.

It had broken the poor devil.

You could cope with pain, fear and humiliation, it was Hell after all. But slides? That was going too far. He'd seen which way the wind was blowing and made an application for a transfer to the Incubuses, citing the need for an opportunity to learn and grow.

He'd hung up his pitchfork and transferred to the incubus department, replacing some dim demon who thought that prodding people in fiery pits was more satisfying than poking women in warm places.

"Dunno what sort of succubus I'd make actually," Smudger said, filling the awkward silence before the questions he really wanted to ask made an escape through his mouth. "A bit ugly, I suppose, and you can get away with that as an incubus. It's manly. Or a bit of rough. But people don't want that in their lady friends."

"I'm not a succubus," replied Lucy.

"But Lucy's a girl's name," Smudger blurted.

"It's a nickname," Lucy said, small frost crystals forming in the air around him.

"Oh," said Smudger, watching the way the snow fell gently through the air to melt a few inches above the rough floor of the cave, hissing away into steam.

"Most people are too polite to mention it," Lucy said, his fingernails subtly shifting in length, becoming long and hooked. "Or too scared."

Smudger hunched over, trying to look small and not worth the effort of disembowelling.

"I wonder what's keeping Bert," he said. "It doesn't usually take him this long to hand out assignments. I bet you've got someone really good, someone pure and innocent, wanting to be ravished by the darkness. Mind, you've got to watch yourself with them. They've been reading all the wrong sorts of books and have no idea how it works in practice. They'll tie you up in complex sexual origami without any thought for your back, and how it's going to hurt in the morning."

Smudger leaned towards his companion, speaking very quietly. "Strictly between you, me, and the doorpost, I like 'em middle-aged, bored with their husband, and just bloody grateful for a bit of a run out at their time of life. They can be a bit frisky, it's true, but they work you smart, not hard, if you know what I mean. They do like to go on top a fair bit."

Smudger smirked, remembering his last trip fondly.

Lucy wasn't listening. He had his head tilted to one side, considering the motivational poster held against the wall by a pair of unmatched hands with shockingly dirty fingernails. The one that said that there was no I in team, and where some wit had added beneath in jagged runes carved into the rock, 'but there is a me'. With an added comment as to where the Devil could shove his poster, none of which was achievable without half a pound of butter, a stick of celery and being able to bend double.

Lucy wasn't smiling.

It wasn't the funniest joke you'd ever seen, not like the one written in blood splatter across the wall by the entrance to Hell, but it was still worth a twitch of the lips.

The Higher Ups were notorious for not having much of a sense of humour.

"This isn't some sort of appraisal is it?" Smudger asked, suddenly struck by a horrible thought. "Or one of those time and motion studies. I'm not that kind of demon." Smudger cringed at the thought of being watched whilst at work. It was unnatural, that's what it was.

"It's a custom job," he added. "None of this climbing aboard and flailing away for thirty seconds. It takes time to chip away at someone's soul, leading them into sin and debauchery."

"It's not an appraisal," Lucy said.

"Phew. I know we've had some management consultants come through recently, but there's no need to be adopting all of their ways. They're a set of right bastards."

"Which isn't a bad thing," Lucy said, confirming Smudger's suspicion that this was a high ranking demon, fully integrated into the hierarchy of Hell.

"I suppose not, not from your perspective anyway," Smudger said generously.

His own view was that there were people for whom Hell was too good, and he'd spent several hours coming up with new and inventive ways to punish people who used nouns as verbs, and who believed a positive attitude could overcome everything.

They were wrong about that, at least as far as pits of slurry were concerned.

"It's not an appraisal," said Lucy, "because those idiots wanted to introduce upwards appraisals, and I wasn't going to stand for that. You do what I want, and if you do it well enough, I don't stick you in a fiery pit of lava until I feel you've purged your offence. What we don't have is touchy-feely nonsense about feeling fulfilled and valued in your work."

Lucy turned to Smudger and gave him a long, hard, considering look. "What we *do* have is quality control."

"Ah," Smudger said, and swallowed hard. "You're not, yanno, Him are you? 'Cos I hear he's blond, and what with the name...?"

Smudger's guts lurched, anticipating being wrapped around a tree branch above a pit. Rumour had it that He'd started taking a more hands-on approach to demon management, with surprise inspections and asking people if they were happy in their work.

There was no right answer to that question. Happy had no place in hell, but neither could you admit to being unhappy in your work, being that it was an honour to serve and all that.

"Would you trust any answer I gave?" Lucy's smile was as pointed as his claws.

"S'pose not," Smudger said sourly. "If you're in disguise, you're not going to say, and if you're not you, you're not going to say, so the only thing I'd trust is if you said you were Him, 'cos then you wouldn't be."

Smudger scowled.

"Probably wouldn't be Him," he added, working through the logic of the propositions.

"They don't call Him the Lord of Lies for nothing," Lucy said, and smirked.

"You won't hear me say a word against Him." Smudger's answering grin was full of sharp teeth. "And I'm sure we're going to be the best of friends."

Lucy indicated with a half shrug that he was not opposed to the proposition.

"So, it's not your first time then," Smudger said. "In fact, you could teach me a trick or two if you were of a mind to."

Smudger tried his best to look like a puppy looking at a biscuit with all the want a puppy can muster but merely succeeded in looking cross-eyed.

He was just grateful that he looked like a demon with his insides still qualifying for the description.

"I thought you were going to teach me a thing or two," Lucy observed mildly.

"Well, that was before, wasn't it? Before I knew who you actually were. I may know a thing or two, but you must have had thousands of women to my hundreds."

Smudger hesitated for a moment. Asking questions was a risk. Questions was close to arguing, and He didn't like people arguing with him. But everyone knew that the Big Bosses liked to talk about themselves, and a demon talking about his illustrious past was a demon not thinking about the wrongdoings of the minion before him.

"I mean, you met Eve, didn't you? You started it all off from what I read, giving the humans free will. It's all rather flattering—more cunning than all the beasts of the field and all that. Even coming from a biased source, that's a good write up," Smudger said.

Smudger gathered his courage together and asked the question. "I've always wondered, though—what was she like?"

The look in Lucy's eye hardened. "Why do you want to know?"

"I just wondered, mate. No offence." Smudger smiled

ingratiatingly. "It's just the biggest blag in history, that's all. But I can see it's all very hush-hush. Need to know, and all that, and I don't need to know."

"She was a nice girl," Lucy said. "Bright. Inquisitive. And just a bit fed up with being expected to do as she was told, just because she'd been made out of a rib. An afterthought, Adam said. Getting it right the second time, she said."

"So it wasn't all manna and figs, even from the start." Smudger shook his head sorrowfully. "It's the same old story—my wife doesn't understand me, my husband doesn't listen to me—it's all so very predictable."

"And useful," Lucy said.

"That too." Smudger grinned. "Though you do have to listen to a lot of complaints before you can get down to business. Usually about loo seats being left up. It's amazing how these little things add up. Makes you glad all we have is a pit for that sort of thing. No one ever complains about leaving the pit edge a bit scuffled, though I suppose being able to swap equipment if necessary helps."

Smudger could tell his companion was not especially interested in the toilet habits of lesser demons. "But you've probably got a gold edged pit to yourself, and no shortage of tongues to help clean up," he said, and then coughed nervously. "Er, so Eve…?"

"So, she was inquisitive, and inclined to resentment, and she had heard the rumours about Adam's first wife…" Lucy continued.

"What, Lilith? I met her once." Smudger twitched, but said nothing more.

"Aware, then, that she was not merely the second attempt at a human, but a second attempt at a wife, Eve was eager to sin, and looking for an opportunity to do so." Lucy smiled at some fond memory, his forked tongue flickering across his lips. "She had tried some mild lies, and found the results agreeable, but was looking to expand her repertoire."

"And had you led her down the primrose path already, or had she taken the first steps herself?" Smudger asked.

"Modesty forbids me to answer." Lucy shrugged. "Someone may have pointed out that where one's partner was already dealing in falsehood, there was no need to strictly adhere to the truth oneself. It would be unfair in the extreme if Eve were to be held to a higher standard than Adam, someone may have added."

"Or even God—not exactly the most forthcoming or reliable chap," Smudger said, and cringed back from Lucy's baleful glare.

"We do not mention that name," Lucy hissed. "Ever."

"Yeah, sorry." Smudger held out his hands in submission. "Don't pay any attention to me. I've got foot in mouth disease. Anyway, you were saying...."

"Someone may have suggested that the rules of the game were fixed, and the dealer wasn't honest," Lucy continued, inspecting his nails. "Someone might have done that."

"But that's essentially true," Smudger said slowly. "Isn't telling the truth against the rules?"

Lucy arched an eyebrow. "Rules?"

"Oh, I see," said Smudger slowly, in the tones of someone rearranging his assumptions about life. "Does this mean that no one has to obey the rules?"

"I would say that an anthropomorphic representation of the powers of darkness may not be fettered by a rule-based approach to being sinful, but you can bet your claws that minions of the powers of darkness pretty much are," Lucy said, and showed his teeth in an expression that was not even attempting to pass as a smile.

"Ah," Smudger said, adding under his breath, "So you're just as bad as the man upstairs, but with added hypocrisy."

"It would be wrong to assume that a rebel was in favour of freedom in general as opposed to a particular, measurable freedom for himself," Lucy continued, ignoring Smudger's editorial comment as unworthy of attention or, perhaps, looked at in the right light, as flattering.

"Message received," Smudger replied sourly. "Loud and clear. Do as I say, not as I do."

"Words to live by."

Smudger muttered something else under his breath, and then added, more loudly, "You were telling me what Eve was like."

"Bright, I said," Lucy replied.

"Not what she was like," Smudger protested. "What she was like. You know." He moved his hands through the air, describing female curves.

"Does it matter?"

Smudger snorted. "Of course it matters."

"I don't see why." Lucy paused. "You don't mean that you actually enjoy mortal women? All those fleshy bits."

There was an awkward pause, whilst Smudger reached for an explanation, any explanation, that wouldn't see him ending up face down in a fiery pit as punishment for sleeping on the job.

"Obviously," he said, speaking slowly in the hope that inspiration would strike. "Obviously, I live to serve my master in all things, and that is the chief joy in my work, but the whole process wouldn't be possible unless I took something of an interest in the woman. No matter how fleshy her bits, or how lacking in scales and leathery wings she was."

"Mmm," Lucy said. "So why do you care what Eve looked like?"

"It is descriptive colour," Smudger replied easily. "Like telling me what sort of tree it was, and what sort of fruit, or what Adam looked like."

Lucy gave Smudger a hard look, but effectively conceded the point by moving on. "He was a big lad and very hairy. Clothes were a definite improvement in his case, so I don't see what all the fuss was about. He should have been grateful for my intervention, but did that stop him whining? No, no it didn't."

"Ungrateful bastard," Smudger said. "And Eve?"

"Eve was just average—average height, average weight, average breasts, mousy brown hair, and average brown eyes—nothing special. Not like Lilith."

"Well, He wouldn't want to make the same mistake twice, would He?" Smudger said. "Not that the red hair doesn't look good on Lilith. Very striking. Very appropriate."

The two demons exchanged looks of common understanding about what that meant.

"Definitely above average intelligence, though. So he didn't learn that lesson." Lucy smirked.

"So, what was the apple...?"

"Apple? There was no apple."

Smudger grinned, and briefly contemplated nudging his companion in the ribs. "Oh, so the rumours about the nibble, being more of an *ahem* nibble than a nibble were all true then?"

"You're not suggesting..." Lucy's eyebrows rose. "It was a pomegranate, is what I meant."

"If it wasn't a nibble nibble, then, what was all the fuss about?"

"The power of free will, the power to choose good or evil, the power to break the rules—all of these things, not just some third rate bunk up against a tree," Lucy said.

"Not third rate, surely," Smudger said, taking the chance to apply flattery to his boss. "Not for her."

Lucy scowled. "Why are people so obsessed with sex anyway?"

"Er, I'm an incubus. It's what I'm here for. It's the job description—sex demon. It's what I think about, it's what I do." Smudger shrugged. "I thought it was because of you and Eve, because no one mentioned pomegranates to me."

"Just apples."

"I thought they were symbolic apples, not your actual apples."

"And what you thought they symbolised was sex?"

"Not so much, to be fair, as the taking the form of a snake and twisting round the tree, but I had supposed sex was the whole point of the discussion," Smudger said. "If it wasn't to do with sex, then why am I out almost every evening making the beast of two backs with a succession of mortals. What's the bloody point?"

"Ah."

"There is a point, isn't there? Because I'm too old to be dealing with existential angst at my time of life."

"Oh, there's a point all right." Lucy didn't scuff his feet along the floor like an errant demonling, but there was a faint air of embarrassment about him that made him look younger, almost innocent. "I suppose I may as well tell you, as long as you promise to keep it a secret."

"May I be struck down with boils if I breathe a word."

"I think we can guarantee that." Lucy's smile was feral. "So, what happened was, I offered the fruit of the tree of knowledge, and Eve did eat thereof."

"So the story goes."

"What the story doesn't mention is what happened next, not accurately."

"Bias in the reporters," Smudger said. "It's an old, old story."

"Eve ate the pomegranate. She sucked the seeds out of the thing, chewed the flesh of the fruit, and licked her way round the rind, juice running down her chin."

"Sounds messy."

"It was," Lucy said. "Very messy, and very hard to hide when He turned up a bit later on one of those carefully unannounced visits."

"What with having no clothes to wipe your hands on. I can see her problem."

"And so could He," Lucy continued. "And all those little lies she'd been trying out just fled from her mind when he asked her why she had sticky fingers."

Smudger snorted with laughter. "I'll bet."

Lucy looked uncertain, as if he wasn't quite sure what the joke was. "And Adam was no help either. He'd been quick enough to help himself to the extra pomegranate, without a by-your-leave, but when it came to owning up to his wrongdoing it was all 'The woman whom You gave to be with me, she gave me of the tree, and I ate' or 'The serpent deceived me, and I ate'." Lucy snorted. "I've never seen a finger so quick to be pointed. If I had been innocent, I would have been mortally offended."

"Instead of which, you were not innocent and immortally offended," Smudger said.

"Indeed." Lucy smirked. "And then He started with the questions, and the passive aggressive oh nobody loves me, nobody does what I say, and Eve said she'd had quite enough of that with Adam, thank you very much, and that was pretty much it."

Lucy shrugged eloquently, conveying his opinion of God's man management style.

"Crash. Bang. Clothes. Thorns and thistles. Flaming Sword. Bring forth children in pain and suffering, don't let the door hit your arse on the way out of the Garden," he added.

"The Flaming Sword sounds like overkill against two unarmed humans. What did He think they were going to do?" Smudger asked.

"Ten minutes of listening to Adam is enough to make anyone reach for the flaming swords," Lucy said darkly. "He was a man who would have been much improved by silence. And he didn't stop whining after the doors shut behind him."

"I know the type," Smudger said. "Nothing is ever their fault, is it? It's their parents, or their children, or their partner, or the boss, or even the dog."

Or God made me do it, Smudger thought. *God made me Fall.*

"And whilst it is pleasant to be given all due credit, this wore out after the first fifteen minutes of complaining. After that, it was just dull." Lucy's hands flexed, the claws on his long fingers suddenly visible. "An argument I made. Pointedly."

"And how did he take that?" Smudger said, eyes wide with anticipation.

"He was utterly unable to take a hint," Lucy replied, his lips falling back to show well-developed fangs. "So, really, he was asking for it."

Smudger leaned forward. "Asking for what?"

"I liked Eve," Lucy said. "She didn't try and point the finger, contrary to the official reports. She wasn't one to blame others. She'd taken that first bite with her eyes open, and she knew what she was doing. I couldn't do anything to counteract His edict, but I could do something… nice for her."

"Nice?" Smudger asked. "You're not telling me you felt guilty?"

The temperature in the cave plummeted to arctic, a burning cold that shrivelled the soul, and made the hairs stand up on the back of Smudger's head.

"What?"

"Nothing," Smudger yelped. "Just being stupid."

Being a blob under a microscope would be promotion compared to Smudger's current status. He was a speck of dirt on a blob under a microscope. He would be sneered at by a speck of dirt on a blob. He wasn't fit to wash the boots of the speck of dirt.

It was only long practice that kept his knees locked so that he didn't fall down, but Smudger hadn't been this terrified since his old Mum had found out about the fling with the slime demon two pits down.

This, truly, was the Lord of Lies.

"I pay all debts," Lucy said, his voice sounding deeper and

oddly plural.

Smudger heard the threat in that. "Yeah," he squeaked. "You're well known for it. Paying your debts. Punishing people, certainly. A gentleman."

Lucy's look could have punched through the centre of the universe.

"And I can imagine that Adam had got on your last nerve by this stage," Smudger added, really wishing he could shut up. "So you had to do whatever it was that you did, just to shut him up. I can see that."

The unnerving, unearthly gaze softened. "There was that."

"I... er... really should be going," Smudger said. "Nice to meet you and all that, but I've got to see a man about a dog."

"Don't you want to know how the story ends?" Lucy asked.

"Mmm, yes, of course." Smudger nodded frantically. He'd do anything, as long as he kept his innards on the inside.

"So, I thought what could I do?" Lucy said, talking as much to himself as to Smudger.

Smudger started to back away, but a clawed hand grasped his shoulder tightly, stopping his getaway.

Lucy leaned into his face, close enough for Smudger to smell his breath and count each of Lucy's yellow, snaggled teeth. "What would really hurt Adam?"

The smell of brimstone sharpened in the air, and Smudger whimpered.

"And then it came to me."

Lucy's grip slackened, and Smudger wriggled free.

"Sex."

"Er, you invented sex?" Smudger rubbed at his shoulder, wincing at the tender spots, where each claw had singed his hide.

"I may as well, for all the ability Adam brought to it." Lucy's grin was wide, smug, and disturbing. "I made Eve's daughters the gift of my demons."

Smudger swallowed hard. "You mean Incubuses?"

"Even so." Lucy patted him on the arm, like a pet that had done well. "All that bringing forth in pain? The least I could do was arrange for a little pleasure first."

"Not so little," Smudger said reflexively, then cringed.

Lucy's hand snaked out again, pulling Smudger to him by the ear. "I am pleased to hear it," he said, right in Smudger's ear. "I wouldn't want to hear that people, and by people I mean you particularly, were slacking off in favour of spending time hanging round the fiery pits poking people with pitchforks, when they should be hanging around the mortals poking people with their own, personal, pitchfork. You're not put here to have fun."

When Lucy let go, Smudger was grateful to find his ear and his pitchfork still attached.

"Right," he said. "Message received and understood."

"Good," said Lucy. "I am glad we had this little chat. Some of the advice I have had recently has suggested that I had a remote and authoritarian management style, and that I need to be more hands-on."

Smudger wheezed, dragging breath back into his lungs and hoping the purple spots before his eyes would fade. He wished very much both for a cigarette and to be a very long way away from his current position and never to have his Lord's hands on him again.

"So," Lucy said brightly, "in line with my current open, hands-on management style, please do let me know if you have any questions."

Smudger swallowed hard. There was no way to win here; asking would be as likely to cause a reaction as not asking.

"But if Incubuses are your gift to Eve's daughters...?" Smudger said, managing to sound enquiring, interested, and enthused without actually asking anything.

"Yes?"

"Well, what are Succubuses for?"

"Revenge," said Lucifer.

WENDY WORTHINGTON

Provender

He was smiling for the first time in years, a full-out grin that hurt his cheeks.

Emily wouldn't even know me, he thought, and that made him nearly giggle. He almost wished he'd thought of smiling for the surveillance cameras, but it was too late now.

The picture they'd captured wasn't bad. Emily would recognize *that*. Maybe she already had. Maybe she was sitting in front of her television, staring at that picture right now. He hoped so. He wished he could see her, see the look of incredulity wash over her smug little face. At first, she'd probably think it was all some stupid mistake. She'd have a hard time believing it was really him, and he wanted to tell her himself how wrong she'd been about him. He wanted her to know the kind of thing he was capable of doing. He wanted to see her tears and her revulsion. He wanted her to feel like she would never be able to stop crying again.

He especially wished he could be there when she opened her freezer. She wasn't going to like that special, nasty little surprise in with all her artificially flavored, frozen almost-food, not at all. Served her right for putting the stupid cat ahead of him. Even if the news stories didn't make her cry, that package in the freezer would do it for sure.

He grinned again, realizing how odd it felt to curl the edges of his mouth upward. It truly was a peculiar sensation. How long had it been since he had even *wanted* to smile? Emily had done this to him, though of course it hadn't been just her. She'd had quite a lot of company over the years, but today was mostly for her benefit. He'd been thinking of her, imagining her all splattered with other people's blood while he worked today. The vision had made him happy, and it made him even happier now. Once she heard the glorious news and saw his picture—*his* picture—she would realize just how powerful he really was. She would be sorry. She would cry and feel sorry. And then she would go home, and she would be forced to think about him for the rest of her long, stupid, miserable life. She would never be able to leave him behind again.

The backpack rubbed against his shoulders as he climbed. He should have thought of the cabin weeks ago. He could have stocked it, had it ready and waiting for him. Instead, he was forced to haul in everything he could carry on this one trip. As it was, he'd had to leave some of the provisions in the bed of the pickup. He'd watched it all burn with some regret. He couldn't risk trying to haul all that extra food into the forest with him, and he didn't dare leave it behind. Waste of a good truck, too, but it couldn't be helped. It wasn't like it had been *his* truck.

He'd thrown in the bag of little powdered donuts as the flames crackled up into the pine trees. They didn't even count as food, just evidence. He hadn't felt bad about those donuts. The growl from his stomach betrayed him for a moment, but he knew it was just mindless biology. He'd learned that lesson early. He had the willpower to wait until he got to the cabin. He'd skipped lunch on purpose. Hunger fueled him right now. Hunger, and a prickly sensation at the back of his neck.

His imagination was working overtime today. Probably just adrenalin, but he wasn't used to being watched. The cameras had made him nervous. He quickened his pace. They were probably following him already. He didn't have time to celebrate, not yet. Too much left to do.

He focused on the sound of the cans and the packets of dehydrated rations in his backpack clunking and scraping against one another as he climbed. *Fourteen dinners, fifteen breakfasts, fifteen lunches.* Enough to get him through the first two weeks if he measured every meal and kept a strict eye on each portion. The pack was heavier than he would have liked, but he couldn't count on adding to his basic supplies until he'd settled in. It wouldn't be the first time he'd made do with what he could scrape together. He was resourceful. He was strong in the ways that counted.

At the top of the ridge, he paused to take a drink from his Camelbak, leaning his M1 rifle against a tree. Maybe he should polish off the rest of the water now. That would lighten the load a little. There was a well at the cabin, so he'd have more once he got there. He took another swallow and stared out at the endless trees.

He probably should have waited until summer. By then, there would be berries and nuts and maybe some things like sorrel and dandelion greens to supplement what he had in his pack, but most of the possibilities out here weren't edible yet. Summer would have been better. But Emily had forced his hand. Emily and her damn cat and all those absurd people she'd worked with, the ones she'd laughed about him with. Today had been coming for years, and he couldn't have waited any longer. This was Emily's fault. She deserved everything.

He tucked the hydration valve back into the strap of his pack. He would save a little water for now. The cabin was still a ways off, if he remembered right. Of course, his legs were longer these days, and the hours he'd put in at the gym this past year had started to pay off. The first time he'd made this hike, he'd been a starved and scrawny kid, huffing along behind his father, expected to keep pace with a grown man, expected to ignore the grumbling in his stomach and keep hurrying along. He hadn't been smiling then.

The thought of his father wiped the smile from his face now. He had him to thank for even knowing about this place, of course, and he certainly knew how to survive until summer because of that bastard, but it wasn't enough to make up for all those nights he'd gone to bed hungry and terrified. He wondered if he could dig the old man up, just to show him the news coverage. Might be worth dragging him out of his grave.

He remembered the surprise on the son of a bitch's face when he'd stumbled back out of the forest holding a fistful of mushrooms, that first autumn. *He didn't even let me eat them,* he thought, his jaw tightening at the memory. *Goddamn son of a bitch. Poison mushrooms, my ass. He just couldn't believe I could do it on my own.* He shivered.

One of the worst horror stories the old man had told him that first night out in the forest came rushing back. Poison mushrooms were nothing compared to some of the imaginary terrors he had filled him with all those years back. Ghosts and zombies and killer trolls and bloodsucking werewolves—the old man had filled his young imagination with gory tales, and he'd been fool enough to believe them all once upon a time. *No more, old man. I'm never falling for that crap again. You can't scare me now. I'm in charge now.*

He shifted the pack on his shoulders. He still had plenty of ammo, so maybe he'd get lucky and be able to shoot a deer in the next week or so, just to get things started. It wouldn't be as satisfying as picking off a human being, but you wouldn't want to eat a human unless there was nothing else at hand.

He picked up the rifle again. It felt solid and reassuring in his hand. *Just you and me,* he thought. His M1 had been his only reliable friend for a long time now. Anybody following him now would be in for a nasty surprise.

A bird above him started a chirruping song, and he paused for a moment to listen. He squinted up at the sun angling in through the foliage. *North,* he thought then, and he set out again.

The ground angled down on the other side of the ridge, rough and overgrown. *Nobody's been up this way for a good while,* he thought, and it was reassuring. He'd be safe up here. Even if the cops found the burnt wreck at the end of the fire road, they'd still have a tough time following him from there. He didn't need a trail, and he was being careful not to leave one. They'd never find him. He was too smart for that.

His boot clipped a rock, and he stumbled, catching himself on a tree and leaving a little chunk of skin on its rough bark. He cursed, brushing his hands together and then sucking on the raw patch to ease the stinging, the tangy saltiness tickling his tongue. His stumble had snapped a new sapling poking its head up through the dead leaves at the foot of the tree. He twisted the branch the rest of the way free with his good hand and used the limb to scatter the leaves into a less damning heap. After a moment's work, he was satisfied that the leaves and the broken twig looked more like the foraging of a wild animal than the tracks of a man on the run.

He glanced back up at the higher ground behind him, once again checking the angle of the sun. He had been walking in a kind of a zigzag for more than an hour. Perhaps it was safe now to choose a more purposeful path. He still had hours of prime daylight, but he would need most of them to reach the sanctuary of the cabin, and then he would still need some light to settle in and erect at least a few wards around the perimeter. Then he would eat. He would sit down and savor every damn mouthful—his stomach could just go on growling until he was safe. It knew how to wait.

The cabin was on the other side of the creek, and the rushing water would slow the dogs if they deployed the canine units on the first pass, but he was still pushing his schedule. Shooting that highway patrolman had slowed down his retreat, but it had felt so damn good.

The stupid cop had been asking for it, after all. He'd been

leaning on the hood of his car, stuffing one of those stupid little powdered donuts into his fat face. They weren't even decent bakery donuts, either, but those useless little machine-made ones that came in a bag, full of preservatives and processed sugar and manmade crap. Not an ounce of nutrition in the whole package. He'd done him a favor. He'd plucked the bag from those fat fingers while he watched the man's life evaporate from his surprised eyes. "This stuff'll kill you," he'd told him, and he'd had a good laugh at his own wit. He'd said it again when he'd tossed the bag into the fire: "This stuff'll kill you."

Not getting the officer's Glock had probably been a mistake, though. It would have been prudent to have a backup weapon. Still, what was past was past. He shifted his pack again and started down the slope toward the water.

He should have been hearing the stream by now. Curious. Maybe the spring runoff hadn't been as heavy as it was sometimes. He'd been here at times when the water had raged up the sides of the ravine, furiously devouring the leaves and twigs and small rocks in its way, but he'd also seen a time or two when it had been the merest trickle. Still, he ought to be hearing something by now.

He stopped again, his eyes darting around the dense vegetation as he strained to pick out the sound of running water. The air was remarkably quiet. Most of the birds seemed to have stopped to listen with him, and the wind was somewhere else altogether at the moment. A single trickle of sweat beaded up on his forehead, sliding down to halt briefly in one eyebrow before running down the side of his nose to his top lip. He licked it away impatiently, the salty aftertaste stinging his tongue, and focused on listening.

At last, he was able to pick out the faintest tremor of what must be water. He let out a puff of air and started down the slope again, deciding to keep to a straight path now. He could walk down the stream for a few yards once he reached it to confuse the dogs before emerging on the other side, but he would need time for the detour. He didn't have the luxury of too many evasive maneuvers now. He shook his head, feeling the tickle at the back of his neck again. Yes, they were definitely following him. He tried to move faster.

The undergrowth was thick here, and he had to choose more than once to bypass the heaviest growth or risk leaving marks of his passage. Most of the patches were blackberry bushes, their stiff, thorny canes barren of berries at this time of year. He marked their positions for the fruiting season, but for now they represented not sustenance but hindrance, grabbing at his flannel shirt and scratching his exposed skin as he skimmed their rough edges, pressing on through the forest.

The water sound was still very faint—the stream must be low. He might have to travel a fair distance along it to cover the scent of his passage. The wind had started up, rustling the trees around him and confusing his sense of what he was hearing. He tried to remember whether the cabin was more upstream or downstream at this point. He had made this trip more times than he could count, but the last time had been the disastrous year that had ended everything with his father, and he screwed his eyes shut, concentrating hard to get through the thicket of memory in order to focus on simple geography. His stomach growled. *Upstream,* he decided at last.

He finally came to the place where the ground started to rise again, but there was no stream running through the lowest point. He stopped and frowned at the small heap of rocks that marked what had clearly once been a runoff of some kind but was now waterless. He listened. The sound he had taken for water now seemed to be just the whistling wind, steady but dry. It had been a couple of years since he'd been back here, and things could change fast in the deep woods. Obviously in that time the water had found new ways to get downhill. It was irritating, but that was the way the world was, even out here.

He started up the slope beyond the rock pile, deciding to keep to a straighter path to make up some time. This was taking longer than it should, and he still had work ahead of him before he could quiet the roaring of his empty gut.

The hill on the other side of the old stream bed wasn't as steep as the one he'd come down. He crested it easily. But it also meant that he wasn't nearly high enough for any kind of a view ahead. The trees here were thicker and darker, and the sun was lower now, too. He wasn't worried so much as annoyed. The cabin was well hidden. He didn't expect to see it much sooner than he got to it, but now he had an itch between his shoulder blades, and he needed to get *on*. He glanced over his shoulder. The forest kept its secrets well.

As he trudged ahead, he concentrated on drawing up a checklist of the essential things he would need to do when he got there at last. The well was around back, covered by a wooden plank, and he would need to make sure he could get to it. The plank might have fallen in or debris might be weighing it down, but the well itself was deep and spring-fed. Even if the rope that reached down into its moist darkness had rotted, he had a spare with him, just in case. That regular, reliable source of clean water was the best thing about the cabin. Here, he could easily ride out whatever storms were left to finish the spring and drift through the ease of summer into the fall before he ever had to start worrying about keeping himself alive.

Once he got there, he would unload all his food and arrange it in order so he could make sure it lasted as long as possible. He would make dinner and silence the now-constant rumbling of his mutinous stomach.

Maybe he could start foraging for extra food in a few days, if the coast was clear enough. There were a few homes near the edges of the wilderness that had proved to be good supply sources before. A couple of those places had vegetable gardens. He'd pick off the first harvest as soon as the early crop was ready, before the idiots who had planted them even realized anything was close to ripe. He knew from experience just how soon you could eat a green tomato and where to dig for new potatoes. He might even start a garden of his own. His father had never let him get that comfortable. A garden would be one more poke in the old man's eye.

Getting more ammo might be the biggest challenge, but he still had quite a lot with him, plenty for hunting good meat. If he was careful, he'd still be able to save enough in case any of the searchers stumbled onto him and decided to try to be heroes. He kind of hoped they would. He hadn't gotten nearly enough target practice in today. Shooting that last cop had been fun. He wouldn't mind another adrenalin rush before the weather turned cold again.

Still, he'd need to get there soon.

The not-water sound was a little nearer now. Now that he could hear it better, he realized it was less regular than a steady stream of water would have been. It was probably an animal foraging through the leaves, a squirrel perhaps, or a good-sized bird. Funny how the smaller creatures could make so much noise. It was nothing alarming, just life in the woods. He stopped paying attention. It wasn't going to lead him to wherever the stream had decided to run these days.

The angle of the sun was sharper now, and the yellow light was starting to shade toward a warm orange. He wasn't going to have as much time as he'd like to scout the edges of the place before settling down for the night, and using his flashlight or even building a fire would be risky before he had secured his boundaries. It would be a dark first night if he didn't get there soon.

He had started up one more slope when he realized the not-water sound was suddenly much closer. It was some sort of snuffling noise in the foliage off to his right. He halted, wary and alert. A distant bird began a tuneless melody, then abruptly cut off its song in mid-note. The wheezy breathing continued, a sniffing sputter moving toward him through the dried leaves. He strained to match it with his memory of the animals he had seen in these woods. Deer were quiet, almost silent, but this was wet and slightly reckless, damper than the bear he had once encountered as a scrawny teenager rooting around for something, anything, to eat. He remembered how they had eyed one another, several shuddering yards apart, before the great beast had shambled off in search of tastier, fatter prey. That was a memory for darker nights, though, not the rosy peach light of early evening.

This sounded bigger and unfamiliar. The snorting, moist exhalations had not altered when he had stopped, so it might be coincidence that it was lumbering in his direction. Still, he could feel the goose bumps ripple up his arms as he tensed, frozen in place, staring toward the sound. Identifying it might give him a cue about his best defense. Should he make himself as small as possible, or try to present as fearsome an opponent as he could? And was the wind blowing his scent toward those sniveling nostrils or carrying it away? His pack felt heavy on his tense shoulders, but there was no way he could afford to abandon the food and run.

He raised his rifle slowly, but held off on releasing the safety, which would make a noise. Besides, he didn't want to shoot for food until he was settled in at the cabin. He didn't have time now to drag an undressed carcass along with him, but just shooting it would be a waste of good meat and a huge marker for anyone tracking him. He forced himself to recognize the irony of hesitating to kill when he had spent the day shooting his way into history. Firing at a dumb beast did not present the same satisfaction as murdering a man. The thought helped to tamp down the panic that was rising in him and threatening his ability to think.

From the snort and sputter of whatever it was, there seemed now to be only the thinnest veil of foliage between them. He braced himself and slid back the latch to release his weapon as quietly as he could, gripping the rifle with shaking hands as the final branches were crushed aside.

The beast stood less than three yards beyond the barrel of his gun. He stared into glittering, grey eyes that reflected the dying sun back at him with a silvery gleam. They were set in a head shaped like globs of sodden, dull clay that spouted a few random tufts of coarse black hair, balanced atop a massive and grotesquely misshapen body. Huge hairy arms ended in fat knuckles that dug furrows in the ground, their sausage shapes convulsively flexing to reveal terrifyingly sharp claws. Two enormous, stubby feet crushed earth, plants, and rocks beneath the creature's hideous weight. Repellent, ashen-grey skin showed sweaty between draperies of stinking animal pelts. It swayed forward, sniffing wetly at him, a dribble of mucus trickling from one enormous nostril down through the crevices of its face to moisten oversized lips that looked for all the world like two great slabs of uncooked liver.

It eyed him speculatively, its strange, silvery eyes running up and down his body, evaluating him. He jerked the rifle in threat, though it was obvious he wouldn't be making any meals out of this beast, whatever it was—the meat would be greasy and fatty and would probably taste of rotting flesh, to judge from the stench wafting off it. As he watched, a massive, wet tongue emerged to lick the bulbous lips. For one brief moment, he and the beast were suspended in time, eyes locked, breath halted, bodies frozen.

In the silence, a long gobbet of thick, greenish drool hit the carpet of dried leaves with a splat.

An old memory suddenly sprang to life, the worst story he fought not to remember, a childhood tale of horror that his father had told him in the dark one night to frighten a piteous young boy already terrified out of his mind. This *thing* was that memory, sprung into solid, nauseating life. *Troll.* The word smashed into his brain and began pounding on every sense. A scream started inside his head, working its way out.

He swung the rifle up and squeezed the trigger, aiming for that colossal, obscene mouth. The bullet lodged in the corner of the creature's jaw, knocking it backwards by mere inches. It recovered its balance, glaring at him with an almost puzzled expression on its hideous face.

He fired again, this time aiming for an eye. The bullet connected, with a sound halfway between a crack and a squish, disappearing into the spongy flesh just below the eye socket and eliciting a low grumble from its target. He pulled the trigger a third time, but his load had been spent, and he could only gape stupidly at the lack of any more profound effect from two point-blank shots to the face.

"Jesus Christ," he gibbered, half a prayer, more a curse.

He reached awkwardly backwards, fumbling frantically at his pack, searching out more bullets or a knife or anything useful as a weapon as the troll lurched forward, its blackened claws stretched toward him, its incoherent growls drowning out the whimper rising in his throat. He gave up trying to find anything else useful and swung the gun toward the troll, trying to connect with a forceful blow, but it grasped the barrel and flung the weapon aside. He tore the backpack from his shoulders and thrust it between them into the grasping arms. The troll wrenched it open, raining down a cascade of tin cans and silvered food packets and a thin spittle of water, batting them all away like so many minor annoyances, stretching through the distractions toward the real provender before it.

In one more inevitable step, it was on him.

Its talons connected with his flesh, ripping through the flimsy cloth covering his arms to shred the muscle and bone and blood beneath. Its colossal mouth opened in a great wave of diseased breath to reveal razor-sharp teeth, their edges encrusted with filth. It grasped his arms in its giant claws, stretching them wide, ripping them from their sockets, opening him to the coming night, laying bare his blackened soul and his howl of terror and his final gasps of existence, releasing his emptiness into the foul air. It sank its jagged teeth into his neck in the warm light of the setting sun, sucking in great gulps of pumping red blood, swallowing whole huge mouthfuls of flesh, ripping away his certainties and his carefully-laid plans and leaving nothing, nothing at all behind.

"Emily," he managed to croak before the last gasp of air left his lungs. A bird in the trees high above him let out a single squawk and then lifted into the air, greeting the sunset and leaving the troll to his dinner.

JONATHAN WAITE

PRETORIUS

We are getting rather good at it, Eugénie and I. We tailor ourselves to the times as the times shape themselves around us. Without wishing to boast, I would challenge any latter-day Sherlock Holmes or Henry Higgins to study us and divine, from our apparel, manners, or even voices, our first beginnings, all those many years ago, in that other country.

Nobody notices older people now-a-days, for one thing. The cult of youth is in full sway. I must say I find myself thoroughly in sympathy. I have always admired the *jeunesse dorée*; a predilection, then as now, purely aesthetic in nature, whatever those prurient gossips at the University might have thought. But now, it seems, my preference is shared by the world at large, and those of advanced age are regarded, not as unfailing founts of wisdom and experience, but as tiresome burdens on the family and the state, requiring constant care and attention, and so are treated as invisible whenever possible.

Sometimes Eugénie is my daughter, or my granddaughter, or my niece; sometimes she puts on a rather fetching nurse's uniform and wheels me around the town in a Bath chair. Everyone looks at her; nobody acknowledges the thin, white-haired fellow under the blanket. Once I might have felt this quite keenly. Once my pride was more fragile. But I no longer crave the ephemeral rewards of fame, or even notoriety. I have seen too much of them. Anonymity is far more discreet, especially when one does not noticeably age. And anonymity, in this modern time, is all too readily come by. I am sure the name of Professor Doctor Septimus Pretorius would mean even less to the average citizen of today than it did in those far-off days when I was a humble toiler in the vineyards of Academe. And that is surely as it should be.

And yet; and yet. I have been thinking for some years about setting down in writing an account of our life together, from its tumultuous beginning to the tranquil repose of today. Who would read it I know not; perhaps only I. Were it to be read—and believed—there can be no doubt that the mobs would once again be on the hunt for us, as in the olden days. Perhaps I simply crave the danger... or perhaps I hope that somewhere such an account might find the sympathetic reader, the kindred soul for whom I have long yearned. At any rate, let us consider this small essay by way of a trial balloon, a dry run.

At the moment we live quietly, as we must, in a cathedral city in rural England—or as rural as England ever gets—and I am what our landlady calls a "silver fox," when she thinks I am not listening. I must confess that the description tickles me to a degree. I dress carefully, as always, and with judicious use of cosmetics I can pass for fifty or thereabouts. Eugénie, of course, is ageless, as beautiful and apparently flawless as a well-crafted porcelain figure, and attracts general admiration even in the hideous fashions of this century, as she did forty years ago in tie-dye caftan and beads, or fifty years before that in the dropped waistline and cloche hat of the flapper, and so on, further back, even beyond the infernal crinolines and corsets of the Empire—I mean, of course, the German Empire. I cannot suppress a thrill of proprietorial pride when I survey her. Really excellent work, for a first attempt, and using a flawed methodology. And so very durable, in all possible senses.

We still look for him, of course. Every weekday morning she and I patronise a "cyber-café" in the High Street and spend an hour or more surveying that wondrous invention, the Internet. It seems, though, as if he has finally achieved the obscurity for which he so yearned. Perhaps he is in Africa, or some other depressed area, aiding the little brown people who seem so tragically unable to manage their own affairs in an orderly manner. Perhaps he has become American, and serves with the troops in one of their numerous theatres of war. They do so admire bigness. Again, I must confess to some sympathy for the preference, though in their case it springs from their lamentable immaturity as a colonial culture. Not that one must call them that. Names are so very important in these superficial times, when everyone is so exceedingly sensitive in matters of terminology and etiquette. So much easier to change the name than the substance.

Then again, he may be buried deep in the heart of one of their vast cities, slaving away at a menial job of work, inhabiting one of those depressing one-room apartments with huge insects in the walls and neon lights flashing in the window all night. That would ideally suit his morose, self-abnegating nature. I imagine him assuming some polysyllabic Eastern European name, to explain his peculiar accent, his monosyllabic delivery. I wish I had had more time to teach him proper syntax.

Sometimes we wonder if he is truly dead, if the titanic engine of his body has failed at last. This, you understand, is a matter of some concern to both of us, since we live by the same process that gave life to him—though of course my own infusion of the vital force came about by accident, in the explosion that destroyed our laboratory. If he dies, then so might we, and I know that I myself still hunger for more life, and still more. There is so much more to see, to learn, to do. I am sure—nay, I know—that my Eugénie feels the same. It is true that no act of man can destroy him—that disastrous affair in Russia proved that—but the ruinous passing of time can surely not be staved off indefinitely, for him or for us. Surely, at some point, the universe will notice us and eradicate the irregularity.

But it has not happened yet, and I am gratified to note no diminution of our faculties. We still look for him, though, just in case.

We remember, you see, his last words to us, that terrible night, as his damaged brain—an assistant's blunder, compounded by Henry's ham-handed surgical technique—finally recovered a shadow of its moral sense; too little, too late, as the modern phrase has it, and hardly an asset in the world that was to come. Eugénie still wakes up screaming now and then, stricken by terror of his hulking figure coming in through the window, seeking to extinguish that which Henry and I kindled at his own urgent instigation. That he would do it we dare not doubt; if one thing about him became apparent in our brief acquaintance, it was the depth and strength of his will. And while, to the best of our knowledge, he has no idea that we survived, there is nothing to prevent his tracking us down as we are endeavouring to track him. It is essential to remain vigilant. We must discover, for our own peace of mind, exactly where he is, and whether he still wishes us ill.

Looking back, I note that I may have given a false impression. It is, of course, quite absurd to imagine that a scholar of such brilliance as I might be content to rusticate indefinitely in the shadows. Naturally I continue my experiments whenever time and convenience allow. My goal remains the same; to penetrate to the innermost secret places of Nature and lay them bare to the admiration of humanity. Once this would have been dismissed as sacrilege or lunacy; now, of course, it is a commonplace idea, as unexceptionable as heart transplants, vaccination, and all the rest of the *apparata mirabilia* of modern scientific medicine. Of course, it does rather take the thrill out of the game when there is no...

transgression... involved. I used to quite enjoy being hailed as a blasphemer.

One must, nonetheless, proceed with caution. The solitary researcher is unheard-of now; science is considered the province of armies of specialists, labouring for the profit of some huge, anonymous corporation, and certainly this method produces results, if only those results that redound sufficiently to the profit of the aforesaid corporation. Fortunately, thanks once again to the marvellous invention of the Internet, it is possible to create such a corporation entirely out of thin air, and I have done so several times. Eugénie is, if possible, even more adept than I at the fabrication of virtual people, imaginary places, histories of events that never happened. I rely totally upon her—upon, I should say, the talents which my genius providently conferred upon her—whenever it becomes necessary to remove to another location where we can begin again.

And so I find myself in command, whenever the necessity arises, of a moderately-sized laboratory of the imagination, staffed with diligent workers in a number of specialities, and producing every so often a modest advance in some technology or other—which I then discreetly sell to one of the real corporations who are better placed to put my discoveries to profitable use. Were I, after all, to approach them under my own name and say, "I have discovered this or that," questions would be asked as to my funding, my background, and other matters which I do not care to discuss. In any case, I have never cared for the tedious rigmarole of registering patents and so on. So I submit to their tender mercies my little advances in the technology of washing powder or petroleum or what have you, and receive some nugatory emolument in return which helps to pay for food and lodgings, not to mention gin and cigars; and we go on.

Of course, this is not the main thrust of my researches, merely a petty but profitable sideline. My goal remains what it always was, to create life in God's own image, and this I continue to do, with a view to understanding and fully fathoming the process whereby I do it. Repeated experimentation, close observation, and minute measurement remain the tools with which I pursue this goal. Infuriatingly, Henry's work remains the more significant contribution. I can grow lives from seed, as always, but without a concentrated exposure to his mysterious Great Ray, they remain disappointingly fragile and transitory, and wither and die in a matter of hours once removed from their protective flasks. It enrages me almost beyond endurance that even though, thanks to my judicious improvements of Henry's original designs, not to mention the ready availability of electrical power these days, I need no longer depend upon the fortuitous proximity of a thunderstorm, the precise nature of the Ray still eludes me. It is certainly not mere electricity, nor is it a form of light beyond the ultraviolet as Henry believed, but what it is—whether, indeed, it is a Ray at all, or some other form of emanation—remains beyond my capacity to determine. Perhaps, had I the facilities of one of those vast laboratories I mentioned, I might come closer to resolving that little problem... but there. Crying for the moon has never been my style.

You may wonder why, since my ambition is so all-consuming, I do not place my knowledge at the disposal of one of those corporations I mentioned, and allow them to uncover the few remaining pieces of the puzzle. Pride, I fear, the sin of Satan. Mine was the discovery—and Henry's, of course—and mine will be the hand that places the final piece. Besides, I have studied the workings of these corporate entities, and I have to say I am not impressed. Mere money-grubbing raised to a colossal scale; vulgar, tasteless and devoid of style. Academic institutions are governed by tiny minds with no will to challenge ancient taboos; charitable foundations exist merely to glorify the name of their founder. The pure lust for knowledge is as alien to them as it would be to a woodworm. I would as soon cast my research notes into the river as throw them away on such *canaille*.

National governments are no better, mindlessly pursuing the adulation of the mob rather than the highest goals of humanity. I can recall very few truly great leaders, men who followed their principles unswervingly without thought of public opprobrium, and even they proved in the end to lack true foresight and are universally despised by those who follow. I pity those of the brotherhood of science who are forced to toil in the service of such lowly spirits as govern us to-day.

But, you say, a man of my abilities, possessed of my knowledge, might rule the world. Oh yes, I know all the clichés about what are called "mad scientists," that is to say, scientists who are not content to believe all that is taught them or to follow the common herd. It is a mystery to me why such a person should ever conceive a desire to assume the intolerable burden of ruling the world; or why, should this bizarre contingency come to pass, it should be seen as such a terrible catastrophe. I see no especial virtue in the current system of government by the drivelling imbecile with the nicest smile, any more than in the old model of hereditary pot luck. On the contrary, should a man of breeding, education, and experience such as myself be so generous as to offer his services as world ruler, I would imagine a really sensible populace would greet the news of his accession with wild orgies of celebration.

But I am not so public-spirited. I begrudge every second of my time not spent following my personal inclination, whether for work or pleasure. I have no interest whatsoever in telling people what to do; it is far more amusing to watch them blunder about, and perhaps to make the occasional pithy observation in passing. Responsibility holds no appeal for me. No, as long as life pulses within my frame, I shall continue to take the path of the lone student of unhallowed arts, the path first trodden by me, and later Henry, all those years ago, and let the world find its own way to hell.

Poor, dear Henry. (I only ever knew him by that name. Apparently there was some juvenile wager with a school friend that if they both attained places at the University they would exchange Christian names. Certainly "Victor" never really suited him, in my opinion. At any rate, I shall continue to call him by the name I know best, and you, my dear reader, will simply have to sort it out for yourself.) Had he survived to behold this epoch in which we live, he would have been as horrified by it as he was by his own brutish creation, which, to be frank, it strongly resembles. I visited him once, some ten years after our last conversation, and besought him to rebuild his machines, subject himself to the Ray. It worked on me, after all. I dwelt lovingly on the glorious prospect of walking through eternity together, he and I and our greatest creation, voyaging fearlessly into futurity.

Of course he rejected the idea out of hand; he called me a phantom, a figment of his own disordered mind. I think perhaps, on reflection, he was wise in his generation, to use the Biblical phrase. Though gentle of birth, and educated by—I flatter myself—the best, he remained to the last, like his father, a superstitious peasant at heart, clinging to his shibboleths and rituals, perpetually stricken with guilt because he once trepidatiously trespassed on territory he ascribed to his jealous God. And as for that simpering wife of his— Well. Need I say more?

I have long been of the opinion that science is a vocation best served by those unhampered by romantic entanglements. Henry disagreed with me from the outset, and look what happened. Elizabeth, with her interference, her selfish demands on his time, and her confounded mystical and moral scruples, jeopardised everything he and I were working for time and again. The only use I ever found for her was as—

what do they say now—leverage, to keep Henry's courage at the sticking place when his own scruples, or more probably his cowardice, threatened to supervene. He had a first-class brain, or upper second at the very least, but no real fibre, no stamina.

Eugénie, now, *there* is a companion truly worthy of immortality. Her flashing wit, as sharp and as swift as the rapier I used to wield in my long-lost youth, her quick perceptions, her boldness, and her capacity to endure, have borne me up through the best of times and the worst, through poverty and pestilence and all the tempests that toss our little barque as it traverses life's ocean. She and I have circumnavigated the world together, from the glittering salons of Paris to the jungles of Peru, from the frozen wastes of Russia to the gimcrack palaces of Hollywood; and always, when I have despaired, it has been she who has succoured me; when my weak human nature has let me down, it has been she who has shown me a way forward. I watch her sleeping and marvel that such a quicksilver spirit can lie so still, so serenely inactive; and then I grow anxious, and check to make sure she is still breathing. Old men—I should say, middle-aged men, laughable though the term is, given our tale of years—are prone to such fears. I know that soon she will wake and dress herself, and with a cheery "Come on, Uncle Sep!"—she calls me Uncle Sep—she will embark on another day, undaunted, indefatigable. I envy her her youth, her... zest. If only... but there we are.

I appear to have digressed at some length. No matter; old—or middle-aged—men are supposed to be discursive, after all. I was talking about my continued researches, was I not?

On the brighter side, Henry's Ray does solve the problem of size that always dogged me in the early days. Subjected to it on a daily basis, my little manikins grow to human stature in a matter of weeks, and their metabolism slows to normal human rates under the drag of the increased body mass. It also helps that my life forms have no troublesome scars to heal, such as marked Eugénie, and of course our prototype. No—they begin their lives whole and healthy, new flesh and bone that has not already undergone the predations of age and death. I always knew my methods would prove the superior; all that tedious stitching, so unnecessary when every cell in a human body contains the germ of an entirely new being. Even now, when Eugénie is in a passion with me and lifts her superb chin, I fancy I can discern—though perhaps no-one else could—the visible remnant of the needlework whereby we fastened her face to her skull. Naturally I do not mention it. I have my faults, but I hope I am never petty.

It is no great matter to acquire suitable materials. This is, above all, an age of carelessness; people blunder through their lives in a sort of semi-coma, discarding viable cells hither and yon. A used paper napkin in a restaurant, a piece of chewing gum parked unobtrusively on a bench, a pair of headphones deemed suddenly less stylish than the ones in the shop window, we are ever on the qui vive for such unintended bounty. I always use tongs, of course. One never knows what one might catch. Happily, disease organisms seem not to respond to the Ray, otherwise the earth would long since have succumbed to a plague of immortal viri from the various deceased malefactors and vagrants used by Henry in his construction. I have no idea why this should be so. Frankly, were I not such a profound sceptic, it might impel me to entertain the conjecture of a special Providence.

The only problem that remains is how to dispose of the successful experiments, but even here we have devised an elegant solution. The cult of youth, as I said, is ever in the ascendant in these latter days, and the young people of this time like to see people who resemble themselves, were they only gifted with flawless beauty. And so, when I have grown and animated four or five interchangeably beautiful boys or young women, Eugénie creates life histories for them, and with some rudimentary training they go on to do very well in the field of the performing arts, such as it is.

Naturally, since they do not age, it is necessary to allow them to fall from favour after a while, but only for a year or so. The public's memory is really shockingly deficient and readily accepts as such anything that it is told is new, and when the latest boy band takes the stage, who will care if some of them look somewhat similar to the overnight sensation of two years ago? And if all else fails, or if they should prove recalcitrant, there is always the old tank of *aqua regia*, blessed eradicator of one's occasional failures. Nobody notices; nobody cares.

It is an amusing hobby for a gentleman, to pander thus to this world's increasingly avid and exclusive desire for entertainment, reduced to the lowest common denominator: endlessly recycled songs performed without wit or élan by endlessly recycled singers. And, of course, there is money in it, far more than in mere scientific research. One craves a little comfort on occasion.

And, while the boys are growing and training, I have the pleasure of contemplating them from afar; their smooth, flawless skin, their limpid eyes, their quick, gracile movements. All too soon it is time to drape their supple bodies in the shapeless clothing of today's youth, teach them to lumber about like adolescent gorillas, drill them in the jarring, charmless doggerel that has replaced the poetry of Byron and Shelley. I do not, of course, interact with them in any way; the encounter would be needlessly embarrassing on both sides. I am privileged merely to oversee their nurture and take what delight I may in the sight of golden, flawless youths as yet unconscious of their own allure.

It is my only weakness.

I once spoke to Henry of a new world of gods and monsters, and to my amusement I see that my prophecy has come to pass, though not quite in the way I imagined. The gods of the modern age are tawdry, half-baked creatures of man's fashioning, mere makeshift puppets of flesh, worshipped with fanatical fervour for a season while they cavort upon the stage, and then forgotten; while the monsters are shadowy, immense entities of terrible power, devoid of physical existence and only imperfectly understood, manipulating mortals for their own simple, brutal ends. It is perhaps no world for an idealist, no world for a soul like Henry, who believed in progress and the perfectibility of mankind. There is no hope here, no clear path to a bright future such as my poor pupil envisaged. But then, I never thought there would be.

This, after all, turns out to be my world, and Eugénie's, a world that might have been made for us to live in.

And we really are getting rather good at it.

ABOUT THE EDITORS

J.L. Aldis' background is in academia, though latterly she has occupied her time learning languages (German and French), translating documents from their source languages into English and from what the writers think is English into actual English. And from Marketingspeak into English, though the authors of these pieces of 'prose' are generally more resistant to improvement. She has also taught English as a foreign language. Thus it is with some relief that she is now returning to her roots in critical practice—turned to positive production—with this collection of short stories. She has found it extremely rewarding to work with a group of authors who are all devoted to writing the best possible stories, and would like to thank them all for their grace under fire. Her heartfelt thanks also go to E.E. Weber, who served as a second (and very astute) set of eyes before each story was finalised, and to Story Spring Publishing for bringing this book to the reading public.

In addition to having studied and written in a variety of genres and styles, including fiction, nonfiction, plays, and poetry, **E.E. Weber** has taught college-level writing and storytelling. She has edited novels, short stories, grants, book chapters, and scientific manuscripts and is delighted to have served as assistant editor for *Thoroughly Modern Monsters*. She is most often found with a dog on each leg and her nose in a book.

ABOUT THE AUTHORS

Jae Eynon is a moderately well-travelled Brit who is glad to be back in England after sixteen years in countries where they don't drink Proper Tea. She attempts, somewhat chaotically, to herd two cats, a pet rat, her children, and her spouse through life with minimal abrasions and fits in writing whenever and wherever she can. She used to be a scholar of Literature with a capital L, but Life (ditto) took her down other paths, and now she both reads and writes fantasy, which is much more fun, as well as—surprisingly—uses many of the skills she acquired picking the Renaissance apart at the seams. Jae can be found at: http://twitter.com/JaeEynon and http://www.facebook.com/jae.eynon

M.R. Glass has been escaping into fantastical worlds for as long as she can remember. Using the threads of myth, legend, archetype, and fairy-tale to weave those worlds into words and images that others can share is one of her greatest joys. She is a psychologist by day and a writer by night and lives in the US Midwest with her husband, three kids, and two extremely furry cats.
https://www.facebook.com/pages/MR-Glass/305635632915237 and http://twitter.com/mrglass4

Antioch Grey is an author and a lawyer who lives in London with her collection of shoes. She has no cats because she doesn't trust them not to be plotting against her and would rather keep a pet blond. Other interests include chocolate and classical statuary, but not at the same time because there's

nothing worse than chocolate smears on statues.
https://twitter.com/AntiochGrey
www.facebook.com/antioch.grey

Murphy McCall is a worker bee by day and a writer by night. *The Freakshow File* is her first foray into publication. She is a displaced Southern Belle who frequents exotic museum exhibitions and keeps Detective Vasquez on speed-dial. You may visit her at https://www.facebook.com/murphy.mccall.3

Abby Phelan is a twenty-five year old student of the arts (archaeology and geography) who has just started her first job and is missing college like crazy. She's spent roughly twenty of the past twenty-five years reading voraciously in a number of genres, with fantasy, science fiction, crime, historical and mythology probably coming out on top.

As a writer, Abby has been dabbling with fiction more or less since she was seven, and actually letting people see the results since she was around sixteen, with mixed results. This is her first published story and comes primarily out of a fascination with the intersection of various mythologies in her native Ireland. And also, it must be said, from a mild conviction that the Port Tunnel is vaguely supernatural in origin.

After many long years in academia, **Caireann Shannon** decided her overactive imagination was much more important than any number of musicology conferences. She ditched her music books in favour of the quill (or laptop) and began by writing internet fanfiction. Having won numerous awards and a loyal readership, she eventually turned to original fiction. She is the author of three novels so far and is represented by a

top London literary agent. Her numerous jobs have included ghost writing for a UK fiction series company. She lives near Dublin, Ireland, with her husband and two sons, and can be found on Twitter under Cai Shannon.
http://twitter.com/caireannshannon

Other than a lengthy detour in Scandinavia and Europe, **Lin Thornhill** grew up in southern California, where she currently lives with her family and their miscellany of pets.

Lin's early professional forays were in the entertainment business. While she has worked on both sides of the camera, it is the written word which enduringly captivates her creative interest. The *Bitter Seed, Bitter Fruit* trilogy was among her first collaborative efforts. More recently she has performed in the triple-threat categories— producing, directing, writing— for *An Unlikely Hero*, a decade-in-the-making documentary featuring the leader of the Filthy 13 upon whom the film *The Dirty Dozen* was based.

Throughout, Lin has turned her hand to the world of speculative fiction. Her Elba universe comes to life in *Emancipation*, the first novel of the *Cohesion* series. She keeps her skills sharp by writing short stories and other pieces of flash fiction. To learn more, visit www.linthornhill.com.

Michaela Vallageas lives in Paris. She's a professional chef, a writer, and a wine buff. From spicy to sour, from bitter to sweet, from pungent to finger-licking delectable, she has set out to savour all of the world, all of the words.
https://www.facebook.com/michaela.vallageas

Jonathan Waite attributes his tallness to his father, his abundant hair to his mother, and his general uselessness to intensive training and long practice. He lives near one of the boring Victorian white horses with his wife, who also writes, and a number of cats, who (as far as he knows) do not. He himself has been writing since the early sixties, but most of his early output is now blessedly lost to posterity; more recent work can be found at http://www.avevale.org/. He also makes music under the name of Zander Nyrond, and some of that is available on Bandcamp. An accomplished performer upon the bockelhorn and Flemish clacket, he once gave an epic performance of Wagner's entire Ring cycle, specially arranged for the latter instrument, to an audience composed entirely of goats; and his one regret is that after a tragic incident in infancy involving an egg-whisk, a packet of cornflakes, and a late-night showing of *Bride Of Frankenstein*, he cannot manage to write five sentences without descending into ludicrous fabulation.

Libby Weber was raised in a log cabin in rural Illinois and spent' her childhood climbing trees, catching toads, and exercising her immunity to poison ivy. After earning a degree in theater, four varsity letters in fencing, and a spectacularly rude nickname from her fellow trombone players in the Northwestern University Marching Band, she followed her heart to San Diego, where she lives with her much-beloved husband/in-house editor and two dogs. In addition to writing and editing fiction, she sings with the San Diego Master Chorale and writes about the arts for the nonprofit news site Voice of San Diego. Visit her website (http://libbyweber.wordpress.com/) or follow her on Twitter: http://twitter.com/thelibbyweber.

Wendy Worthington is that rarity in Hollywood: a working actor. She has acted in more than fifty TV shows, from her first guest appearance on "Murphy Brown" to recurring roles on "Suddenly Susan," "Ally McBeal," "So Little Time," "Ghost Whisperer," "Desperate Housewives," and "Bones," and in numerous sketches on "Jimmy Kimmel Live." Under Joss Whedon's direction, she sang on "Glee," and has her own trading card as the villainous lunch lady from an episode of "Buffy the Vampire Slayer." In films, she has worked with Steven Spielberg ("Catch Me If You Can"), Robert Zemeckis ("Cast Away"), and Clint Eastwood ("Changeling"). She has also appeared on a few cutting room floors, including opposite Tom Hanks in Jonathan Demme's "Philadelphia." On stage, she appeared in the world premiere of Charles Busch's "Die! Mommy! Die!"

She is repped by Eleanor Wood at Spectrum Literary Agency, with murder mystery novels set in the film industry (starting with *Die Laughing* and *The Hollywood Finger*), and her first murder mystery short story, "Snow in Winter," was published in the anthology *Death on a Cold Night* by Elm Books. Her short play, *Company Business,* was a finalist in the Actors Theatre of Louisville's Ten-Minute Play Contest in 2008.
https://www.facebook.com/wendy.worthington.37

ABOUT STORY SPRING PUBLISHING

We hope you've enjoyed *Thoroughly Modern Monsters*. We're pleased that it—our inaugural publication—attracted so many excellent authors who produced such wonderful stories.

A quick note about our editing decisions. You may have noticed that we utilized two different editing standards: one for American writers and one for the Europeans. We value authorial voice as much as we value standard spellings and punctuation. So, rather than substantially change the European authors' voices by altering their spellings and grammar, we opted to maintain their distinctive style, even going so far as leaving many of their pacing commas as written. The Americans were edited to the *Chicago* standard, also keeping authorial voice in mind.

Story Spring Publishing is the brainchild of two writers and inhabits the space between traditional publishing and self-publishing. We publish interesting, engaging books with diverse, well-developed characters and worlds. We aim to provide a high-quality reading experience, regardless of whether the reader is holding a book or reading a screen.

You can find us on Twitter:
http://www.twitter.com/storyspringpub
and Facebook:
http://www.facebook.com/StorySpringPublishing

Our website is www.storyspringpublishing.com.

Made in the USA
Lexington, KY
15 December 2014